THE HANDMA...

It was rumored ...ra
Lynn, was slated to receive the Rebel Forge Busi-
nessperson of the Year award, something that she'd
yet to receive in all her years as a small-
businesswoman. The reason for the slight was obvious:
there was bad blood between my sister and Eliza
Glade, a woman who ran the chamber of commerce—
along with her businesses—with a velvet fist.

Sara Lynn frowned. "If you haven't heard the rumors yet, you will tonight. Bailey and I are completely
and utterly finished. I will never be able to get the
image out of my mind of him in Eliza Glade's
embrace."

I was shocked but finally managed, "Are you positive you want to be here? Eliza's going to be making
the presentation." I couldn't imagine my sister onstage
with her worst enemy in the world.

Sara Lynn stood her ground, though. "I won't let
that woman deprive me of this evening. I did nothing
wrong, and I won't scuttle away to a corner and
hide."

She left the table for a minute, out of earshot.

"There's a good turnout tonight, isn't there?" said
Aunt Lillian.

Her friend nodded. "I think half of them are here
to see that niece of yours onstage with Eliza."

They were just starting to serve when Sara Lynn
rejoined us, without her husband in tow. She looked
more shaken than I'd ever seen her, but it was clear
that further conversation wouldn't be welcome.

I heard a scream from the kitchen.

"Eliza's dead!" the woman's voice shouted. "Someone stabbed her in the heart."

And that's when all hell broke loose. . . .

TEMPEST'S FURY

NICOLE PEELER

www.orbitbooks.net

Copyright © 2012 by Nicole Peeler
Excerpt from *Blood Rights* copyright © 2011 by Kristen Painter

Orbit
Hachette Book Group
237 Park Avenue
New York, NY 10017
www.orbitbooks.net

Orbit is an imprint of Hachette Book Group. The Orbit name and logo are trademarks of Little, Brown Book Group Limited.

The publisher is not responsible for websites (or their content) that are not owned by the publisher.

The Hachette Speakers Bureau provides a wide range of authors for speaking events. To find out more, go to www.hachettespeakers bureau.com or call (866) 376-6591

Printed in the United States of America

First edition: June 2012

10 9 8 7 6 5 4 3 2 1
OPM

*To my big brother,
for a lot of reasons.*

TEMPEST'S
FURY

CHAPTER ONE

It was times like this I wished Hallmark made a line of "So your supernatural daughter is going off to fight a supernatural war" cards, because I certainly didn't know how to say that to my father. Especially not over my cell phone, after I was already overseas.

"So what are you doing in Britain again?" My dad asked skeptically, as soon as I told him I'd landed safely.

For a split second I considered telling him the truth. But I didn't want to give him a heart attack, especially so soon after he'd just been healed. So I took the coward's way.

I lied.

"Oh, you know. Just doing some supernatural stuff. But safe stuff, of course. Safe, supernatural stuff."

I'm not really *lying*, I consoled myself. *I'll be safe as houses with Blondie and Anyan.*

And I knew I would be. Anyan was a fierce warrior—a barghest, with not only the ability to change shape between a sexy man and a fierce doggie, but also the ability to tap into two elements: earth and air. That made him super strong, as most of us could only tap into one. Mine was water, of course, since I'm half-selkie. Don't club me because I'm beautiful.

Blondie, meanwhile, was something older and stronger than anyone else I knew. She was an Original, and I'd only recently learned what that really meant. Turns out she was one of the first humans to have access to magic, and she could use all magic in a way no other creature could. Even the Alfar, who could manipulate all four elements and were usually our (rather shitty) leaders, had their limitations. Blondie didn't. But it was even more complicated than that, as Blondie was the reason we were all the way we were. She'd been conned into using an artifact—the horn of a really ancient magical creature—that hadn't worked as it was intended. Instead of being the powerful weapon she'd been told it was, it had caused the Great Schism. That was when all the supernatural folk went from being like Blondie is, with access to all that power, and became as we are now: divided into different factions with different powers.

"And who are you working for, exactly?" my dad asked, still sounding skeptical.

"Oh, just some powerful supernatural people. But they're good. Definitely good. I think you'd like them."

Oh, and "they're" under your feet, I considered adding.

For the creature who had sent us to Britain was the very same creature who lived beneath Rockabill. If Blondie was ancient, this thing was prehistoric. No, it was pre-humanic—it existed way before the Earth even looked the way it does now. Not biological in a sense that we understood, it did still have a body that lived underneath most of the Eastern Seaboard. But it was actually a being of pure Earth and Water. That didn't mean it could just manipulate earth or water, as supes like me could. It meant it *was* Earth and Water—its parents were the actual elements that created our planet.

So it was big, and anything but bad. I'd been in its mind, and it was the closest thing to "good" I could imagine. It was also as close to omniscient as we could hope for, under the circumstances. So if it said, "go to Britain and start a war," we damned well knew we'd better get to Britain and start a war.

"And you've got everything sorted for your visit? You have a ride and everything?"

"Of course!" I said, confidently.

I hope so, I thought, less confidently. I'd gotten through customs just fine, despite being nervous as shit. Now I was supposed to be meeting a contact, for whom I had a code word, but I'd walked out of Heathrow's customs area to find myself alone. As for Anyan and Blondie, they were coming in on separate flights—all part of our attempt to sneak into the country. We were going in with our magic dampened, under assumed names, and alone. I was posing as a college student, which wasn't much of a stretch.

"Anyway, Dad," I said, trying to wrangle control of the conversation. "I'm fine and I'll stay in touch. And you can always call my cell if you get worried. But what about you? Isn't today your first day?"

"Yup," he said. "I did all the other training already. Today Grizzie will work with me on all the coffee stuff. She's determined to make a barista out of me."

"It's easy, once you get the hang of it. And, hey, you

can start drinking coffee again. Enjoy the fruits of your labors."

My dad had only recently been healed of the heart defect that had made him an invalid for more than a decade. The supes had healed him, and glamoured the whole town and medical system to believe he'd always been healthy. But that had left him without his disability checks, and without a job. My leaving on the creature's mission had actually worked out well, in that he'd been able to slot into my spot at Read It and Weep.

He was also getting back into doing all the stuff he'd once taken for granted. My dad used to love coffee, but for a very long time he'd only been able to drink the very watered down, mostly decaf version I'd made for him at home. But now he could go nuts, if he wanted.

"Well, we all miss you, even if it is fun working in the bookstore," my dad said. "Grizzie and Tracy want you to know that you can come back anytime, without me losing my job. With Tracy having the twins, she'll mostly be at home. So they'll need an extra set of hands."

I grinned. What would happen when I returned had been a concern for me, and there it was—solved.

"Tell them I love them. And I love you too, Dad. I'll call you whenever I get a chance. Oh, hey, I think I see my ride."

There was a shifty looking woman with crazy raven-black hair scanning the concourse. And I mean she was shifty, for real. She was wearing a massive military-style trench coat that was moving oddly on her body, as if she had an extra something or other stashed on her back.

"All right, hon. Call me soon. I love you."

"I love you too. Bye, Dad," I said, as the woman caught

sight of me and gave me a small nod. She walked towards me and I flipped my phone shut. When she got close enough, I looked around furtively before skittering up to her.

"Pachanga!" I shouted, causing the crazy-haired woman to cringe. Maybe I was a little loud, but I was so relieved my ride had shown that I was a little slaphappy.

I also wasn't entirely sure what "pachanga" meant, although I knew it came from *Dirty Dancing*. So it was either a kind of dance or a euphemism for female genitalia. But it was now our chosen code word, with which I was supposed to identify my contact in London.

That very contact raised her coal-black eyes to mine. "Nobody puts Baby in a corner," she repeated, leaving me free to blurt out my next question.

"Are you a selkie?"

The woman shook her head. Up close, she was totally emo: a huge fountain of dyed black hair spilled around her face and down her shoulders, in teased-out waves like David Bowie's in *Labyrinth*. Her already dark eyes were rimmed with tons of black makeup, and she sported a lip ring and another in her nostril.

"Sorry, no. I'm Magog, and I'm a raven. Not a selkie." she said, in a singsong accent I recognized as Welsh from watching *Torchwood*.

"A raven?" I asked, disappointed she wasn't a selkie but excited to find out what a raven was. Meeting new supernaturals was what I liked best about my mother's world, except for when they tried to kill me.

"You'll understand, later. Don't want to frighten the humans," she rasped, twitching her lips at me. It wasn't a smile, just a cynical twist of the lips that said, "Here's where a normal person would smile, but I don't do such things."

"Um, okay," I said, before realizing I'd not yet told Magog my name. Nor did I know who she was, besides a raven.

"My name is Jane. And who are you, exactly?"

"Your ride," she said, as I stared about, looking for some sign that I was really in another country. Unfortunately, Heathrow just looked like any airport in any city. "I'm one of your party's contacts. I'll take you to our safe house, and the barghest and Cyntaf will follow."

I blinked, unsure who "cunt-uph" was, exactly. But it sounded naughty.

"Uh, cunt-uph?" I hazarded.

"Cyntaf. It's Welsh for 'the First.' "

"Ah," I said. "You mean Blondie."

"Blondie?"

"Yes. That's what we call her. The tattooed lady," I added, when it was obvious Magog still wasn't comprehending. After a second, she gave that cynical little half-twist of her mouth again—her "not smile."

"Blondie, yes. That's perfect. Blondie could . . ."

"Party, I know," I said, with a sigh. "I've heard it before."

"Well, here she's Cyntaf. If you're set, let's head out to the van."

With that, Magog turned briskly on her heel, clearly intending me to follow. It was only then that I noticed how grotesquely the coat bulged up over her neck and shoulders as if she were a hunchback. My curiosity surged as I remembered what she was. Ravens, after all, had wings.

I couldn't wait to see them.

* * *

"Are we here?" I asked.

Magog nodded, as silent as she'd been on the drive over, and I craned my head to get a better view of the building Magog had pointed to as we passed. But we were at an odd angle, parked well away from our destination despite there being room to park in front. Plus, the little white van we were driving had no windows in the back, and no matter how I moved around in my seat, I couldn't see much. I finally gave up, suppressing a sigh as I turned to sit normally again.

To be honest, our drive through the night streets had been disappointing. I'd peered out of the windows, hoping for a glimpse of Big Ben, the London Eye, or Westminster, but we seemed to crawl along darkened suburban roads surrounding the airport for hours in inexplicably heavy traffic, getting no nearer to the city. Still, the views were interesting. The street signs were new, not to mention everyone was driving on the wrong side of the road, which freaked me out every time we turned. Plus, what with the steering wheel being on the right hand side, I kept thinking small children and dogs were driving, or that cars were magically driving themselves while their human passengers sat with bored expressions. The houses were also definitely Not American: most seemed to be row houses, their front lawns paved to hold one of the tiny cars that seemed to be everywhere.

That said, the vast banality of the 'burbs—while not particularly inspiring—had given me an inkling of London's size. I'd only been in a few "real" cities in my life: Boston, Montreal, and Quebec. Chicago we'd only driven around, never even entering the city proper. After Rockabill, the cities I'd visited had seemed enormous. I realized now, however, that they were really baby cities, barely out of diapers. London must be a *city*, with a mass of people so huge I found it slightly terrifying.

A sudden desire for the emptiness of my ocean struck me, and I wondered how we'd be able to do anything covert, let alone start a war, in a place as tightly packed as London.

Magog and I sat in silence for about twenty minutes, unbroken except for my initial attempts at conversation—which were rejected—and then my occasional sleepy yawns. I tried to focus on what we were doing here, on what little Blondie had told us, but I found my thoughts continually reverting to happier things. Things with big noses, like Anyan Barghest, for example.

It was during one of these sleepy, Anyan-related reveries that I saw headlights pull up behind me. Magog perked up, peering carefully into her rearview mirror before she exhaled with relief.

"It's them. We can go in."

Pushing open my car door I hopped out, then indulged myself in a long, hard stretch. I paused at the top of my stretch to take a deep breath. The air smelled of pollution, but also of water. I could smell river water, and ocean water, and rainwater. The air was saturated with moisture, bathing me in a delicious tingle of power. I closed my eyes to enjoy both that tingle and the ache in my limbs as I stretched, only to find Anyan had appeared and was watching me with a sensual little smile pursing his lips.

My belly burned with lust for that damned man, as my heart picked up its pace in my chest. Anyan and I had been friends, with the hint of something more on the horizon, when we'd both been attacked a couple of months back. I'd saved us, barely, but nearly killed myself doing so. When I'd woken up, everything was suddenly so intense between us. He'd watched me lie in a coma for a month, and had obviously come to some decisions about us on his own. But for me—the one sleeping—no time had passed at all since we'd exchanged those first tentative touches.

I'd woken up to him wanting me with a hunger I couldn't help but match, but I also couldn't entirely understand.

Having read way too much for my own good, I knew that a thousand motivations that had nothing to do with me could have created his sudden interest: my saving him, his seeing me almost die, my vulnerability in that coma.

But I didn't want a man who thought he owed me, or wanted to save me. And even though all of Anyan's actions towards me up to that point had been anything but paternalistic, I still worried. A worry compounded by the fact that, while I was still at the stage where I wasn't sure if it was okay to touch him at all, let alone in public, in reality we'd already have had sex if we hadn't been interrupted by Blondie. And we'd been interrupted to go to another country, to start a war. One in which I was supposed to be some sort of Joan of Arc figure, hopefully minus the horribly painful death by burning.

To say we had some issues to work out was an understatement. But when Anyan looked like he did now, all rumpled and gorgeous in a pair of low-riding jeans, with his bright blue T-shirt making his iron-grey eyes extra cold and inscrutable, I knew the only thing I wanted more than world peace was for those cold grey eyes to warm when they met mine.

He held his hand out to me and I took it without thinking, moving closer to him as I did so.

"Good flight?" he murmured, brushing my hair back from my face. The gesture was ironic, considering his own curly black hair was sticking up like that of an electrocuted poodle. An adorable, electrocuted poodle.

"Long," I answered. Before I could help myself, I said, "And I wish you were on it."

"Me too. I worried about you."

"It was fine. Easy. Magog was there soon after I got in," I said, gesturing towards the raven who was removing both my backpack, a big travel one I'd borrowed from Anyan, and her own to carry them towards the house.

"Good," Anyan said, letting his finger trace down my jaw. I wanted to take it in my mouth, even as I wanted to ask him what he felt, even as I told myself to simmer down. We were sorting things out for ourselves and I needn't rush things.

But I didn't do or say anything. I just watched him watch me, wondering what he was thinking. And whether it involved the misuse of whipped toppings.

"Come on, then," Magog rasped, from under the cold light of a streetlight. "Let's not dawdle."

Anyan picked up the pack he'd dropped, as well as another box, laden with official looking stickers. I grabbed that one from him under the auspices of being helpful, but it was really because I wanted it back. The box contained my labrys, my champion's ax, and I'd missed it. I'd agreed it was better that Anyan bring it into the country as he was a real weapons expert, and would be able to convince any suspicious parties that his falsified credentials as a museum curator were actually real. But just because I knew it was better he carry the ax didn't mean I'd liked being separated from it.

Once we had our stuff, we trudged up the sidewalk to the front door. I could feel a camouflaging glamour swirling around us: the first time I'd felt any magic from anyone since we landed. Even Blondie, who usually glowed like a sparkler, had kept all her power dampened. But now she was waiting for us under cover of glamour, Magog and another stranger waiting patiently beside her.

When we got close enough to greet each other, I noticed that Blondie looked no worse for wear after her transatlantic flight. Even her pink Mohawk was perfectly spiky, and her oversized jeans and tight maroon long-sleeved T-shirt looked fresh. I felt like I'd been rolled around by hobos on a sidewalk somewhere, and wondered how she did it.

That said, my attention was quickly pulled from the Original to our newest addition. He was huge, first of all. He towered even over Anyan, and was nearly as big as the spriggan, Fugwat, although not as wide.

He was also a curious shade of grey and bald as a bowling pin. I could see black lines covering his skin, more like striations than tattoos, even over his face and down his neck. His eyes were the same shade of grey as his skin, and his features were small and stubby in his big head.

All in all he was massive and terrifying, like the Devil's bouncer. I was glad he was, at least ostensibly, on our side.

"That's Gog Coblynau," Magog said, "And he's mine."

As a student of mythology gone a bit obsessive about the subject when I learned of my mother's world, I recognized the word "coblynau." In human myths, they were Welsh mining spirits or gnomes. I figured that meant, in supe terms, that Gog was an Earth elemental. Come to think of it, he did look a bit like something you'd find in a mine.

I nodded, acknowledging Magog's words and her claim. She could have Gog. I wanted a coffee.

Gog laid a hand on the door, and I watched, fascinated, as the wood stretched and reformed itself to open a passage without actually unlocking the door. As he did so, the black striations spraddled across the back of his head—more like tattoos than veins, but not quite either—glowed a dull black, casting his grey skin in an eerie pallor.

When there was space enough for us to enter, he motioned us through.

Once inside the house's slim, long hallway, I peered around. There was a small room to my right that was clearly a living room, and then a small kitchen behind it. A tiny, steep staircase was in front of me to my left, leading to what I assumed were two bedrooms the same size as the living room and the kitchen. Everything was painted cream, and I recognized most of the furniture as Ikea.

I was also pretty sure we weren't supposed to be there, not least because Gog and Magog were doing the same thing I was—peering about like they'd never seen the place.

My suspicions were confirmed when I felt a sweep of power from Blondie, testing for other forms of life. When she found nothing, she nodded to Magog, who reached into her coat's massive pocket and pulled out a coal-black rock that was big enough she handled it with two hands. She laid the rock on the shelf of the radiator by the front door, touching it lightly as she squatted down to murmur to it, imbuing it with the power of her breath. Nearly all winged things were Air elementals, and Magog's whispers were laced with a strength that made me shiver.

As soon as she was done, I felt a *whoosh* of power emanate from the stone, and then the street noise disappeared entirely. Then Magog took off, moving around the tiny house quickly, as if scouting.

"A shield, called a nullifier," Gog said, his voice as gravelly as his skin. Magog, already done looking around the downstairs rooms, whooshed past us as she headed upstairs. "We use them to make safe houses. If anyone is nearby, this house looks like a dead zone, even if we're using our power."

I nodded as if I understood, wondering what we would do now.

"You settle yourselves," Magog said, her footsteps pounding on the stairs as she dashed down from her second story investigations. "Clean up, do whatever, but try to disturb as little as possible. I'll pop over to the shops for supplies. There's a double bedroom, a single, and the couch in the lounge folds out to a double, I'm pretty sure. Feel free to claim which room you'd like, but leave a double for Gog and me."

With that the raven was off, but only after Gog had reopened the door in his odd way. It was only then I noticed the alarm system installed next to the front door. It was blinking away in safe mode, content that no one had gotten in on its watch since the door had never, technically, been opened.

"You and Magog take the double upstairs. Blondie can have the single. Jane and I will take the lounge," Anyan said to Gog, after which Anyan shot me a look as if to ask if that was all right. I smiled my acquiescence, hoping I didn't look like a girl who'd won the lottery.

"That works," Gog rumbled, shouldering his and Magog's packs.

"Um, Gog?" I asked, despite the fact I probably didn't want to know the answer. "Are we supposed to be here?"

The grey man turned to me, his brows furrowed.

"Are we . . . guests?" I asked. "Or did we break in."

Gog smiled, a real smile unlike Magog's, and I saw that he was missing his bottom front teeth.

"Oh, we're not guests, Miss. We definitely broke in."

I squelched my alarm at the alacrity with which he said that we were committing what had to be felony, even in Europe.

"How did you find it?" Anyan asked, casually.

"Facebook," Gog said. "You'd be amazed at what people put on their walls. This young couple is enjoying a weekend in Amsterdam. It was very nice of 'em to let us know exact dates, don't you think?"

I shook my head, very glad that for all intents and purposes, I lived in 1996. Having no friends, I'd never been up on social networking.

And now I had no inclination to start.

CHAPTER TWO

What is a lounge?" I asked, turning to Anyan. "I like the sound of it. I'm hoping for something in purple velvet, personally."

Sorry to crush your dreams, but the lounge is that room," Anyan said, pointing to his right. " 'Lounge' is just British for living room."

"Oh," I said, trying not to sound disappointed as I schlepped my backpack into the decidedly non-purple and non-velvety "lounge." I left the pack near the wall by the door, but took my labrys case with me. I sat down on the couch, and set the case on the brass-and-glass coffee table. Tearing through the various pieces of official-looking tape keeping it shut, I finally pried it open.

The ax didn't look like much: rough-hewn, double-headed, and not at all fancy. But I felt a sense of peace as I touched the handle, caressing the old wood with a gentle touch. It glowed faintly, just for a second, as my skin made contact and I felt an answering spark of power deep in my chest.

Content that it was unharmed after its long journey, I shut the case again and stood up.

"I need a shower," I said. "Really badly."

Anyan nodded from where he stood rooting around in the large backpack he'd brought.

"Me too. It's probably upstairs." Then he looked up to meet my eyes and I flushed at the heat I saw in them.

"It's probably not the best idea, under the circumstances," he said, moving towards me. I didn't know whether to back up or launch myself at him. "But I love the idea of conserving water..."

"Going green, are we?" I said lightly, despite the tension in my belly.

"Yes, obviously, and so showering with you would really be the right thing to do. To reduce my carbon footprint, and all." His voice was getting growlier by the second, and my lady Jane growled back in sympathy. He was close to me now, his big body dwarfing mine. For a second I imagined climbing up him like he was a vine, then I reimagined that scenario with both of us naked, and then I shivered.

"And I do have a terribly difficult time washing my own back," I said. "I always miss places. End up smelling like a goat..."

He chuckled as he stepped so close to me that the tips of our shoes touched.

"I can always count on you to say something sexy," he said.

I blushed. "I know. I'm very smooth."

"You are smooth," he murmured, leaning down to brush his lips against my forehead. "Smooth and soft and warm. I could touch you forever..."

And with that his lips found mine. The kiss was gentle, but his lips moved against mine with an authority that made my own knees weak. When he pulled away I whined, till he nuzzled away my protests with that big, crooked nose.

"Jane, we should talk," he said, his voice dark with lust.

"Hmm?" I said, dreamily, rubbing against him like an overzealous cat and not caring one bit.

"We should talk," he repeated, his voice slightly strained. "I think we need to..."

"Get a room?" said a new voice: one that didn't belong to any of the people I knew were in that house.

Anyan and I raised shields, looking towards the door to the lounge. There stood a little being, no taller than three feet, which looked like the classical incarnation of a cauldron-stirring, Shakespearean witch. Its skin was a crazy mottling of blue and purple, with hair that streamed up in haylike stalks like a homemade Troll doll. It was bent, wizened, and its nose tapered in front of it like a lewd, homegrown carrot. Its clawlike blue hands clutched a walking stick and its beady yellow eyes flicked across my skin in a way that made me feel even dirtier than I did after the long flight.

"Hiral," Anyan said, greeting the little creature in an exasperated voice.

"How did you get in here?" I demanded, stepping away from Anyan and getting ready to make a mage ball.

"I was invited," the creature said, "despite the cold greeting I'm currently enjoying. And there's not a door in this kingdom that can keep me out, pet," Hiral responded in a voice that was squeaky and unpleasant, before stumping painfully into the room. On further consideration, something about the little creature's voice and mannerisms told me that it was male, although I wasn't entirely sure until he paused to give his balls a bold and thorough scratching. After which, he looked around until his eyes lit on the beanbag propped in the corner of the lounge.

"Ah, perfect," he said throwing his staff on the beanbag before settling himself down with a long sigh. "Yes, this will do."

Then he looked from Anyan to me, his yellow eyes twinkling. When he smiled his teeth were long, crooked, and black with rot.

Anyan looked at Hiral for a long minute, but the little creature just kept grinning at him. His smile wavered, however, when Anyan strode forward purposefully. Causing Hiral to squawk like a chicken, Anyan picked up the beanbag, Hiral and all, and carried it into the kitchen. He set it in an out of the way corner, tucked behind the table.

"Perfect," said the barghest, dusting off his hands. He turned on his heel to stride back into the lounge, closing the pocket doors that divided our room from the kitchen with a definitive *clink*.

"The lounge is ours," Anyan said, in a faux-evil prince voice that made me giggle.

"That it is. But we have to clean up and we have to be ready to talk to Blondie. So anything else will have to wait." I said, albeit regretfully, as I moved towards my suitcase to dig out my toiletries and something comfortable to wear.

"You're right. Good idea," Anyan said, following my lead and opening his own backpack. But he didn't sound like he believed what he was saying. To be honest, I didn't believe what I was saying. Part of me was sick of waiting, while another part wanted to figure out just what I wanted from the word "wait."

The truth was that I'd been relieved when Hiral had shown up. Redefining "coitus interruptus" had been the running joke of my time with Anyan in Rockabill, before and after I'd been attacked. We'd finally get a chance to have some alone time and something or someone would interrupt. It was like all the forces of the universe had conspired together in a massive cock-blocking scheme. It had sucked, yes, but it had also meant that Anyan and I were sort of permanently, deliciously stalled between desire and consummation. I found myself terrified at the idea that we might now have the chance to dive into something.

For as much as I wanted Anyan, I knew that we did, indeed, need to talk. The last year of my life had been crazy, and I'd gone from being a cautious person to living like life was a swimming pool and I was in a belly-flop contest. I had no regrets, but Anyan was different.

There were things I wanted to say to him, before we plunged into any metaphorical deep ends.

I just had to figure out what those things were.

I nibbled on a biscuit, watching Gog's large grey form bustle about preparing a pot of tea. The rest of us were sitting around the small kitchen table of the house we'd commandeered. Blondie sat across from me with Hiral at her side—the two seemed to be very close chums, something I couldn't understand since the little creature had gotten no less unpleasant since he'd arrived. It turns out Hiral was a gwyllion, which was a type of mischievous spirit in Welsh mythology. The reputation for mischief was well earned, I'd realized, as I'd watched in horror as Hiral licked every single chip from a bag of "crisps," putting them back into the bag as he did so.

I planned on throwing that bag out before we left, feeling sorry for the poor humans whose house we'd already misappropriated.

Magog had taken the head of the table to my right, leaving the left for Gog as Anyan sat with me on my side. Both the barghest's and my heads were wet, although we hadn't "conserved" any "water." Still, it felt good to have changed into comfies, and Blondie and Anyan had done the same. Hiral, however, had already been dressed in what appeared to be a burlap sack, and Gog and Magog were wearing everything they'd come in with, including their coats.

I wonder if they ever relaxed, those two.

Once Gog had placed the teapot on the table and settled his big bulk in his chair, I turned to Blondie.

"So what, exactly, is going on?" I asked, relieved finally to have the chance to get some answers.

Blondie turned to me, placing her hand on mine.

"All of this involves the Red and the White."

I cast a querulous gaze down at our hands, before raising my eyes to meet hers. She obviously thought I might flip out when she'd said that, but I was clueless.

"The Red and the White? Isn't that a novel by Stendhal?"

Everyone looked at me like I was smoking the rock right there at the table, except for Anyan. He gave me the look he gives me when he realizes there is something important I don't know, and that he probably should have told me.

I sighed, but it was more tired than frustrated. The fact was that I'd had to pack a lifetime's learning into less than a year when it came to my supernatural heritage. Gaps in my knowledge were more like crevasses, but that was only to be expected.

"You've really never heard of the Red or White?" Blondie asked, making a cat anus face.

"Nope. Never."

"Really?"

I flailed my hands at her, impatient. I hoped I hadn't been dragged halfway across the world—and out of Anyan's bed—for vague premonitions of dread. "Why would I say I'd never heard of them if I had?"

"Yes. Well. Think *Lord of the Rings*'s Ring Wraiths."

"Okay."

"Now think Ring Wraiths with death-rays for eyes and the ability to shoot nuclear warheads out of their wazoo."

"What?"

Magog's coat stirred as she shifted, her rough voice interrupting Blondie.

"Making light of this situation isn't helping, Cyntaf. She needs the facts."

"Magog's right," Anyan seconded.

Blondie shrugged, changing track.

"The Red and White are children of original Great Elementals, just like the creature underneath Rockabill."

"They're also Earth and Water?" I asked, confused. How could creatures that were kin to the gentle being under Rockabill be monsters out of legend?

Blondie shook her head, snorting a humorless laugh.

"No. All of Earth and Water's children ran the gamut from harmless and gentle to powerful and gentle. Fire, as

I'm sure you know from the creature, spawned all sorts of evil creatures on its own. Air, meanwhile, did not have many children: she was never as...together, shall we say, as the other Elementals. She was also powerful and distant, which made her very attractive to a being as covetous as Fire."

I frowned. Fire was, from all accounts, a nasty piece of work. Something told me it wouldn't be pleasant to be coveted by Fire.

"When Air resisted Fire's advances, Fire grew enraged. Fire raped Air, and from that union spawned two creatures," Blondie said.

My mind spun with the implications of Blondie's words. I'd been so close to the being living under Rockabill; I'd shared its mind. I understood how it wasn't like us. It wasn't a creature of genes and DNA. It was as much spirit as substance, and its spirit was that of its parents.

"The creature under Rockabill," I said, trying to articulate what I knew to be true, "it was born of Earth and Water. It was born of love and union. It's because of that it was good. So to be born of Fire and Air, and born of violence..."

"The Red and the White weren't beings you'd invite over for tea," Hiral squeaked, sloshing his own cup in the air and causing it to spill. Blondie absentmindedly mopped up his mess with her napkin.

"Wait," I said, finally catching up with what Blondie had been leading me towards, "the Red and the White are *those* creatures? That came from Fire's raping Air?"

Blondie nodded grimly. "To our people, the children of Fire and Air were known as the Red Queen and White King. Begat in violence, they reveled in their birthright."

"So what did they do?"

"They did everything hellish that you could ever imagine," Blondie said, her voice sad. "From the moment they were born they were bent on destruction."

"So where are they now? What happened to them?"

"They were destroyed, many times over. But each time, they'd rise again. This cycle repeated itself, for countless centuries. At first, there were enough of the children of the other Great Elementals to take them on. As that generation died out, however, it was up to those that remained—first those of us who had powers, pre-Schism, like me. What you call 'Originals' nowadays. Then Alfar and their armies."

"That was till Cyntaf," interrupted Gog, his low voice thick with admiration as he stared at Blondie adoringly. I noticed she flinched under his gaze.

"What did she do?" I asked the coblynau.

He turned his grey face towards me, his striations pulsing as he began talking, a physical manifestation of the excitement I could hear in his voice.

"She destroyed 'em, she did. For good. We've not heard a peep from 'em since she battled 'em, as our champion."

My ears perked up at the word "champion," and I looked enquiringly at Blondie. But I wasn't the only one.

"Wait, that was you?" Anyan asked.

Blondie nodded and Anyan studied her for a moment. "This is all starting to make sense," he said, eventually.

"What makes sense?" I asked, utterly confused.

Blondie thought for a moment, then sighed. "This is silly. There's an easier way to do this."

The Original stood and turned her back to us, only to strip off the tight, long-sleeved black T-shirt she now

wore. Descending from her shoulder blades like trailing
wings or drooping vines were two tattooed dragons: the
left one white, the right one red.

I stood, moving toward her as I knew what to do. I indicated the others should follow my lead. When I was
behind Blondie and close enough to touch, I raised my
fingers to her inked skin.

It was time for a little show and tell.

My raised fingers made contact with the warm skin of
Blondie's back, and then I was no longer Jane True.

*Standing in a field, the bodies of the fallen all around
me. I saw the corpse of the power-mad idiot who'd let
himself be seduced by the voices, and had released the
Red and White from their slumber.*

*But his death gave me no pleasure, for now only one
thing mattered: stopping the monsters.*

I can't do this, *I told the voice in my mind.*

[You have to,] *the creature responded, its voice as
calm and loving as possible.*

They are too strong, *I said, even my mental voice weary.*

[Yes. They are. But I will help. My cousins must be
stopped, and hopefully for good, this time.]

*The creature's voice went silent, but I still felt its pres-
ence in my mind. My head turned without my willing it,
and I knew it was using my eyes to scan the ground in
front of me. My gaze lit on the rough-hewn, double-
headed ax of a dead goblin.*

[That will do,] *the creature said.* [Pick it up.]

*I did as the creature asked, bending down to pick up
the labrys. As my fingers made contact with the smooth
wood of the haft, I felt a burst of power so strong as to be
painful surge through my body.*

[Steady now,] *the creature said.* [This will hurt.]

The power grew, screaming out of me with my own cries of pain. My hands, controlled by the creature, gripped the labrys. It burned with power: power that I fed from a source I couldn't understand—a mixture of the creature's power and its connection to water and earth.

[Water and Earth to fight Air and Fire,] *said that voice in my head when the pain finally began to recede.* [A weapon for a champion. In this battle: that champion is you, my child.]

The weapon was light in my hand, and I felt it was a part of me. I swung it, experimentally, and it sizzled through the air, glowing with power. Knowledge also became mine: knowledge of weak points, places that were vulnerable, and how those vulnerabilities could be exploited.

Hmmm…I thought, putting it all together. We've chopped them up before, but we've never done it quite so…thoroughly.

[The weapon will indeed make you thorough. We already know dissecting the beasts is not enough to contain the enemy,] *the creature warned.* [They have learned to call too effectively, and too many are willing to risk themselves putting my cousins together for the power they offer. We must make their inevitable destruction more permanent.]

I nodded, understanding. Nothing could kill the children of Air and Fire. But that just meant we had to be ever more creative in our approach.

Hefting my axe, I strode forward. I could see both the King and Queen—Red and White—at opposite ends of the battlefield. Siblings and lovers, they used humans and supernaturals alike to stage their deadly games of chess. Creating strife, fueling wars, whispering in dark voices of plots despicable and weapons obscene, the spawn of violence begat the violence that was their nature. Always on opposite sides of the battle, they would come together at the end to fuck over the carnage they'd inspired.

Let's see how powerful they are without a torso, *I mused, feeling my labrys pulse with my own strength, my own determination. Then I cut to the left, towards the King. He was the weaker of the two, and I'd seen the Queen tear one of my best friends apart with her bare hands.*

I was saving her for dessert.

CHAPTER THREE

I, Jane True, came back to myself with a gasp. Crowded around me, all with a hand on Blondie's bare back, the others also came to themselves one at a time.

"Bloody hell," rasped Magog. "You took on the Red and the White single handedly?"

"Hardly," Blondie said. "I had help."

"The labrys was yours," I interrupted, feeling like a thief.

"It was," Blondie said. "But I gave it up centuries ago, and gladly. You are its champion now, Jane."

"I don't understand," I said. "You just gave it up?"

"It's got a life of its own, in many ways. You'll see. When I needed it, and it thought I was what it needed, it was there for me. Then, one day, it wasn't. The Red and the White had been defeated for so long, they'd become only stories to frighten children. I guess the labrys thought its time was over. Now that it knows its not, I guess it needed a new champion."

"But why?" I begged, suddenly seeing an out...and it was an out I desperately wanted. "Why can't I give it back to you? Why can't you be the champion again?"

Throughout my pleading, Blondie had been patiently shaking her head. "Not how it works, Jane. It chose you. Which tells me that this war doesn't need me, at least not in that capacity. Besides, it's not mine to give away or to take. It's the creature's, and he gave it to you."

I started to argue with her, ready to remind her that the idea of me with an ax, fighting the forces of evil, was patently ridiculous. It was like arming a wiener dog with lasers. Before I could start, however, Anyan's elbow nudged me in the ribs. Only then did I look around to see Gog, Magog, and Hiral staring at me with rapt attention.

"So the stories are true," Gog rumbled. "Another champion has arisen." The coblynau gave me a speculative stare, his striations pulsing darkly.

Then he stood up and bowed.

To me.

And then Magog followed him.

I stared at their bent heads, horrified.

"What are you doing? Get up!" I demanded. The sight of them genuflecting before me was terrifying.

"We've been waiting for you," Magog rasped. "You are in our stories. You have been foretold."

Panicking, I looked to Blondie for help. The Original merely shrugged.

"It was pretty obvious that someone, sometime, would manage to cobble together the Red and the White. And at that point we'd need a new champion. It wasn't exactly divination to put that together," she said.

"Wait," I said, Gog and Magog's strange behavior

abruptly forgotten, "what do you mean by *cobbled together*?"

Blondie began talking as Gog and Magog took their seats again, exchanging long looks with each other.

"You already know, Jane, how there are relics of dead Elemental beings that have enormous power."

I nodded, remembering what I'd seen in Blondie's tattoo of the Great Schism—the moment when the humans originally gifted or mutated with the ability to use some of the elemental forces around them had been split up into the factions we now knew. She'd used the horn of a dead Fire elemental, the fossil of a being that had been pure elemental force.

"Yes, I know their bits can pack a punch. But you said *cobbled together*. Are you saying that if we put together enough parts of those creatures, they'd live again?" I hazarded.

"In the case of the Red and the White, yes. Think about it," Blondie said, wearily. "Those creatures were not... us. They're not necessarily organic. They're born of the powers that shaped life; that shaped our planet. And they're elementals. Does fire ever truly die? Can you kill a breeze?"

I shuddered.

"So is it just the Red and the White, or can all remains come alive again?" I asked, horrified. Because if so, we were fucked. Our every waking minute would be spent on an endless hunt: Jarl and Morrigan trying to uncover and awaken various bits of dead things, while we tried to stop them.

"Thankfully, it's just the Red and the White," Blondie said, much to my relief. "Most are really dead. For the children of Earth and Water, death was always final, even if their remains carried power. As for Fire, eventually even the fiercest blaze can be tamped out."

"What about Air?" Anyan asked.

"That's where it gets tricky. The bad news is: it's impossible to kill Air's children. The good news is: it doesn't matter. They all sort of dissolved of themselves, eventually, joining their mother in the wind."

What Blondie said was sad, but also poetic and rather beautiful, and I could see we all thought it so. Except for Hiral.

"Don't look relieved," the little creature squeaked in his horrible voice, his long nose bobbing obscenely. "What Cyntaf is about to say is, 'Well, almost all.' She likes to do that, you know."

Blondie gave Hiral a dirty look, to which he responded with a backwards peace sign, his long, blue-clawed fingers almost as long as his forearms.

"Well," Blondie said, her voice laced with sarcasm, "almost all, indeed, when it comes to the Red and the White." Then her tone grew serious again. "They'd be destroyed, but—like air feeding a fire—they would rekindle. So we tried imprisoning them. Always, inevitably, they got free. Usually by convincing some human or supernatural to help them. Even the few times we'd managed to sort of chop them up, before I had the weapon, they just dissolved and reformed somewhere else in a few decades time," Blondie said.

"Cyntaf, we don't understand," Magog rasped, interrupting Blondie. "Our legends say you destroyed them, as the champion..."

"The legends lie. I didn't destroy them," Blondie corrected. "The labrys just gave me the power to chop them up into so many pieces, so quickly, that parts of them were like slurry."

I grimaced at that image, imagining a Slurpee of Evil.

"So why innit that destroyed? It sounds destroyed to me," Gog said.

Blondie shrugged. "The ax was the most effective weapon we'd ever used, but still there were parts that wouldn't be…slurried. And even some of the destroyed parts kept coming back together, like in a modern-day horror film. Something about the ax kept them bound to that cut up form. So we divided them up and hid the pieces, as far and as wide as possible."

"What happens if they get put back together?" I asked.

"That's the thing," Blondie said. "I don't think they can be. There was enough that we really *did* destroy, and that couldn't reform. I don't know how they can be put back together. But someone's looking for those pieces, anyway. And the pieces like to help."

"Help?" Anyan asked.

"Yes. That's the problem with the Red and the White. Well, that's the other problem besides the fact they're pure evil and they enjoy bloodshed and carnage—even cut up they can still speak to people. It's like they send off vibes that make people want to help them, oftentimes without knowing what they're doing or why."

"So you cut them up a while ago, but they've still been able to get people to do stuff for them?" I asked.

"Exactly. I cut them up nearly four centuries ago. But they've still been responsible for most of the greatest atrocities in human and supernatural history. One or the other has a body part that's found, and it starts whispering, and next thing you know some human or supernatural has gone batshit and started a war."

"Does that explain Hitler?" I asked, wondering at the historical implications of Blondie's words.

"No, unfortunately. That was pure human crazy."

"So whom did the creature send you to?" Anyan asked, interrupting me before I could start listing historical maniacs to see if they were evil supernaturally or au naturel.

"The contact I was sent to by the creature was a museum curator. A mortal. His specialty is relics."

"I'm assuming you mean the body parts of purported saints, and not supernatural relics?" Anyan asked.

"Yes, human saints," Blondie replied. "He told me how he'd been interested in them for years, but it wasn't until he found a certain relic—a hand that was supposed to be some woman martyred in the fourth century—that relics became an obsession. And not just any relics."

"Let me guess," Anyan said. "He suddenly discovered he had a burning desire to collect everything he could find of that particular saint."

"Bingo," said the Original. "Even though it wasn't a particularly important saint, nor was there any reason to put it together, he just suddenly really wanted to do so."

"It's funny how such whims ripen, when the Red and the White are involved," Hiral squeaked. I noticed with irritation that he'd eaten the entire plate of cookies.

"So where are all the relics he found?" Gog asked. A question to which I wasn't sure I wanted to know the answer.

"One day a few months back, a beautiful blonde woman arrived at his door. He described her as a shorter version of 'that pretty elf queen from the *Lord of the Rings*.' "

I groaned. That was almost definitely Morrigan: she of the beauty and the evil.

Blondie's eyes flicked to mine, acknowledging my guess as to this mysterious stranger, before she continued: "She expressed a desire to own his relics, and suddenly he realized he no longer wanted them. After years of tracking them down obsessively—even mortgaging his home to pay for some—he suddenly couldn't care less about them."

"He sold them to her?" Anyan asked, with a distinct growl backing his words.

"Yes. For quite a nice sum, actually. He was no longer in the hole," said Blondie.

"So we assume the bad guys have at least most of one of the sets of relics?" I said.

"At least," replied Blondie. "But I'm afraid he had the complete set, or near it. Otherwise why would he feel he could give it up? I don't think the relics would let go of a human who'd done such a good job finding them to start with. Not unless they had reason to."

"Why are Morrigan and Jarl doing this?" Anyan asked. "They already have power, and could get more if they wanted it. They can't think they'll be able to control the Red and the White if they're awakened."

Blondie shrugged. "Who knows what they think. Remember, the Red and the White are masters of seduction. We don't even know how they do it—do they promise things, or just plant a seed in the mind? And we know so little about Morrigan, especially. She was just a typical Alfar monarch, until the day she killed Orin.

"The fact is that throughout history people have been willing to fight and die for the Red and the White,

including people who should have known better. My
guess would be they don't *plan* on actually resurrecting
the Red and the White. Maybe they think they can just
use the relics to amplify their power. But we can assume
that no matter what Morrigan and Jarl think they're planning, the Red and the White are planning something completely different, and using the Alfar to get it."

"So where does this leave us?" I asked.

"Well, we know what they're looking for. We know
we're behind. That said, I think I have a place to start—a
source at the British Museum. But that can wait until
tomorrow," said Blondie.

"We know our mission, then," Anyan said. "We have
to stop Morrigan and Jarl from getting any more relics.
And we've got to try to get back what they do have."

Blondie nodded, but Gog looked pensive.

"How do we even know the relics can be used?" asked
the coblynau. "You said parts was destroyed. How can
they be put back together with parts missing?"

Blondie frowned. "People do it all the time," she said,
gesturing towards the Ikea furniture. "And besides, even
if the Red and the White can't be resurrected in their
entirety, that doesn't mean some of that power can't be
channeled. Even a little bit of their strength would make a
formidable enemy nearly impossible to beat."

"So what exactly can the Red and the White do?" I
asked. "And what of their powers do you think Morrigan
and Jarl might be able to control if they put enough of
them together?"

"They could shapeshift," Blondie said. "But they
nearly always chose the form of a dragon. They have huge
Elemental control over Air and Fire, obviously. They *are*

Air and Fire. They're also really seductive. There's something about them that gets under the skin. It's like a form of hypnosis.

"As for what Morrigan and Jarl will be able to do with those parts, who knows. But obviously those parts have power, still, if they're working their magic on people like that curator. I'm thinking Morrigan and Jarl will be able to glean quite a bit of power from those pieces, even if they're not able to resurrect the Red and the White entirely."

"Great," I said, before looking around at everyone. "So to summarize, the Red and the White, forces of ultimate evil we thought were destroyed, might manage to resurrect themselves. Even if they don't manage that, their bones might still be used for unspeakable violence. And we have to stop that from happening."

"But even if we're too late, you can stop them, Jane. As the champion." Gog looked pleased at having put two and two together. I glared at him.

Despite the fact he seemed to be a nice coblynau, I suddenly wanted to punch him in the face.

When Anyan practically tossed me onto the sheets the second we'd made up the Hide-A-Bed, I thought he'd changed his mind about the whole talking thing.

The libido was all for buttering the barghest's bread, but my brain was siding with my virtue on this one. I was ready to take charge by being very good and not attacking Anyan back, when he had the audacity not to attack me in the first place. Instead, he cuddled me close and started talking.

"I was so scared when you were in that coma," Anyan murmured, his breath feathering my lips as he kissed me gently before finishing his thought. "When you woke up, I thought I had to grab you, gobble you up, then and there. But here you are. Still with me."

His iron-grey gaze rested on me while his fingers trailed over my cheek, down my jaw and neck, finally sliding over my arm. Meanwhile, he'd also managed to touch on about six of my current issues.

"Is that what we were doing in Rockabill?" I asked, seizing the opportunity to try to understand how he felt about me despite how good his hands felt on my flesh. "Grabbing each other?"

"I think that's certainly one way to describe it," he said, chuckling, but I didn't laugh with him.

"Was that all it was?" I asked instead, my voice betraying my nervousness.

"What do you mean?"

"I mean, was the way we were, or, um, the way you were with me, just because of the attack?"

"I'm sorry, Jane, I don't understand what you're asking," he said. His eyes betrayed only curiosity and his fingers never stopped their comforting caresses.

I took a deep breath, realizing belatedly that we were, indeed, plunging headfirst into a Real Talk. "What I'm asking, I think, is if whether the attack, or what happened after, is why you . . . liked me so much when I woke up."

Anyan's expression changed from curiosity to confusion. For a split second his fingers stopped tracing patterns on my skin, but then just as suddenly his expression cleared and he was shaking his head like he couldn't believe what I'd just asked.

"Oh, Jane," he said, shifting me around so he could see my face better. "You really can be an idiot."

The "idiot" gave him a hard pinch in the soft flesh of his side. He yelped, grabbing my hands in a gentle wrist-lock. He used the leverage his grip gave him to pull me close enough our noses were brushing against each other.

"Do you really think I care about you just because you were knocked out for a month?" he asked me, softly.

"I was in a coma," I said defensively, rolling as far away from him as I could with my wrists still in his grip, which was only on to my back. I couldn't really care less about the terminology, but I was miffed he'd called me an idiot.

"And it was terrifying," he said. He rolled closer to place one of his big hands on my belly. "I was scared every minute you were lying there. But it did give me a lot of time to think."

I shifted my chin to stare over my other shoulder, suddenly unable to look Anyan full in the face.

"See, that's where our stories diverge," I said, to the table lamp next to me. "I didn't have that time. To think, I mean. I was dreaming, and not even my own dreams, but the creature's."

Anyan's fingers, which had begun a restless little dancing caress, stilled on my stomach.

"Are you saying that you don't feel anything for me?" he asked. If I hadn't known the barghest so well at this point, I wouldn't have recognized the flatness in his voice.

"No," I said quickly, rolling over to face him so that he could see my own expression. "That's not what I'm saying at all. I'm saying that, from my perspective, one minute we were a possibility, and the next moment I woke up and we were naked. Well, I was naked. How come you're never naked?"

"Focus, Jane," Anyan said, his voice all rumbly where I'd ended up pressed against him.

"Right, sorry. Anyway, what I was trying to say is that I want to know why. What changed when I was asleep? Why me? Why now?"

"Because you deserve it," he said, leaning forward to nip at my lower lip.

"What does that mean?" I mumbled, against his lips, then pulled back enough to say what I was most afraid of. "Do I 'deserve' it just cuz I saved us? Because I got hurt?"

"No, you daft girl," he said, nipping again at my lip, this time more sharply. I felt an answering twinge in my belly.

"It's not just because you got hurt, or because you saved my life. It's because of everything you are, and how I feel when I'm around you."

My eyes must have been big as saucers as they ever so slowly met his.

"The reason I want to be with you, little minx, is because you make me feel relaxed in a way I haven't, in a really long time. At the same time, you make me feel focused, like I finally have something I really want again. When I'm around you, I have no idea what you'll do next, or how I'll react. It's like you strip away all my experience."

Not all his experience, hopefully, butted in my libido.

"So," he continued, first taking my chin in hand and turning my face, because I'd gone back to giving him my nervous side-eye, "while you were lying there, in that coma, all I could think about was how my life would change if you were no longer in it. I realized how much I'd come to want you—to see you, to talk to you, to touch you. And I knew that if you died in that bed, in *my* bed, I'd be really, really pissed off."

I couldn't help but giggle. "Royally pissed off?"

"Royally," he replied, but while his tone was light his expression was very serious.

"Would you have run off to expose your sparkly chest to the humans in Italy?"

"What the hell are you talking about?"

"I guess you probably didn't read *Twilight*."

He didn't bother to answer, but kissed me instead. I kissed him back. It felt like we were agreeing on something, and it felt good.

"So," he said, pulling back just enough to speak but leaving his forehead resting against mine, "can we date?"

My heart practically exploded in my chest. My breath caught; I might actually have hiccoughed. A thousand responses raced through my head even as my brain threatened to shut down and do a cerebral happy dance.

Naturally, the most inappropriate response possible won the short but intense battle for utterance. My heart may have felt like it was buoyed on the wings of a thousand intoxicated doves, but I couldn't let him know that and still hold up my head.

"What?" I asked, pulling away from him. "You're like four-hundred-million years old. And you want to *date*?"

He gave me the stink eye.

"Seriously, you're so *old*. What did people do for dates when you were a puppy? If you club me over the head and take me to your cave, I'll be traumatized. You can't pull that shit on a girl who's half seal. We have a history."

"Jane, I'm serious."

"So am I! Seriously, you're *old*. And you want to *date*.

When we've almost already had sex and there's a war about to start, or started, or who knows what. And you want to *date*?"

Anyan's long nose twitched as he sniffed, clearly offended.

"What's wrong with dating?" he asked.

"You're *old*," I said. "Old people don't date."

"I'll give you old," he said, and suddenly I was on my back and Anyan was hovering above me.

Score one for the libido, my brain said, admiringly. Said libido bowed deeply, while my virtue threw up its hands in defeat.

Anyan's hands found my hair, knotting themselves in my still shower-damp tresses and tugging gently. I sighed, arching my back up to press myself into his body, and then his lips were on mine. Unlike our kiss before, this kiss was a hungry one: all teeth and tongue. I answered him with a ferocity that didn't surprise me. I felt like a starving woman, and Anyan was my wheel of brie.

His mouth made its way over to my ear, sucking and nipping gently at the lobe before he worked himself down my neck. I knew I was in trouble when his gentle kisses turned into a rough bite at that soft spot where my shoulder met my neck, and I nearly bucked him off me it felt so good. He had this domineering way about him that totally ketchuped my tater tots—it was like he knew what I wanted more than I did.

It was scary, and gorgeous, and gods it felt good. So I was as surprised as Anyan when I stopped him by gently pushing on his chest.

"I think we should wait," I said, when he'd backed up enough for me to look him in the eyes.

"Wait?" Anyan asked, looking confused.

"I can't believe I just said that, but yes. The thing is, I don't want this to be Ryu all over again."

A stormy look passed over the barghest's face when I said my ex's name, and I cursed myself.

"I mean, you're not Ryu, and I don't feel about you the way I felt about Ryu, and I can't believe I'm still saying the name 'Ryu.' I'll stop now. But I actually liked what you said. About dating. About getting to know each better and taking things as they come. I don't want to take things slow, or fast, or whatever—I just want things to be right."

Anyan sighed, rolling over onto his side and cuddling me close.

"Using the dating thing against me, eh?" he asked. I smiled against his pecs, wishing we were naked and biting but also knowing that how we were right now was how it should be.

"Sorry, but I do think it's a good idea," I said, raising my eyes to meet his.

"Don't be. You're right. And besides, this will be more fun."

"Fun?"

"Yes, fun. This means that I get to work to seduce you."

"Ooh la la," I said, raising my chin to kiss his freshly shaven jaw. Anyan let me kiss him, then he withdrew, looking down at me with a predatory little grin.

"I'm serious, you. I admit, my seduction skills are a little rusty. But I'm going to look forward to getting you alone whenever I can, and making you want me. Eventually I'll get you to where you're begging. And then, little girl, I'm going to show you what begging really means."

With those words the barghest ran one big hand slowly

down my back to cup my ass. He squeezed, the look in his eyes making me want to call out for a tarp.

I think I wheezed.

"Now go to sleep, Jane. Tomorrow I'm going to start training you on that ax."

Anyan rolled over to sleep, leaving me staring at the ceiling.

Even my libido was fairly certain we were in way over our heads.

CHAPTER FOUR

Anyan was using his coach voice, but a quiet version as we were in the postage-stamp sized backyard of the house we'd misappropriated. Luckily it had a very high privacy fence around it—otherwise the neighbors might have looked out to see what looked like a reenactment of Conan the Barbarian Midget.

"Good, but keep your right wrist strong," the barghest told me. "You don't want to let the head waver: you want the blade to cut true."

I frowned in concentration, feeling the sweat on my brow streaming down my face. At that point in our practice, my wrists, forearms, triceps, and shoulders felt like they were on fire, while my abs and lower back ached with a dull pain. But I did as I was told, steadying my right hand up the haft of the labrys well above my left, then slashing forward, bringing my right hand down the haft as I did so, so that it met my left.

"Better. But we'll need quite a bit of practice to get

those arms strong enough," Anyan said. "Had enough for today?"

I nodded quickly, wanting to sit down on the ground and not move till someone fetched me. Instead I let the double head of the labrys clunk on the grass, with the haft resting against my leg as I fanned my sore hands in the air.

"Blisters?" the barghest asked.

I nodded, miserable.

"Here, let me," he said. Soon, his big hands were around mine and then I felt the warm tingle of his healing powers sweep into my skin. I sighed, rocking back on my heels and shutting my eyes wearily.

I'd slept well the night before, despite what had been a rough half hour full of mad hypnagogic fantasies all beginning with some ridiculous premise, like my sleep-walking, or getting up for a glass of water, or needing to pee. Each fantasy ended the same way, however, with my coming back to bed only to trip and fall onto Anyan's penis. Luckily, my overtaxed sex drive was combated by sheer weariness and jetlag, so sleep eventually crept up on me like an over-the-hill ninja. When I really dreamed, it was of sitting with a black dog in a sunlit meadow, while bees buzzed around us and flowers bloomed. When I woke up, I felt like I'd been given a portent of good things to come.

There was no lounging in bed for me, though. Anyan had immediately scooted me into breakfast and then, as soon as I'd finished eating, ordered I get dressed, bring the labrys, and follow him outside. I thought he might be interested in a first date of naughty ax-play, but instead he just wanted to start my lessons.

Lessons I very obviously needed. For the only other

time I'd fought with the ax, I'd let the creature take over my body. In that fight with the now deceased Phaedra, I had been amazing—only it wasn't, of course, really me. It was the creature, controlling me through my mind. But it wasn't there to help me, now. I kept reaching towards the place in my mind where I knew I could contact my ancient friend, but all I got was the mental version of sleepy static, with an occasional flash of a dream or a faint emotion.

It had warned me it was going to sleep, and, in fact, had wanted me to destroy the last sigil that could free it because it wanted to be able to sleep deeply, in peace. But I hadn't thought it meant it would fall off into some kind of coma.

Which left me in charge of its power: its own champion, with no idea what I was doing or how I was supposed to do it.

Awesome.

At least Anyan was a good teacher, and knew how to ax-fight. The part of me that went squishy when I thought of him thought about the fact that Anyan was good at everything, and that he also looked hot while he was being good at things. For example, watching those long arms, roped with muscles, swing that ax around as he demonstrated the various moves I would be learning had left me no more enlightened about what to do with the labrys, but it had left me slightly breathless. And pretty sure I knew what to do with the barghest, if not the ax.

Sop him up with a biscuit, the libido purred, borrowing Grizzie's favorite phrase.

"Jane?" Anyan's voice interrupted my reverie, and I looked up at his face. I realized I'd been staring at his hands on mine. And might have been purring.

"Hmm?" I asked, dreamily.

"I said that you're all healed," he must have repeated, his eyes crinkling with laughter at my reaction to him. But before I could be at all offended he thought my overt lust for him was funny, he brushed a kiss against the knuckles of my right hand. "And now I want to see you charge up this thing. I want to see how it works," he continued, as he dropped my hand and moved away a step. "How much power you have, as well as control."

So I dutifully raised the ax so that its double-head was about level with my eyes. Then I closed my eyes, and reached out to it . . .

The power was immediately there, and even through my eyelids I could see the charge that had lit up the labrys. I felt its force lick up and down my spine, incredibly strong and both mine and not-mine. It was like I was pregnant with a life force that was both part of me and utterly foreign.

"That's enough, Jane. Can you shut it off?"

I frowned again in concentration, my eyes still shut, as I pulled my inner focus away from the power now residing within me. After a few seconds, the light in front of my eyelids dimmed, and the world was plunged into darkness. I blinked my eyes open slowly, letting them adjust to the dawn light and focus on Anyan.

The barghest was matching my expression, frown for frown.

"How do you do it?" he asked. "How does it come to you?"

I lowered the ax slowly, then let its double-head rest against the floor again. I thought hard, trying to figure out how to articulate what it felt like to access the power with which the creature had gifted me.

"It's like there's a door in my mind that I can open or shut. Behind the door is the power."

"It's as simple as that?" Anyan asked.

"Yes and no," I replied. "Because I feel like that's all I can do, shut it off or turn it on. I don't know how to *use* it, really. Although I guess we'll never need a flashlight..."

"Can you ask the creature?" Anyan interrupted. "Because you're going to need full access to that power, as soon as possible."

I tried that place in my mind that had once held the creature's communication.

"Nope," I said, shaking my head. "I think it's sleeping. Really, really deeply," I added, when Anyan looked like he wasn't going to take "sleeping" as an answer.

"Damn," he said, looking at me with concern. I saw, then, how worried he was about me. In turn, I realized why.

"I'm being set up as some kind of hero, aren't I," I asked, my voice small.

His only response was a somber nod.

I suddenly wanted very much to sit down, so I did. Dragging the ax behind me unceremoniously, I walked to the small set of steps leading from the house into the garden and I sat down heavily. Anyan followed, squeezing in next to me and wrapping an arm around my waist. I let my head fall on his chest.

We sat there in silence, for a moment. I don't know what Anyan was thinking about, but I was thinking about what it meant for me to be a hero. It took a few minutes for me to realize I had no idea, but I knew whom to ask.

"What does it mean?" I asked quietly, peering up at him.

"What?" he asked.

"Being a hero."

Anyan thought for a minute, and when he responded his voice was serious.

"It can mean a lot of things. In this case, though, it means a lot of things it shouldn't. It means that people are going to want something from you. They're going to want you to be someone in whom they can invest their hope. But this is also the Great Island—a country legendary even by supernatural standards for its politicking. Many of our monarchs and monsters have emerged from this place.

"That's why we're here, probably," Anyan said, stroking a big hand down over my hair like he was petting a cat. "It's said that whoever holds the Great Island holds the power of our kind. So it's no coincidence that any large battle fought would be fought here."

I shivered at the words "large battle," and his grip on me tightened, the hand in my hair still stroking gently. Then his fingers found my chin, and he raised my gaze to his.

"So your having the power of the champion means that people are going to want to use you, here. People will want either to take your power, or to make you work for them, or to knock you out of the game. In the New World, the politics you've seen are nothing compared to here. There is space to breathe and to be left alone, for the most part, where we grew up, and beings like us came to the New World for the same reasons humans did: to be free. But here, everything is ancient."

I nodded, understanding to a certain extent. "I think it must be the same for humans, in some ways," I said. "The difference, you know, between Americans and Europeans."

"Maybe," Anyan nodded. "Certainly Europeans have to deal with a lot more history every day, in a way Americans don't so much. But there's one important difference."

I cocked my head curiously, enjoying Anyan lecturing me. He didn't talk this much that often, and I loved this chance to see the side of him that was wise and patient.

"British history is not only long but also alive in many ways, yet all but the most recent players are dead," he said. "Imagine if in their parliament, there still walked Henry the Eighth, or Queen Elizabeth, or Shakespeare, or William Wallace?"

Suddenly understanding, I blanched. "That's what it's like for the supes," I said, "Isn't it? The Alfar that lead them are the Alfar that have always led... and there's no where to escape them, on an island of this size."

"Exactly." His lips pressed against my forehead, and I snuggled closer. "History isn't really history, on the Great Island. It's more like the supes here live with multiple presents layered one on top of the others, making the future hard to imagine and the past impossible to escape. It's why there are so many fullbloods here, like Gog and Magog, in the rebel camp. Halflings have it rougher than ever here, but so does everyone else."

"So what do we do?" I asked.

"We trust no one but each other, and maybe Blondie. While she definitely wants something from us, at least I think we know what that 'something' is. As for everyone else, even if they're otherwise decent creatures, they *will* have an agenda, having grown up here. They will have something they want from us or for us, like Blondie does, but we'll have no idea what it is until it's too late."

"Trust no one," I repeated, feeling like I was in an episode of the *X-Files*. I looked up at Anyan. "Is that it?"

"Nope. You might also have to save the world."

"Oh?" I said, trying not to show my fear.

It's not going to happen, I told myself. *We'll stop Morrigan and Jarl way before they got anywhere near resurrecting the Red and the White. We'll get back whatever bones they've managed to run off with, and we'll hand them some whoop ass on a plate.*

I'm never going to have to play hero.

Bolstered by those thoughts, I managed to laugh at Anyan. "Gotcha. Trust no one and be prepared to save the world. Anything else?"

"Keep nudging the creature. See if it wakes up, ever. I know it wants to sleep, and it's obviously not engaged with this world the way it was when Blondie was champion. But we're going to need it. In the meantime, we'll get Blondie to help train you with the labrys—maybe she knows more than just how to make it light up."

"You bet she does," came a voice behind us. It was Blondie, looking muzzy as she sipped from a steaming mug.

"There's coffee inside," she said, gesturing towards the kitchen. "Then we gotta go."

"Where to?" Anyan asked, hoisting himself to his feet before giving me his hand to help me up.

"The British Museum," the Original replied, as she walked in the house.

I couldn't help it. The part of me that would much rather be a tourist than a champion flushed with anticipation.

I got to go to the British Museum. I just hope no one there wanted to kill any of us.

*   *   *

"Wow," I said, as I walked through the gates.

The British Museum was the sort of outrageously imperial building that was all the more impressive for its age. The great stone pile before me, a monument to empire and cultural commerce, was the inspiration, the architectural Platonic ideal, for the places of civic pride with which I'd grown up.

The outside of the building was all pillars and long low stairs leading up to the main floor. A huge courtyard, partially flanked by the museum's huge wings, was already full of tourists. Armies of Italian school children milled around, steadily encroaching on my personal space, and I wondered what on earth we were doing here. There were too many normal humans, surely, for anything of supernatural interest to be in the British Museum.

That said, Blondie had warned us to mute our mojo, so there had to be something or someone we were avoiding.

We pushed forward through the crowd, heading towards the bronze-and-glass doors into the entryway of the museum. I half-expected the doors to lead us into some magical realm the humans couldn't see. Upon pushing our way inside, I was instead greeted by a security guard who asked to look in our bags. Luckily I'd left the labrys in Magog's van, which Gog and the raven were guarding, as that would have been awkward to explain.

Hiral ignored the guard entirely, striding boldly forward. Still, even though I felt no magic coming off of him and he was, for all intents and purposes, a tiny blue-and-green monster, no one paid him the least bit of attention. I wondered what gwyllion were, with magic so infused in their blood and body that they used such powerful mojo without actually using it.

Once the guard was done with the rest of us, Blondie strode forward through what had been another, interior courtyard of the building, but had been glassed in to make an enormous covered square.

A vast floor of white stone flowed toward a round structure in the center of the square, with a soaring net of glass-and-steel serving as its roof. At the center of the square stood what had been the original Reading Room of the British Library, before the library had moved to its new digs near King's Cross. There had always been a circular structure standing there, even when this was an open-air court, but now it was multistoried and gleaming white, rather than the weathered stone it had been.

An actual thrill flowed up my spine as we moved towards the old Reading Room. It no longer remotely resembled the space where the likes of Virginia Woolf and Karl Marx had sat, but those walls had still housed the finest minds of multiple generations laboring at their great works.

The respectful hush in the Reading Room told me I wasn't the only one left a bit *verklempt* by my surroundings, and I knew the gaze I was casting about was probably a ridiculously reverent one. That said, the room deserved some reverence. A vast, intricately decorated domed ceiling lorded over a room full of exhibition items in glass cases. While I was a bit disappointed that it was more museum than library, by this point, it was still gorgeous.

And for a second, I tried to imagine myself in a lady's day dress, rather than my jeans and long black sweater.

The fantasy ended, however, when I was unable to get rid of my new red Converse, even if it were only in my imagination.

Virginia Woolf would totally have rocked Converse, I told myself, wondering whether the others would let me nose around just a little.

Unfortunately, Blondie was all business as she strode purposefully towards the back of the room. Hiral was already waiting for us, picking his teeth with a long fingernail, his expression bored. Anyan followed sharpish, but I trailed behind, peering greedily into cases. Eventually, Blondie sent the barghest to fetch me. He did so sweetly, taking my hand with a caress of his thumb on my palm that made me want to follow him anywhere.

That said, I did wonder if I'd ever get a chance to see any real sites before I had to leave Britain.

Blondie paused at a back wall of the Reading Room. She peered up at the ceiling, which was dotted around its edges with plaster moldings that resembled the enormous plastic molding in the center of the dome. Then she began herding us together, staring the whole time at the ceiling and lining us up with something only she could see. Anyan ended up crowding right behind me, while Blondie pressed in from the side. Hiral was standing between our legs, an uncomfortable fact I did my best to ignore. Eventually, the Original looked around surreptitiously, and I felt the faintest of glamours waft off of her, her power a gentle supernatural wind against the hairs on my arms as she camouflaged all four of us.

Only then did Blondie lean forward and breathe on the wall. A glyph appeared, similar to the one I'd seen when we were hunting the creature, except this one was smaller and looked more modern. It also wasn't touch activated, as Blondie used only a soft puff of breath and a few whispered words before it started glowing.

I'd been expecting the wall to open, revealing a secret corridor. Instead, I nearly screeched when I felt the floor move. Belatedly, I realized why Blondie had bunched us up the way she had.

Instead of there being a secret door, we were standing on a secret platform that began to descend, very slowly. Light still filtered in from the hole in the floor above us, but soon that was blotted out as either another floor or a glamour covered up the entrance. I felt a moment of panic and I clutched Anyan's hand, not knowing if I was allowed to create a mage light or not. But Blondie did it for us a second later, and we descended in silence, Hiral's mad blue hair tickling my bare forearms. Eventually, I had to ask.

"Where the hell are we going?"

Anyan opened his mouth, about to answer me, when Blondie stopped him with a finger on his lips.

"Let her see it for herself," she said. "It's more impressive that way."

For a second it looked like he was going to protest, and I *definitely* wanted to protest. But then he smiled, and nodded.

"You're going to love it," he told me, and that was all he'd say.

I grumbled, wondering what the hell was awaiting me as we crawled downward at a ridiculously slow pace. Any irritation at how slow we were going ended however, as the platform emerged from the tunnel we'd been in into a vast room of books.

A frightening sense of vertigo hit me at the same time as did awe at my surroundings. I realized only then that we must have been standing on magic, for there was no apparatus under or above us that I could see. Despite the slightly braver part of me that wanted to look around, the scared-shitless part of me squeezed shut my eyes until I felt Anyan's hands steadying my shoulders and, even more comforting, his Air magic wrap around me, binding me tightly to him in a security blanket of mojo.

My eyes opened and I smiled at him gratefully, only then daring to indulge my curious side by looking around, albeit carefully.

If I'd been a bit disappointed at the only moderately library nature of the former Reading Room-turned-exhibit, this room more than made up for it. Typically Alfar in that its design seemed to ignore the laws of physics, we descended past stories of books. There were so many, in fact, that they were soon towering above us, bending with the roof into entire arches of shelves, multicolored leather book spines defying gravity by being shelved normally, if apparently upside down. Huge ladders on complicated tracks crisscrossed not only the walls but the ceiling, as well, and I shuddered at the thought of climbing all the way up one of those to get a book on the ceiling.

When we were finally at ground level, the magical platform dissolved, leaving us standing on a lush burgundy carpet. More low carrels of books dotted the vast space before us, creating natural little divisions between clusters of seating options. The time range of the furniture ranged from modern, if very chic, sofas to the little leather and wood chair-hammock thingies I imagined had been the thrones of Celtic kings. There were also low tables, desks, and conference tables, offering different options for working or reading. Sconces holding mage balls lined the room, bathing everything in their warm and welcoming light, and at the very center of the room there was a fire pit, around which were low couches lined with pillows.

The fire pit was a bizarrely seventies Playboy touch, but it worked, not least as the flames of the fire were a supernatural kind that wouldn't actually burn down the library.

Standing there, I felt almost overwhelmed by the room. It was the ultimate library, heaven for a girl who considered herself a strong contender for the ultimate reader.

"Do you like it?" Anyan asked, his voice teasing. Looking up at his iron-grey eyes, I realized I was beyond words.

In response, I could only moan.

I was pretty sure I'd just had a nerdgasm.

CHAPTER FIVE

What is this place?" I breathed, when I'd gotten my brain back online.

"It's our Great Island's Great Repository," came a woman's alto voice from a high-backed chair almost directly to my right. I couldn't see her, as the chair had its back to us and she must have been seated. But then the voice stood, and turned, and I found myself staring into my mirror image.

For there was Jane, just as I'd last seen her in my reflection: the same long black hair with bangs framing her face, the same black eyes in which the pupils were barely discernible, the same heart-shaped face with its familiar plump cheeks, high cheekbones, and button chin, followed by my equally familiar curvy figure. Except where I was wearing jeans and a long black wool sweater, and my red Converse—my official Ninja gear—she was wearing a simple grey sheath dress. The sheath did nothing for me.

You've definitely put on the weight you lost sleeping, my brain observed. *And then some.*

It's cushion, harrumphed my libido. *For the pushin'.*

"Ummmmmm," I said, stupidly, as my mirror-image cocked her head at me.

"Yes?" the image asked, as I continued saying, "Ummm."

I looked over at Anyan, and then the other me also looked over at Anyan.

"What the hell is going on?" I demanded, as the not-me version of me rolled her eyes and walked from behind the chair and away a few paces. After a few strides and a few seconds, I realized that the not-me was changing. Soon enough, an utterly nondescript woman stood staring at me. When I say "nondescript," I don't mean average, I mean she completely defied description. One minute I thought her hair was mouse-brown, and then I decided it was dull blonde, and then I decided it was more of a dull grey. Similarly, her eyes kept changing. From dreary hazel brown, to watery blue, to insipid green. Her figure and facial features appeared to morph between all styles of average. Indeed, that was the woman's only defining characteristic, what with all the changes: the fact she was utterly average, at all times. I would forget her face the minute I walked away from her, even if that face hadn't been changing before my very eyes.

"Still here then, Sarah?" Blondie, now standing slightly behind me to my right, asked the woman.

A rueful smile crossed the woman's shifting features.

"I'm married to the knowledge, Cyntaf," she said, in a thick Scottish brogue. "You know that."

"Aye, Sarah. I do," Blondie said, her own accent morphing to match Sarah's. "Come and give us a hug, then."

Sarah walked past me to get to Blondie, and I watched, alarmed, as her figure changed swiftly back into mine as she got closer. Then she was past me, and herself again, but then Blondie was holding another Blondie tight, stroking a muscular little hand over the side of her twin's head, below her Mohawk.

The Blondie that was really Sarah was shivering, clinging to our original Original like a woman lost at sea. Our own Blondie's eyes held both grief and wariness.

"It's been so long," the Sarah-Blondie whispered.

"I know," our own Blondie replied. "I'm sorry."

"I've missed you."

Our own Blondie's response was to kiss Sarah-Blondie, the Original's body melding seamlessly and comfortably against her very own shape.

I felt a hand touch the small of my back and I looked up to meet Anyan's gaze. He looked as curious and as uncomfortable as I did. When we heard whispers coming from the pair in front of us, we both turned our backs. With Gog and Magog guarding the little white van, only Hiral was with us. But he was eyeing what now sounded like a rather heated reunion with lascivious glee, and I felt Anyan use a heavy swath of power to turn the little creature around so he was also facing the door we'd just entered. Hiral looked around just long enough to stick out his long, black tongue at Anyan before he wandered forward to begin browsing through book shelves as if doing so had been his original intention.

"What is she?" I whispered. The way Sarah had morphed her shape hadn't been like a shapeshifter—I could tell she'd no more controlled it than did a chameleon changing colors.

"A doppelgänger," Anyan said. "They don't really change shape as they do automatically invoke a glamour so powerful you could even touch it. It's strong mojo, but I'm sure you can imagine how it makes people uncomfortable."

I nodded, remembering what it felt like to look into my own eyes. But, then again, Blondie seemed to have no trouble. My libido couldn't help but wonder what it was like to make love to oneself, which totally shorted out my brain. Stuck on that one thought, I didn't hear whatever clued Anyan in to the fact the little reunion was over and we could rejoin the party. But I automatically moved with him as he steered me back to the two women.

Sarah had moved away from Blondie, so that she was herself again, whatever that was. Her form was still shifting, more erratically and wildly than before, but it eventually began to slow down until the shifts were again subtle. Blondie, meanwhile, looked grim. I wanted to hug her, unsure what was going on but knowing that not a lot shook her up. Yet whatever there was between her and the librarian had done so.

"So," I said, to break up the tension, "I'm Jane."

I didn't go to shake the doppelgänger's hand, or anything, as I knew I'd end up shaking my own.

"And I'm Sarah." Sarah's eyes slid over me curiously, before darting to Anyan.

"And you are Anyan Barghest," she said, a note of awe in her voice. A stack of books came winging from somewhere on the ceiling, to land in a stack at her feet.

"Anyan the Great," she said, picking up the first book. "This details your greatest triumph, when you ended the reign of Drina the Despotic. And here," she said, throwing the first book on the floor only to pick up the second and third, one in each hand. "Here we have an exposé on your early life, and another detailing your skill as a strategist." The books joined the first on the floor, and then a bunch of paperbacks floated up in front of our faces. They had lurid covers featuring a hunky man who was sort of Anyan-esque, wearing a black wolf pelt. "My favorite, the romance series featuring the dreaded Fanyan Barghest, loving his way through all of the courts."

I cocked an eyebrow at Anyan, who looked suitably mortified.

"Total fabrications," he told me, blushing a rare shade of beet.

But I was less surprised by the fact someone had tried to turn him into a supernatural Fabio than I was that he had a critical (and not so critical) volume of work dedicated to him. I'd been told he was a hero, over and over, but I never saw that version of Anyan. The version of Anyan I knew, my Anyan, never took himself that seriously.

"And my favorite," Sarah said, floating a huge, leather-bound tome towards me. I plucked it from the air, and nearly tipped over it was so heavy.

"The definitive biography. Everything you ever wanted to know about Anyan Barghest is in those pages," Sarah said.

"And we don't have time for reading," Anyan said, his voice firm. He held out his hand for the book, and after a long second I handed it to him.

I put a damper on my brain, not letting it jump to the thousand, mostly horrendous, conclusions on which it wanted to pounce, like the fact the book would prove Anyan was quite the Casanoghest, or that he had a thing for livestock, or was a known cannibal.

You have the man in front of you, I told myself, firmly. *You don't need another creature's version of his life. He gets to tell you that himself.*

Feeling better, I winked at Anyan before turning back towards Sarah.

"What's a Great Repository?"

Sarah's ever-changing eyes met mine, and for a second they again flashed large and black, mirroring my own. I shivered, but then they shifted again and she was bustling away from us towards a cart stacked with stuff. There were really ancient scrolls, and equally ancient roughly bound books. There were also a few more properly bound books, but they, too, looked incredibly old. Incongruously, the final articles on the shelves were what looked like modern-day, if outdated, textbooks.

"What your human history calls Great Britain, your supernatural side calls the Great Island," Sarah said, acknowledging my human ancestry far more gracefully than did most other supes. "It's unique as, due to geography, supernaturals and humans grew together through their formative years. While that changed, and the relationship has since evolved, there is still a symbiosis of cultures here on the Great Island greater than anywhere else on the planet."

"What does that mean?" I asked.

"Basically," Blondie said, taking a seat at one of the nearby long, low tables that peppered the room, "supes aren't entirely in the closet, here. Long ago we ran around free with the humans. That's why there's such a strong fairy mythology. We were the Fair Folk, the Tylwyth Teg, et cetera."

"But not everyone knows about us now," I said.

"Magog said she had to hide her true form from the humans."

"True," Sarah conceded. "There grew to be too many problems between our kind and humans. Our numbers were shrinking, while the human population kept growing. Tensions kept increasing, but when Christianity finally took hold on the island we knew we had to go underground. Imagine what the witch trials would have done to our people?"

My lips twisted in silent acknowledgement. "But we're standing in the middle of the British Museum, in a room that's apparently run by the supernatural, for the supernatural. That's not really underground. Well, we are underground, literally, but you know what I mean."

Sarah smiled at me, her face again flashing into my own before shifting. I was never going to get used to that. "Our leaders recognized early that the feudal system respected power, and that it could keep secrets if the benefits for doing so were obvious. Despite all the political changes here on the Island for human society, some things haven't changed, and respect for power and lineage is one of them. Let's just say we've made it worthwhile for this human government to keep our secrets, although there are often slips. Why do you think the British are still so obsessed with fairies, and stories of strangers from other worlds popping round to save them?"

"Oh my god, is Doctor Who real?" I asked.

"The Doctors are actually a team of different Alfar who handle situations that, in reality, are probably the fault of the supernatural community to begin with. But yes."

"Whoa," I said, awed out of my little mind. "Awesome. Can I meet them?"

"Yeah, no," said Anyan. "As they'd probably kill us on sight."

I sighed, all fantasies of becoming the Doctor's next sidekick blown away by the fact that, apparently, the Doctor would blow me away.

And not in a fun way, my virtue warned my libido, which had perked up at the word "blown."

"So the government knows about this room?" I said.

"There's a very secret part of a very secret part of our government that knows about it, yes. In fact, most of that secret part of the government is secretly made up of supes, but that's a secret."

I shook my head, resetting my rattled brains.

"Huh?" I asked.

"Basically we've weaved ourselves into the echelons of human power in a way unheard of in other countries. The closest approximation of what we've done here on the Island is in your North America, but because you're all in different Territories there's been no single, top-down infrastructure to embed in your human governments. Therefore your supernatural communities mostly use their positions in human government to monitor and to cover things up. Here on the Island, we can make things happen."

I frowned at Sarah, unsure how I felt about that bit of information. But she ignored my expression, and continued talking.

"This room is, in many ways, symbolic of our relationship to the human inhabitants of our Island. One can see it as built inside the human edifice, yes. But one can also see it as having the human edifice built around us, with us as its backbone—its core."

"And here is housed the greatest compendium of supernatural knowledge ever gathered in one place, since the Great Library in Alexandria burned," Blondie said, moving towards Sarah who, alarmingly, again began to look like Blondie the closer the Original came towards her. When Blondie was standing next to Sarah (who was now fully Blondie) she leaned in to kiss her doppelgänger on the cheek. "Whilst Sarah has been its prisoner."

"Its curator," Sarah corrected, laughing, but our own Blondie's expression told me she hadn't been joking. I realized at that moment there was something else going on here, something I didn't understand. I filed that information away to ask Blondie about, later, if I had the chance.

Okay, I was also really curious about Sarah, and their relationship. But I liked to hide my nosiness behind legitimate questions, whenever possible.

Anyan cleared his throat, obviously trying to head off any pity party before drinks could be poured.

"So what are we doing here?" asked the barghest, pointedly.

Sarah straightened, walking back towards the little cart she'd been hovering around since we walked in.

"You're here because rumours have been spreading about the Red and the White. I knew someone would come to me, eventually, for information. So I began compiling everything we have."

"And?" Anyan prompted.

"And, a book is missing."

"Who cares?" squeaked Hiral, doing a strange magic-fueled hop to stand on the table next to me. He sniffed his long blue nose and again scratched at what I imagined were his equally blue balls. "It's a library. I bet books disappear all the time."

Sarah gave Hiral a long look, and then took a very small book off of the shelves behind her. She tossed it to the gwyllion. Hiral's long blue fingers snatched it out of the air and he looked at the doppelgänger curiously.

"Try taking it out, gwyllion," she said. "Even with your powers—your being able to get in anywhere you want and hide yourself—you try leaving this library with that book."

I watched in a combination of alarm and respect as Hiral disappeared, and I mean disappeared both physically and magically. It was like there was nothing in that room with us except for a high-pitched, maniacal giggle that was making its way swiftly towards an open set of double doors on the far side of the library.

Then we heard a howl as the laughter hit the lintel, and suddenly Hiral—now entirely visible—was shooting across the room, his little form smoking as he shrieked in pain.

"Like I said," Sarah said dryly, as we watched Hiral's huddled form pant and swear from the patch of rug he'd finally landed upon, "a book is missing. A book about the Red and the White. And as you have seen, it's not easy to get a book out of this room."

"What book was it?" I asked.

Sarah paused, as if trying to figure out how to word what she wanted to say. When she did start speaking, the look on her face was confused, but it was as if she was as baffled by her confusion as she was actually confused.

"This is where it gets tricky," she said. "The fact is, the book shouldn't be important."

"And why is that?" asked Anyan.

In response, Sarah began to lay out all the books and scrolls lying in front of her. The majority seemed to have been made in batches of the same time period, and most were really old looking. Anyan walked over to flip open one of the actual bound books, and it revealed an inside full of beautiful illuminations, like in the Book of Kells. Then all of the reading material made a huge jump in time, to what looked like the relatively old, but still very much modern, textbooks. Indeed, the only thing the old stuff and the new stuff had in common from here was that it was all dauntingly thick, with the last, modern hardbacks being about the same size as my compiled Shakespeare.

"These are all the exact same book," Sarah said. "They're the sort of textbook version of the Red and the White, updated through the centuries as they've been resurrected. Many of our kind have a copy of this book already—they're sort of the supernatural version of, say, *War and Peace*. It's a daunting read, so not everyone picks it up, but enough people do that it's hardly rare. And pretty much everyone's been forced to read it at some point or other, as part of their schooling."

"Do you have supe school?" I asked.

Sarah gave me an exasperated look. "Of course we do."

"And you all read this book?"

"Yes."

"So why steal it?"

"Exactly."

"Was there something special about the stolen copy?"

"I can't think of how," Sarah said. "It's definitely one of the new versions that's missing. I know that. But they're all supposed to be the same book. They have to be the same book."

Here Sarah's brow furrowed, as if she were concentrating on something. "I know they're the same book," she said, "because I wrote the last version. I modernized the language, and I researched what was written in the past, and I told what happened to the Red and the White after they were destroyed by Cyntaf..."

Again Sarah's voice trailed off, and she stared at the textbooks in front of her as if she weren't entirely sure she'd ever seen them before. The way she was acting, it was like someone who'd been way too heavily glamoured for way too long. But that sort of glamour-abuse only happened with humans, at least that I knew of. I snapped to when Sarah started speaking again, rubbing her hands down the front of her dress as if she wanted to make sure she was still all there.

"Those are the official library copies. They were all donated by our central press at the same time that they were published. I remember receiving them, and I remember glancing through them...they were all the same. There wasn't a hollowed out part with a treasure map or anything. And they were what I wrote."

Sarah should know if they were what she wrote, but there was a questioning note in her voice that made me raise my eyebrows, and she kept looking over at the books like they might bite her. Something fishy was going on.

"So what you're saying," came Anyan's rumbling voice, "is that someone risked all that security, and wasted all that power, to smuggle out a book that anyone can just come in here and read on their own."

"Now you see why I contacted Cyntaf," Sarah said. "I don't lose one of my charges lightly, and everyone knows that. For someone to risk the wrath of my Repository to steal something so common, something about the Red and the White..."

"It has to be *un*common," I said, glancing at where Hiral still lay, his burlap garments still smoking. I moved forward to the table, picking up one of the remaining modern textbooks.

"Looks like we've got ourselves some reading material," I said, settling myself into the chair next to me. Anyan picked up another copy, as did Blondie and Sarah.

Without another word, we all started reading.

CHAPTER SIX

There's nothing here we don't already know," Anyan said, tossing his book on the table. "It's the same story we've always heard."

I glanced up at the barghest, then back at the book. Unlike Anyan, I was fascinated by what I was reading. I still knew so little about the supernatural world. To find all of this information laid out in this easily accessible narrative was awesome.

"I know you're probably enjoying the history," Blondie said to me, softly, "But I'd skip to about chapter thirty-five. That's where all the newish stuff is."

"Hmm?" I asked, distractedly.

"We should all be concentrating on what happens after chapter thirty-five," Blondie said, this time louder, to address the whole table. "That's the most recent part. They must have stolen the new book for a reason, instead of taking one of the older ones. Let's assume the information they want is in a new section, written after the last hard bound one, over there, and work backward if we don't find anything."

I dutifully flipped forward, hoping I could take the whole book with me when we left, and even Anyan picked up his own copy and went to the relevant section.

We all read in silence, for about another twenty minutes.

"Still all the same," Anyan said. "The bad guys are still the bad guys, and we still beat them using a combination of Alfar cunning and Alfar power. Same old story."

The frown that had appeared on my face as I started reading grew deeper as Anyan articulated what was bothering me about the text. "But that's not the story, is it? I thought Blondie told us the story. With the slurrying, and her as the champion. She's not Alfar."

Blondie chuckled. "Yes, well, history is written by the winners, and the Alfar, for all intents and purposes, are always the winners. They couldn't have some wayward Original winning, now could they?"

"So they lie?" I asked.

"Yup," Blondie replied.

"What do they say?"

"Oh, I'm still in it. And I wield the labrys, and it makes me the champion. Only I'm not an Original, in their version. They never say exactly what I am, but they imply I was just a weak Alfar. It makes for a rocking story— average person turned hero, armed with a magical weapon that can defeat the greatest evil. They just lie about where the power of the labrys comes from."

"Ohhhhh," I groaned, as a bunch of wobbly things that had been bothering me fell into place. "That's why Anyan knows about the Red and the White, but he didn't know

Blondie destroyed them. The story you know is the lie?" I asked the barghest. He nodded.

"But they call you Cyntaf, here," I said to Blondie. "Do they know you're an Original?"

"Some, like Gog and Magog, have figured it out. Those whom I know really well. But most don't think about it. They think all *Cyntaf* means is that I've been around a long time, and that's enough for them."

"What do they say about where you got the ax?"

Blondie snorted. "There's no mention of the creature, at all. Instead, I'm imbued with the power of Alfar monarchs past, who all got together in a ghostly cabal and granted me their undying favor."

"Wow. So you're still the champion, but in the official version you're the Alfar champion?"

"Yes. The Alfar are powerful and they think ahead. Or at least they try to. This trick bit them in the butt, in the end. After all, it eventually came out that I was really affiliated with the rebels, and here I was the champion. Made the Alfar look bad. None of that's in the official version, obviously, but it used to be a big deal."

"So they lie, like they did with your story, in every single book?" I asked.

"Basically, yes," Blondie said.

I looked over at the cart, and then walked to where Sarah had packed the other books. She'd left them bundled by time period.

Picking up one of the ancient bound ones I said, "So, when will this one end?"

Blondie peered over at me. "That's the one that ends with my story. But there's nothing past the actual fight in that version."

"What about this time?" I asked, pointing to the books that looked significantly older than the previous batch.

"That one will tell you the Alfar queen at the time did it, but it was really a group of mixed factions, including me. We'd cobbled together quite a few relics of other Elemental children to win the day," Blondie said.

"So all these books will tell me that the Alfar did it, alone?" I asked.

"Yes," Sarah said.

I picked up the first volume of the second bound batch, and started reading the very last chapters. Sure enough, the story was about a brave Alfar queen who led her people in battle and saved the day. Any mention of other factions was slight, with the Alfar dominating the action.

So I picked up the next volume, and it was the same deal. Same story, written in the exactly same language. An exact copy, to be precise.

It wasn't until I picked up the fourth of the five volumes that I noticed something different. I was reading the same line I'd already read three other times, "... and the Queene did spake her ire, calling forthe fire," when the type set shifted. It was only the slightest change in spacing, but I'd majored in English, so I'd seen all sorts of font-shenanigans pulled by my fellow classmates. Still, I nearly didn't see these, as they were in a volume that pre-dated the sorts of professional printing presses that kept everything nice and uniform. Yet there was definitely a distinctive spacing change to a sudden patch of language that was also very new.

For this line read, "... and the Queene did spake her ire the creatures united called forth the power in their relics calling forthe fire."

I blinked, unsure what I was seeing, then felt my spine tingle as I looked a few lines down to see another bit of odd spacing, and the once familiar phrase, "...the fire it did blaze like the sun, and it smote the wily minions," changed to, "the fire it did blaze like the sun and the relics, united, created a force so powerful and it smote the wily minions."

"Crafty motherfuckers," I breathed. I kept skimming, only reading the bits with the odd spacing, and there it was, all in front of me—the real story of what happened that day, not the fake, Alfar version of history.

"It's so Alfar," I said, holding up the book and speaking loud enough that the others could hear. "It's just like what they did with the creature."

The others were looking expectantly at me and I walked towards them with my prize.

"They covered up the truth, and they hid something in plain sight in such a way that they could find it again, if they needed it. They know they need to manipulate the truth, but they also know they might need that very truth, some day. So they hide it right there were everyone can see it, just like they did with the creature."

"What'd you find, Jane?" Anyan asked, impatiently.

"It's all right here," I said. Then I changed my mind and trotted over to grab the first book of the batch that I'd looked at. "Look at this paragraph," I said, pointing out the one line about the Queene I'd latched onto in the beginning. "Now look at it here," I said, pointing at the slightly different one in the fourth version. "Keep reading, but only read what's kind of weirdly spaced compared to everything else. You'll see."

While the others read, out of curiosity I went to the

remaining books of that series. They were like the first three I'd read. Only that fourth version had been different.

I was listening to the murmurs at the table behind me as I looked over the scrolls. As these were handwritten, there were no spacing clues, but I quickly found a single scroll with some little decorative, Book of Kells-esque squares in the margins that indicated where something new had been stuck in.

"They really are evil geniuses," Anyan said, his voice tinged with admiration.

"The Alfar?" asked Blondie.

"Yeah," answered Anyan. "If they'd created a secret room in which to hide this information, someone would have found out and needed to break in. Because that's what people like me do. We're nosy. But instead, they work it into a book everyone already knows about, and has already read as a kid, and won't ever pick up again because it was ruined for them in school."

"Like *Catcher in the Rye*," I exclaimed. "Everyone gets that book too young, and teachers inevitably screw it up trying to make it 'nice.' That book is brutal!"

Everyone ignored me. Anyan continued.

"They hide the real information in these books, knowing no one is ever going to come reading these textbooks. To top it off, they don't even keep them. They *generously* donate them to the Great Repository. No one is *ever* going to crack open one of these books."

"Wait, but what's in the missing book that's so important that *we* don't know?" I asked. "After all, we have Blondie. She was there. What can the book tell us that she can't? And we have the person who wrote it!" I said, pointing at Sarah. "She can . . ."

"Sarah wouldn't have been responsible for the changes," Blondie broke in, using a sharp voice that brooked no argument. Her vehemency was odd, against her laid-back, surfer-girl persona. But she didn't meet my curious gaze, instead obviously avoiding my eyes as she continued talking.

"As for what the books might have contained, it's obvious: what happened to the pieces."

"Oh," was my only response. I was busy sticking more questions into my "ask Blondie later" file.

"I didn't take care of that part," she continued. "I was pretty badly wounded. The Red got me right before I took her down, and there's something about that bitch's claws that wouldn't heal right. It wasn't a mortal wound, or I'd be a goner. But it was bad enough, and I had to heal the old-fashioned way. So the bits were gathered up and distributed by others."

While Blondie was talking, my eyes flicked over to Sarah. She looked disturbed, her face scrunched up as if she were trying to remember something.

"So we need that book," Anyan said. "For all we know it contains the exact locations of every piece of chopped up bad guy that's out there."

"Where do we start?" I asked, eager to follow up our first real lead.

Sarah pursed her lips, and then smiled.

"What they always do on *Taggart*, with the CCTV footage," she said. I had no idea what she was talking about, but I followed her anyway.

"It's this Scottish police show," Anyan explained patiently, as we walked through back hallways of the British

Museum towards the room where Sarah said the security footage was held. "It's a good show, but also really quirky as they have this rotating roster of like twenty Scottish actors they keep killing off, so one guy dies as a bum in one episode, then you see him die again as a rich exec in another."

Anyan kept talking as we all took seats in front of a bank of small televisions, five twelve-inch monitors in a short row, and Sarah started fiddling with a central keyboards station.

"And there's this great tag line," Anyan said, suddenly affecting this really bad Scottish brogue. " 'There's been a mur-der,' and they say it each time, in this thick Weegie accent…"

The barghest was adorable when he geeked out, and I resisted the temptation to scratch him behind the ear as I watched Sarah and Blondie begin scanning through CCTV footage from around the museum.

"We need Magog," Blondie murmured.

Anyan chuckled, "Yeah, she can do it way better. 'There's been a mur-der.' "

"We need her to help us look through these tapes, barghest, not to say your stupid tagline," the Original said huffily. "Hiral, go tell Magog we need her," she told the gwyllion. "And take her place as sentry, would you?"

The little man grumbled under his breath but dutifully stumped off.

Sarah kept cycling through the various pieces of footage, shaking her head as she did so.

"I've gone over this a thousand times," she said. "There's nothing."

"Maybe," Blondie said. "But if there is something you

missed, Magog will find it. She's the eyes of a carrion bird, after all."

I couldn't help but make a face at that, one that I pulled up short as the carrion bird herself walked in.

She's pretty hot for a vulture, my libido said.

Not a vulture, a raven, my brain reminded me.

And you think everyone's hot, my virtue told my libido, snottily.

My little mental battle went on, unnoticed by anyone else, as I gave up my chair to Magog. The dark-haired girl sat down with a careful adjustment of the wings under her massive coat.

Sarah started up the series of videos on all the different monitors again. I moved around to watch Magog's black eyes flicking over the various screens. She did so with a serene expression, however, as if she were not at all over-whelmed by the process.

"Faster," Magog said, indicating to Sarah she wanted the videos put on fast forward. Sarah shrugged, and the images on the screen began to blur in front of us.

"Again," Magog said, when the thirty minutes sur-rounding the time the books must have been stolen had been gone over. Sarah hit another button, and we watched Magog watching.

"Again," Magog said, a final time. For about halfway through this viewing she raised her hand and said "stop" in a voice that brooked no argument.

The images froze. It was an outside shot of the docking bay that stood on the left hand side of the museum. There was a large truck parked next to a bunch of motor scoot-ers, all of their mirrors practically tangled together they were so close.

"Back up a bit," Magog said. "Then play it again, slowly."

Sarah did so, and we watched as absolutely nothing happened. But Magog grinned fiercely, her small mouth stretched into that humorless grimace I'd come to associate with her.

"There," she hissed, pointing at a scooter's mirror. "In the mirror."

Sarah played it again and, sure enough, there was a flash of something reflected in one of the motorbike's mirrors, even though nothing appeared in any of the others.

"How did that happen?" I demanded, thinking in horror of all the times I'd had semi-public sex with Ryu, after he'd assured me that his glamour meant no one, no camera, no nothing could see us.

"It's a reflection of a reflection of a reflection of a reflection," Blondie explained as Sarah saved the image to a thumb drive that she took over to a larger computer on the wall. "Sometimes, in such circumstances, our magic peters out after so many reflections."

I frantically tried to remember if Ryu and I had ever had any fun house sex, as Sarah loaded various programs onto her computer until she was ready to enhance the picture. I decided to worry about any possible YouTube videos of me engaged in "hide the fang" until later, as we watched Sarah work.

She was pressing buttons, and the little scrap of image kept getting larger and more defined, until we could see a bit of a face. I thought it was still really blurry, but it was enough for Blondie.

"Alistair, you little shit," growled the Original.

Sarah looked at Blondie curiously.

"You recognize him?" she asked.

I thought it was rather obvious the answer was yes, but I kept quiet.

"He's a petty criminal. Hands for hire. But I would have thought he had the good sense and nose for trouble to stay out of this one."

She sighed, straightening. "Magog, will you call some of your contacts, see if they know where Alistair is squatting nowadays. They may know him as Fingers or Ali Baba or dead meat if I don't find him soon." Magog nodded, pulling out her cell phone and heading into the hallway.

That left the four of us, with Sarah staring longingly at Blondie.

"Um, why don't Anyan and I head outside. Round up the troops," I said. "Let 'em know we're coming…" I grabbed Anyan by the elbow, but he looked at me as if he didn't understand what I was doing.

"Give you two some time alone," I said for his benefit, jerking my head at where Sarah was giving Blondie mooneyes.

"Oh, yeah," he said, finally cottoning on. "We'll go outside. Meet us … whenever."

"Smooth," I muttered as we walked into the hallway, past Magog who was busy hissing threats at someone in the phone.

"Yes, well," the barghest replied, "not all of us can be as smooth as Smooth Jane True."

I couldn't help but giggle, and he put his heavy arm around me drawing me close against him.

"So what's the deal with those two?" I asked, as we

headed down the small hallway towards the exit that led into the public areas of the museum.

"I don't know exactly, but I know they've been a thing for a very long time. That says a lot about how much they like each other. Sarah's been working in the Repository for nearly her entire adult life, and dating a doppelgänger is sorta off-putting for a lot of people."

"It would definitely put a whole new spin on 'self-love,'" I said, pushing open the doors at the end of the hallway, where we reentered that vast white space of the museum's main inner courtyard.

"I guess Blondie's been alive long enough that she can stare herself in the eye, even in the bedroom."

"That's deep, yo," I said, tickling him in the ribs. He grabbed my offending hand and raised it to his lips, only to graze his teeth against my knuckles.

I definitely wheezed that time, and for once I couldn't think of anything snarky to say in response.

We were also nearly to the main entrance, and the cool spring air and soft sunlight coming in was very inviting after so long spent in the climate-controlled environment of the museum.

Dragging Anyan forward, I suddenly really wanted to be outside, and looking around at London, a city I'd barely gotten to see. And I wanted to do it with the man at my side.

"Let's go sightsee a little," I said, turning around to walk backward as I pulled Anyan forward. "Just a teeny bit. We'll tell Gog. We can be back in twenty minutes."

Instead of listening to me, Anyan was making a face. A face that didn't bode well for my sightseeing idea.

"Where *is* Gog?" he asked, and I turned my head around, still walking backward and dragging him with me.

I looked around for the coblynau, hoping he hadn't wandered off so we were stuck there. *If we could just have twenty minutes…*

But that thought was short lived. It died with the feel of a hood falling over my face and a stabbing little pinch in the back of neck. Suddenly unable to use my legs, I toppled backwards as someone very strong grabbed me from behind.

CHAPTER SEVEN

I don't know what they'd given us to knock us out, but it was powerful. One minute a hood was thrust over my head, the next minute I was sitting, tied to a chair, and feeling very, very groggy.

"Jane?" came a voice next to me. It was muffled, but it was the barghest.

"I'm here," I said. "Are you okay?" With every word I spoke, the stale air in my hood blew around my face. *Being hooded isn't nice*, I realized. *And neither is being tied to a chair.*

"Are you naked?" I asked Anyan, my drug-addled brain supplying me with terrible images.

"What? No? Are you?" he asked, his tone harsh with worry.

"No, but the way we're tied up, in chairs, made me think of that new James Bond. With that horrible ball-busting scene."

There was silence beside me. Maybe I shouldn't have mentioned ball-busting.

"Anyan?" I asked. Still no reply.

"Look, even if they bust your balls, I'll still like you," I said, helpfully. "I'll totally help you recover," I added, when he still didn't reply.

"Will you please just stop talking about ball-busting," Anyan said eventually, in the measured tones that told me I was *theeees* close to a spanking.

So of course I kept talking, my tongue fueled by nerves and loosened by whatever had knocked us out.

"If you have a seat bottom, I'm sure they're not going to bust your balls. I think it has to have the seat removed, to work. Do you have a seat?" I asked.

I heard some heavy breaths, muffled by his hood.

"I have a seat bottom, yes," he said, eventually.

"Oh, good. So do I. Phew!" I said. He didn't reply. Maybe it was time to change the subject.

"So," I said, "Who do you think are our kidnappers?"

"Why don't you ask them?" Anyan said. "Since they've just come in to sit in front of us."

Oops, I thought, closing my mouth with an audible clink of my teeth. Anyan's heavy breathing hadn't just been because he wanted to throttle me. He'd been trying to smell through the hood.

"Very good, Anyan Barghest," said a man's voice in front of me. "And do you know who I am?"

"Of course I do, Jack. So how about you stop this charade?" Anyan's voice was low, menacing.

"Phil," said Jack's voice, in clear command.

Suddenly, the hood was whisked off my head and I sat, blinking in the dim light. When my eyes finally adjusted,

I looked around, observing that we seemed to be in some sort of empty warehouse with concrete floors and very high ceilings. Looking to my left, I checked to make sure Anyan had also had his hood removed. We both looked each other over carefully, assessing any possible damage, then turned to face forward towards our kidnapper. I knew there were people shuffling around behind us, but the man in front was clearly in charge. Plus I was tied up in such a way that turning around would have been difficult.

Jack wasn't that big, but he was lean and looked tough. His tousled blonde hair spoke of a boyishness that did not match the wry twist of his sharp features, or his cynical, probing blue eyes. Despite his small size and casual demeanor, he also radiated an air of menace, as if he'd do just about anything to anyone under the right circumstances.

I hoped these weren't the right circumstances.

"Jack Young," Anyan growled. "Why have you kidnapped us?"

Startled, I realized from the full human name that the man in front of us was most probably a halfling. Full supes only used one name and their faction to identify themselves, which was why I was Jane True and Anyan was Anyan Barghest.

The man gave us a feral smile, and, for a second, fire licked over his arms. But it wasn't flame-fire; it was a strange, magical looking blue fire. Either that or it was so hot it burned blue.

This was the exact sort of situation under which I didn't enjoy, so much, meeting new supernaturals.

"I should be the one asking questions, barghest," Jack

said. His tone managed to be entirely nonchalant and entirely full of threat, all at the same time. "After all, you're on my turf."

"You don't own London, despite what you think," said Anyan.

"Maybe not," Jack replied. "But I own the dark heart of London. The dark heart that you've been scuttling across since you arrived. Now, I'm asking you nicely, why are you here?"

"Nothing that involves you, or your so-called cause. Let us go."

Jack pursed his lips, looking between Anyan and me. "Let *you* go? Maybe I will let you go. And maybe I'll keep the girl."

Anyan actually growled at that, but I rolled my eyes. Something about the way Jack bantered with Anyan let me know he wasn't going to hurt us. Enough people had tried to kill me, after all, that I *knew* murderous intent.

I also realized I really wasn't happy about being kidnapped.

"Thanks, but no thanks. This *lady* is not for keeping."

Jack actually smiled at that. "And who exactly is this *lady*?" he asked, placing the same emphasis on the word that I had.

"My name is Jane," I said, leaning as far back in my chair as I could to effect an air of casual disregard. "And you're Jack. There's a nursery rhyme there somewhere."

"And what are you doing here, Jane?" Jack was watching me with appraising eyes. He'd probably assumed I'd be a gibbering wreck by now, but he didn't realize that being abducted had become almost a hobby for me.

"I'm a tourist. I'm sightseeing. And what is it you do, Jack, when you're not abducting innocent tourists?"

Jack looked slightly less amused with me as he answered.

"I'm a simple businessman with strong ties to my community."

Anyan snorted as I asked, "What community?"

"The halfling community. Which I think is probably *our* community, is it not, Jane True?"

I hadn't given him my last name. *Uh-oh.* Jack paced towards me, his gait like that of a lion. I have to admit, if he didn't radiate brutality I'd have been attracted to him.

I'm attracted to him because he does *radiate brutality*, cooed my libido.

Shut up, you idiot, chastised my virtue.

I, myself, stayed mum.

Kneeling before me, Jack put his hands on my knees. I grew distinctly uncomfortable, not least because I was reminded of Conleth, the crazy ifrit-halfling who'd also kidnapped me and also tied me up.

"Between us," Jack murmured, his blue eyes spearing my own black gaze, "I represent halfling interests, both officially as well as, well, let's just say unofficially. For that I'm called a rebel. But I like to think of myself as a patriot."

And with those words he lit himself up like a blue Roman candle. On the one hand, it was an impressive sight. On the other hand, it was definitely the wrong move to make with me.

In a flat out panic, I was suddenly back in that dank warehouse with Conleth, and my mojo reacted before my brain. Automatically reaching into that place of power inside me left by the creature, I pulled all of the water out of the air like I was some mighty supernatural sponge. And then I sent it crashing into Jack, as if two enormous bucketfuls of water appeared out of nowhere, on either side of him, pouring towards each other. He was left on his ass—drenched, spluttering, and with his fire totally squelched.

There was furious movement behind me until someone had a hold of my hair, yanking my head back hard. Then there was a knife at my throat and Anyan was shouting and I was pulling with all that force again...

"Enough," barked Jack from where he was sprawled on the floor, his air of authority strong despite his now sodden nature.

"Let her go," Jack finished, his voice gone smooth and quiet again. "Miss True is our guest, after all."

He stood, careful to keep his feet under him on the now slippery concrete floor.

When he was standing, Jack walked towards me, placing a hand under my chin. I stared up at him defiantly, ready to lash out with my mojo if I had to.

"A guest with a lot of power," he murmured. "How surprising."

Then Jack turned on his heel, pacing a few steps away as if trying to decide what to do next. Keeping his back turned, he gathered his power around him before a short burst of flames left him entirely dry. Only then did he turn around.

"I'm very sorry to have frightened you," Jack said, in the slick tones of a politician apologizing for something he'd actually loved doing.

I shook my head. "You didn't frighten me. I just... react badly to ifrits," I said.

Smiling, Jack echoed the shake of my head with his own wry little movement. "Not an ifrit, darling. I'm wyvern," the man said, clearly expecting me to be impressed.

"Isn't that a snake?" I asked, just as Anyan said, "And nahual, and human."

Jack's carefully schooled expression flashed just a glimmer of annoyance, and I wonder which of us had gotten to him. Or maybe it was our tag-team irritation offense, something Anyan and I should probably patent.

"It's not a snake. It's more like a dragon," Jack said, petulantly. "And I've never hidden my mixed blood."

"Why don't we show *her* blood, boss?" said a ridiculously accented man from directly behind me, the man who must have held the knife to my throat. Despite that, however, I suddenly couldn't take him seriously as he sounded like an evil Dick Van Dyke. He had one of those accents I couldn't help but assume was a joke.

I resisted the urge to crane my neck around. Instead I gave a heartfelt sigh, as if bored to tears at the thought of another person threatening me with bodily injury.

"Phil, be good," soothed Jack. "Come around and meet our guests."

From behind us walked Phil, and I couldn't help but stare. He was tall, and skinny as a rail, but what made his look was the shiny lamé green suit he was wearing, with no shirt underneath. He was, however, sporting a top hat that had a matching green lamé band around it. I thought he looked ridiculous, until his tongue flicked out at me.

It was a snake's tongue. *Naga*, I thought, gathering my power again for a strike.

"No need for that, Jane," came Jack's charismatic

voice. "We know the trouble you've had with nagas, but Phil's a halfling. One of us."

Snark battled smarts for a second, and snark won. "Um, if there's an 'us,' why are *we* tied up?" snark asked from my own mouth.

Jack smiled at me, but ignored me, as he brought forth his other two compatriots from the shadows. "Adele Norris," he said, gesturing to a very plump, sweet-faced black woman who waved a cat's paw at me. She was obviously a nahual halfling.

"And meet my brother," Jack said. "Lyman Moore."

Like his brother, Lyman was slight, although he had a bit more weight on him than did Jack. He was wearing antique looking circular glasses, and a somber, old-fashioned dark suit. He was also smiling broadly, but apparently at nothing in particular. It wasn't a scary smile, just inappropriate.

"Aren't you really half-brothers?" Anyan asked, conversationally. I saw Jack's mouth twitch again, in annoyance, before it reset. "Or quarter? I never could figure out what you call two men who share a grandfather. Although I guess he's Lyman's dad, no? And your grandfather? I can't keep it straight."

An obviously irritated Jack was nearly answered, when Lyman put a hand on his brother's arm.

"My father was the last full-blooded wyvern," Lyman said, quite calmly. "And his son was Jack's father, yes. But we are brothers." Lyman was now standing in front of Anyan, and despite the fact his weird, placid smile had never changed, I could tell he didn't like the barghest one bit. And from Anyan's own expression, the feeling was mutual.

The barghest was about to respond when there was a tremendous crash from the glass ceilings above our heads. I ducked my face, although the falling glass was nowhere near, just as Blondie and Magog came swooping in: Magog on coal black wings so enormous they dwarfed her, and Blondie on the same angelic white wings she'd used to fly me over the Sow just last week. They looked liked dueling angels in a movie, but they were obviously on the same side as they landed next to us, supernatural weapons called forth and charged up with mojo.

"Jack, what the fuck do you think you're doing?" Blondie asked, her voice almost friendly. Almost.

Jack smiled at the Original. "Cyntaf! So good to see you. It's been too long. And Magog. What a surprise." The rebel leader's eyes were hard as he looked at the raven.

Blondie's only reply was a cocked eyebrow.

"I am sorry for detaining your friends," Jack said. "It's just that here you are visiting, and you never came to say 'hello.' I was hurt."

"I'm sure you were, Jack," Blondie said, dryly. "Why don't you untie them?"

Jack paused for just a second before nodding at Phil. The suited man's snake tongue flicked out at me in annoyance, but I felt the ropes tying me to the chair uncoil and then start to slither off of me. The effect was definitely like that of snakes against my skin, and I tried to put on a brave face.

"There, now. Your friends are free. So why don't you tell us what you're doing here?" Jack asked again. This time, however, his voice was laced with an edge I didn't like. Blondie helped me to my feet, as Magog did the same for Anyan. I wasn't sure how long we were out, but standing didn't feel so natural at the moment.

Blondie ignored Jack, making a fuss looking me over, making sure I wasn't hurt. Only then did she turn to Jack, although she kept an arm around my waist to keep me steady.

"If you know, you'll be involved," the Original said, grimly. "And this isn't some political game this time, Jack. It's bigger than all of us."

Jack paused, as if assessing his choices.

"My turf, my problem," he said, finally. Adele had the good sense to look nervous.

"It's the Red and the White. Someone's trying to wake them," Blondie said, her tone serious.

"Bullshit," Phil laughed, his garish green suit reflecting the dregs of sunlight coming through the now shattered ceiling. "Them's children's stories, meant to scare younglings who don't know no better."

But Blondie didn't laugh at the joke, and neither did Jack who was watching the Original with thoughtful blue eyes.

It was Lyman who finally broke the silence.

"Well, isn't this a pickle," he said, still grinning inappropriately.

Jack nodded. "It is indeed. I'll need to look into this claim."

And with that he strode forward to shake first Blondie's hand, then mine, then Anyan's, and finally Magog's. He was like a politician mopping up the dregs of a long parade route. I was so surprised at this turn of events that I shook his hand like it was completely normal to politely see off one's abductor.

"I'm sure we'll run into each other again, soon enough," he told me with a wink, before turning to Blondie. "Cyntaf, I'll be in touch. Nice seeing you."

And with that he was off, striding out of the double doors that appeared to be the only exit, his entourage trailing behind him like some bizarre Benetton commercial.

Blondie let go of my waist and stepped away from me, frowning in thought.

"Who the fuck was that?" I asked, rubbing my chafed wrists.

"He's the leader of the rebel forces here on the Island," Blondie said, wearily. It took me a minute to get what she was saying.

"Wait," I spluttered, as my little lightbulb finally switched on.

"Those are the good guys?"

CHAPTER EIGHT

But if they're the good guys, the brave rebel halflings seeking justice, who the hell are the bad guys?" I asked, scampering to keep up with Anyan's long strides. It was just the two of us and we were walking away from the flat Gog had misappropriated for the evening. It was a small, two-bedroom affair in the London borough of Islington, a place that was definitely more urban than where we'd stayed last night.

"Things aren't that easy, on the Island. The good guys aren't too good, and the bad guys aren't much worse. And we're here." Anyan said, even as he realized I was practically jogging. He slowed his pace and took my hand. "Jane, welcome to our first date."

"Huh?" I asked, totally surprised. I'd been expecting some sort of rebel mission when Anyan had told me to get dressed to go out. I hadn't realized he meant "go out" as in on a date. I looked down at my long purple cardigan, covering a black T-shirt and leggings, and prayed I was dressed appropriately. Then I looked up. What I saw made my palms damp and squished all concerns regarding appropriate dress under a pile of latex.

"Um, Anyan, that sign says 'S&M.' I'm not against a little playtime, but if this is your idea of a first date, what on Earth do you do for the second?"

"While I'm now looking forward to exploring your definition of 'playtime,' it stands for Sausages and Mash," Anyan said, chuckling evilly. "I'm just taking you to dinner, Jane."

"Oh," I said, embarrassed. Not least because all I'd had to do was look through the windows to see S&M was a diner, with nary a flogger or bound-human-figure in sight.

Anyan swatted me on my butt as he opened the door. "In you get, little minx."

I did so, telling the hostess we were two, even as I marveled at the turn of events. *From kidnapping to going on a date with Anyan. If my life is anything, it's never boring.*

The hostess showed us to a little table with its booth-seating cut into the corner, which meant we could sit sort of next to each other. The restaurant was shabby, but super hip, built on a base of diner furniture and diner kit that had been all sexed up with lush extras, like odd paintings and beautiful, if slightly random, throw cushions.

The waitress left us with menus after we each ordered a beer.

"I can't believe we're here," I said, still delighted.

"Well, we had to eat. And I figured you needed some downtime after today. I'll take you swimming tonight too."

"Thank you," I said, meaning it.

Anyan looked up from his menu and smiled at me. "Oh, don't thank me. I'm also being greedy. I wanted some time with you, without the others. Now what are you going to order?"

I blushed, looking down at my menu and trying to focus on the food, which wasn't hard, because as soon as I saw my choices my stomach started growling. The menu was not fancy at all, with all British classics like fish and chips and pie and chips. But one of my cardinal rules in life is to always order the specialty, which was clearly sausages and mash. And yet, that still left a lot of sausages to choose from. There were the traditional sausages—Cumberland and London traditional. There was also a vegetarian option that looked delicious, mushroom and tarragon. Then there were the specials—bold, very not-American choices like leek and caerphilly, a Welsh cheese, or ale and Bramley apple.

I wanted them all, but I also knew I was being greedy. Then Anyan's deep voice rumbled from next to me.

"Why don't I get the three-sausages and mash with the special sausages, and you get the same thing with the traditional ones, and the vegetarian, and we can share?"

At his words, I nearly choked on my emotions. *You're perfect*, I thought, even as I said, "Yes, sharing is my favorite."

The way I saw it, one of the single greatest advantages of being in a relationship was that you got to eat off the other person's plate. That Anyan might share my view was dizzying.

We ordered when the waitress brought our beers. After she walked away, Anyan and I clinked glasses.

"To our first date," he said, giving me a sly little wink. I giggled, and we sipped our beers.

"And to not getting kidnapped again. I promise not to

drag you anywhere without being more careful," I said. Anyan clinked my glass again, but shook his head as he did so.

"That was as much my fault as yours, Jane. I was complacent, thinking we'd managed to sneak in without anybody knowing. And I depended on Gog and Hiral, but Hiral's undependable and I shouldn't have left Gog without real backup."

Poor Gog had felt terrible about letting us be captured. When he'd caught up with the rest of us—a little dazed still from having been knocked out with a much larger dose of the same tranquilizer Jack and his gang had used on Anyan and me—he'd acted so guilty I'd had to tell him to shake it off. It wasn't his fault. He'd been knocked out too.

But I had my doubts about the gwyllion.

"Where do you think Hiral is?" I asked. There'd been no sign of the little creature since Gog was attacked. Gog had seen the gwyllion approach Magog and take her place on the other side of the wide doors. But when Gog had looked again, Hiral was gone. Upon turning to find out why, the cobylnau had felt the dart in his neck.

"Who knows," Anyan said. "Hiral has his own ways."

"Can we trust him?" I asked, cutting to the chase.

"Hiral? It depends on what you mean by trust. He'll steal your wallet and you can't depend on him to be where he's supposed to be. But he'd never betray us to Alfar like Jarl and Morrigan."

I frowned, wanting to protest us putting any faith in someone who had such a flexible definition of "dependable," but Anyan obviously wasn't in the mood to talk about Hiral. He was looking at me in the way he did that made me feel I was brand new.

"You were very brave back there," Anyan said, surprising me.

"What? I didn't do anything."

"Yeah, you did. You were cool as a cucumber."

"I knew they weren't going to hurt us," I protested, but Anyan was having none of it.

"Shush," he said, leaning forward to kiss me into silence. It was a quick peck, but it worked. I was staring hungrily at his mouth as he continued.

"Your instincts have developed. And your reflexes. The water trick was awesome."

Still staring at his mouth, I smiled. "Thanks, but that was more panic than plan. Jack totally reminded me of Con."

"I bet. But you probably would have knocked a real ifrit out with that much water. You'd have taken Conleth no problem, were he around today."

I shrugged, not wanting to talk about Con. Everything Anyan was saying was nice, but it wasn't what my libido wanted to hear.

What it wanted to hear was that he wanted me. That he needed me. Or that he'd brought handcuffs.

We both fell silent, gazing at each other hungrily when the waitress came over with our meals. Then I switched to gazing at my plate hungrily.

Anyan's hand found my thigh under the table. He squeezed gently, bringing my attention back to his face.

"We'll eat, and then I'll take you swimming," he promised. "This date's not over yet."

My belly did a little flip-flop over the subtle promise in his words.

When I dug into my meal, I wondered if there were any other kinds of sausage in my immediate future.

It made a nice change from worrying about evil beings, possible traitors, and kidnappers.

Anyan shifted me in his lap, obviously not caring I was still soaking wet from my swim. The rough denim of his jeans scraped against my legs, and I again wondered why he was always clothed and I was always naked.

Seems unfair, that, my libido whined, to which even my virtue agreed.

We were sitting on the wooden dock overlooking one of Hampton Heath's little ponds. Originally man-made clay pits, they'd long since reverted to nature. While the power they gave me wasn't anywhere near that of the ocean, a nice long swim had still charged me up, especially as I was already so much better at pulling power out of the water-saturated air.

And we were finally, absolutely alone. Even if we were technically in public, the ponds had long since closed and we had a nice strong glamour swirling around us in case anyone had the same hankering for a late night swim that I had.

As if to remind me just how alone we were, Anyan's fingers were busy stroking down my arms, the side of my neck, from my thighs down from where the sweatshirt I'd used as a towel stopped covering me. His touch spoke of affection and possession, a heady mixture of emotions mirrored in his eyes, which he kept locked on mine.

"I'm getting you all wet," I murmured, feeling it all was too intense. All I'd had to dry off with was Anyan's sweatshirt hoodie, and he'd manhandled me into his lap while I was still dripping.

He smiled, and I realized I'd opened myself up for about a hundred wisecracks.

"It's okay," he said. "I like you wet and slippery."

I squirmed. That was Anyan's superpower, apparently—making me squirm.

The barghest's nose twitched, and his lips bowed in that little intense moue they did when he was being sexy. I felt his fingertips rove higher, slipping under the sweatshirt to brush across my belly. I wished they'd rove lower, to where I was aching for him.

"Well, you're an inconsiderate date," I said, although my voice was a lot rougher than it should have been. "Don't even bring a girl a towel..."

"Who says that wasn't on purpose?" His big hand started to gather the sweatshirt up, in a clear bid to take it away from me.

"Oh no, mister," I said, moving with the sweatshirt so that, in a flash, I was no longer cradled in his arms but straddling his thighs, my face inches from his.

"The whole point is that we're supposed to be getting to know each other," I told him.

"We are getting to know each other." He pressed a kiss to my jaw but I pushed back on his chest.

"The key words are 'each other.' You already know me. I want to get to know you better. Maybe I should go check out one of those books," I added at the last second, wondering how he'd react.

For a second Anyan's grey gaze looked uncomfortable, like he wasn't sure where I was going to go with that idea.

"You could," he replied, eventually, carefully. "I can't stop you. But I wish you wouldn't."

"Why?" I challenged.

He chuckled. "You can stop that sordid imagination of yours, little minx. There are no harems or anything like that. In fact, there's nothing you'd read about the 'Anyan' of those stories that I probably won't tell you about, myself, at some point.

"Although 'Fanyan's' a different story."

I couldn't help but giggle at his joke, but I was still curious.

"So why can't I read them, if they don't lie?"

"Because they don't lie, but they're not honest either. I did do those things, yes, but not in the light each books casts me. Those authors all wanted to see me a certain way: as a hero, or a master strategist, or a cruel genius, or a patriot to the Territory.

"But I was none of those things. I was someone doing a job, for reasons that were sometimes admittedly rather noble and sometimes kinda shitty. There were times I knew exactly what I was doing, and it was pretty smart, and other times I made that shit up or I did something insanely stupid that worked because I was lucky, not wise. But those things never get talked about. All of those books want to make me the perfect *something*: whatever it is that floats the author's boat. But I'm not a perfect any-thing. I'm just me."

"Oh I *do* like you. You're so clever," I cooed, running a finger over his lips. Anyan could be scary, and he could be sexy. It was when he was so casually clever, however, that I wanted to pickle his gherkin.

He nipped at my fingers playfully before he met my eyes, his iron-grey gaze serious and unyielding.

"And that's why I like you, Jane. Because you've only ever seen me, not the things people tell you I am. You've heard all sorts of nonsense, but you just shrug it off and refuse to believe it."

"Anyan," I protested, "I don't *not* believe it when I hear good things about you. I know you're all of those things."

"Yeah, but you don't *treat* me like that. It didn't faze you when you discovered I was famous as a supe, or even when you realized I was famous as a human artist. You always treated me the same."

Only then did I really get what he was saying—the huge backdrop of Anyan's life that, up till then, I'd either ignored or been oblivious.

"You're a *celebrity*," I said, only then able to contextualize the Fanyan books and the biographies. "You're like a supernatural what . . . Winston Churchill? Only hot? Do girls want you to sign their chests?"

"I'm not a celebrity, it's different. It's just . . ."

"Whatever, you're totally a celebrity. You should get a Beaver haircut. Or Bieber? Whoever the hell that boy is with the silly hair. I could flat iron it for you."

"If you don't stop right now, I'm going to turn you over my knee and spank that little bottom of yours."

Dead silence.

"Um, Anyan," I said, when I could breathe again. "Threatening me with a spanking is the number one way *not* to get me to stop doing something. That's like saying, 'Stop, or I'll give you delicious chocolate cake.' "

"Oh yeah?" The barghest said, growlingly, pulling me up his lap suggestively. But I stayed his arms.

"So when *are* you going to tell me more about you?" I asked.

He smiled at me affectionately. "In their natural time, Jane. As things come up."

For a second, I wanted to push. But I could also see, from the look on his face, that now was not the time to ask him to share his secrets. It wasn't his fault that he knew all of my secrets and I knew none of his. He'd known everything about me before I even knew him—the circumstances of our relationship meant he hadn't had to earn my trust, although time and again he'd proven to me he deserved it.

So I didn't resent having to earn his. After all, that was exactly the reason I'd wanted us to take the time we needed, however long that was.

Not that I couldn't still torture him, just a little.

"But I want to know important things," I said, gazing deep into his eyes, "For example... what you like."

I undulated my hips against his as I said the last bit, before leaning forward to nip, very gently, at the soft flesh of his ear lobe.

"I want to know what turns you on." His big hands flexed on my hips as I breathed over the shell of his ear, letting him feel my breasts press against his chest as I kept my hips moving.

"I want to know how to make my puppy growl."

With that I kissed him hard on the mouth, raking my nails gently down over his T-shirt covered back.

"Bad girl," he rumbled, as he used his strength to topple me backward and his earth magic to cushion our weight as he landed on top of me.

"This isn't letting *me* get to know *you*," I pointed out, as his mouth found that place on the side of my neck that made me whimper.

"Oh gods, Jane, the answer to all those questions is you. You turn me on; you're what I want; you make me growl."

He punctuated his words with feathery kisses on my neck.

"You're mine, little minx," he said, and that's when his teeth found my neck, marking me possessively.

I moaned, bucking against him and feeling taken and wanted and so turned on.

His tongue licked away the sting of his bite, even as I felt his knees nudge mine apart. I opened for him, and he settled his hips against mine. The rough denim of his jeans pressed against my softest parts, and I shivered. Nonetheless my hands quickly found his ass, pressing him tighter against me as his mouth found my nipple.

He used his lips and teeth in a way that made me swoon, and it was with the utmost regret that I informed him of what my hand on his ass was telling me.

"You're vibrating," I murmured.

"Fuck it," was his only response, as he dove for my other nipple.

Yes, fuck it, my libido encouraged.

But both my brain and my virtue knew that wasn't a good idea. So I pulled out the offending cell phone to see the screen.

"It's Blondie," I said. "She's called twice."

Anyan sighed into my cleavage.

"Now she's texted," I said. "Should I read it?"

"Yes," he mumbled, clearly defeated. I pressed a few buttons while my libido cursed me roundly.

"She says, 'Where are u? Alistair squealed...sort of. We've got an early start tomorrow.' "

Just as I was finished, the phone buzzed again with another message.

"This one says, 'stop humping xxx.' "

Anyan's weight shifted, so that he could lounge on me, using me as a convenient pillow.

"I think I hate her," he said with a sigh.

"I know," I said. "But I think I'm getting a splinter in my ass, anyway. And we went plenty far for a first date. You don't want me to think you're slutty."

Anyan moved, and then stood to help pull me to my feet. His hands brushed down over my butt.

"I think you're splinter free, and I also think you're going to like me slutty."

"Yes," I said, giggling. "I think I *am* going to enjoy that."

And with that I hugged him close, cinching his waist in a tight grip and burying my face in his chest.

"So are you enjoying dating?" he said, his voice happy as he pulled me closer.

I laughed. "Yes, I am. And I'm looking forward to the next time. Maybe you can crank up your Victrola and we can waltz whilst my governess chaperones."

His fingers traced down my spine, and it was his turn to grab my ass.

"I always did have a bit of a governess and her sweet young charge fantasy," he murmured, lowering his mouth to mine.

"It's because you're old," I murmured against his lips, before I let him kiss me.

All I got for my joke was a sharp, none-too-gentle smack on my ass. So I made another. And another. Till Blondie texted again, and we had to go plan for tomorrow.

CHAPTER NINE

"Seriously, I never want to leave," I murmured, as I pressed my nose against the glass case.

Anyan rumbled something conciliatory, but I only had eyes for cheese.

We were at Borough Market, this high end, posh food market. The night before, while Anyan and I were on our date, Blondie had called on Alistair, the guy she'd fingered as having stolen the library book from the Great Repository. Unfortunately, as his freshly bloated corpse attested, she was about three or four days too late. He'd died rather horribly, it appeared, after quite a fight. While she could hardly mourn the passing of a professional petty criminal who should have known better than to play with the big dogs, she did thank him for two things. First of all, he'd left out a drained charm—a simple heart pendant that she could sense had recently released a tremendous amount of power. That cleared up the mystery of how he'd managed to steal the book, since the Alistair she'd known had only been gifted with pretty good glamouring skills, very sticky fingers, and a considerable amount of chutzpah. The second thing for which she was grateful was just how good a fight he'd put up. For at some point during the struggle, the little notebook in which he'd kept his appointments had gotten knocked behind the stove. After fishing it out, she saw that Alistair had an early morning meeting at Borough Market, for the next day. Considering that all he'd had in his fridge were cheap lager and Tesco generic Scotch eggs, she highly doubted he was visiting the market as a foodie.

One thing he hadn't done, unfortunately, was hide Sarah's missing textbook so well that his attacker couldn't find it. But the fact the textbook was missing didn't have Blondie worried, mostly because she knew who had stolen it and killed Alistair. After all, the only other thing missing was Alistair's perpetual partner in crime, Reggie. While Alistair had been the (admittedly rather small) brains behind their criminal partnership, Reggie was the muscle. Reggie, like Jack, wasn't a big man, but he was equally vicious. Reggie also had far less control than Jack did, which was borne out by the fact Reggie liked to masturbate over his victims after he killed them, something both gross and unwise in a world that understood DNA.

Unluckily for the victim, and despite having worked together for so long, even Alistair didn't warrant any special dispensation from Reggie's "usual treatment."

Murdered by his partner, Alistair was now stinking up his empty flat, while Reggie undoubtedly planned on cashing in on what must have been a job so big as to tempt them away from their usual petty shenanigans and rocket them into the big leagues.

Which meant that our team just had to wait for the hand off.

And I got to ogle the cheese.

I knew I should probably take today's mission more seriously, but I was in such a good mood after last night's date. It had felt like a real date, and it had finally really felt like I was in the UK. Up till then, we'd just been running around like headless sheep. But last night, sitting in that very English diner eating very English food, I'd remembered I was somewhere I'd always wanted to visit.

After which, canoodling with Anyan had been brilliant. He was making sure we did what I would have thought impossible—really getting to know each other despite all the chaos of this situation.

Plus, from what I'd understood, today was going to be a simple case of thump the minion. We'd wait till the courier came for Reggie's prize, only we'd be waiting. Then we'd have both the book, and hopefully a soon-to-be-squealing insider telling us everything he or she knew about Morrigan and Jarl's plans.

There was no way I was wasting artisanal British cheese over a mere minion.

"Would you like a sample?" the man behind the counter said. I think he just wanted to get me away from the glass of his display case. I might have drooled on it.

"Can I?" I asked, beaming at him.

"Of course. What would you like?"

"What would you recommend?"

"How about a bite of this Stilton," he said, after a brief consideration. "Everyone loves a Stilton."

He passed me a tiny wedge and I actually saw stars

when I placed it on my tongue. It was sharp and delicious, with that unmistakable blue-cheese tang.

"Mmm," I purred. "Moldy."

"And this is a bit of Wensleydale," he said.

This bite was crumbly but creamy, all at the same time. No wonder Wallace liked it so much.

"Would you like a bite, sir?" the man asked, offering Anyan his own small wedge. I watched Anyan take it, greedily eyeballing the cheese as he took a small bite, and then offered me the rest. I ate from his fingers, only just refraining from licking them as I did so.

Anyan laughed. "I think we better take some home," he told the man. "Wrap up four or five of your favorites, if you don't mind."

The man nodded and then began scanning his selection as if he were a master craftsman figuring out which tool would be the best for a job.

"I warn you," I said to Anyan, sidling up to stand close to him and craning my neck to see his face once I'd done so, "if you feed me good cheese, you'll never get rid of me."

"Is that all I have to do?" he asked. "What happens if I sweeten the pot with some of that bread and homemade chutney over there?"

My eyes followed where his fingers pointed and my mouth began watering like a fountain. I was so distracted my libido answered for me.

"Then I'll sweeten your pot," it said, much to my virtue's evident consternation.

All I got in reply was a growl and a fierce kiss, but those little tokens of affections were almost as satisfying as the Stilton.

Soon enough I was clutching a bag of incredibly stinky cheese, which had cost Anyan what might have been the GDP of some tiny country somewhere. "Artisan" apparently translated as "fuck-off expensive." I considered putting the bag in my backpack, but I didn't want anyone to see I was carrying around an ax when I unzipped it. Plus I didn't want to risk the cheese next to the ax-head.

So I hung onto my prize, happy to play the part of the tourists we were pretending to be. As good as his word, Anyan steered me over to look at another stall's chutneys and dried fruits when he received a text.

"There's action near Roast," Anyan said. "Our man's showed up, and he's clearly waiting for someone."

A second later, Blondie called and Anyan answered. After a minute, he said, "Agreed. We'll head that way."

I cocked my head at him as he replaced his cell in his back pocket.

"Reggie's got the book. There's no sign of the courier, but they'll show up soon enough."

Browsing along as we went, we slowly meandered our way through the market. I realized how strangely relaxed I was, as we wandered around the delicious smelling stalls. If I ignored the kidnapping—which really hadn't been much of a kidnapping, really—nothing much had happened on this trip except for a cool visit to the museum. I could almost pretend the barghest and I were just a couple on holiday, enjoying the sights

It was only when I saw a flash of something moving above me that I was reminded we were on a mission. Magog, I knew, was covering the rooftops. Borough Market felt like it was open air, but most of it was really part of an old, awesome structure with rooftops high over our heads. Only the occasional girder would remind one to look up, and admire the view.

I sighted Blondie and Gog next: Blondie was wearing her hair down, instead of in a Mohawk. If you didn't look too close she looked like a young, blonde businesswoman, dressed as she was in a conservative suit she'd stolen from the owner of the flat we'd commandeered last night. She was sitting, sipping a coffee and pretending to read a paper. Meanwhile, Gog was standing a few feet behind her, wearing green coveralls and a brightly colored vest that marked him as a Council employee. A close-fitting black cap pulled down low over his neck disguised the majority of his grey skin, and he kept his head bent low to hide his face. To complete his disguise, he was busily sweeping around a set of trash cans.

I could see the creature that had to be Reggie—a rather seedy looking character standing in an awkward spot by a couple of vending machines selling water. According to Blondie, Reggie's lineage was a hodgepodge of various factions, and the only way I knew he wasn't human was the very faint glamour sparking around him to dissuade humans from coming near.

The only creature not accounted for was Hiral, who was nowhere to be seen. I wasn't even sure if he'd come with us, however. He'd shown up the previous evening, with no explanation as to where he'd been all day or where he'd gotten to when we were kidnapped. I wasn't impressed with his lack of answers, but everyone else seemed to take it in stride as "just Hiral for you."

When we'd left for today's mission, he'd just grunted and waved his long-fingered hand, as if to say, "I'll join you later. Maybe."

I shook my head, again wondering why everyone appeared to trust the little gwyllion, when something else caught my eye.

"What's a butty?" I asked, pointing at the sign for a cart also labeled "Roast." I guessed Roast was the larger restaurant, and this was its food cart.

"It's a sandwich, basically," Anyan said. "But on a roll."

"Are they good?"

"Why don't you find out," Anyan said, archly, as he led me over to the small stand.

A short while later, I was in heaven.

"If you were a bacon butty, I'd marry you," I told the barghest, although he probably couldn't understand me as my mouth was so full.

"I have no idea what you just said," he told me, confirming my suspicions. "But you look happy."

"I've never wanted to marry a sandwich," I said, around another huge mouthful, "but this is like sex and flour."

"I'm sure, dear," Anyan replied, patiently, but I could tell he was carefully monitoring our surroundings. I took another huge bite just as he swore, and began inching me behind one of the larger girders supporting the market's roof.

I chewed as I moved, but when I saw why we were hiding, even that most delicious sandwich turned to ash in my mouth. I hastily swallowed, tamping down on my reflex to throw up a shield and prep a mage ball.

"Morrigan," I murmured, for sure as shit there she was, right in front of us.

I couldn't believe I'd been so arrogant, thinking this

mission would be easy. I should have knocked wood—and by wood, I mean my wooden head. It had just been so tempting to think, this morning, that this would be a vacation. That we'd spend the rest of our time here going on dates and occasionally working, only to have the relics plop in our laps with little effort.

Plus, we'd all been so sure the Alfar would send someone else. Alfar *never* did things for themselves when they could send a minion. They just didn't. So why *was* Morrigan here, anyway?

She looked gorgeous, of course, but very different than she had at the Compound. Her lithe figure was clad in a beautiful green dress that clung to her form on top, but swirled out into a kicky, fun little skirt that came just to her knees. The outfit was capped off by a pair of toweringly high heels: all gold but for a matching green jewel pattern in a T-bar across her arch.

I couldn't stop staring at her, my eyes roving, taking everything in. It was shocking to see her again after everything that happened. The last time I'd clapped eyes on her, after all, she was murdering her husband and king, Orin. But now, here she was—not only looking happy, but *really* looking happy, in a way that wasn't at all Alfar.

What happened to the dead-eyed, mostly comatose woman who'd drifted around the Compound making vague pronouncements on issues I thought she didn't really give a shit about? That Morrigan had been replaced by a sharp-eyed sex-vixen.

The two guards flanking her were goblins, their tall, bony frames clothed in the sort of anonymous dark suits worn by the Secret Service. The goblins' yolk-yellow eyes scanned the crowd ceaselessly, and they looked ready to take care of anyone they might come across. Behind Morrigan were another three guards: I couldn't tell exactly what factions they were, yet, but they looked just as serious in their own dark suits as did the goblins.

My eyes itched to return to Morrigan, but I refused. Instead, I carefully assessed our surroundings and our positioning.

Gog was still doing his sweeping thing, but his body was stiff. Blondie was watching the proceedings from over her newspaper, the tension in her arms betraying her awareness. Out of the corner of my eye I saw Magog, shielded from Morrigan's party by a massive steel buttress, edge her way forward. She wasn't wearing her overcoat, and her wings fell about her like a wash of coal.

We had good placement in the market, I decided, but the location itself was the worst place to be for a real fight. At twenty minutes after eight, Borough market was already bustling with stall owners and employees, a few tourists, and quite a few people on their way to work, picking up a coffee at one of the various little cafés dotted here and there.

In other words, there would be quite a lot of collateral damage if this turned into a shit storm.

"What do we do?" I whispered. Morrigan was talking quietly to Reggie, who was clenching something inside of his coat, his arms wrapped around himself protectively. "We can't let her get out of here with that book," I hissed, just as Blondie put down her paper and made a series of gestures that looked like the signals of a catcher in baseball.

"And we're not going to let her," Anyan said. "Time to get that ax out, Jane. Just don't do anything crazy."

Without thinking, I hastily shrugged off my backpack and unzipped it to get to the labrys. Blondie was standing, and Gog was unscrewing the wooden handle of his broom from its brush. Meanwhile, Magog was inching forward on her little platform, obviously getting ready to fly.

I swore as the zipper stuck, finally wrenching it free so I could open my pack. The labrys felt like it was waiting for me; like it was calling. With tangible relief I pulled it out, feeling its heavy weight go light in my grip as its magic melded with mine.

"Ready?" Anyan said, his voice gone low and growly.

I nodded.

"Watch for Blondie's signal," he said.

"What's that going to be?" I asked, only to have my question answered by Blondie herself.

For suddenly the woman dressed like a conservative exec lit up like a Christmas tree, and the Original lofted one of the most potent mage balls I'd ever laid eyes upon. It was easy to forget how powerful Blondie was, as she never threw her weight around. But feeling the power radiating off that orb was a sharp reminder that the Original was something other than we were, and not to be taken for granted. I watched in awe as she lobbed her supercharged mage ball straight at Morrigan.

Less fun to watch was one of the goblins throwing himself in the way of the missile, and the way he exploded in midair, body parts flying everywhere. His shields had been no match for the Original's power.

The next few minutes were a complete blur. Magog shot past us, harrying the two guards that had been behind Morrigan before they were knocked away by the blast.

The raven herded them away using rapid-fire mage balls that flowed like machine gun bullets from her hands.

Gog, meanwhile, was taking care of the remaining goblin, who'd armed himself with a sword he'd pulled from somewhere inside his suit jacket. The coblynau had unscrewed the handle of the broom, and had reinforced the wooden handle with his own powerful earth magics. It glowed a dull green as he battled his opponent, their hits blurring they were so quick.

That left Anyan and me to handle the remaining guard, and Blondie to take Morrigan and Reggie. Considering Reggie was way out of his depth here, that should have been easy.

In fact, I was pretty confident striding towards the remaining guard, who was pacing towards us manfully. Granted, I was behind Anyan, whom I figured would do all the work.

Left to handle the big guns, Blondie was making a bee-line towards Morrigan. The Original's arm practically blurred as she threw those crazily powerful mage balls.

This should be over quickly, I thought, only to have my world—quite literally—thrown upside down.

I landed, with a painful thud, upside down on top of Anyan. Nothing had broken his fall, and when I'd managed to scramble off of him—I was reeling like a drunken sailor—it took him a second to get to his feet. When he did he looked pretty bashed up. I felt a strong pull from his earth magics as he healed himself, then did the same to me as a precaution.

Only then did I register what happened. It was like a bomb had gone off, with Morrigan at its epicenter. And yet she was left standing, laughing maniacally like some stereotype villain as she surveyed the chaos she'd created. The stalls immediately surrounding her were overturned, and I saw a number of forms strewn about. I hoped they were all just knocked around, like us, and not dead.

Very dimly I thought I heard a variety of sirens, car horns, and some screams, but it was like I was underwater.

"What the fuck was that?" I shouted, or at least I thought I had. My voice sounded far away, so I shook my head trying to clear my hearing.

"Morrigan," Anyan mouthed. I shook my head again and forced myself to yawn, and suddenly the world was blaring with sound. "Doing something she shouldn't be able to do, even as an Alfar. Where's your ax?"

I frowned, looking around till I saw the labrys's handle sticking out from underneath a recycling bin that had blown towards us. I went to grab it, feeling a wild power surge up my arm as I did so.

"Whoa!" I shouted, feeling like I'd just stuck my finger in a light socket. "It's not happy about something!" I told Anyan, as the labrys urged me forward. But I dug in my heels, watching as Morrigan tucked something large under her arm.

A book.

"Oh, hell no," I yelled, and this time I charged with it as the labrys carried me forward. Anyan followed on my heels.

Catching sight of me, Morrigan grinned. That grin faltered, however, when she saw what I was carrying. The labrys had lit up when I'd grabbed it, but now it went supernova as if recognizing an enemy.

Morrigan took off, so ridiculously spry on her high heels that I found another reason to hate her. Two of her remaining guards joined her as she ran, stumbling a bit themselves. She'd obviously not shielded them from whatever blast she'd set off.

We were snaking our way through the market towards the little café called Monmouth that had delicious coffee so strong I'd earlier dubbed it "colon blow." Morrigan, meanwhile, was still in the lead. But pumped full of ax-mojo, I was running far faster than I normally could, and we were quickly shortening her lead.

Before I could bask in our triumph, however, two shiny black sedans roared up onto the street in front of us and the doors were thrown open. Getaway cars.

"Oh, hell no!" I shouted, putting some of my own power into my strides. There was no way Morrigan was getting away from me: not now, not after all she'd done.

And not with that damned book.

Moving away from Anyan, I shot forward and I swear I was barely a few yards from Morrigan when she turned to raise her arms, and I hit a wall. Not a metaphorical runner's wall, mind you. It felt like the evil Alfar queen had raised an invisible brick wall in front of me. I bounced off it, hard, but used both my own mojo and that of the ax to stop myself flying backward.

I don't know, at that point, whether it was my own anger or the ax possessing me, but much to my surprise I found myself striding forward like Xena, brandishing the labrys, which was almost blinding in its radiance.

"Get...back...here," I snarled through gritted teeth, applying the ax to the edge of Morrigan's shield. The Alfar's little smirk vanished as the labrys's blade began to penetrate through her shield. She scrambled backward, diving into one of the cars. I strained forward as the car revved its engines tauntingly and sped off into the morning.

The shields dissolved with an audible pop, and I found myself catapulted forward to sprawl in an undignified heap on the pavement in front of me.

"Motherfucker!" I yelled, popping up to my feet on a wave of pure adrenaline. I shook my labrys at the retreating cars, gibbering insanely. Just as I was considering throwing the ax at Morrigan's retreating sedan, I saw the trunk pop just a tiny bit. Hiral's long nose poked through the gap, and his little eyes leered at me as he gave me a wicked smile.

Before I could figure out just whose spy Hiral was, exactly, I heard a scuffle behind me. As I turned around, I felt the now familiar prick of a needle in my neck, and a hood being thrown over my head.

CHAPTER TEN

I came to, spluttering, when someone very rudely threw a glass of water in my face. Hearing a similar spluttering from beside me, I turned to see a very angry looking Anyan. Unlike me, he was gagged.

Before I could say anything to the barghest, we were both blinded by ridiculously bright floodlights. I winced away from the light, feeling like I'd been hit by a truck and wondering if maybe those were its headlights.

"Why are you kidnapping us again?" I raged, despite not being able to open my eyes. I felt as mad as I had watching Morrigan split. Even madder, since we might have had a chance to catch up with her if Jack hadn't insisted on playing his little games. "You've already abducted us once, isn't that enough? And where the hell is my ax? And my cheese?"

I waited for Jack's smarmy politician's voice, but the voice that floated to my ears was not Jack's. Instead it was smooth, cool, and calm...Alfar calm.

"I am afraid, Miss True, that we have neither cheese nor an ax." At those words, my heart dropped. My first outing out with the labrys and I'd lost it? Awesome. The voice in front of me, however, was still talking so I forced myself to listen. I told myself that at least the bad guys didn't have the ax, and there was a good chance one of my friends had found it.

"Furthermore, you are also mistaken regarding my own identity, and the nature of the situation in which you now find yourself." Hearing those flowing, formal cadences I knew it definitely wasn't Jack behind those lights, and I knew whoever it was had to be Alfar.

"Huh?" I said, stupidly. I'd been so sure it was Jack and his cronies, again, that hearing a strange voice—a strange *Alfar* voice—threw me off my game.

"You have not been kidnapped illegally, as your language implies. Rather, you have been lawfully detained by the leaders of this realm."

Oh, shit, I thought, my mouth going dry and my heart pounding in my chest. Angry noises were emanating from where Anyan sat beside me, but I couldn't make out anything he was trying to say.

"For what?" I forced myself to say, trying to sound jaunty rather than scared shitless.

"You tell us," the voice replied. "You may start with what brought you here, and why you are on our soil."

"Your soil, huh?" I said, still trying to sound confident. I was trying to suss out who I was dealing with. For while "our soil" left little doubt that our kidnappers were connected to the Alfar rulers of the Great Island, I didn't know how high up the food chain they really were.

"Tell us why you are here, Jane True," the voice said,

ignoring my own questions and refusing to play. "Or we will be forced to come to our own conclusions. Conclusions that you will not like."

I shut my eyes, the lights too bright. And I started talking.

"You see," I said, "I've always really loved Britain. I've watched all the mysteries on Masterpiece Theatre, and I can't get enough Wallace and Gromit, and I really have to congratulate a culture that puts baked beans on toast and calls it dinner..."

"That is enough," the Alfar voice said, grown slightly sharper. "Are you claiming to be a tourist?"

"Yes," I said. "I even bought cheese. Are you sure you didn't see my cheese, by any chance?"

"You are lying, halfling," another voice pronounced. Lower than the first, it was still Alfar-cool, if not as calm as the other voice.

"Me? Lie? Do I look like a liar?"

"You claim to be a tourist to the human Great Britain," said the second voice. "And yet you have only done things related to our supernatural Great Island."

I scoffed openly at that mark, trying to roll my eyes but the light was too blinding.

"Let us see," the second voice continued. "We have reports of your associating with known supernatural rebels. We have you in the company of the Original known as Cyntaf—and yes, we know what she really is, even if she tries to hide it. We have you visiting the Great Library. And we have you engaging in a firefight in Borough Market, in clear view of humans, risking our people's careful arrangement with the human government. Shall I continue?"

I sat still, knowing I'd been paddled way the fuck up shit creek already.

"We also know, Jane True, that you come from the Territory formerly held by Orin and Morrigan. We know that Orin is dead, and that you were witness to that event. We also know that your former queen, Morrigan, has been sighted on these islands and that she was *also* involved in that firefight at Borough Market. What do you have to say on this matter?"

"Nothing," I mumbled, looking down at my tied-up feet like a petulant teenager. "And she's not my queen."

"What did you say?" came the first voice.

"She's not my queen," I said, more loudly. "She's a murderer and a..." I didn't know who these people were, or how much they knew, or how they'd react if they did know the truth about the Red and the White. So I pulled back.

"She's a murderer and a very bad lady," I said, instead. I knew I sounded silly but I didn't care.

"So you are not working with the Alfar known as Morrigan," the first voice asked.

"Hell no," I said.

"Are you working against the Alfar known as Morrigan?" the first voice asked.

I realized too late that my silence was as much an answer as any I could have given.

"Interesting," said the first voice. "Cut the lights and prepare the prisoners."

Someone did cut them, and my dazzled eyes were plunged into an acute darkness. I blinked, only seeing muzzy bits and pieces of things. Then I felt another needle at my neck, and I swore. Then everything went even darker, albeit a different kind of dark altogether.

*   *   *

This time I came to with another wet face. This one, however, was because I was thrown at the water rather than the other way around. Anyan and I had been tumbled into a wet ditch on a country road, presumably rather far from London. We'd been ejected from the back of a white van similar to Gog and Magog's. It wasn't our friend's, however, as the unfamiliar license plate and the rough treatment attested. They would probably have allowed us to get out ourselves, not thrown us out.

Anyan was also stirring, and I made my way over to him. Together, we struggled out of the ditch and onto the dirt next to the paved road.

I called Blondie as we walked down the road to where there was a bus stop. My phone wasn't one of those fancy smart phones, with a map, so we had to use the shelter to tell her the name of the stop, and what route it was on. Then we took a seat.

After giving us a quick healing—we were both grotty and out of sorts from all the rough treatment—Anyan snuggled me close, wiping my forehead clean and then kissing me there.

"Was that The Alfar Powers That Be?"

Anyan only nodded.

"Do you know who it was, exactly?"

"Yep," the barghest said. "I recognized their scents and their voices. That's probably why they gagged me. You, Jane True, warranted an abduction from none other than the Alfar Leader of this territory, himself."

"The king?"

Anyan's chest rumbled as he sighed. "Nothing as straightforward as that, I'm afraid. There's a saying, here, that 'Whosoever holds the Island holds the Race.' You can probably guess how that's caused a lot of problems. There was always some crazy who wanted to be king or queen of the mountain, and they were constantly attacking whoever ruled the Great Island."

"So then how is that dude the leader?"

"Leader, Jane, with a capital 'L.' It's all because of semantics. Long ago the Alfar realized that calling anyone king or queen of the Great Island was just asking for trouble. So they changed the word 'king' to 'Leader.' "

"That's lame." I said, looking up at Anyan and wrinkling my nose.

"Yes, but it worked," he said, then kissed me on said appendage. His mouth lingered, and I felt my body flush.

After all the adrenaline of the day: the firefight, then getting kidnapped, then getting thrown out of a moving vehicle, I shouldn't be surprised at what happened next.

I pounced.

My mouth was on the barghest's, and I was kissing him as passionately as I ever had. I suddenly really wanted him. Maybe it's because I wanted to know he was alive and well, or maybe because we'd just had such a crazy day together and the one thing I'd come out of it realizing was that I could rely on him always to be there.

We'd even gotten kidnapped together, twice, as if our abductors knew we went together like a horse and carriage.

Anyan kissed me back, just as passionately, helping me swing my leg around so that I was straddling him on the bench. His hands cupped my bottom and I moaned into his open mouth.

Then a passing car honked, and I realized we'd both forgotten a glamour.

I lifted my face, giving a finger to the car, then looked back at him with a sigh.

"Maybe this isn't the best time," I said, sliding off of him to sit next to him on the bench.

"No, it probably isn't. You'll just have to wait for our next date."

I grinned. "When will that be?"

"Soon as I can finagle it, little minx. We can shoot for no interruptions, for that one."

"Nobody likes interruptions," I said, solemnly.

"No. How am I supposed to make you beg with someone blowing up my pager?"

"You are so *old*," I said, laughing at his nineties-speak. "Now tell me about the Leader."

So Anyan did. Apparently the Leader was your typical Alfar, but more savvy than most. The Great Island wasn't an easy place to rule, so there couldn't be the sort of All Powerful But Completely Out of Touch rulers that our own continent's territories were known for.

The leader's name was Luke, and the other voice had been Luke's own second, Griffin.

"Griffin's an interesting Alfar," Anyan said. "Extremely powerful, but also really with it. He's probably the edgiest Alfar I've ever met. He's also really smart, but he's tremendously conservative. He doesn't want anything to change the status quo, ever, and he wholeheartedly believes in the superiority of purebloods."

"He sounds like a charmer," I said dryly.

"That's the funny part," Anyan said. "He is a charmer. He's one of the most personable, interesting Alfar you'll ever meet. He's engaged, fully, with reality in a way the rest of his kind eschew. Yet he's still totally Alfar in his thinking."

"Well, it makes sense," I said. "After all, that system rewards him for being born himself. Why would he want it to change?"

"It's still amazing that beings like Griffin can constantly be faced with facts that challenge their worldview, but remain oblivious."

"It happens all the time, Anyan. Although I'm happy to hear it's not just humans that are so blind."

"Anyway," Anyan said, "They're obviously aware something's up, and they wanted to find out what it was."

"So they kidnapped us?"

"I think they kidnapped you, really. I was just thrown in because I was with you. I think you present them with the real mystery: what are you doing here and why? The rest of us are known around these parts. They probably figure we're just spying for the rebels, or the Territory. But you they don't understand, and your being here makes us being here look more suspect."

"Okay," I said. "So how did I do?"

Anyan shrugged. "I think you did well. You didn't give anything really important away, and we're alive. I'd count that as a success."

"But I lost the ax," I said. "And the cheese."

"We don't know you lost either, yet. Maybe they were picked up by the others. Plus I don't think the labrys is the type of thing to get itself lost. And I can always buy you more cheese."

"You'd do that?" I said, impishly, beaming up at him.

"Of course," he answered, with an expression that was so affectionate my heart lurched like a drunk on a bender. Then it realigned itself as I remembered something important.

"Wait, who will The Powers That Be side with? Us or Morrigan? She is Alfar, after all."

"That, my dear, is a good question," Anyan replied, gone serious again. "And one we still can't answer. But I think we can be fairly confident that even the Alfar here can't be stupid enough to want the Red and the White to rise again."

"Ugh. I don't like relying on 'confident.'"

"Neither do I, but we'll have to for now. At least until they show their hand."

I made a disgruntled sound, expressing my unhappiness with our situation.

"So you've met the rebels and you've met The Powers That Be. Which do you like better?" Anyan asked.

That was easy.

"I'm thinking neither group is going to end up on my Christmas list."

Then, with a sigh, I finally brought up the thing I'd really been dreading acknowledging.

"We have to get that book back."

Anyan nodded. "I know."

"I don't want to have to be a hero," I said, my voice small.

The barghest put his arm around me, drawing me close.

"I know," he said.

I let him hold me like that, till Gog showed up in the white van to carry us away.

CHAPTER ELEVEN

That we'd been kidnapped by the Alfar Leader didn't impress any of our new friends. Apparently, they'd all been kidnapped at sometime or other by TPTB. Neither were they impressed with my news about Hiral having hid out in Morrigan's trunk.

Turns out the gwyllion had already called. He was in Brighton, where he'd discovered Morrigan had her hideout. From what Blondie had told me, the Red and the White had always had a slight obsession with Brighton, and had tried to use the human king, King George IV, as one of their resurrection tools. He hadn't found any of their pieces, but he'd commissioned dragons everywhere throughout the Brighton Pavilion.

As for our current mission, the others had picked us up with our bags already packed and our train tickets already bought. I was hugely relieved to discover we were already on track to get the book back, the bones back, *and* kick Morrigan's admittedly rather fine Alfar ass.

Unfortunately, however, my friends had neither my cheese nor my ax. I did a pretty good job of flipping out when I discovered I was now a weaponless champion, but Blondie assured me cryptically that all would be well—that the ax would find me when it was needed and that it wasn't going to lose me so easily. Since I still had no idea where it was, however, I didn't find her words particularly comforting. Instead, I went right ahead and kept freaking out until she yelled at me that I wouldn't live to see the labrys returned to me if I didn't stop irritating her.

When I still didn't stop she sighed.

"Do you *feel* like it's lost?" she said. "I know you think it's lost, but do you *feel* like it's lost?"

I paused at her words, and buried my instinctive response to shout, "yes, I know it's lost so it feels lost." Instead, I tried to feel for the ax, as I could do when it was in my hand.

"No," I said, surprised. "It doesn't feel lost… but where is it?"

"It takes care of itself," she said. "You'll get it back when you need it. Now shut up about the damned ax."

So I tried to put a cap on my nerves by concentrating on the other thing I was feeling quite strongly, at that point: my hunger. Luckily, I'd been assured there'd be snacks.

So soon enough I found myself on the hour-long train ride to Brighton. We'd gotten a whole table to ourselves, with four seats around it. Anyan and I sat facing backward, while Blondie and Magog sat across from us. Gog was going to arrive in Brighton a few hours after we arrived, with the little white van and some other rebel fighters to help pad out our numbers.

My table, unsurprisingly, was soon littered with empty packets of food strewn in front of me. Anyan had taken me to the Marks & Spencer food hall in the train station, and I'd gone a little crazy. They just had the most amazing looking sandwiches, and salads, and desserts. Not to mention all these fancy chips and sweets. I suppressed a contented burp and then leaned back in my comfortable seat, feeling almost relaxed—no small feat for someone who was on her way to confront her worst enemy and who'd managed to lose her most important weapon.

But at least we were on track as far as our mission was concerned. I was also warm, and fed, and while still worried about the labrys, I made myself feel better by touching on that place that told me it wasn't missing, even if it wasn't exactly here. I'd also been assured by Anyan that not only would I get to swim in Brighton, but that I'd get to swim in the ocean. That made me more than happy. Ponds and rivers were one thing, but nothing could compete with the ocean when it came to her awesome power.

So I munched, and dozed, and recharged my physical batteries, knowing I'd get to recharge my magical ones soon enough. The others did the same, although maybe with less munching.

Eventually, however, all the juice I drank caught up with me and I got up to go to the potty. I had to walk into the next train carriage, through these little doors that opened with a hush of air like those on *Star Trek*'s spaceships.

Ambling slowly, I enjoyed the view of the British countryside while waiting patiently for the person already occupying the toilet to finish.

I tried not to think about how gross the bathroom

would probably be. While British trains were one hundred percent better than American trains, there was still enough rocking that I imagined boys would have difficulties.

So I concentrated on the music coming from my old iPod to distract myself, leaning over the empty seat next to me to get a better view. Then I heard a flush and the sound of a lock turning, and I straightened up just as the bathroom door opened.

Only to find myself staring into the cruelly beautiful eyes of Graeme, the rapist incubus.

He clearly was no more expecting me than I was him, and we stared at each other for what felt like an eternity. His once perfect features were strangely waxen, courtesy of his having been horribly burnt by Conleth, the ifrit-halfling. But other than that he looked the same as the last time I saw him, and very much alive. I'd really been hoping he hadn't made it out of the tunnel collapse that Phaedra had described before she, herself, bit the big one.

I stowed my iPod and headphones in my pocket, taking a careful step back as Graeme finally registered my presence with a slow smile and a wave of his juju. Both were as dark and sadistic as I remembered them.

"Jane," he said, taking a step towards me.

"Graeme," I acknowledged, taking another step back.

"It's always a pleasure to see you," he said, increasing the roll of his pain-drenched magics against my shields.

"I'm afraid I can't say likewise," I murmured, pushing back with my own power. I wasn't the same Jane he was used to beating up, and the sooner I let him know that, the better.

That said, I had to think carefully. There was a whole

train carriage full of people sitting around me. They hadn't noticed anything too out of sorts as of yet, but they would if Graeme and I started throwing magic at each other.

"Why don't we take our conversation over there," I said, nodding towards another set of doors that led into the roomy little compartment between carriages where people could stash luggage and wait to disembark the train.

"Trying to get me alone, Jane?" Graeme asked, licking his lips in a way that made me shudder.

"Actually, yes," I replied, sidling past him and pressing the little button that let me open the door.

When it was shut behind Graeme, I turned to him. I didn't actually know what the fuck I was planning to do. I just wanted him away from all the vulnerable humans. I'd found out that at least two innocent bystanders had died at Borough Market, with two more still in hospital with severe injuries. There wasn't going to be a repeat of that around me again, if I could help it.

So I lured the enemy away from the civilans, and then realized I had no idea what to do. Naturally enough for me under such circumstances, I started babbling.

"On your way to see Morrigan?" I asked. "Is she your boss, now that Phaedra's dead?"

Graeme's mojo tightened around my shields, but they weren't getting past. Nor was he stupid enough to do that mind trick he liked to play, not after I'd nearly broken his little brain the last time he tried it on me.

"Is Phaedra definitely dead, then?" he asked.

"Yes," I said. "Oh, yes." I'd seen the little Alfar who'd been Graeme's superior speared by one of the creature's tentacles. It wasn't a sight I was apt to forget anytime soon.

Unsurprisingly, Graeme wasn't too fazed. All he did was shrug.

"I figured as much," he said.

"So now you're working for Morrigan, I take it? Oh, wait, you were always working for her, weren't you? We liked to think you were Jarl's, but it was Jarl and Morrigan together all along, wasn't it?"

Still Graeme said nothing, although the mojo brushing against my shields was getting increasingly ugly.

"My real question is," I began, suddenly wishing I had the ax, "who's really in charge, amongst those two? In other words, Graeme, are you Jarl's bitch, or are you Morrigan's?"

Graeme's lips twitched, and he lunged for me, using a combination of power and brute physical force. But my own shields were strong, and even though I wasn't as charged up as I wanted to be, I still had more than enough power in my reservoirs.

Holding the incubus back with my mojo, I looked him in the face as I asked him again what I wanted to know. I figured I only had a few seconds till my cronies felt all the power being bandied about and came to investigate.

"C'mon, tell me," I repeated. "Are you Jarl's or are you Morrigan's? Who really wears the pants in that fucked-up family?"

Graeme snarled again, his waxen face horrible in the canned light of the railway car, and he really poured on the juice. He was trying to force his way through my shields, and although they were staying strong I wouldn't be able to hold them indefinitely. I also didn't know why my friends hadn't already come.

My eyes flicked to the little door and Graeme grinned.

"They're not coming, you little halfling cunt. I've shielded this whole compartment. They think you're safe. But you're mine, you little whore."

I really want my ax, I thought, starting to panic. I was doing everything I could to hold Graeme, but just like I knew his tricks, he knew mine. He wasn't letting me reach out to the water around him to trap him, as I had before, nor was he letting me find a gap anywhere in his own shields through which I could force them open.

What kind of champion am I? I realized, fear arcing up my spine. *I can't even beat Graeme, and I've lost the fucking labrys…*

[Just call for it, my child,] came a sleepy voice in my head.

Creature? Is that you? I asked, almost crying with relief. It could help me.

[Am I Creature, now?] it chuckled, although the sound was dreamy. [Your fear woke me. You needn't be afraid. Your weapon is merely waiting for you. Just call for it. It wants to be with you.]

Call for it? I thought. *How the hell do I call for it?*

But I could feel the creature was gone, already back to snoozing.

Putting another flood of power into my shields and managing to push Graeme back a few inches, I ignored the rage and need to hurt me written all over his face and called to my ax.

Um, Ax? Are ya there? I could use you right about now.

Nothing. So I tried again.

Oh, Aaaa-axxxxxx. Are you there?

Still nothing. And with every second that ticked by Graeme was gaining the ground he'd lost. My power was draining fast and although I could pull a little bit from the air, the dry, air-conditioned environment of the train wasn't helping me out much.

With a brutal shove, Graeme inched forward even more, till we were practically nose-to-nose, separated only by our impenetrable shields. Problem was, I didn't know how much longer mine would remain impenetrable.

The incubus shoved again with his dark force and I felt a weak spot, right in the center of my protections. I moved more power inward to reinforce that weak spot, but Graeme took advantage of that shift and began eating away at the edges of my shields.

I swore, starting to panic, and with a thudding heart I really, really, really wanted my labrys. I felt a tingle, when I did so, so I urged my wild emotions on, letting myself really *need* my ax. At the same time, I pictured myself holding it.

The problem with our magic, however, was that it took a lot of control—control that powerful emotions or a lack of concentration made difficult. I'd learned to do quite well with manipulating emotions and power at the same time, but even I couldn't compensate for a total lack of concentration.

Feeling my shields buckle, then collapse, terror chased through me as Graeme's hand closed on my left arm, yanking me forward.

I called one last time, with all my need, all my fear...

But I was just as surprised as Graeme when, with my right arm, I raised the double-headed ax between us.

"What the fuck?" he hissed, as I laughed uncontrollably, relief flooding through me so powerfully I nearly went to my knees.

Being on your knees in front of Graeme, however, was not a good idea, so I chose the more sensible route: I called out to the ax with my power, watching as it lit up, its own power lapping eagerly at me like a joyous retriever.

I missed you too, I thought. *Now let's get rid of this bad man.*

Graeme had let go of my wrist and had backed up a step when the labrys appeared. Then he'd backed up again when it lit up. In fact, he was backed up all the way against the door that led off the train.

"It was nice seeing you, Graeme," I said. "Do remember to mind the gap."

And with that I punched, hard, with one wave of power at the button that opened the train's door. Sparks flew from it as it must have shorted out. At the same time, I punched with another wave of power right at Graeme's shields.

Suddenly unbalanced as the door behind him was forced open by my magic, I didn't really need to shove that hard to push him off the train. Not that I was sorry for doing so as I watched his body arc through the air. Walking forward to poke my head out of the open door, my hair whipping around my face, I watched with a feeling of immense satisfaction as Graeme landed with a thud a good distance from the train track.

I backed away from the door, then, and hit the button that made it close. They did, and suddenly the little room was completely quiet. Only then did it hit me what had just occurred.

I had kicked Graeme's ass.

I had kicked *Graeme*, my nemesis's, *ass*.

And it had felt *so good*.

First I did a ridiculous happy dance. Then, hugging the labrys carefully to my chest, I let it feel how grateful I was. It seemed to respond, in its way, and I felt a tingle of satisfied power rush through me. I was just about to rush back to the others and let them know that I, Jane True, had just *kicked Graeme's ass,* when I realized that I *still* had to pee, only now I had an enormous ax to contend with. I let it feel my frustration, then watched as it melted away. When I panicked and called back to it, fearing I'd somehow offended or rejected it, it reappeared in my hand.

I grinned when I realized what was going on. I not only had a weapon, I had a clever weapon.

Experimentally I dismissed it again, and it dutifully disappeared. Again I called for it, and there it was. I dismissed it once more, and then headed through the inner doors to where the bathroom was. Once inside the bathroom, I called for it again. Despite having moved locations, it came to me there in the bathroom. I was so happy I kissed it, feeling a warm tingle in my lips where there should have been cold steel. I dismissed it one last time, finally relieved my aching bladder, and then went back to rejoin my friends.

They were all as I'd left them, somehow oblivious to what had occurred. Graeme's shields must have been really strong, and I think that once the labrys had shown up it had taken over for them. Lucky for me, it was better at this game than I was.

I sat down across from Blondie and next to Anyan, trying to keep my face neutral.

Then I made the labrys appear on the table. They all hissed with relief, although Blondie didn't look at all that surprised to see it.

"Told you it wouldn't lose you," she said.

"Yes, well, you were right. Also, the creature spoke to me. It's already back asleep but it seems that if I really freak out it feels it."

"Why'd you freak out? Bathroom that awful?" Anyan asked, obviously torn between worry and confusion at how even a train bathroom could be so bad my fear of it could wake an immortal being from its sleep.

"The bathroom wasn't nice, but it was more the fact I ran into Graeme that did it."

"You ran into Graeme?" Anyan asked, sharply.

"That I did."

"What? Are you okay?"

The table went silent, but I was only seeing Anyan by that point. His iron-grey eyes were so worried.

"I kicked his ass, Anyan. Like, totally kicked it. Like, I can't believe I kicked it so hard. It was *awesome*."

I knew I was babbling like an idiot, but Anyan was grinning as if I'd brought home a trophy.

"Did I mention I totally kicked Graeme's ass?" I concluded, lamely, my own smile growing to match the barghest's. Anyan's kiss was so fierce it took me by surprise. But even more shocking, to me, was just how proud I felt when he said his next words.

"And you say you're not a hero."

CHAPTER TWELVE

My evening swim at Brighton Beach was heavenly. Rocky as hell, but heavenly.

The moonlight was strong, casting shadows over the pebbles as I stood there, counting crows. Well, only one crow. Magog was my babysitter for that evening. She was obviously not impressed with my love of the water, and sat huddled inside her massive coat with her wings shifting around her like she had anacondas hidden under her clothes.

The others were strategizing and reaching out to various contacts, trying to cobble together some extra help. Gog was on his way with four other rebels, but we knew we needed more.

Graeme, after all, had seen me on the train to Brighton, which meant we couldn't count on the element of surprise to be on our side.

Instead, we needed greater numbers, a good plan, and hopefully for Hiral to come through as our man on the inside. That said, we'd not heard bupkes from the gwyllion since he'd let us know where Morrigan had holed up.

I took that time to swim and swim and swim, partly out of necessity as I needed to be strong, but also partly because it was the first time I'd seen the ocean since arriving in London. Granted, I'd only been here a few days, but I missed the sea.

So I frolicked, and charged up my powers, and generally tried to relax. I felt like all I'd done ever since I woke up from that coma was to run around like a headless chicken, but here in the water it felt like I had some time to myself and that things would wait for me, on land, till I was good and ready for them.

That feeling of security was an illusion, of course, and when I did finally walk up the beach, I found Blondie waiting impatiently for me.

"We've gotta go," she said. "You're needed."

Automatically, I touched that little part in my mind where I could feel the ax waiting for me to call it forth. I wondered where it actually was, like on another plane or something, before I reminded myself that down such roads lay madness.

"Did Hiral contact you? Are we going in?" I asked, instead of thinking about the labrys's secrets.

"He did. And it's not good. It seems that Morrigan's getting ready to move out tomorrow. And she definitely knows we're here—Hiral saw Graeme arrive at the estate. But she doesn't seem to care."

"And that's bad?" I asked.

"It tells me she knows something we don't about either their strength, or their numbers, or something. They've

got something they're hiding—something powerful—
'cause even Morrigan wouldn't be that arrogant."

I thought about the strong, sexy Morrigan I'd seen at
the market. She seemed so changed from the Morrigan at
the Compound, but that Morrigan had been a lie. She'd
been posing as your typical Alfar for the gods knew how
long…we knew nothing of the real woman underneath
the facade that had fooled us for so long.

"I don't know," I said, shaking my head slowly and
voicing my thoughts. "Maybe she is that arrogant. We
don't know the real Morrigan at all, do we?"

Blondie shrugged. "True. But we can't make any
assumptions. We need to plan and we need to motivate.
We've rounded up a bunch of fighters, and Gog's brought
in our own people from London. But they need a pep
talk."

"And you want me to hear it?" I asked.

"No," Blondie said, "I want you to give it."

And with that she was striding towards the street at the
top of the beach, where Gog waited in the little white van.
I followed behind, demanding to know what Blondie
meant by me giving the troops a pep talk.

She ignored my questions till we were in the van, and
then Gog took off, darting through darkening evening
streets.

Only then did she turn to face me.

"Our people need to see you, Jane. They need to know
you're on our side and that you're ready. They need to see
the champion."

My first reaction was to tell her she was nuts, but then I
realized that was my purpose, after all. I was a figurehead—
this operation's Joan of Arc, minus the martyring (hope-

fully). But still, I was Jane True...who the hell was going to be inspired by me?

"Are you sure they'll care?" I asked. "I mean, I don't exactly look like a champion..."

"Nonsense," Blondie said. "Already people know about the things you did, outing Jarl. And they know the story of the champion, and they'll recognize the power of the ax."

I frowned at Blondie, not believing her.

"Cyntaf's right," Magog said, her raspy voice unfazed. "They'll believe the labrys. And we need something to believe in," she added, reachingouta small hand and placing it on Gog's thigh as he drove.

For his part, Gog looked at me in the rearview and gave me a wink and a tooth-deprived smile.

I wanted to argue more, or at least ask exactly what part I should play. When Anyan had called me a hero after battling Graeme, that had felt good. But kicking the ass of one's nemesis was a lot different from being asked to persuade other people to fight. Unfortunately, before I could air my concerns, we were already at our destination: a terraced house in Hove, next to Brighton.

Following the others, we made our way down the steps into a basement apartment that reeked of cat piss and probably hadn't seen a paintbrush since it was built. We walked through a low door and then into a small foyer that had crumbling tile and no furniture. Blondie led us further into the house, down a narrow hallway that led into a large, if disheveled and filthy, kitchen.

Sitting around on chairs, on countertops, and even on the dirty floor, were about twenty beings. They were a mix of identifiable, probably purebred creatures loyal to the rebel cause and other beings that might have been half-lings or purebloods. Everyone had the same expressions on their faces, however: boredom that turned to curiosity mixed with a tangible element of fear as we entered.

I hung back, uncomfortable with my role in this room. I didn't even know what we were doing, and I was supposed to be leading these people? Luckily, Blondie was more than happy to do the talking.

She walked around, first, like a politician, greeting individuals and shaking their hands, or offering them a hug. Only after she'd said hello to everyone did she come back towards me. Blondie didn't yet single me out, however; instead she started talking.

"My friends, my comrades," she began. "Thank you for coming this evening and for volunteering to help."

A few people looked at each other, as if they were still on the fence about the volunteering part.

"We are facing an enormous challenge, and one that many of us thought would never happen again. The Red and the White are rising."

Everyone shifted around at that admission, and the level of tension in the room rose palpably.

"Many of you are probably wondering what that actually means. Very few in this room were alive the last time the Red and the White appeared, and they have not been our enemies for entire generations. Instead, other enemies have arisen and it is to combat those enemies that you took your places as soldiers.

"In fact, many of you are probably wondering whether the Red and the White have anything to do with you. Why you should care. Why you should waste your resources fighting something that's not necessarily Alfar."

Most of the faces, by this point, were watching Blondie with rapt attention. She really knew how to work a small room like this, and her charisma was undeniable. But only a few nodded at her words. I realized that the rebels, while Blondie's natural allies, weren't necessarily *our* natural allies in this fight. After all, the Red and the White weren't the enemies that the rebels had been fighting for so long.

So while it made sense for Blondie to go to the soldiers she knew for help, we were going to have to work to convince them that this really was their fight.

"Make no mistake," Blondie said, "The Red and the White must be fought. And while they are not being awoken by the Alfar that rule this land, they are being raised by Alfar who have proven themselves, time and again, to be the enemies of halflings and those they believe to be lesser factions. The two Alfar seeking to raise the Red and the White were responsible for heinous crimes against our halfling brethren, and now they seek even more power. Power that, if achieved, would make them nigh on unstoppable.

"So I would ask you to expand your definition of 'the enemy.' The Alfar who rule this Island may be cruel and power-hungry, but nothing you know can prepare you for the depths of depravity that will be unleashed if the Red and the White are allowed to rise."

"I entreat you to join with us. Help us defeat those Alfar who've come to our Island, seeking to destroy it. For that's what the Red and the White will do. They won't discriminate. They'll destroy everything. Human, supernatural, Alfar, and halfling. We'll finally be equal, but it will be in death."

Blondie's speech was making an impact, and I could see the fear in the eyes of the people sitting before me. I also knew that these were, as Blondie had said, soldiers—they were not civilians, easily scared. But as Blondie made her speech I tried to think through what the Red and the White meant to the people of this Island. They were a combination of history and bogeyman . . . it was as if Adolf Hitler were threatening to rise from his grave, only armed with all the power of the damned. I realized that we were asking them to fight the creatures of legends—the stories they spoke of in hushed voices.

We are asking them to fight, I thought. *And some will die.*

It was only at that moment that I realized what we were doing in that little basement apartment. We were creating the first cadre of soldiers for what would become an army. An army that we would lead into a battle with unspeakable power and evil, and an army made up of individuals who might die in that fight.

Only then did I understand what it meant to be Joan of Arc. I'd been so busy making martyring jokes that I hadn't thought through what she'd been responsible for, which was leading people to kill others and be killed, themselves.

My skin had grown clammy, and I felt woozy—my head spun suddenly in the oppressive, smelly air of the tiny room. It was like I was very far away when Blondie turned to stand beside me, her arm around my waist.

"But do not think you are alone, my comrades. Do not think we have been abandoned, and do not think we have no hope. For just as the Red and the White rise from legend, so does our champion!"

And with that, Blondie pushed me forward gently. Yet I still managed to stumble, my legs gone numb as I saw the faces peering at me.

Just as I thought they would, their faces showed a mixture of uncertainty and dread. I looked over at Blondie, pleadingly.

"Call the weapon of the champion, Jane," Blondie said, smiling at me with encouragement. "Show them the labrys."

And so I did. I reached into that place where I knew it waited, and I called.

It came to me, and I held it aloft.

The room, quiet before, went as silent as the grave. I could feel all eyes on me, their uncertainty changing to something else.

"Light it," Blondie murmured. And as if answering her command, I felt the power of the creature thrust itself through me and into the ax.

The light it gave off was almost blinding, and there were shouts as faces were averted. I didn't understand what they were shouting about, as my own eyes had been forced to shut at the brightness of the labrys. But as I toned down the power, getting it under control and dialing down the light pouring forth from the ax, I saw the faces of the soldiers in that room.

They were looking at the labrys, at me, with rapt faces, all traces of doubt or fear wiped clean away. Some even had tears in their eyes, and one tough-looking woman was openly weeping.

If the Red and the White were creatures sprung from legend, so was the champion, the person they'd been taught about as children. I thought back to all of those books in the Great Repository, those textbooks they'd all been forced to study that talked about the champion and her power. No wonder they reacted to me as if I were King Arthur brandishing Excalibur.

Blondie's hand closed on my shoulder from behind me as she stepped forward to join me.

"Who fights with me, fights with our champion. Who fights with our champion?" the Original called.

A loud howl tore through the chest of an incredibly beefy man sitting front-and-center. "Me!" he shouted, beginning to pound his fists on the floor. Others joined him, either stamping their booted feet or slapping their hands on walls or tables.

"Me! Me! Me!" they chanted, declaring their allegiance to their champion.

"Who will follow us to victory!" yelled Blondie. The chant continued, swelling in volume and speed until it was deafening.

Looking out at that audience, watching me with adoration, tears burned in my eyes.

CHAPTER THIRTEEN

I still felt nauseated, but the cool water on my face helped. Bent over the sink, I filled my palms with another handful to splash on my cheeks, before drinking deeply from the faucet. Then I raised my still dripping face to the mirror, looking into my own eyes.

"What the fuck have you gotten yourself into?" I whispered to myself. But I had no answers.

"Jane?" Anyan called from outside the bathroom door just as he knocked, softly. "You all right?"

I opened the door for him, and he frowned when he saw my face. I probably looked as good as I felt.

We'd returned only moments ago from the little apartment where I'd met the troops. We were staying in a lovely big town house courtesy of one of Blondie's local contacts, and I should have been thrilled that Anyan and I finally had our own bed with it's own en suite bath. But I couldn't care less.

All I could think about was the fact this war was real,

and I was supposed to be leading it. Even if it was only supposed to be in spirit, that felt even worse, somehow. I felt like I was posing as something that would get those people killed.

Pushing past the barghest, I made my way over to the bay window that was the showcase of our room. It looked out over a lovely Georgian square that, bathed in moonlight, reflected an ordered calm the opposite of my roiling emotions.

Meanwhile, Anyan took a seat on the bed, waiting in his patient way for me to start talking. Eventually, I did.

"You called me a hero when I faced Graeme. I felt like a hero, at that moment. But that was personal, and I kept it personal. I can't lead those people to fight my fight."

Anyan thought about what I said, before finally speaking. What he came out with surprised me. "You have to stop thinking any of this is about you, Jane."

A million rejoinders flashed through my mind. *Of course it was about me! They killed my mother! They raped my friend! Jarl's nagas were going to kill me like they did Joe Gonzalez from Shreveport! It's always been about me!*

But I managed, if only just, to say none of these things. Instead I narrowed my eyes at Anyan, waiting for him to continue.

"I know it looks like it's about you, but you're just like the rest of us—caught up in this massive shit show that's obviously always been about something a whole hell of a lot bigger. You're involved, yes, but in the same way we all are. If anything, you're a victim. You didn't ask for Peter Jakes to finger you as a halfling, but he did. You didn't ask for Jakes to get himself murdered in your town, but he did. And you didn't ask to find his body. But you did. And that's how you got involved. But you didn't *start* any of this."

I winced, realizing that Anyan had managed to nail my emotions with more accuracy than I ever could. I was horrified about leading those people, yes. But I also felt guilty—a guilt so profound I couldn't even acknowledge it to myself. To do so would be to sink under its weight.

"Haven't I?" I asked, harshly. "What if I'd not found that body, and Ryu never came to Rockabill, and Jimmu had killed me? None of this would have happened."

Anyan shook his shaggy head, his grey eyes sad.

"No, Jane. Your death wouldn't have changed anything. All of this would have happened anyway, and probably faster. Up until you came along, we thought that Jarl was working by himself, doing evil shit because he could and because he had a typical, Alfar-purist agenda. But it's never been just about Jarl, Jane. He's part of something huge, and part of something that has nothing to do with us.

"Think about it," he continued, when I frowned. "Think of what's happened in the past few months. Has any of it really been about Jarl, at all?"

I thought, as he'd asked, and then I said, "No. It's been about Morrigan, hasn't it?"

"Yes," he said. "Morrigan has been in the shadows, this whole time. We always thought it was about Jarl, but it's really been about Morrigan, the Red, and the White. And none of us had a clue. For all we know, she orchestrated all Jarl's crazy just to serve as cover for what she was doing with the relics. Or her madness infected him. Who knows."

"But what does that have to do with the people we met in that room?"

"It's simple, Jane. We've all been victims of Morrigan. We've all been put into a position we don't want to be in, because of Morrigan. We've all been forced to take on new roles, because of Morrigan.

"So now you need to ask yourself," he said, "What you want that role to be."

"I don't have a choice," I said, frustration lacing my tone. "I got conned into taking that stupid ax."

"No," Anyan said, and his voice was adamant. "You've always had choices, Jane. I said earlier that you were made into a victim by Jarl. But is that what you remained?"

I'd made a face when Anyan had said the word "victim," and I suddenly started to understand.

"I'm nobody's victim," I said. "But I'm not sure about being a hero, yet, either."

"I think we're *all* gonna have to be heroes, if Morrigan gets her way and resurrects the Red and the White. Otherwise, we're all fucked—humans and supernaturals, alike. So when the beings in that room volunteered to fight, it wasn't because of Jane True. It wasn't even really because you have an ax, or you're called a champion. Yeah, knowing you're the champion might have made them feel a little more hopeful, but they volunteered because they know their history, and they know what will happen to everyone they love if Morrigan gets her way."

"It's not about me, about Jane True, at all," I said, finally getting it.

Anyan held out his hand to me from where he sat on the bed. I moved forward to take it, and he pulled me down to sit next to him.

"Nope, it's not about you. It's about survival. And you're no more a victim than they are, Jane. You've never once backed down, even though you were scared. You've never once put others ahead of yourself, when it came to danger."

I didn't point out that I'd hidden behind Anyan, himself, at least five dozen times this week. He was on a roll of Jane Adoration, and I was enjoying it.

"So just be yourself, Jane. Don't stress out about being anything else. You've done heroic things dozens of times, when you've had to. I've got faith in you. And if what those people need right now is some of that same faith, that idea of a champion, are you really going to take that away from them?"

I shook my head. "No, sir." And I wasn't. I still wasn't happy about my role as champion, but everything Anyan said had made sense. This chaos was happening with or without me—and if I needed to step up and shoulder my part of the load, that's what I'd do.

He smiled down at me, and then his mouth was on mine. The kiss was gentle, affectionate, and lingering. It also took me down to the bed so that, with a little adjusting, we were lying side by side. His favorite soft Eukenuba shirt was against my cheek as my body instantly relaxed against him.

"Is it wrong that I like it when you call me sir?" he asked, cuddling me close.

I giggled, but my laugh turned into a yawn. I was suddenly exhausted both physically and mentally. Today had been fucking crazy, even for all the recent crazy days we'd had. We'd fought Morrigan first thing that morning, then been kidnapped, I'd had that confrontation with Graeme, then there had been the whole thing with the rebel soldiers.

In technical terms, I was pooped.

I was also finally alone with Anyan, in our own bed-room, replete with all the privacy in the world.

So it was with much regret that I nodded off, fully clothed in the barghest's arms. I slept deeply and dream-lessly till I awoke the next morning to find myself alone in that big bed, wondering if my libido would ever speak to me again.

My dad was talking so fast I could hardly understand him.

"Linda Allen reads the craziest books, have you ever actually read one of them? And oh my God have you seen what Miss Carol orders? I think my eyes about near fell out. But we miss you and the girls are fine, although Tracy is about as big as a house by now, and Grizzie's acting like she's okay, but I can tell she's freaking out, and she wants to paint the baby's room with murals of what she calls 'cavorting nudes,' but Tracy is putting her foot down..."

I listened, patiently, until he took a moment to breathe.

"Dad? How many coffees have you had today?"

"I don't know. Why do you ask? What does it matter?" he said, hyperactively and evasively.

I sighed. For the past fifteen years my dad hadn't been allowed more than one cup of mostly decaf coffee a day, because of his heart condition. But now that he was healed, all bets between him and coffee were appar-ently off.

"Dad, just tell me. How many have you had?"

"I had some for breakfast, obviously. And then one at work. And then Grizzie was teaching me how to make dirty images with cinnamon on the foam—which she's unsurprisingly really good at—and so we had to drink what we used to practice, and then the boys called up from the fire station for some coffees, but then they had a call out, so they were going to go to waste, anyway, so..."

My father continued motormouthing away like a Valley girl on meth, while I frowned and shook my head. I hadn't thought through the consequences of leaving him alone in a state-of-the-art café. After all those long years without real coffee, training him to be a barista had been like teaching a junkie to cook gourmet crack.

My dad was now talking about his plan to reorganize the bookshelves by size and shape, when I interrupted him more forcefully.

"Dad, I really think you should talk to Tracy and Grizzie before you do any reorganizing. And maybe sleep first, before even bringing it up. Have you been sleeping, by the way?"

"Of course I've been sleeping. Why wouldn't I be sleeping?" he said, clearly lying.

"Great. Is Griz there? Or Trace?"

"Yup, want me to pass the phone?"

"If you don't mind. And Daddy, I love you."

"I love you too, baby girl."

With that the phone was passed, and I heard Grizzie's unmistakably husky voice purr down the line.

"Jane. My darling. What are you wearing?"

"Nothing, actually," I said, grinning. It was true. I'd just gone for a swim on the beach, again, and was basking in the sun, on a towel and under a heavy glamour. Only the occasional dog of a passing jogger seemed to notice me, pulling on their leashes to get to what their owners perceived as an empty patch of Brighton's pebbly beach.

"Mmmm," she growled. "My lady bits are straining at the thought. Are yours straining, as well?"

"They were strained the moment you got on the line," I said, giggling away. We shared a laugh, but then I got serious.

"You've gotta cut my dad off, Griz. He can't handle all that coffee."

Grizzie groaned. "I know. I caught him taking sips from people's orders before he delivered them, yesterday."

"Make him decaf for a few days without telling him, till he's back under control. Then let him know you made the switch. I bet he'll be fine after that."

"If he's not?"

"We stage an intervention," I said, only half-joking.

"Awesome. I have just the intervention outfit."

"I'm sure you do. Listen, everything else okay there?"

"It's great. Other than the coffee thing, your dad's fit in perfectly. And it's nice to have a man around, actually. He's been super with the ladies."

"What?" I said, sitting up so fast my head swam.

"We had a load of tourists in from Bangor yesterday— little old ladies who came to see the Sow and breathe the sea air and have a lobster dinner. Your dad was selling them all the shit we haven't been able to move since we got it in. You know those hideous aprons with the lobsters wearing bikinis?"

I shuddered. "Yes."

"He sold five of them. And those stupid snowglobes that are supposed to be sand and look like Florida, but with 'Rockabill' written on them. He sold eight of those. He told the old ladies they would look nice on their nightstands, and then he winked. They snatched them up like they were winning lottery tickets."

"Oh," I said, trying to picture my dad winking. "Wow."

"He always was a ladies' man," Grizzie said. But then she paused. "Wasn't he? It's like I can't really remember, for some reason..."

"Oh, he always had his ways," I said, interrupting before Grizzie could explore the gap in her memory that was my dad's recent history.

"And Tracy's all right? The babies?" I continued, keeping her off the scent.

"Oh, everyone's fine. Tracy's fat as a walrus and can you believe she wants to paint the baby's room yellow? I mean, how pedestrian can we get..."

Grizzie chatted away for a while, until a few people came in for coffee and she had to get between my dad and their mochas. I hung up with her after promising to call again in a few days, and then lay back down on my towel.

Ladies' man? I thought. *My dad?*

Then I grinned. The thought of my dad happy, and with someone else, filled me with glee. It had taken me a moment to readjust to the dad I'd known—besotted with my mother and unable to think of anything but her eventual return—with a man who could charm old ladies into buying tchotchkes. I hoped he'd keep charming them. And that one of them, eventually, wouldn't be so old. And would see what a great guy my dad was.

Because he was. He was kind, loyal, gentle, and unbelievably open-minded and generous for someone who'd grown up with so little and known such hardship. He deserved happiness to go along with his newfound health.

My phone rang again, and I absentmindedly picked it

up and flipped it open. I was half-expecting it to be my
dad, calling to say good-bye after Grizzie hadn't passed
the phone back to him. Instead I heard the jeweled tones
of a woman's cool voice.

"Is this Jane True?"

My heart nearly stopped beating.

On the other end of that line was Morrigan, or I was a
monkey's uncle's robot sexdoll from France.

And I don't speak French very well at all.

CHAPTER FOURTEEN

This is Jane True," I said, my brain nearly fizzing it was going so fast. But my voice was steady, even if my heart was pounding. I looked around frantically for Magog, but she'd wandered over to buy an ice cream from a man with a cart.

"Hello, Jane. So nice to hear your little voice again."

"Morrigan?" I asked, my voice almost, but not quite, cracking. She sounded gorgeous, even over the phone.

"Oh, I'm flattered. You recognized me!"

"Yes, well. You have a way of making an impression on people."

"Is it my natural grace?" I thought about her grace, which was, indeed, very memorable.

"I think it's more the killing of your husband in front of a room full of people, and then running off with his brother."

"Oh. Well, if I'd known that would have such a big impact, I would have done it ages ago."

"Why are you calling, Morrigan?" I asked, cutting to the chase.

"I have something you want," she said.

The book, I thought.

"Yes, you do," I said.

"I didn't expect to find it, and I'm very impressed by it."

"Okay," I said, having no clue what she was talking about. Maybe she meant that she didn't expect to find the code hidden inside of the book? But then why did she steal it?

"That said, it smells bad. And it's rather rude."

At those words, everything clicked and my heart sank. *She doesn't mean the book. She means Hiral.*

"So, I have something you want, which I don't particularly want. And you have something I want. I'm thinking a trade is in order."

I thought quickly. I had no idea what on earth we could have that she wanted. But should I admit that? Or should I try to blunder through, acting like I knew what she wanted, when I really knew nothing?

"We have something you want," I said, as much a possible statement as it could, possibly, be a question.

"I want to talk with you, Jane. I want to open up a dialogue. And your smelly little rat-faced friend, here, is a good way to do that. I won't kill him. I'll even give him back to you, unharmed. Consider it a reward for coming to see me."

"All you want to do is talk?" The idea was fantastic. I wanted to talk to Morrigan, too. I bet we could work a lot of stuff out, if we could just sit down and talk.

"Believe it or not, yes. I used to want to kill you, I won't lie. But you've become ever so much more interesting than that plebeian little child who wandered into my Compound, so many months ago."

"Thanks for that."

"Don't mention it," she said, and that's when it hit me. Alfar never used contractions. Morrigan had definitely loosened up.

"So what do you say?"

"My conversation, for Hiral?" I asked, again, to clarify. "That's it?"

"Yes."

"What conditions?"

"You'll come to my estate, obviously."

For a split second, that sounded like such a good idea. We could have some alone time. Really get to the bottom of things.

What the fuck is wrong with you? my brain demanded, forcing me to think logically.

"You've got to be kidding me. You want to talk so bad, we meet where I say."

"Fine," she said, "But within reason. It's got to be open, and public, and not owned by any of your riffraff."

"Okay," I said, thinking hard. Problem was, I had no idea what there was in Brighton or what would be the best place to meet, strategically. "Um, can I get back to you?"

"After you've had time to consult your barghest? Not a chance. You wanted to negotiate conditions, Jane—so negotiate."

"Fine," I said. "Um..."

Then it hit me.

"Brighton Pier," I said, grinning at my genius. "Meet

us at the pier, at midnight. Bring Hiral, and he'd better be unharmed."

"Brighton Pier it is," Morrigan said, then her line went dead.

"Brighton Pier?" Anyan demanded. "Are you crazy?"

I blinked. I'd thought it was a smart idea. I'd bolted the two blocks back to the house we were staying at, Magog following on my heels and shouting for me to stop. But I hadn't slowed down till I was sitting at the beautiful house's round kitchen table where Gog, Anyan, and Blondie were already strategizing.

"What's wrong with the Pier?" I demanded.

"What's wrong with the Pier? How about the fact that there aren't even any really solid structures to use as cover. And how can I call the Earth if I need it?" the barghest continued.

"Plus they could just burn the whole thing down around us," Magog said, her voice strangely bored at the idea. "That's what happened to the other Brighton Pier, you know. Burned up, right into the sea."

I gulped. I hadn't thought about that.

"Stop arguing," Blondie said. "What's done is done. At least we're not going to Morrigan's estate."

I didn't tell them how I'd almost said yes to that idea. I had no idea why on earth I would have said yes—it was obviously the stupidest idea possible.

"We'll get Hiral back," I said instead.

Blondie sighed. "How the hell did he get captured, anyway? I've seen him walk through enemy camps, whistling, without being seen. Something's not right."

"Do you think he betrayed us, Cyntaf?" Gog said, his

tattooed face sad at that thought, but also resigned, as if betrayal was something he took to be part of life.

"No. Hiral would never join the Alfar...any Alfar. But something still isn't right...however, none of this matters. What matters is figuring out a plan. A good plan. A plan that won't get us all killed."

She paused, picking up a saltshaker that stood on the table in front of us.

"This is Jane," she said, placing it in the center of the table.

I gulped, as she put other objects around the saltshaker after naming them. But the saltshaker that was me remained at the center.

"Um," I asked, when it became apparent that she wasn't moving me out of the way. "Why am I at the center, again?"

"Because you're who she wants to talk to, Jane. Plus, where's this shitshow going to go down?" she asked.

"Brighton Pier," I said, wanting to scream. "I know it was a bad choice, I get that already, but..."

Blondie cut me off with a look.

"But nothing. You picked a pier, babycakes. And you're our only Water Elemental."

I sighed, suddenly hating my own idea with the strength of a thousand suns.

It was May, but in Great Britain that didn't mean it was spring. The wind whipping over the pier was vicious, shot through with a razor's edge of cold that even I felt, despite my selkie blood. Not wanting to waste energy on keeping myself warm magically, I pulled my hoodie tighter around me, wishing for the thousandth time that I'd brought a proper jacket. I envied the night watchman we'd glamoured to sleep in his warm little booth, looping his CCTV cameras so they'd show the same ten seconds of nothingness for however long it took us to face Morrigan.

Other than the sleeping guard and the trespassing, we hadn't gone to much trouble to disguise ourselves. We didn't figure we'd get out of tonight's meeting without a fight, but we also didn't figure that was such a bad thing.

We had some of our best soldiers—mostly the ones Gog had brought in from London—watching the front of the pier, so that Morrigan's peoples couldn't drive up a truck loaded with explosives or anything. And I'd spent the previous few hours setting various water snares around the perimeter of the pier, so nothing was getting to us that way.

The way we figured it, without cheating we were an equal match for Morrigan and her people. As long as they didn't come with an entire army, we might as well meet them and see what they wanted. If it *was* a fight they wanted, that'd be all right by us too.

So although I was front and center, I knew that at my back stood my friends and our new allies. Plus, with Anyan and Blondie standing directly behind me, I couldn't help but feel confident.

We'd decided to meet Blondie at the very back of the pier, where it was more open air and had more of a carnival atmosphere, with a roller coaster and everything. The front and middle parts of the pier were mostly made up by a covered market, which would have been no good for fighting.

Wrapped up in my own thoughts, I flinched when a mage ball suddenly winged its way from far above my head to land with a sparking thud at my feet, but only a little. It wasn't an enemy's missile, after all, but Magog's. The raven was perched far overhead on top of the roller coaster, keeping a sharp watch for our guests. The mage ball at my feet was her signal they'd arrived.

A large wolf came streaking up to me before changing into a man, breathing hard from his sprint. Anyan and Blondie moved forward to hear our nahual scout's report.

"It's her," he said, through his panting. "It's only her, with Hiral on a lead, and five other guards."

I frowned. Five other guards? That wasn't a lot. We had at least twenty people stationed throughout this pier, and five more guarding the foot of the pier. We also had Anyan Barghest, the fiercest living warrior of the time, and an actual Original, whose power easily rivaled that of an Alfar monarch.

I know Morrigan's arrogant, I thought, *but she's not crazy. Blondie's right—something's not right.*

Anyan was obviously with me on that one, because he made a series of quick gestures that sent most of our soldiers melting into the darkness around us. If Morrigan was planning a surprise, we may as well hide some of our own aces along with our sleeves, for good measure.

Magog flapped down from her position on top of the roller coaster to join me, and I took a moment to admire her natural form. Her wings spread out in an enormous inky spread. She was wearing leather pants and a thin leather breastplate, and I saw that her feet were the scaly black feet of a bird, long toes and all. But it didn't make her any less beautiful.

As if to counter Magog's raven beauty, I saw movement from the corner of my eye and I faced forward to find the equally beautiful, but golden Morrigan striding to us. She was wearing a lovely cream pants suit, with towering high heels and her long hair pulled up into an enormous, supremely sexy twist. Her emerald eyes shone with curiosity as she strode forward, hips moving like those of a cat-walk model. It was only when she was a bit closer I could see her dragging Hiral behind her. He was on a dog's leash, with a collar around his neck, and he looked about as pissed off as I'd ever seen his always pissy little face.

I would be angry too, however, if I were being dragged around like a recalcitrant puppy.

"Jane," Morrigan said warmly. "It's a pleasure to see you."

For a moment I thought she was going to come up and hug me, but she stopped a few yards away. I marveled at my own disappointment.

You want to punch her in the eye! I reminded myself angrily. Still, I watched her with rapt attention as she looked around at my friends.

"You've brought your little buddies. Anyan," Morrigan said, nodding to the barghest whose bristling presence I could feel only a few feet behind me. "And Cyntaf. Always a pleasure to see you, Original."

It was only in her greeting to Blondie that Morrigan's carefully friendly facade slipped, and for a second we saw the venomous creature lurking under her skin.

Of all the people here, I wondered, *why does she hate Blondie the most?*

It felt strange, not being the one hated most by the Alfar in the room.

But a second later Morrigan had slapped her party face back on and was waving into the shadows.

"And hallo out there! To all you little hiding monkeys! I see you, you silly things."

Laughing warmly, as if we were all in on her joke, she turned again to face me.

"Well, Jane, you came. Just as I asked. Here's your naughty pet," she said, holding forth Hiral's leash. I raised an eyebrow.

"That's it? You're just giving him to us?"

"Of course, silly!" she exclaimed, as if I were obviously crazy to mistrust her. "I said I would, didn't I. Now come take his lead." Morrigan's accent had suddenly gone British, another mystery. She'd always spoken with a flat, American accent, but now she sounded like the Upstairs part of *Upstairs, Downstairs*.

I inched forward, hearing Anyan growl behind me as I did so. But I went anyway, carefully erecting my most powerful shields. It wasn't hard with all the water saturating the ocean air.

To my surprise, Morrigan did nothing but calmly hand me Hiral's leash when I walked forward. I dropped to one knee, undoing the collar as quickly as I could, and then let him run away behind me towards our friends.

"Now why on earth would you let that smelly thing run free?" Morrigan mused. "Oh well. You have what you wanted. Now do we get to talk?"

"Sure, Morrigan. Now we can talk," I said, refusing to let my voice betray just how much I wanted to talk to her. "But no funny business. And I can't imagine what you have to say to me."

"Me?" She asked, her gorgeous gemlike eyes huge and innocent. Except that now, upon being closer to her, I realized that those emerald eyes were slit, like a cat's.

And didn't they used to be blue? I remembered, suddenly.

Who cares, my libido purred. *They're beautiful…*

"Of course I won't pull anything funny. I only want to talk," she said. "In private."

And with that her hand closed on my wrist and everything went black.

CHAPTER FIFTEEN

I was proud of myself that I didn't panic when it went black. Mostly my composure could be attributed to the fact I recognized this darkness: it was like the blackness that Blondie took me to when she'd wanted to talk.

Which means I hadn't actually gone anywhere. Indeed, Morrigan was still standing exactly where she'd been, a few feet from me. Her green eyes watched me, undoubtedly hoping I'd freak out and she could use my panic to her advantage.

But instead I took a deep breath, and gave her my falsest smile as I pulled my wrist from her grasp.

I'd remembered Blondie explaining to me how this mind trick worked, back when we were in that cave and she was about to send me to meet the creature. She'd needed to talk to me, so she'd put everyone in that cave into their own little illusory box. They couldn't attack us, but we couldn't attack them, either. She'd explained how the trick actually worked—that the best she could do was to put everyone in their own mental space, but that meant that they were still where they'd been standing. They just couldn't see anything, like I couldn't see anything.

Thinking hard, I tried to figure out how to use that information.

I was also trying to figure out how Morrigan had learned this particular trick. It had not been a part of her repertoire, at least that I knew, before she left the Compound.

"Well, Jane. Isn't this nice? Just the two of us. Like we used to be, when you came to visit." Morrigan's accent was still upper-crust British, and it flowed from her lips too naturally to be faked. The Alfar queen was full of secrets, apparently.

I narrowed my eyes. "I thought you said no tricks, Morrigan."

"Oh, don't be such a stick-in-the-mud. This isn't a trick! It's a little gift—the gift of privacy."

"I'd rather not be so private with you."

"You wound me, Jane. You really do. Now, talk to me. Tell me why you're a part of this rabble, a sweet girl like you?"

I stayed quiet. I didn't even know what she was asking, exactly, so I couldn't have addressed her question if I'd wanted to.

"I hear rumors, Jane," Morrigan continued, unfazed by my silence. She paced in front of me, slowly, as if deep in thought.

"I hear that you have a weapon. That you were given power. Is that true?"

I touched the part of me that was the creature's, that held the ax, and I was glad I'd kept it hidden for our meeting.

"I've always had power, Morrigan," I said, instead of the whole truth. "But because I'm a halfling, most of your kind refused to see it."

Morrigan smiled. "Touché. But I'm not talking about normal power. I think you know that. I think you know I'm talking about the power of the champion."

"Me?" I scoffed. "The champion? I know you realize how ridiculous that sounds," I said. After all, it was ridiculous that I was the champion. True, but ridiculous.

Morrigan's mouth pursed in a grimace of concentration as she turned to look at me, her eyes narrowing.

"And yet you seem different, halfling."

"Having your mother murdered and your best friend raped will do that to a gal," I said, fury inflecting my voice.

"This is war, Jane. People die. People get hurt," Morrigan said, taking another step closer. "And you do look harder, yes. But there's more. There's power..."

Before she could continue, I also took a step back, towards where I estimated Anyan should be standing, in his own little box. I didn't know if I was moving only mentally, scooting a little image of myself around in my mind, or if I was actually moving. But I figured I had to be moving in the real world, since Blondie had brought me those milkshakes at that Ben & Jerry's, the first time she'd used this trick with me all those months ago in Rhode Island.

"Speaking of changes," I said, trying to keep Morrigan distracted as I took another step backwards. "You're different too. You're dressed a bit like the sleazy hanger-on of a movie villain, to be honest. I mean, you're hot, but you definitely look less regal and more high-class hooker."

Morrigan hissed at me—and I mean hissed—and took another step towards me that I balanced out with one of my own, backwards.

"Plus there're the speech patterns. You were totally Alfar before. And now you're all casual—almost human. And a British human, at that. Which is weird, Morrigan. What have you been up to? Or were you always just a big phony?"

Morrigan hissed again, and I could have sworn she was growing. Her pants suit definitely looked a little strained at the seams.

Those angry green eyes were larger now, in a face that was elongating.

"And what is it with those eyes?" I asked, taking another long few steps backwards, right towards where I knew Anyan should be standing, assuming that he hadn't changed position and that I was actually moving. Otherwise I was going to have a very irate Alfar chasing me around my own mind for what could be millennia.

"They were blue," I said. "You definitely had blue eyes…"

"And now I have green, yes," Morrigan hissed, through a mouth gone decidedly snoutlike. "Would you like a closer look?"

At that second two things happened. First, Morrigan's neck elongated like a jack-in-the-box's, springing her gaping jaw towards me, her mouth suddenly full of very large teeth. I tumbled backwards to avoid their snapping cruelty, only to fall into my own familiar man-wall, Anyan Barghest.

As if I'd popped a bubble, the illusion around me shattered as my body touched Anyan's. And then all hell broke loose.

"What the fuck?" Anyan shouted, pulling me back and away from the decidedly non-Alfar Morrigan standing in front of us. "Alfar can't shapeshift!" he yelled, clinging to logic, as he sent a volley of mage balls winging at her, as well as a powerful battering ram of power using his elemental control over the air. Barghests were one of the very rare beings to control more than one element, besides the Alfar, who controlled all four.

Even Blondie looked scared, standing there with wide eyes. Her mouth was moving and I realized she was saying "no" over and over again.

Meanwhile, Morrigan kept growing. Her clothes were splitting at the seams, and her face wasn't at all human, anymore. Her mouth kept elongating until it was like a long, thin muzzle while the rest of her face receded as if wrapping itself around a huge torpedo. Her shoulders were rounding, hunching as they grew in size. Her tailored cream coat ripped all the way, falling down to pool around her wrists as her body ratcheted forward, as if breaking in two at her lower back.

She howled, then, a sound of agony and release as her hands began to lengthen into long fingered claws. Her high heels ripped apart as scaled toes burst forth, scrabbling for purchase on the wood of the pier. Her forearms and calves rippled upwards with muscle as she began to grow at a ridiculously fast rate. The rest of her clothes shredded around flesh now mottled with what looked like freshly forming scales.

Her guards had fanned out behind her, mirroring our own forces that had taken position behind Anyan and me. But their side didn't look like they were about to faint, as virtually everyone on our own team did.

Anyan called for us to raise shields, and we did. Then I wove my water power through them, coating our defenses with as many layers of my force as I possibly could while Morrigan just grew, and grew, and grew.

It was only when the mottles turned all the way to scales, and the form before us reared up to roar at the heavens that I realized what we were dealing with.

Morrigan had just changed into a dragon.

An enormous, scaly, motherfucking dragon.

A red dragon.

A red dragon, I thought, my mouth going dry as I realized, for the umpteenth time in the past few days, something I really didn't want to realize.

For sure as shit, the dragon that had been Morrigan blazed crimson in the night sky. She looked more like the color of old blood in the moonlight, but I knew she'd burn like fire in the sunshine.

Suddenly, it all made sense. The physical differences— the eyes, the attitude, the clothes; the speech patterns; the seductive charisma.

The bones have a way of drawing people to them, I remembered being told.

Before us roared the reason Morrigan had searched for the bits and pieces of a dead queen. And why those pieces would want to be found, when they were missing parts and couldn't be resurrected as they once had.

They didn't need to be resurrected.

All they needed was a willing host.

Morrigan had become the Red Queen.

As if to remind us that she had, indeed, turned into a motherfucking dragon, Morrigan chose that moment to rear her head back, and then unleash a stream of fire that began burning everything in its path before it lighted on our shields.

Blondie pushed forward, her power booming out as she strengthened our defensive barriers. Her power was enormous, but I could feel the force emanating from the Red.

Even with the Original's tremendous strength, she was going to need help against the dragon. So I focused the strength of my water, reaching into that space left in me by the creature, to saturate the air around us and keep us cool and moist. Or at least moist, for the heat was terrible.

We were also burning down Brighton Pier.

"Pull the ax!" Blondie yelled.

"No," I shouted, "it's what she wants! She's showing her hand, hoping we show ours!"

"We're not going to have any hands to show if we're all dead!" Blondie replied, the sweat on her brow attesting to how much energy she was using by holding the bulk of our shields against the dragon's fierce flames.

I looked at Anyan, and he nodded. So I reached into that space hidden deep inside me, calling on the labrys and the creature's power. Both responded with a surge, and suddenly I was holding a beacon of light in the darkness.

If I thought the labrys had lit up before, I now knew the real meaning of the word "supernova." The ax was so bright that I imagined it could be seen throughout Brighton, certainly, and I hoped it wouldn't be seen all the way out in London.

Something told me the Alfar Powers That Be weren't going to be too happy with us for destroying Brighton Pier, only a few days after destroying Borough Market.

But the ax wasn't listening to me. As it had that day outside Roast when it had undoubtedly recognized a truth the rest of us couldn't see—that Morrigan had become its ancient enemy, the Red Queen—the labrys took over.

And it wanted to fight.

It was pulling me forward, straight at the dragon. I was screaming and literally digging my heels into the ground, trying to stop my forward momentum. If I went past our shields, the damned magic ax would be dragging a selkie shish kebab, not a champion.

But it pulled me forward effortlessly until with my last scream it took me past our shields. I poured as much strength into my own shields as I could as I squeezed my eyes shut, ready to be roasted. And yet, although I did feel an increase in temperature, I definitely wasn't on fire.

Cracking open a single eye, I could see that the ax's power was streaming forward towards the dragon's maw, pushing back the fire emanating from it like they were two hoses trained on one another.

The dragon took a step back, its fire cutting out abruptly as it tried a more physical approach. Rushing towards me, its head lowered, it slashed with teeth and claws and the impact on my shields was like being hit by a thousand linebackers. My protections held, but I was being battered like a hamster in a ball when Blondie, Anyan, and Magog came to my rescue.

Out of nowhere, the snakelike shape of the roller coaster track ripped off its legs and came lurching out of the darkness to wrap itself around the dragon. Blondie had enchanted it so that it moved like a snake. Magog, meanwhile, darted above it in the night sky, helping direct it with her air magic while Anyan aided Blondie by helping to strengthen the wood of the roller coaster with his earth powers.

The roller coaster wrapped itself around the dragon again and again, enclosing it in a cage of wood.

"It's not going to hold!" Anyan warned, pulling me against him as we backpedaled towards the end of the pier.

Back to where the water lay, waiting for me.

I scrambled through the tottering remains of the roller coaster, which fell around us as we ran, bouncing off our shields. There was a tremendous crash behind us and I craned my head around, nearly slipping on all the debris, to see the dragon shrugging off its wooden prison in an explosion of fire and wood. Its enormous tail flexed and lifted, batting Magog out of the sky like it was swatting a fly. The raven fell into a little booth, upon which the dragon was about to pounce. Blondie and I both sent powerful volleys of magic straight towards it, trying to distract it before it could end Magog.

The blasts hit the beast, and it turned towards us—but its green eyes narrowed on me when it caught sight of its true enemy. Blondie scampered off to help Magog, leaving me with an impetuous labrys that raised itself in my arms as if taunting the creature. I groaned, wishing the ax would stop volunteering me for things. Despite the ax waving my arm around like I was imitating Queen Elizabeth, I kept climbing away, trying to get as close to the water as I could before the dragon-formerly-known-as-Morrigan caught up with us. Anyan was a step in front of me, helping clear the way with powerful scoops of his magic, his shields doing the bulk of the work to keep us from getting our heads bashed in by the crumbling vestiges of the roller coaster.

Not for the first time, I thanked my lucky stars the barghest was on my side.

Unfortunately, there's only so far you could go trying
to outrun a dragon on a pier, before you ran out of pier.
We were at the very edge of the water, and Morrigan was
coming along quickly, breathing fire at our heels.

"You are mine, Champion!" The dragon growled, ter-
rifyingly loud. I also hadn't thought a dragon could talk,
but I should have known better than to assume.

I wasn't sure where Blondie was, but Anyan was busy
trying to use his shields to push back as the dragon tried
to push forward, all while still protecting us from Morrigan's fire. He wasn't going to be able to do much more to
stop the Red's head-on assault, so it was up to me.

Luckily, all that fire had given me an inspiration, and
with the ocean behind me, I had more than enough of the
wet stuff to play with.

So I reached, as hard as I could and with all of my own
power and that of the creature's, towards the sea. I could
feel her answer within my bones, a split second before an
enormous wave came surging up behind me. But it wasn't
a normal wave: it didn't rise and fall as a wave should.
Instead it floated in the air, growing in size, until it resembled a massive wall of water.

Using another massive surge of power, I envisioned the
water forming itself into a tongue, and then I sent it lapping straight at the enemy.

The dragon that had been Morrigan gave a rather
undignified squawk as the water came towards it, and it
tried to back peddle ineffectually. The wave caught the
dragon despite her best efforts, and I heard satisfying
hissing sounds as she got well and truly drenched.

That day, I learned a wet dragon is a sad thing. Coughing and spluttering, the dragon tried her best to create fire from a belly that only spat and sizzled. Morrigan gave me a furious look as I strode forward, labrys at the ready. When she saw Blondie also coming at her from where the Original had been healing Magog, Morrigan snorted wetly before crouching and spreading her massive red wings. With a few powerful wing beats and a huge surge of magic, the Red Queen was airborne, taking with her our chance of getting back that damned book.

Lofting the labrys, I prepared a massive strike that I doubted would have any effect on the beast's shields, when I felt a little hand tickling the back of my knee. Jerking involuntarily, my magic died as I turned to find the gwyllion staring up at me.

"Let her go," Hiral said, spitting an ugly yellow glob of mucus onto the wood of the pier in front of him. "I only let her catch me so I could steal what ye wanted." And with that, he pulled a bundle of paper out of the crotch of his pants.

I nearly kissed him. I nearly kissed the papers. Then I realized where both had been, and I checked myself.

CHAPTER SIXTEEN

He might have been smelly and blessed with a singularly unpleasant character, but Hiral was an excellent spy. Having realized there was no other way, he'd used the chaos of his ransoming to steal the pages from the stolen book, with which Morrigan never otherwise parted. She'd only given it to one of her most trusted henchmen after stepping out of the limo they'd driven to the pier, knowing that she was probably going to go dragon and dragons don't have pockets.

After she'd made that hand-off, and the chaos of the battle had started, it had been child's play for Hiral to pinch the book off the guard, rip out the pages he knew were important, and put the book back where it belonged. If all went well, Morrigan wouldn't even notice anything was missing until we'd foiled all of her evil schemes.

Before the gwyllion had gotten captured, however, he'd made a few more important discoveries.

"Jarl is Morrigan's prisoner?" I asked, incredulously.

"Aye. He's treated like a guest, but the kind of guest who's not allowed to leave the room or go anywhere without guards. And he's not the arrogant shite that led in your Compound, either. He's terrified."

"What happened to scare him like that?" Blondie asked. Hiral snorted.

"I'd think my lover becoming a bloody great dragon might have that effect."

"No," I said, the truth popping up its head and giving me a raspberry. "It's obvious, isn't it? Morrigan's the Red Queen, but Jarl's still Jarl."

"And the Red Queen needs her king," Anyan said, running his fingers through his shaggy hair. My own fingers itched to do that for him.

"Which is why they needed the book," Blondie added, pulling me back to the conversation.

Magog nodded as we talked, but Gog looked confused, bless him.

"What's going on?" he asked, when it was obvious more clarification wouldn't be forthcoming, otherwise.

"They must have been able to cobble together enough of the remains of the Red Queen to transfer her power to Morrigan. Morrigan must have been willing to let the Red in. Maybe she didn't know how thoroughly it would take control," Blondie explained to the coblynau, patiently.

"But Jarl saw what happened to Morrigan, and he's no longer quite so willing to become the White King. And they obviously don't have enough of the White, yet, to make the transfer. That's why they needed the book, to find the missing pieces."

"So we've got to stop them from finding those pieces," Gog said. "And save Jarl from becoming the White."

I made a face. "I wouldn't refer to it as 'saving Jarl,' " I said.

"But that's what we'd be doing, Jane," Anyan said. "He'll face another sort of justice, if we succeed, but we do have to save him from Morrigan."

"Why don't we just kill him?" I suggested, unapologetically and ruthlessly.

"I doubt Morrigan actually needs to use Jarl for the White, although she obviously wants to. If we kill him, she'll just find another vessel. We need to focus our energies on finding the missing pieces, using the book, rather than waste energies on vengeance," Blondie said, in a voice that brooked no argument.

I grumbled internally, but I also understood that she was right.

"So let's get to it," I said, trying not to pout that we didn't get to go ahead and kill Jarl. "Let's go over those pages and see what there is to see."

Blondie pulled them out of her backpack, where she'd been keeping them, and spread them out on the table.

"And you're sure she hasn't gotten to act on any of this, yet?" the Original asked Hiral.

"I don't think so," he said. "She got back to the estate, and there was some trouble with Jarl. He'd killed a few of his guards and she was very irritated with him. She spent most of the time I was there 'punishing her naughty boy,' " Hiral finished, punctuating his sentence with air quotes.

I made a face, even as I bent low over the table to examine the papers.

It wasn't hard to find the bits we were looking for as they were marked off by that subtle spacing difference, which was obvious if you knew what you were looking for. I read the spaced-out selections for my friends, ignoring the rest of the text as it was nonsense. It was fun to read, if a bit challenging, as the language was still written in an archaic style even though the spelling had been cleaned up to modern standards.

"The original one did loft the weapon that made her champion...and did use that weapon to cleave the beasts in twain...after which she did hew through their necks... and their limbs...and then continued to dissect them until nothing was left but those bits too small to cut... until those in attendance saw the bits reforming...all of the body drawn together as if by a greater power...its parts surging towards one another..."

I made another face, not enjoying the idea of "surging parts."

"...Cyntaf did continue applying her blade...yet the parts would not cease their movement...and her own wounds were grievous and deep...as her strength faded our wise ones knelt in prayer to the Elements...and were blessed with the idea to travel forth with the pieces of the White and the Red...dispersing them throughout the lands...None would know where the others went...their hiding places were secrets unto themselves...the only place they would be shared would be here, in this secret volume...compiled by the scribe whose mind, as is traditional, would be cleansed...and whose body, again as is traditional, would become a prisoner of this text..."

My words trailed off as I realized who they were talking about. "The librarian!" I shouted, feeling so angry with the Alfar for ruining another person's life out of their own greed for knowledge they knew they shouldn't use, anyway. "The doppelgänger, Sarah. She's the one whose brain they cleaned out, isn't she? And she's trapped in that library?"

Blondie's face was sad as she nodded her head.

"I realized long ago she's trapped in that library, and why. She's not the first, either. There have been many other librarians before her. I knew they kept Alfar secrets, but I didn't know how they did it. I didn't know about the books they wrote."

"Does she even know why?" I asked.

Blondie shook her head. "She just feels like she has to be in that library all the time—she was reconditioned to believe it's her great task. She never truly questions her duty. Her mind isn't capable of doing so. Even if she read this, she'd forget upon turning the page.

"What happened to the other librarians?"

"They ceased being useful."

I grimaced at Blondie's words, grumbling about the Alfar as I found the place I'd stopped my reading. Then I continued, although my words held an edge of bitterness.

"...the Red is hiding in places unseen, places much seen, and places not to be seen..." I made a face, but continued through the short but totally confusing little riddle that followed. The riddle was obviously meant to give us a clue as to where the Red was hidden. None of us paid too much attention, however, as we were too late to stop cobbling together the Red, anyway. It was the White that mattered. When I started in on his section, I slowed my reading so we could take it all in.

"...the White, the male force, was ever more its mother's son than it's father's..." I read, from the very first section of spaced-out commentary.

"So the White was more Air than Fire," interpreted

Blondie. We all nodded in agreement as my eyes sought out the next section.

"...it was believed to speak less quietly than the Red, who reached out even to those whose mission was to hide it..."

"Meaning the Red could communicate better than the White, which makes sense," said Anyan. "It was able to get itself put mostly back together on its own, before Morrigan showed up. They were both always good at seducing humans and supernaturals to do their bidding, but from all the old stories the Red was always the talker."

"...and yet many of those sent away with the pieces of the White disappeared themselves, or were found hoarding their treasures...keeping what should be lost...and there was even murder and mayhem enacted amongst the bearers...and many lives were lost...my own orders to continue recording these newest locations were made despite my protestations...I think even my own leaders are infected..."

I looked up, startled, to see Blondie frowning, and then looked down to read more. The language changed, here, as if Sarah were writing it herself rather than recording the words of another.

"....they demand this knowledge be recorded, and I have neither the strength of magic nor will to negate demands made to me by magic...but words are open-ended...they hold many meanings...and I may record without revealing, if I am clever..."

My heart beat faster, liking Sarah more and more. She'd suspected her leader might be under the Red and the White's spell, and had tried to keep concealed the information they wanted revealed. She'd done everything she could against beings far stronger and more ruthless than she.

"...there are whispers...that the White, although silent, speaks as loudly as the Red...already that which was purposefully lost has disappeared, found although that should be impossible...So I will reveal less than I was bid, under the assumption that those giving me the commands are lost...recording only *something*, rather than everything, knowing that should this knowledge be needed, or wanted...that one piece will be as good as all pieces... hide a single piece and hide them all...or find a single piece and find the rest..."

I frowned, confused. "What's she saying?" I asked.

"She's saying, I think," Blondie replied, "that she's going to fulfill the rules of her assignment by giving the information she was bade. But she's only going to say where *one* piece is buried, and she's not going to make it easy."

"So she fulfills her assignment, but not really," Anyan said. "But what about the stuff about the single piece?"

"That's easy," I replied, having just figured it out. "That's how she fulfills the letter of the spell. If one piece is found by those who want to keep the White from being resurrected, then that piece can be hidden again so that it can't be assembled. But if the people searching for that piece are doing so to put it back together, that piece will probably lead them to the other pieces, on its own. It wants to be reassembled, remember? Just like the Red. So having one piece means that the one piece *can* help find the rest, so she's doing what the spell asks her to do, technically. But it also means people like us can find the piece and hide it again, like Sarah wants. She has to reveal something, as she's been commanded, but she's trying to reveal as little as possible. Now let me finish this.

"...the heart of the White is buried with the proof that even those who kill kings fall themselves... their progeny no more immortal than they... the pure of soul as vulnerable to worms as those they murder for corruption... And that's it," I said, after carefully scanning the next few pages. There was nothing more written.

Everyone watched me flip the pages, looking as confused as I did.

"Sorry, folks, that's all she wrote. And it doesn't help. All we now know is that the secrets Sarah was asked to keep involved the location of the relics, and that she was bade to write them in the books. But she didn't, and she made her clues obtuse on purpose. Then her memory was wiped."

Magog's raspy voice echoed Blondie's obvious disappointment.

"The tombs of political megalomaniacs are a dime a dozen here on the Great Island. Between human leaders and supernatural ones, I can think of a dozen possibilities off the top of my head. We need to narrow it down."

"We need," rumbled Anyan, "to talk to Sarah."

"What good will that do if her memory's been scrubbed?" I asked.

"Brains aren't easy to wipe entirely clean. Traces of things come back, just in odd ways. Sarah might not know what she knows, but she might be doing something that tips us off. We need to talk to her."

"And fast," Magog said. "Because if we need to talk to her..."

"So does Morrigan," Blondie said, already moving for the door.

*   *   *

Once again, we were too late. I was beginning to feel like
that was our modus operandi, as really bad superheroes:
"Too Late To Save Shit! But We Gave It A Go!"

Sarah was in very bad shape when we arrived. At first I
thought she was dead, as she was laying in a fetal position
in a huge pool of blood, her arms wrapped around the
center of her body. A horrible smell permeated the air—
shit, and blood, and fear. For a terrible second I was back
in the Healer's mansion, surrounded by his victims and
his instruments of torture. My head spun, but Anyan's
hand on my nape settled me until my concern for Sarah
could do the rest.

It was only when we were closer and could see her failing powers attempting to change her into versions of all of
us, that we realized she was still alive. But barely. Her
eyes were closed, and I prayed she had passed out. The
pain must have been excruciating.

"Shit," Blondie swore, diving in with hands and healing powers extended. But when she managed to peel Sarah's arms from her body, we saw how bad the damage
was. A slash across her body had her guts spilling out. I
was no doctor, but I knew enough about anatomy that I
understood, from the smells in the room, that Sarah was
not long for this world without some major magical intervention. But her wounds resisted even Blondie's powerful
healing magic.

"It won't close," the Original sobbed, tears streaming
down her face as she pressed Sarah's guts into her belly
and held the wound shut.

Anyan, unspeaking, added his power to hers, but still
nothing happened.

"The Red did this," I said, remembering what I'd read in the history books. I choked back the bile that rose in my throat, as Sarah didn't deserve any weakness from me, and continued. "Wounds from her claws won't heel with normal magic."

Blondie looked at me, her face splotched and swollen in grief.

"Try the ax," she said. "Try the creature's magic."

I did as she asked, calling forth the labrys and pulling on its power. I glanced at Anyan, who directed all that strength for me in a healing spell.

Still nothing happened.

"Call an ambulance," I urged. "Call the human paramedics. They'll know what to do."

Blondie gave me a stricken look, before she turned to Magog and nodded. The raven frowned, but eventually she stood with her cell phone, then began pressing buttons and speaking rapidly as she left the room.

When we turned back to Sarah, we saw that she had come to. Her eyes were opened, her gaze resting on Blondie with an expression curiously serene. She reached with shaking hands to touch Blondie's face as she tried to speak. Her fingers left streaks of blood, like exclamation points, down Blondie's cheeks.

Slowly, weakly, Sarah began speaking.

"I don't know what she wanted," she whispered. "But I think I told her what she needed. She seemed pleased with me. Then she did this. She asked, about my research, so I told her. Have I ruined everything?"

At those words, fat tears spilled from Sarah's eyes. She probably couldn't even remember what she might have ruined, magicked as she was by Alfar spells. But she knew the stakes were high and that something had obviously gone the wrong way in that room.

"No," Blondie said, nearly choking on her words. "You haven't ruined everything, beautiful girl. You were brave and strong, as you always were. And clever. But we must know your research too. Where is it?"

"She took my laptop, but I have Dropbox. Check my work comp. My password is Cyntaf."

Sarah's body convulsed then, with pain or in the throes of death, I don't know. Blondie cried out as if she were the one wounded, and I realized I was crying. Even Hiral looked misty-eyed. Only Anyan's face showed grim resolve, but I knew inside he would mourn this brave woman who'd risked and lost so much, simply because she'd been given an arbitrary task by the Alfar.

The doppelgänger died a few seconds later, her excruciating whimpers something I will never forget. Blondie held her hand throughout. Only with her death did Sarah's face stop shifting entirely to settle into that of a thin, plain girl.

Covered in blood, Blondie sat back on her ass with a thud, looking at Sarah's body with the expression of a lost child. My heart nearly broke, and I went to crouch behind her, wrapping my arms around hers. She was shivering.

Anyan stood, then, and went to the work computer. He pressed a few keys, moving the mouse around a bit.

"She was working on a biography of Anna Gibson."

Then there was more punching of keys, and some more mouse movement. Then he had what we needed.

"Anna Gibson was Cromwell's granddaughter. She has a tomb in Bloomsbury. We have to go now."

Blondie visibly shook herself, lurching out of my arms as she stood.

"Tell Magog to stay and take care of the human police."

Anyan looked uncomfortable for a moment, but when he spoke his voice was gentle.

"She didn't call an ambulance, Cyntaf," he said, using the name that had become Blondie's formal moniker, even for us. "You know that."

My own expression revealed my confusion as Blondie looked like she'd just been slapped. Then she nodded as if accepting a heavy burden.

"Of course," she said, her voice dull. "How silly of me."

And then she walked out of the room.

I stood, trotting after Anyan who'd followed Blondie.

"What just happened?" I asked, tugging on his elbow.

The barghest looked at me sadly, letting the emotions he hadn't shown to the others show to me.

"She was as good as dead when we got here. Magog would never have risked revealing the location of the library to average humans. She probably called Jack to alert Griffin to get a clean up crew into the library. And a new librarian."

"But why?" I said, asking so many different things at one time.

"With a wound like that, which can't be healed by magic and that's obviously not natural, we die. There are no hospitals for us, not unless we know it won't get out of hand. We can take care of a lot of things with magic, but lighting up every police scanner in the area with a murder is too much for us to cover up without a massive amount of work. Blondie knew that when we walked in and her healing didn't work. She knew, but she didn't want to know."

I blinked, feeling about a thousand emotions crashing over me at one time. But I was still blindsided by the force of Anyan's anger at the words he spoke next.

"It's what we do best, letting things die," he said, bitterness lacing every word.

I'm ashamed to admit it, but all thoughts of Sarah flew out of my brain as I slammed once again into that impenetrable wall which was Anyan's history. It didn't happen that often, but when it did, man did it hurt.

What had he suffered? And what had it done to him?

CHAPTER SEVENTEEN

Crouching low behind one of the many small crypts dotting the former graveyard, I kept my eyes on Anyan, waiting for his signal.

We were in the cemetery in Bloomsbury, named St. George's Gardens, where Anna Gibson had once had her tomb. It was a lovely place, long since turned into a park. All of the crypts' bodies had been removed, and the headstones had all been relocated to line the park's stone walls. Only the crypts remained, in various states of disrepair, while in front of the tombstone-lined walls gorgeous gardens full of roses would soon bloom. Taken altogether, the place was a lovely—if melancholy—haven in the middle of the city, although its beauty was currently marred by the enormous magical dome that had appeared near one of its stone walls.

Morrigan and her people were using the ultra-powerful version of the nullification-charm that the rebels used for their safe houses. Unlike ours, which only showed a blank magical space, Morrigan's made a *real* blank space. It looked as if a dome of onyx had fallen in a wide circumference around what must have been Anna Gibson's former crypt.

I kept my eyes on Anyan, and when he nodded at me I pulled the labrys out of its hiding place. One minute my hands were free and the next I was holding the double-headed ax, its power lighting up the park around me. That said, it was bright, but not *too* bright.

It doesn't seem to be going crazy, like it would if Morrigan were around, I thought. *But maybe the shield she's using is that strong.*

Once I was holding the ax, Anyan nodded again, holding up one finger, then two, then three. My muscles tensed in anticipation as he nodded one last time, sharply, motioning towards the black dome.

Then I was racing towards it, labrys aloft, as Anyan ran one step behind me, Blondie flanking the barghest. When we were close to the shield I cleaved with the ax, carving out a rough-hewn circle with its power. It cut through the shield like butter, despite all the power that had gone into that inky barrier.

As soon as the hole was cut, I stepped back as in charged Blondie and Anyan, mage balls at the ready. I heard Anyan swear, Blondie sigh, and then I heard the Original shout, "All clear!"

I made my way into the shield, first gesturing into the darkness for Gog, Magog, and Hiral to follow. Our rebel allies were waiting in reserve, ready to pounce if anyone escaped the shield with any relics.

The inside of the shield was eerie, as it looked and felt like a piece of the outdoors had suddenly been roofed in. I also saw that the tomb in question had already been desecrated, its stone covering pushed off. The lid had cracked, lying broken on the ground.

"It's empty," Anyan said, before swearing angrily. Blondie had found the source of the shield, a pretty blue rock sitting on top of another gravestone. She touched it, and suddenly we were outside again. But not alone.

Jack Young and Lyman stood right where our entry hole had been, Lyman smiling at us as if we were all about to throw a baby shower. Phil the naga-halfling and Adele were standing on what had been the other side of the shield, blocking us in. Meanwhile, our good friends Gog and Magog were holding a struggling, spitting Hiral. Gog, at least, looked faintly apologetic but Magog was as cool as usual over their betrayal.

"How nice to see you again Anyan and Jane," said Jack. "And you, Cyntaf."

We moved into a tight bunch, me keeping a firm grip on the labrys.

"Magog," said Blondie, her voice tight with emotion. "How could you?"

Magog stood silently as Jack *tsk*ed.

"Don't blame the raven, Original," said Jack. "Magog's a good soldier—a good *rebel* soldier. And I'm the leader of the rebels, as you need to remember. Besides, this is only a friendly visit."

"Oh yeah?" Blondie asked, her tone dripping sarcasm. Meanwhile, I was suddenly putting together how we'd been kidnapped that time outside the British Museum. We'd been set up then too. My eyes met Hiral's gaze. He was obviously furious at Magog and Gog from the way he was staring at them, and I felt guilty for having doubted the gwyllion's loyalty.

"Of course," Jack said, smiling broadly as he moved towards us. Blondie followed his movements while Anyan and I stayed facing Lyman. We knew who the real threat was, in terms of an actual attack. Lyman, meanwhile, was still smiling politely, just as he had when Anyan and I had been abducted. But I could feel his power lapping at my shields, and it was considerable.

"You folks have been busy," Jack said, leaning over the tomb to get a look at its lack of contents. "First Borough Market, then Brighton Pier. Now you've destroyed the grave of poor..." Jack took a moment to read the side of the tomb, "poor Anna Gibson."

Jack turned to me, his smile gone.

"You're a very naughty tourist, Jane True."

I shrugged. He was right. We had blown up pretty much every place we'd gone, so far.

"What do you want, Jack?" Anyan said, obviously weary of the other man's games.

"I want some answers, barghest. Like what a dragon was doing flying away from Brighton Pier. Dragons haven't been seen for centuries, not since the Red and the White flew over the skies of this Island, killing whomever they clapped eyes on. And yet you're supposed to be stopping those monsters from awakening. So why don't *you* explain to *me* what happened."

"Don't act like you don't know, Jack. I'm sure your little spies have already told you everything," Blondie said, giving Magog and Gog a disgusted look.

"Actually, they haven't. They've been very remiss about reporting in. I haven't been able to get in touch with either of them, till Magog called me about that unfortunate librarian. Which made me curious as to your progress...or, judging from the state of Brighton Pier, your lack thereof. So I thought I'd pay you a visit, and I asked Magog to text me and let me know where you'd be this evening."

We processed this information, especially the fact that Magog wasn't the total turncoat we'd thought her to be. Finally, Blondie spoke.

"You're right about us being too late. The former Alfar monarch, Morrigan, has become the Red. We figure there wasn't enough left over for them to remake themselves. But there was enough remaining to possess a vessel."

Jack paled visibly, but his voice was still under control when he spoke. "So the Red is unleashed. And the White?"

"Still not entirely assembled. That's what we were doing tonight—trying to head off Morrigan before she could find another piece of her consort," Blondie said.

"Then the pieces are still out there," Jack mused, walking towards his brother. He and Lyman met each other's eyes, and Lyman nodded.

"The pieces are still out there," Jack repeated, "which means their power is still available."

Blondie shook her head, her face betraying her contempt.

"That's not how they work, Jack, and you know it. We can't use the power of the Red or the White; they use us."

Jack made a dismissive motion with his hands.

"So we've been told, Cyntaf. But such information comes from those we know lie to us, all the time. Maybe they don't want us to have that power."

Blondie strode towards Jack, her posture menacing. Jack's followers moved in, as well, flanking their leader as the Original got up in his face.

"You're not that dumb, Jack, so stop acting like you are. You've read the history. You know what happens when the Red and the White walk the earth. This isn't some political game."

"Everything's a game, Cyntaf. And I like winning," was Jack's reply, his politician's smile unwavering in the face of Blondie's ire.

"You'll be used, Jack," Blondie replied. "Just like they use everyone. I'm sure Morrigan thought she was in charge, too, until she became the Red."

"But I'm not 'everyone.' I lead the rebels. I *am* the rebels. Morrigan must obviously have been weak, but look at the power she now wields." Jack said. "And you need to remember your loyalty, Cyntaf. You fight with *us*; you fight for *our* cause. Help us get the kind of weapon that will seal our destiny."

I had to hand it to Jack. His voice oozed sincerity even as his face glowed with an almost messianic belief in his own message. Something whispered to me that Morrigan had probably been as sure of herself, and of her ability to control her new "weapon," as she cobbled together the Red.

But while I distrusted Jack's grip on his own reason, I had to give him credit. He remained remarkably calm when a new voice shot through the little cemetery.

"Your destiny is to serve, halfling," came a bored, Alfar voice from out of the darkness that I recognized from our second kidnapping. It was the Leader's second, Griffin. I squinted around, trying to get a glimpse, but I saw no one.

"We also do not appreciate such conspiracies taking place under our very noses," came another voice, this time that of the Leader, Luke, himself.

Then, as if by magic—although I felt nary a tingle of actual power, five tall shapes disattached themselves from the darkness around the cemetery and flowed towards us.

In the lead was a muscular blonde, who would have been ruggedly handsome except for the fact that his countenance was more like that of a mannequin than a man. A step behind him strode a slightly taller, slimmer figure. This man had beautiful fey features and jet-black hair, cut so that it brushed his cheekbones. His features were schooled into a typically vague Alfar expression, but his eyes betrayed him. They were sharp, assessing everything around him.

He must be Griffin, which left the blonde to be the Leader, Luke. Behind the two leaders were three obvious Alfar flunkies. They were dressed in suits, and had a very Secret Service air about them.

"Well if it's not our glorious Leader," Jack said, affecting calm. But his body had gone tense, and his people clumped behind him like a bunch of grapes. If grapes could look like they were about to panic, that is.

"Can it, Jack," said Griffin. Jack looked surprised at such a human expression coming from an Alfar, and I couldn't blame him. Griffin, meanwhile, looked pleased to have startled the wyvern-halfling.

Lyman, of course, kept the same friendly smile stuck on his face that he'd had the entire time. His eyes, hidden behind a glare on his glasses, could have been closed for all that his facial features reflected the scene in front of him.

Griffin stationed himself in front of the rebel knot, while Luke wandered over to peer into the empty crypt.

"The real Anna Gibson's bones would have been cleared

out years ago, when the humans made this into a park. But they had long been replaced, anyway. That said, we only kept the relics here a short while," he said in his flat Alfar voice. "Whoever opened this tomb was disappointed."

"Then you knew of this hiding spot?" Blondie said, her voice sharp.

"Of course," said Luke, calmly. "Your librarian did a good job fighting her commands, but we had no trouble seeing through her ruse. Over the past few hundred years, she has written over twenty full-length treatises on Anna Gibson. She never understood why, and we wiped her memory after each. But it kept her busy."

Anyan put a restraining hand on Blondie's shoulder, just in time. Blondie looked like she had a hankering for Alfar-kebabs, and I'd felt her powers rise along with her anger as Luke casually discussed their manipulation of the woman she'd obviously cared for very deeply.

Griffin, however, was not so reasonable.

With an audible *boom*, the Alfar second's power mush-roomed around him. Magical reflexes quick as a cat, Blondie's power met his, halfway. Anyan retreated to me, and we built our shields tightly around ourselves. I saw Gog and Magog do the same, protecting Hiral within their barrier.

What was going on between Griffin and Blondie was less of a duel, and more of a game of chicken, or tug of war. They weren't fighting with each other, just exerting a steady magical pressure, trying to get the other's shields to buckle.

I don't think, until that time, I'd ever felt the extent of Blondie's magic. She'd done lots of cool things I couldn't do, and I'd felt her power often. But she'd never really had to extend herself. In fact, the times I'd really seen her fight, like she had against Phaedra in the caves leading up to the creature's lair, I'd later learned she'd been pulling her punches. She couldn't destroy Phaedra because I had to face Jarl's evil little crony myself, in a showdown for the labrys.

This time, however, Blondie pulled nothing. Her power was staggering, and I enjoyed watching Griffin's eyes widen as he realized he was completely outmatched. Also realizing Griffin's plight, Luke's slow Alfar reactions finally kicked in, and the leader lent his power to his minion.

Blondie remained unfazed, simply pouring on more mojo until the rest of us had to physically move away, taking our shields with us, or be crushed.

I watched, alarmed, as one of the crypts standing between Blondie and the Alfar crumbled, and then a second. There was no doubt Blondie was going to win this little showdown, but I worried the only real loser would be this otherwise lovely little park that we'd already damaged.

Finally, after an excruciating wait, Griffin raised a palm to yield. A second later, Luke did the same. Original and Alfars all cut off their magic, and the rest of us had to amp up our shields not to stumble forward, sucked into the void left by all that power disappearing.

Blondie, Luke, and Griffin all stared at each other, until some unconscious signal let the rest of us know the pissing contest was over.

"So what did you do with the remains of the White?" Anyan asked, bringing the rest of us back to the business at hand.

"They are hidden," Luke said. "And hidden well." He took a pristine white handkerchief out of his pocket to wipe off his hands, even though he hadn't actually touched anything. Then he held it aloft till one of his flunkies retrieved it and gave him another, fresh one.

Huh, an OCD Alfar, I thought. Somehow, that combination didn't surprise me.

"There is no such thing as a good hiding place," Anyan said, his voice eminently reasonable. "You know that. Already the Red has been awakened."

"So we heard," Griffin said, his own voice venomous. "Our forces have been busy wiping memories of dragons from the minds of the good people of Brighton and Hove."

"Then you know the truth," I said, tired of playing these Alfar games. Nothing ever happened when they were around—that was their real magic. They ground life down to its nubs, so nothing could ever happen. "You know that Morrigan is already the Red, and she plans to awaken the White. She's already got her vessel picked out and everything. We have to stop her, and no amount of hiding the White's remains will work. Not when the White wants to be found."

Luke and Griffin both looked at me, Griffin's face revealing a hint of surprise as if he found it curious I could speak in whole sentences.

His words, when he addressed me, were delivered as one would speak to a mildly retarded child.

"We found you in the presence of known rebels, discussing the rebel's desire to obtain the White's remains for their own uses. Why on earth would we help you?"

I nearly screamed in irritation.

"We're not on their side!" I shouted. "They ambushed

us, just like you ambushed us. They kidnapped us, just like you kidnapped us. Basically, to us, you're the same people. You're all the people who are stopping us from doing our job, which is to save your island, and your ass, from the beings *you* were too incompetent to keep from being found!"

So maybe yelling at the Alfar Powers That Be wasn't the best idea, but I wasn't known for my tact. I was also very pissed off at that point, and so was the labrys. With my last words it lit up like a UFO, casting its light directly in the faces of Luke, Griffin, Jack, Lyman, and their assorted entourages.

All the various beings threw their arms over their eyes as I wrestled with the ax for control. Eventually it calmed down, and I dimmed it till it was more like a pulsing, handheld nightlight than a spotlight.

Everyone lowered their hands from their eyes, staring at me with a variety of different expressions. Lyman, of course, was still smiling as if nothing had happened. Luke kept up his facade of Alfar calm, although he was frowning slightly.

It was Griffin and Jack who stared at me like foxes who'd caught a rabbit and weren't sure which delicious morsel to bite into first.

They see power, I realized. *It's not me. They just see the power of the champion.*

I felt sick, watching those two and realizing the truth of what Anyan had said to me, just a few nights ago, about the different forces wanting to use what I held.

"Just a tourist?" Griffin said, his tone dry.

I gave him a cold look, and then asked the labrys to remove itself. It did so begrudgingly, as if it knew I was in trouble. Unfortunately, it wasn't smart enough to realize that any trouble I was in, was because of it.

"This isn't about us," I said. "Well, it is about us, because we'll probably be the first to die if Morrigan achieves her mission."

Everyone cocked his or her head at me, and I realized I was, once again, taking the circuitous route.

"What I'm trying to say is that you all need to put your personal politics aside for this, and let us go. We need to stop Morrigan. Not because we believe in the rebels or we believe in the Alfar, but because she's going to wipe out *everything* if she gets her way."

"And you want nothing from your situation?" Jack asked, his politician's smile really getting under my skin. "You only want to stop the Red and the White? You're not enjoying any of your new found power?"

I looked at him like I would kill him, if I could.

"No," I said, my voice brittle. "I'm not enjoying any of this."

He didn't look like he believed me. And neither did Griffin.

"We need to know where these pieces of the White ended up," Anyan interrupted, indicating the empty crypt. "And we don't have time for this squabbling. While we argue, Morrigan's making headway."

Griffin and Luke exchanged inscrutable looks, until Griffin nodded imperceptibly.

"You realize how much humans love old bones, yes?" asked Luke. We all looked at him, nonplussed.

"I believe they refer to them as 'relics,'" clarified Griffin.

"The bones of purported saints, collected by the

Church and venerated," Anyan explained for everyone's benefit. I gave him an odd look. "There's a lot of beautiful Christian art," the barghest said, answering my unspoken query of how the hell he knew anything about human saints.

"Well we decided that the best place to hide something was in plain sight," Luke continued, as if none of us had ever spoken.

I sighed. "You really love that method, don't you?" I asked, but was ignored.

"So we added the bones from this compromised crypt to the bones in a far more secure, well guarded, human establishment. The type of place that supernaturals would never look, and the type of place that has all sorts of bones to throw off any attempts to discover the White's resting place."

"And where is that?" Anyan asked patiently.

"I believe the humans call it Notre Dame."

I raised my eyebrows. Looked like we were going to Paris.

CHAPTER EIGHTEEN

The nice thing about the Alfar being involved was that they had nice rides. The helicopters they'd lent us were whisking us away to Paris in record time.

The bad thing about the Alfar being involved, was that the Alfar were involved. Griffin was staring at me from across the expanse of the helicopter as if he were contemplating how best to put down an arthritic old milk cow that had long since ceased producing.

I kept smiling at him pleasantly, wondering if I could make the ax suddenly appear, hovering over his man parts.

For just a split second, the air shivered over his crotch. I gasped, pulling back my magic even as Griffin looked down, then back up in alarm. Recovered, and with the ax safely stowed in its magic mind box, I beamed back at him.

Frowning, he looked away.

That'd teach him to taunt the zoo animals, I thought,

cuddling against Anyan who was wedged next to me. The barghest kissed my forehead gently, and when I raised my face to his, he nuzzled my nose with his own crooked schnoz. He drew back to smile at me, and my desire for him hit me like a ton of bricks.

I couldn't hear anything in the helicopter: between the headphone thingies we were using as ear protection and the noise of the helicopter, we were all deaf. There were microphones on the headsets, but they miked into every other headset on the helicopter. Good for going into battle; bad for intimate conversations with the man you'd give your left buttock to maul. Luckily, however, Anyan knew all my strengths and weaknesses, as he and Nell had actually had me write them down in essay form as part of my training. So he knew that lots of underwater training with Trill had made me an excellent lip reader.

"I want you," he mouthed, slowly and carefully, shifting in his seat a bit so I could better see that wide, sensual mouth.

"I do too," I mouthed back, aware of his gaze on my lips. My libido pondered whether there was a subtle way to mime a blow job on a helicopter stuffed full of friends and foes, but my virtue squashed that train of thought like a health inspector might a lamed cockroach.

So instead I looked him as deeply as I could in the eyes without actually headbutting him, trying to open up that window into my soul…where, realistically, my libido was doing the humpty dance while dressed in Milkbone pasties and a thong.

"Liverpool here," said a voice over our headphones, interrupting the moment. "Liverpool" referred to one of the four helicopters in our convoy. And no, the Alfar

weren't fucking around—we had a full contingent of their
best soldiers going with us, as well as the members of the
rebel party who had insisted they take part. I could tell the
Alfar had wanted to tell Jack to shove it, but Anyan
explained to me that politics on the Island were carefully
kept in balance by giving the rebels careful, small
acknowledgements—enough to keep them happy and
feeling part of a process, but not enough to give them any
real power. This particular mission was an easy way to
make them feel included and keep an eye on them, without actually granting them any extra authority.

"We're nearing Paris, but we're getting reports of a
security risk at our intended touchdown. Proceed or pull
back?" asked the pilot of the other chopper.

"Proceed, but carefully. Make sure the humans see
nothing."

My eyes left Anyan's as I turned my body to stare outside my window. Just as the pilot said, what had previ-
ously been farmland, and then suburbs, was now definitely
city. And we weren't the only thing in the sky.

In the distance I could see at least three other choppers
going the same direction we were, and I thought I saw
what looked like a fighter jet. My mouth went dry as I
thought about what could possibly be happening that
would require a military presence at all, let alone that big
a military presence.

Reaching for Anyan's hand, I scanned the horizon. The
barghest rested his chin on my shoulder as he did the
same.

It was, of course, Magog who spotted something first.

"Goddesses bright," swore the raven from where she
sat next to Griffin. I glanced at her sharply, but her eyes

were wide and focused on the distance. I hadn't spoken to Magog since we'd discovered she'd squealed to Jack. But, in all honesty, I knew my anger wouldn't last. I didn't envy her, being caught between so many different loyalties.

Sitting on the other side of Magog from Griffin sat Jack, who caught my eye and again gave me that politician's smile. I glowered at him, but it was only when I saw that mask slip to be replaced by sheer horror that I knew we were well and truly fucked.

Taking a deep breath, I turned my head slowly towards the window.

A chorus of obscenities rang out over my headphones as the various pilots caught site of what awaited us.

So that's what it takes to get the military in town, *besides student riots*, I thought. *A dragon attack.*

Perched on top of an already flaming Notre Dame crouched the Red Queen's dragon form. She was even bigger than she'd appeared to us at Brighton, having no space issues to accommodate. The city skyline was now her playground, and while she wasn't quite as big as Godzilla, she was pretty godamned impressive.

"What the hell is that?" One of the pilots asked.

"Our destination, gentleman," said Griffin, pressing down on the little speaking button on his headset. "If you will find a convenient place to land, I think we will be safer on the ground. And we will need to have this Territory's ground forces ready to take us to the site and debrief us."

We watched the dragon knock what looked like a toy chopper out of the sky—we were still fairly far away—and then eat another one.

"Yes sir," the pilot said hastily, giving a string of

incomprehensible commands to the other pilots listening in.

The pilots dropped us off on the massive rooftop of a local hospital that was only a few blocks from Notre Dame. We made our way downstairs past the few startled doctors and nurses who hadn't gone to huddle up next to windows to try to catch a glimpse of what they'd heard was happening at the cathedral. When we got downstairs, there was already a small cadre of French supes waiting for us.

"Bonjour," said a slim and handsome man, with a strong Gallic nose I couldn't help but appreciate. He was clearly Alfar, the power swirling around him identifying him with its mixture of elements. I took a moment to ascertain our current situation while he continued speaking in a rapid French the rest of my group clearly understood.

Around us humans in civilian clothes or cars were traveling as fast as possible away from the barrage of noise we could hear from the cathedral, including screams, explosions, gunfire, and something shouting very loudly. At the same time, humans in various uniforms raced or drove towards the melee in official looking vehicles. Some of those vans were obviously news crews.

In other words, there were humans everywhere: snapping pictures, filming, and calling loved ones and friends with eyewitness accounts.

There wasn't a supernatural force on earth that was capable of covering this one up.

Why would she do this? I thought. *Why would she show herself like this?*

Then I realized that by "she" I was thinking of Morrigan. The Morrigan I thought I'd known never would have exposed her kind to humanity. And maybe the Morrigan I hadn't known—the Morrigan who made a deal with the Red—wouldn't have, either. But the Red Queen was clearly in charge, and she just wanted carnage.

And if carnage was what she wanted, there was no better way to get it than to expose the supernatural world—to show one group of people another, different group of people. Especially if that other group was *really* different— maybe with different colored skin, or a different way of worship, or the ability to shapeshift into a motherfucking dragon.

The Red had last been destroyed long before technology. She could rant and scream all she wanted in a village many hundreds of years ago, and all the supes had to do to mop up was glamour a few hundred people. Even in a major city of the time, any appearances she made could eventually be wiped clean away. But nowadays, with Morrigan's understanding of modern technology behind her, the Red knew she could make quite a splash by showing up on the roof of a major urban tourist-site.

Yeah, I thought. *The humans are going to be pissed, and scared, and even more pissed about being kept in the dark. They're going to want revenge, and their world cleansed, and for everything to go back to normal.*

And the Red was going to love every minute of it.

That was when the debate changed to English.

"You can't do this," Blondie was saying. Anyan clearly had her back, as he was standing behind her bristling with menace.

"We can and we will," the French Alfar said. "This is not our fight."

"What do you mean this isn't our fight? She's the Red! She'll destroy this city, maybe this country, and that's just her alone. When she awakens the White, we all fall!"

"She will have her fun, and then she can go away. We can fight her in our own way, later. She has already compromised us, but she can be explained away as a myth come to life…a freak of genetic history that survived, maybe in Loch Ness to give the humans a thrill, and that can be hunted down. If we try to stop her now, we expose all of our kind."

Suddenly, I realized what was going on. The Alfar didn't want to intervene, and that clearly included Griffin, who was nodding his head vehemently along with his French counterpart's every word.

"You have got to be kidding me," I said, not entirely meaning to talk out loud.

"I'm sorry?" The French Alfar asked, as if I'd farted on his shoe.

"You have to be kidding me," I repeated. "This is a joke. You can't let her get what she wants and you can't let her destroy this city. All of those people in that square will die. The soldiers, and policemen, and firefighters. They're just doing their job, and they'll die because they came across an evil that we helped to create."

"We are not responsible for that creature," the Alfar said disdainfully.

"That creature is part of where our power comes from," I said, stepping up to face him down, nose-to-nose. Well, nose-to-midway-up-his-tie.

"And who are you, little girl?" He asked, his otherwise perfect Gallic nose wrinkling in such a way that I no longer found it so admirable. "Who are you to defy me, in my own Territory?"

That's it, came a clear voice in my head, one that I only vaguely recognized as my own. *I'm tired of this horseshit.*

And with that I pulled, calling the labrys to me. Sensing its enemy nearby, it came to me fully lit, its power emanating from it in waves so powerful the air shimmered.

The native Alfar sprang back, Nose giving me a look like I'd pulled a ferret out of my cooter.

I hefted the ax to lay it over my shoulder, as if I were one of Disney's seven dwarves with his pickaxe.

"I'm the champion," I said. Then I looked at Blondie and Anyan. "You ready?"

When they nodded, I grinned at Nose. Then I started running.

We'd only made it a few paces before the Alfar threw up a shield to stop us. I wish I'd seen their faces when the labrys cut through it like it were paper.

I kept running as hard as I could, knowing I was getting closer when a few human police tried to stop me, although they did so while giving me a wide berth due to the fact I looked like a madwoman carrying an ax. I felt Anyan throw up a hasty glamour for that last block, and I turned to see who else was with us.

The rebels were there, Jack and Lyman lit up like blue-flamed candles, Lyman's light so fierce it burned my eyes. Gog and Magog were also along for the ride, and I could see Hiral's mad blue Troll hair flopping around like a bad rug on Gog's head. Gog was carrying the little gwyllion on his shoulders. To my surprise, Griffin was also following us, though he didn't look at all pleased about it.

Finally, we turned the last corner to pop out onto the deep square that surrounded Notre Dame Cathedral.

The fallen were everywhere, bodies littering the ground. Some were obviously dead, others grievously wounded. And depending on how many of those wounds had been inflicted directly by the Red's claws, we wouldn't be able to heal all of them with magic.

"Plan?" I shouted, the labrys trying to drag me forward to meet its enemy. Digging in my heels, I prayed someone else had an idea.

"We need air, we need power, and we need water. We've got air," Blondie said, pointing at herself, then Magog and Anyan. "And we've got power," she said, pointing at the ax. "We just need water."

I let my head loll back, shutting my eyes and opening my senses. I could feel water, from both underneath me and farther away, higher up. There was water under the catherdral, which I'd later learn was the Seine. And a storm was brewing, close but not yet here. A plan brewed up within me, but I'd need both the water under Notre Dame and the storm...

[Call it], rumbled a sleepy voice in my head.

Whaaaaa? I asked immediately, trying to capitalize on the brief period the creature was responding.

[Call the storm. It will come. Let the labrys guide you...]

Opening myself to the power of my weapon, I let it reach up and out. I felt my arm rise to the sky as my senses traveled the water molecules all around me to where they joined, miles away, with the storm clouds seeding high above the land.

And then I pulled, like an overly competitive ex-jock at his company picnic's tug-a-war.

As I worked, I talked. Well, in my head.

Nice of you to show up, I told the creature.

[The dreams,] it said, sleepily. [Everyone's dreams. Disturbed...a dragon...]

Not just any dragon, I told it. *But the Red.*

[In front of humans? The media? I see it reflected in those screens you call televisions, monitors...]

I thought a grim affirmative at it, the mental version of a nodding head.

It's perched on one of the most popular landmarks in the human world. It couldn't have attracted more attention if it were directed by Bruckheimer.

[You must stop it,] the creature told me, grimly. [You must stop it, and you must prepare. This won't be hidden. I can feel humans everywhere, taking in this scene and I can feel their fear...]

Yeah, well, we're not big fans of the unknown, I told it, acknowledging a sad fact of my human heritage.

[You will be important, Jane.] It told me, all trace of sleepiness gone from its mind. [Even more than you are now. You must be the face of the supernatural world, as the humans understand it. You must confront the evil of the Red, and then you must appear before the cameras. They must understand you mean to help them.]

I swallowed noisily, my power over the storm faltering as I panicked. What did he mean I would have to talk to the cameras? I was no spokesperson. I was a halfling, a nobody, a pathetic little half-selkie from Maine...

And then I saw it. The perfection of it: the big eyes, the tiny build, the Converse and the small-town past.

I was the perfect ingénue. The baby-faced, doe-eyed innocent who no one could fear.

"Motherfucker," I snarled, even as I reached with all

my strength back up into the heavens. The storm obeyed like an eager puppy.

[I never fucked my mother,] the creature said, quite seriously.

It's an expression of frustration, I told it. *I don't want this.*

[I know,] it said, sadly. [But I will help. I will read as many minds as I can. I will help you understand what people are worried about, so that you can address them. It is what you call now a…marketing strategy, yes? I will help you market my children to the humans, so that they understand us. But now you must get the Red off of that rooftop.]

Aye-aye, cap'n, I thought wearily, feeling the creature again drop out of my mind.

"Jane? Jane?" came Anyan's voice, intruding into my thoughts. He'd obviously been calling my name for a while, as he was clearly worried.

"You'll have your water in about five minutes," I said brusquely, looking to Blondie. "Are we going to get this show on the road?"

"We were waiting for you, babydoll," said the Original. As she sprouted her enormous white wings, Magog threw off her overcoat, revealing her own beautifully feathered appendages. I heard the humans gasp around us.

"No glamours?" I asked.

"It's a little late for that," Anyan said, nodding towards the gigantic, ravening dragon.

Now that we were closer and I wasn't communing with the creature and the heavens, I could hear that the shouting had been the Red, all the time. In between gusts of fire and kicking various beautiful parts off the ancient cathedral, she was screaming her brains out.

"Where is it! Where is my love! I'll find him if I have to tear this city apart you puny mortals..."

I sighed. She sounded like a bad Syfy villain. Why did we never fight anyone who had any really good lines?

"The rain's almost here," I said, stepping forward and brandishing the labrys. I could feel its glee at facing its ancient enemy. "Let's do this."

"Hey, Morrigan!" I shouted, waving the ax like I was an air-traffic controller. "Down here!"

"You!" The dragon shouted, craning her bullet-shaped head on her long neck to peer down at me. "Where is the White!"

Around me, various humans were scampering away, or—unsure of our motivations—were setting themselves up to take a shot at us. Gog responded with a massive pull of earth power that ripped up the paving stones around us, separating us from the humans' guns with three walls of dirt and earth magic. I could hear the guns firing, but I trusted to my own manifested shields as well as Gog's to keep me safe as I strode forward within my little open-ended box of earth towards the dragon.

"I have no idea!" I shouted back at the former queen turned giant lizard. "But I do know where something else is!" With that I waved my labrys at the dragon, tauntingly.

The Red's only response was to breathe a wall of fire onto my friends and me. We kept it behind our shields, but it got more than a little toasty inside our protections.

When she was done, I gestured to Blondie, Anyan, and Magog. The storm was right above us. The sky had been getting darker throughout the last five minutes, and now it was pitch black. The wind whipped through our hair while thunder boomed. I raised my labrys to the sky and felt a bolt of lightning bounce down and through me, absorbed harmlessly by the power of my weapon.

Then I called forth water, catching the water in midair and stretching it into a rope.

Beside me, Magog and Blondie launched into the air, their wings and magic swirling the dust around us. Anyan, standing to my left, took my hand, focusing his own control over the air into the night sky.

Meanwhile, I kept calling. More and more water poured from the sky as I wrung out the clouds one by one. Leaving it hovering in midair, I slowly built the water into a thick wall of dragon-quenching wetness.

A wall that Blondie, Anyan, and Magog began to push forward, towards the Red. Laughing—an alarming sound coming from a dragon—the Red barely even bothered to back away from the water as it moved towards her.

"What is this, halfling? Think you can shower me again? I'm not that stupid."

And with that she breathed fire at the wall of water, dissipating a big chunk of it. I pulled it back together, thickening it as much as I could, and we continued its advance. Still laughing, the Red blew another huge gust of fire. More of my wall dissipated, but it nevertheless forced her back one more step. She blew again, and again, until my wall of water was nearly spent.

But with each blast, she took another few steps back. Until I had her where I wanted her.

She hadn't seen the other wall of water I'd pulled up from beneath the cathedral, nor did she feel me pull it up as I was expending so much strength doing the trick with the storm. And, luckily, she remained oblivious until I swamped her with it, cupping the river water with a thousand tiny hands of power to make it linger longer on her skin. And then I pulled down Gog's walls and shouted towards the human forces who'd managed to pull themselves together while the Red was preoccupied with me.

"Shoot!" I yelled, lofting the shining labrys. "Everything you've got! Bring the rain!"

I had a thing for modern military epics, and I'd always wanted to say that line.

Much to my surprise, the humans did shoot. And the Red, saturated with the element that canceled out her powers, couldn't raise any magical shields. Most of the bullets seemed to ricochet off her tough scales, but she was still definitely getting hit in her more vulnerable areas.

But I think it was the rockets that made her leave.

Tanks had rolled up, armed with much bigger guns than what a human would carry. And they weren't immodest in dispensing their load.

Roaring in pain, the Red reared back, her mighty tail crashing through one of the great towers of the cathedral. With a few more destructive swipes, she readied herself before launching into the air. The missiles attempting to take her down failed, and flying helped her dry off and collect her mother's power. I could feel her pulling force from the air around her, and then she disappeared.

We waited for her to reappear like the serial killer in a horror film, but she must have been too wounded in body and pride to return.

Only then did I remember the other part of my job. I'd never wanted to do anything less than what I did, then. I smoothed down my shirt and then my hair, turning to Anyan after I did so.

"Do I look all right?" I asked. He nodded, totally confused at my sudden and inappropriate vanity.

I made my eyes big and sweet as they would get, and then I strode past the soldiers to the media.

Baby seal to the rescue.

CHAPTER NINETEEN

The camera really did add five pounds. Two of which appeared to be in my eyeballs.

"Ohmigod," I said, groaning and burying my face in Anyan's biceps, "the only thing bigger than my hips are my eyes. It's like a manga character came to life and discovered fried chicken."

Anyan chuckled, but his hands reached down to caress my thighs. "I like everything on you that's big, and I like everything that's little. You look fine."

I felt a flush of both heat and affection for the barghest, who always seemed to know the right thing to say to me. Sighing, I snuggled back into the V of his long legs, using his chest as my backrest. He enfolded me in his arms, and I finally felt brave enough to turn my face back to our television.

It was nice and large, as we'd holed up in an incredibly expensive hotel. After all of the hullabaloo with the media, I'd allowed Anyan to whisk me away. The barghest

glamoured us as we darted across a busy street with a lot
of trucks, making us invisible so that those following
would think we'd either disappeared or gotten into one of
the cars. Then he'd taken me directly to a very fancy
hotel, gotten us an enormous suite, and called the others
to tell them where our new, luxury hideout was for the
evening.

We had then commandeered the biggest, swankiest
bedroom, where Anyan had immediately turned on the
television.

And there I was. I did look a bit disheveled, although I
suppose that was to be expected considering Notre Dame
was a smoking ruin, and there were various men and
women running around behind me carrying medical
equipment and stretchers. The only reason I wasn't being
arrested was the powerful repulsion glamour Anyan had
set around me, keeping everyone but the cameramen
away.

Now safe in our room, Anyan and I watched as I stood
silently, the studio news anchor speaking in French. In
real life, the cameramen had been slow to get a mic to me,
until Anyan had drawn their attention to me even as he'd
kept the police away. It was convenient, as it gave the
anchor time to brief everyone on what had happened,
while I blinked owlishly at the media.

Just as the anchor's words ceased, my own lips started
moving. A second later the sound began.

"...situation is under control. I repeat, the situation is
under control. I know what you saw today is frightening,
and that some will believe that life as you know it is forever changed. But please listen to me when I tell you that
all is as it was before, and that you are safe."

I was interrupted by a shout from one of the camera-
men, asking me who I was in French-accented English.
On camera, my eyes darted offscreen. I'd been looking to
Anyan, who had nodded at me to continue.

"My name is Jane, and I work for a force that is here to
help. What you saw today might happen again, but we are
on your side. There are people working for you, working
to…"

Here my words trailed off and the tiniest frown crossed
my lips. The creature had been helping to feed me lines,
prompting me with ideas that it was gleaning from human
minds. What he'd asked me to say made me uncomfortable, but after a short pause I said it.

"As I was saying, there are people working to take
down the forces of evil and bring peace to the world. We
are those people, and we will do everything we can to
make you and your families safe. Thank you for listening,
and, um, have a good night."

And with that, I vanished, leaving the news station's
cameras panning back and forth wildly, trying to figure
out where I'd went, even as it recorded other cameras
doing the same thing.

"I sounded like an idiot," I said, into the silence of the
room.

"No," Anyan said. "You said what needed to be said.
But if this footage has aired here, it'll air any second in
the rest of the world if it hasn't already."

"I have to call Ryu," I realized, as the implications of
everything I'd just done came sweeping over me.

Anyan didn't protest my need to talk to my ex. Instead
he handed me my phone from where I'd set it on the nightstand, understanding the seriousness of the situation.

"You were amazing," Ryu said, in lieu of a greeting. I scrubbed a weary hand over my face, feeling Anyan press a kiss to the top of my head and suddenly fiercely glad that he was there.

"Thanks Ryu, but…"

"I'm serious," Ryu interrupted, my ex's smooth voice purring as sexily as it ever had. "We were all watching the news, thinking 'What the hell are we going to do,' and then you were there."

"Listen, I appreciate it, but…"

"It was really perfect," Ryu repeated, not letting me finish. I don't think I'd ever heard him this pleased with me. "So how do you feel?"

"You really wanna know?" I asked.

"Of course. Tell me."

I shook my head, once again marveling at how someone I'd spent that much time with, and someone who I knew really had cared for me, could still have no idea who I was or what I wanted out of life. I couldn't help but compare Ryu to the man silently holding me, keeping me from flying apart in terror over what I'd just brought down on myself and my loved ones.

"Ryu, I'm terrified. I'm glad I could help and everything, but I'm terrified about my dad and my friends. Any second now someone's going to identify me, if they haven't already, and that's why I called. I need your help. You need to get to my dad, make sure he's safe. Same with Griz and Tracy. You gotta make sure the humans in my life aren't mobbed or used against me."

"Oh," Ryu said, less buoyant now that the other shoe had dropped.

"Exactly," I said, dryly. "I'm terrified that my dad's

going to get sent to Guantánamo, or kidnapped by some loony supporter of Morrigan's. I'm also terrified I ruined my human life, and at the end of all this shit I'm going to have to go into hiding."

Ryu was silent for a moment, undoubtedly processing what I'd said.

"I didn't think of any of that. Caleb's in the area, with Iris, and I'll send him over to the bookstore to get your dad and the girls somewhere safe until we know what'll happen. Then I'll send a crew to do damage control."

"Thanks," I said, meaning it. I had to give Ryu credit—he'd been incredibly kind to me ever since he'd become co-leader of the Territory, with Nyx, after Morrigan murdered Orin. I do think part of his equanimity was that he was just so busy in his new role. Busy, but also really, really happy, which I think said something about his priorities. Ryu had loved me, in his own way, but he'd always loved power more.

I never could have made him as happy as his current position did, and that fact had to be as clear to him as it was to me.

"But you did do a good thing, Jane. We've got time, now. If you'd just fought off the Red and left, can you imagine what would be going through people's minds? But while everyone was going over your footage a million times, we were able to get in touch with our contacts in the human governments, start working things out."

"How are you going to play it?" I asked.

"We're not sure yet. Everyone's seen everything at this point. The footage has gone viral on YouTube, and more stuff keeps getting put up all the time. If it was just the Red, we might have been able to contain it with just an 'extinct species not really extinct' story, but with all of you involved, we'll need more."

"We had to do it. We couldn't let her destroy Paris." At my words, Anyan's arms around me squeezed gently.

"I agree. And what's done is done. So we have to turn this into an opportunity, somehow."

"Are we coming out of the closet?" I asked.

Ryu was silent again, thinking. "Maybe" was his eventual answer. "At least in a limited way. We'll see how everything pans out. A lot is going to ride on you, Jane. You've got to stop the Red, and quickly, before all hell breaks."

"Well, the good news is that I don't think she'll be showing up as a dragon anytime soon. That shape's too vulnerable." I'd been sorting through all of my impressions of our recent battles, and they were only now making sense. "I think she's more Morrigan when she's human, and more Red when she's the dragon. And the Red is so powerful, yes, but she's not built for stamina. She's built to wreck shop, get destroyed, and then rise again. It's fire, after all. And air.

"She's also Morrigan, though. When she's Morrigan she's less powerful, but she's also less vulnerable. I think the Alfar makes the Red smarter too. She was trying to be subtle, do things under the radar, until she let the dragon out in Brighton. I think after this defeat, the dragon will let Morrigan take control again. Which means we won't have a giant fire-breathing lizard on our hands, but we'll also have a smarter enemy with a lot more staying power."

What I said made sense, but I knew not to have too much faith in logic. After all, the whole point of the Red was that she didn't make sense, so I could be completely off base. At the end of the day, all we could do was wait and see what she did next.

"We'll see," Ryu said, echoing my own doubts. "Hopefully you're right. But in the meantime I've got to get to Washington and your group has to stop the Red. Call me again if you need anything else."

"Thanks. Let me know if anything comes up at home."

Ryu promised he would, and with that we said our good-byes.

I let my arm flop down on the bed. I felt a hell of a lot better after talking to Ryu and making sure he'd take care of my dad. Who would, if I was lucky, never even know what was going on until everything was over.

Closing my eyes, I let myself finally relax.

The best part was that I was already lying up against Anyan, so relaxing meant cuddling back against him, even closer. When I raised my face to his for an upside down kiss, his lips were there immediately. I'd only really wanted a comforting peck, but next thing I know I was straining up against his mouth, unable to resist the lure of the barghest.

And then my phone rang. Again. I broke off the kiss to look at my screen.

"It's my dad," I said, swearing.

"Uh-oh," Anyan said, bracing me against him. I desperately, if rather stupidly, hoped that I wouldn't need the bracing. Maybe my dad was calling to ask me where I'd hidden a saucepan, or something.

Needless to say, that wasn't the purpose of his call.

"Hey, Dad!" I said, brightly.

"Dragons, Jane? Dragons?" He sounded really angry.

I gulped. "Um, yeah, sorry. I was hoping you wouldn't see that."

"The whole world saw it, Jane. You had an ax. And there was a dragon."

I closed my eyes, grateful to feel Anyan squeeze my free hand in his own strong fingers.

"Yes, well. I'm okay."

"You're obviously okay, but that's not the point. What are you doing?"

"What I have to, Dad."

"What do you mean, 'what you have to'? You just recovered from nearly getting killed. And now you're trying to get yourself killed again?"

I took a deep breath, trying not to lose my shit. My dad had every right to be surprised and angry.

"Dad, I've gotten mixed up in some stuff that's bigger than me. I didn't want to be involved, but we can't help what life brings us. So now I'm just doing my part."

As I said those words, I realized they were true.

I am *doing my part.*

"You're my little girl, Jane. What are you doing fighting a dragon? With an ax?"

I couldn't help but smile. Even I knew I looked ridiculous with the labrys.

"Dad, I love that you still think of me as your little girl, and I wish that we were having the 'independence' conversation about something normal—like going away to college or moving out of the house. But my life's not been like that, ever. And I have to live it, Dad. I've been chosen to do something that I have to do. That dragon you saw, she's the person responsible for mom's death."

"Revenge won't make you feel better…" My dad began, but I interrupted.

"It's not revenge. It's salvation. I've been given the power to stop her, and I'm one of the only people who can. And yes, I know how ridiculous that sounds," I acknowledged. "But you're going to have to accept this."

"You could be killed."

I closed my eyes at the bleak tone of my dad's voice. "I know. But I don't plan on dying, Daddy. And I've got Anyan with me, and Blondie, and lots of other powerful people. I am going to be fine. It's you I'm worried about. Caleb's on his way over… you remember Caleb?"

"No pants, goat haunches?"

"That's the one. He's going to come over and take you somewhere till this blows over. Ryu's also sending some people to take care of Grizzie and Tracy. The media may come to Rockabill, looking for answers about me."

"I have no doubt Linda or Stuart has already called them to ID you," my dad said dryly, a hint of his old humor returning. I snorted in agreement, thinking almost fondly of my old Rockabill nemeses.

Even Linda's better than a dragon, I thought.

Now Stuart, on the other hand…

"You really have to do this, Jane?" he asked.

"Yes."

"And you'll try to stay safe?"

"Of course."

After a moment, he sighed. "What am I supposed to do?"

"Keep busy," I told him. "Try not to think about it. Design Caleb some kind of genital covering." My dad chuckled at that.

"Can I talk to Anyan?"

"Sure, Dad. I love you."

"I love you too. Stay safe. I mean it."

"I will," I said, passing the phone to Anyan as I extricated myself from between the barghest's thighs. I got up and grabbed a bottle of water from our room's fridge. I took a long drink, listening as Anyan said the occasional "yes, sir" and "no, sir." Eventually he said, "I promise," and then he said good-bye and hung up.

"What did he want?" I asked, as the barghest set my phone down on the hotel's nightstand. He held his hand out to me and I went to him gladly, letting him pull me down on the bed.

"He said to take care of you, or he'd kill me," Anyan said, nuzzling my ear.

I smiled. "Did you tell him it's my job to save all of you?"

"Your dad is human and of a certain generation. He believes males should take care of females."

"Thanks for clearing that up," I said sarcastically, then sighed as Anyan suckled at my earlobe before nipping. I let my head fall back as his lips found my throat.

"You do realize that by 'taking care of me,' my dad didn't mean with sex?"

"You'll fight better if you're relaxed," Anyan said, chuckling evilly. His hands were at the waistband of my jeans, his clever fingers undoing my zipper.

Make-out! Make-out! Make-out! my libido chanted, doing a happy-libido dance at the sound of my fly opening.

And then it nearly keeled over when someone pounded at the door.

"Jane? Anyan? You decent?" came Blondie's voice, but she was already opening the door to our suite's room.

"Jesus, get a room," she said. "Oh wait, you *do* have a room. Sorry."

Laughing at her own joke, she came and plunked down next to us in the bed, putting her arm around me.

Anyan did my pants back up, although the Original eyed him reproachfully.

"You don't have to do that," she purred, waggling her eyebrows at me. "Sex is good for relaxing after battle."

"What did you find out, Cyntaf?" Anyan said, pulling me closer to him and away from Blondie. She sighed, wiggling closer anyway.

"The problem with coming to town and landing on a building, then tearing it up, all while shaped as a dragon, is that you rarely get a chance to read signs."

With that, Blondie pulled a flier out of her back pocket, handing it to me. I unfolded it, unable to stop the laughter that bubbled to my lips.

"The relics are on a tour," I told Anyan, passing him the flier. "Like a rock band, only bones. A real, honest-to-gods tour."

Anyan's wide mouth pursed as he read the fine print.

"They're arriving in York this week," he said, moving to stand. "We've got to go."

"Now?" I asked. I'd had hankerings for another date. A Paris date.

My only answer was their retreating figures. That's when I decided this mission officially sucked. After all, I'd come to Paris, and I'd barely had one iota of romance.

Not to mention any stinky cheese.

CHAPTER TWENTY

Apparently, the Alfar were rather pissed at me, so we had to take the Eurostar back to London. It was an amazingly short ride, and there was actually very little tunnel. I thought we'd be underground forever, and was prepared to deal with much claustrophobia. Instead, I barely even noticed when we went in, let alone when we came out.

There were seven of us on the ride home, so we had two tables to ourselves. Blondie, Anyan, and I sat at one table, while Gog, Magog, Lyman, and Griffin sat at the other

Griffin and Lyman were our devil's bargain. We got to work without a full contingent of rebels and Alfar shadowing our every move, but we had to take both second-in-commands. Meanwhile the rebel leader, Jack, and the Alfar Leader, Luke, were going back to England to meet with the human prime minister. As the territory with the most established connection to its human counterparts, the Great Island was leading the clean-up operation necessitated by Morrigan's attack on Notre Dame.

Blondie was snoozing, waking up occasionally to stare at her phone. I was happily eating the stinky cheese and baguette that Anyan had bought for me at the train station as a consolation prize. Anyan was watching Griffin and Lyman speculatively, while Griffin and Lyman watched each other with distaste.

We were a regular dysfunctional Brady Bunch, but with more magic and fewer bell-bottoms.

"What's the plan?" I asked, after I'd finally had enough and pushed the wedge of brie away. Then I started in on the bunch of grapes we'd also bought.

Anyan turned back to me, cadging his own grape before responding.

"We'll be met at the train station with our luggage, and then get on a train to York. And hopefully we'll hear from Hiral soon."

"I gotta say, he's an annoying little shit, but he's good."

Anyan nodded. "The best. At both annoyance and espionage."

That's why we were missing one foul-smelling little gwyllion. Hiral had managed to find where Morrigan's entourage was watching her tear up Paris a safe distance away. They'd apparently looked as horrified as we had. She was full of surprises, that dragon, even for the super-naturals she worked with.

Hiral had made himself useful and invisible, hitching a ride with Morrigan's entourage when they'd left with the dragon's own departure. Now we were waiting to see what he discovered as we made our way to York, in the far north of England.

"So we wait for Hiral to tell us more about what Morrigan's up to, and we try to nab the bones from the Minster?"

The Minster was York's great cathedral, where the relics were appearing that week.

"Yep. We'll need to do it as quietly as we can, after what happened in Paris. No more news crews."

"No," I said. "No more news crews."

"Blondie, can I use your phone?" I asked, leaning over the table to nudge the Original.

She pulled it from her pocket and punched in the code to unlock it, before handing it over.

"Thanks," I told her. She only grunted and closed her eyes again in reply.

"I'm going to do some research on the Minster," I told Anyan, as explanation for why I wanted Blondie's iPhone instead of my own crappy, but sturdy, cell. I stared at the screen for a bit before looking at Anyan helplessly. "Um, if you'll help me..."

Anyan smiled at me, his grey eyes warm with affection. Granted, I think he thought it was cute I was so incompetent with technology, but it was still sweet. He then showed me how to work the touchpad of the phone, pulling up Safari and then Googling what I told him to. First I made him look up the Minster for me, where we found a link for the tour, itself. It even had its own Facebook page.

Centuries dead bones have a Facebook page, and I don't, I marveled. Then I thought about the way we found housing, and congratulated myself roundly.

The bones we were chasing after were purported, at least according to the humans, to be the bones of Saint Nicodemus. I wondered if they'd always really been the White's bones, or if the Alfar had done a switch. If so, I wondered what they'd done with the "real" saint's bones.

Something tells me they wouldn't go through too many pains to make sure they were safe.

Anyan kept the phone, going where I asked him to, or punching new things into Google. Eventually, I started making him pursue completely random shit. For while he did so, I marveled at his hands, imagining them running all over my body with the same surety with which he worked the phone.

"You're drooling, Jane," said Blondie, her husky, sleep-roughened voice cutting through my reverie.

"Hmm?" I asked, completely distracted. Blondie sighed, mumbling something about selkies before raising her voice so I could hear it over the quiet clatter of the train.

"You're drooling. You two need some alone time before you combust."

I made a face, partially to punctuate the irony of the Original who was a one-woman cock-blocking machine encouraging us to have some "alone time."

"Oh really?" I said, but my sarcasm was lost on Blondie. So I switched to the other issue I had with my current naked barghest obsession.

"I shouldn't be thinking about anything besides our mission," I said, guiltily.

"Nonsense," Blondie said, before yawning so ferociously her jaw popped. "The only thing that goes better with battles than blood is battles and sex. Battles and bloody sex."

"Ew," was all I could come up with in response to that piece of "wisdom."

"Hey, indoor plumbing's a recent luxury," the Original told me, at which point I remembered she actually had the invention of the toilet inked on her skin as a magic-video-tattoo.

"It's true," Anyan rumbled, his big hand finding my knee under the table. He worked his fingers into the joints in a mini-massage that made my whole leg relax. "Sex has gotten a lot cleaner. It used to be way grittier."

"More real," Blondie disagreed, eyes shining with memories.

"Grittier," Anyan insisted, obviously not caught up as fondly in memories of post-battle-sexytimes-past as Blondie was.

"I rarely like the word 'grit' unless it's preceded by 'cheese,' and accompanied by some sort of barbequed meat," I said, throwing that out there in case anyone cared. No one did.

"And my point is," Blondie continued, "that you shouldn't feel bad about wanting to feel alive at times like these. Or wanting to enjoy your body."

"It could, after all, be blown to bits," was my wry aside.

"Exactly! We could all die tomorrow." Blondie's tone was almost happy, her eyes still focused inward as if remembering all of her glorious moments as a warrior.

I wanted to tell her that such things were easy for her to say. She was, after all, the most truly immortal being I'd ever met. Even Alfar's bodies eventually wore out. Yes, it took millennium. But they wore out. Blondie, however, had been kicking around the earth since the dawn of man. I don't think she thought much about death or mortality, except as an interesting and noble, if entirely foreign concept . . . like I might think of flying. Or going on a diet.

So it was easy for Blondie to talk about death and how to deal with it rearing its ugly head. It might be a fascinating concept for her, and presumably she could be killed under the right circumstances, but after all these years she wasn't exactly dancing with death. She and death weren't even sleeping in the same bedroom anymore.

I said none of these things. Instead I said, "Yes, well, there haven't been many opportunities for romance."

"Romance?" The Original chortled, taking me literally. "Romance? Of course there's no time for romance. But who needs it! Every single place we've stayed in has at least one good closet or wardrobe." She looked at me meaningfully. I looked back, confused, until my libido delicately pointed out the obvious.

Nearly choking on my own tongue, I looked over at Anyan, worried that he would be nodding along with Blondie's words. Maybe doing it in wardrobes was the thing to do when on a mission? It wasn't exactly finding Narnia, but it was still good use of the space.

Luckily, however, Anyan looked just as horrified at Blondie's suggestion as I knew I did.

Would he even fit in a wardrobe? I wondered.

I dunno, but I'm willing to find out. My libido said, always ready to take one for the team.

No, was my virtue's only response. But it was a resounding no.

"I remember this one battle, when there was no place that wasn't covered with carnage for us to go, so we climbed the trees instead..." I listened to the Original regale us with stories of warrior-tree-sex with only half my attention. The rest of me was thinking through what Blondie had said. The fact was, I desperately wanted to be with Anyan, but mostly because he was Anyan. If we'd stayed in Rockabill and not had all this drama, we would definitely have been lovers since the night Blondie interrupted us.

And yet, shouldn't things be different, considering everything that was going on? This was end of the world stuff we were dealing with. Then I kicked myself, mentally. Everything, after all, that I'd been involved with over the past year had felt huge—from finding out about my mom's supernatural heritage to becoming a part of this big conspiracy. There hadn't been a moment that didn't feel as if it were virtually the end of my world. So yeah, I had this new huge role, and there was this dragon running around, but I felt confident we'd handle it just as we had the other huge problems we'd dealt with. My role was certainly bigger now, but I was also stronger. Now that I thought about it, I felt less overwhelmed than I had with Ryu in those first days of our relationship, when I'd gone with him to the Compound. That had felt terrible— I'd been terrified, utterly alone, and totally out of my depth. Now I knew I was stronger, and I was used to overcoming big obstacles.

"You might be right about the romance," I blurted out, interrupting Blondie. "But I think we should still do things for the right reasons, rather than just because we can."

Blondie arched an eyebrow. I blushed. Anyan's nose twitched, then twitched again, then again. I thought it might twitch off.

The Original was just about to come back with a retort when her phone made a honking sound, her ringtone for a text message. Anyan passed it over.

"Hiral," she said. "He needs us to meet him. He wants us now . . . he says it's urgent." There was another honking sound and she moved the phone in order to see something horizontally rather than vertically, so it must have been a picture. Her face paled, she swore, and her phone was back in her pocket.

Next second, she leaned over the aisle towards our strange bedfellows contingent.

"Sorry folks. I've been playing by your rules, but desperate times and all that. I'll call you shortly, let you know where we are so you can meet back up with us and spy properly."

They looked confused as she held out her hands to Anyan and me. As soon as we took them, I felt the familiar *whoosh* of power that let me know we were being apparated. We ended up in the drawing room of the beautiful Brighton town house in which we'd stayed. The occupant, a wealthy nahual-halfling, looked up hastily from where he sat on his sofa, perusing the *Guardian*. Apparating was only really safe for places a person knew well, so we hadn't been able to go to Hiral directly. But the gwyllion must be in Brighton or Blondie wouldn't have brought us back here.

"Sorry," Blondie said, as the man put aside his paper. "We've got trouble at the Blackwell Estate. Can we borrow your car?"

Within minutes we were purring along in a beautiful old Rolls-Royce. Considering we'd destroyed everything else we'd touched—including entire buildings—since we'd crossed the pond, I was keeping my fingers crossed the car survived the trip. After driving for about thirty minutes down sleepy country roads, through a few villages that looked perfect for murder intrigue à la Agatha Christie, we pulled the car over and parked. Reading directions from her phone, Blondie led us out of the car and across the lovely, expansive field to our right. The very, very expansive field to our right.

We walked for at least as long as we were in the car, cutting across various fields. I could tell we were nearing the sea—my selkie senses tingling at the nearby ocean.

"Where are we going?" I asked, finally. Both Anyan and I were so used to following Blondie around we'd not bothered till the walk was starting to get a bit ridiculous. I was built for comfort, not for speed.

"Hiral's found the enemy," the Original said, grimly.

"Morrigan?" I asked.

"And her followers," she said.

"Followers?" Anyan asked.

Blondie's only response was a tight nod, her face grim. But she also passed Anyan her phone after tapping away at its screen.

The swearing that came out of his mouth was almost operatic in both tone and passion. I was almost afraid to look at what had made him so upset, when he handed me Blondie's cell.

Usually blessed with a thoroughly piratical panache for the expletives, I couldn't even swear at what I saw. Instead I stopped dead, staring.

"Are those . . . ?" I started, unable to continue.

"Supernatural warriors come to do the Red's bidding? Yes," Blondie said.

I handed her back her phone, scampering along beside her, praying that what we'd seen was a distortion of the truth. Some trick of Hiral's phone, or the distance, or something.

But as we climbed a steep, rocky little outcrop, coming to rest on our bellies so we could peer over it, my heart dropped.

That's no trick of the light, I thought. *That's an army.*

We were lying on an outcropping that overlooked a huge drop towards a valley cut deep into the British seaside. The ocean was to our right, bright and glittering in the very late-afternoon sun. The stone beach led up to a smoothly grassed lawn, and then up to a vast country estate.

Well, I assume the lawn was smoothly grassed. Or it had been. Because now, surrounding everything, were hundreds of tents and trailers. Everything was precisely lined up, and I could see—even from that distance— various supes sparring or working out around the perimeter of the encampment.

There were a crowd of satyrs all standing around as two of their lot sparred with each other, enchanting their horns so that they were doing the magical version of that *Wild America* rams-fighting scene.

In another group, goblins were paired off, dueling with a variety of nasty looking weapons, all charged and glowing with mojo.

Even in the skies, a group of harpies dove at one another, while another group of what looked like angels— human bodies paired with a motley assortment of wings— but I assumed were nahuals practiced flying.

"Wait, why are they all separated by faction?" I asked, finally processing what I was seeing.

"I dunno," Blondie responded, her pert features tight in a frown. "That's new. The Red and the White never cared about factions or anything like that, before. They were all for wholesale slaughter, after all."

"That must be the influence of Morrigan," Anyan said.

"Which means she *is* in there, somewhere," I added.

"It's like that, all around," squeaked a new voice: Hiral's.

He'd popped up right next to me—uncloaking or whatever he did, without any warning. I was so intent on the
sight in front of me, however, that I didn't even jump.

"Who are they?" I breathed. "And why are they here?"

"They're here to follow the Red and the White," said
the gwyllion. Even his funny, high-pitched voice sounded
grim.

"What do you mean, 'follow?'" Who the hell would be
stupid enough to hitch their wagon to primordial forces of
chaos?

Blondie sighed, shaking her head. I couldn't tell if she
was frustrated with my questions or the people below us.

"It happens every time. Some are religious zealots—
we're just like humans, and we have our nuts who want
to see the end of the world. Some just follow whatever
appears to be the most powerful thing in the room."

"And some are idiots," Anyan finished.

At that point, I felt a bit like I was having some sort of
medical issue. My skin had gone clammy and my heart
was beating incredibly quickly. All I could see were all
those supes...that army.

"So when you said war, you meant a *war*?" I asked, my
voice small.

"I'm afraid so," Blondie said.

I'd known things were serious, and I knew people
would die—I'd already seen a massive amount of
collateral damage from Morrigan's actions. But that had
been one person—albeit in the shape of a dragon. I
couldn't begin to fathom the chaos created by two armies
clashing.

Suddenly feeling overwhelmed, I turned to Anyan.

"I think I'm ready for that wardrobe now," I told him,

gravely. Even if we weren't going to have sex in it, it would make a good hiding spot.

"Well, that's not going to happen," Blondie interrupted. "This changes everything."

It speaks to the depths of my discomfiture that I did not call her Captain Obvious for that last statement.

"What do we do first?" Anyan asked, all business.

Blondie pursed her lips, clearly thinking. Then she nodded to herself.

"We make our own," was all she said, as she began sidling backwards down the outcropping, so that we didn't stand up on the ridge for all to see.

"Our own what?" I asked, following her movements.

"Our own army, Jane. And you've got to help."

CHAPTER TWENTY-ONE

Blondie didn't waste any time. The second we'd gotten on the train from Brighton to London, she'd been on the phone—cajoling, threatening, and bribing various supernatural leaders to get them to meet with her. And there were a lot of phone calls. In fact, the only reason she didn't bother wasting her energy apparating us directly to the capital was that she needed this meeting to be way bigger than the one we'd had before.

She wasn't dredging up a few extra soldiers. She was creating our own army.

When we did finally all meet, the room was hot and crowded, packed with people milling about. We were back in Bloomsbury, very close to where Anna Gibson's grave had stood, at the London Welsh Centre. It was a stout, grey-stone building, housing a huge, second-floor social club with space for dances, weddings, and the like. But even in that large space we were packed to the gills. Despite the number of people, however, everyone seemed to know everybody else, although I could tell they weren't necessarily all friendly. In fact, there was a lot of posturing, posing, and sizing one another up.

Speaking of sizing everyone up, I couldn't help but gawk at the spectacle of all the Great Island's rebel leaders contained in one room. I'd thought that the parties thrown at the Alfar Compound in my home Territory had been garish, but nothing could prepare me for the rebel version. Realizing now that things had been kept toned down for delicate Alfar sensibilities, I found myself spending a lot of time either blushing at, confused by, or in awe of the costumes and shapeshifting shenanigans pulled by the various halfling and pureblooded rebels milling about the room.

I'd never been to a fetish club, but I imagine that if every fetish in the world were represented in one room, that might look a little bit like what was on display tonight.

To be honest, the sight scared the shit out of me. Not because I was intimidated by the sexiness, but because of what we'd just seen at Morrigan's compound. The goblins she had on her side were practicing how to kill with vicious efficiency. Ours were dressed like leather daddies. And those minuscule harnesses weren't even good protection.

How were *these* creatures going to become our army?

So I tried to stay out of the way as I watched our satyrs toss their horns flirtatiously, and our harpies compare the feathers—as in the human fashion trend—in their hair, and our nahuals try to out-naked each other with their creative costuming, all the while trying hard not to think about those *other* satyrs, harpies, and nahuals. Luckily, dressed as I was in my very vanilla jeans and black

T-shirt, at first, I'd been mostly ignored. I didn't have the labrys out, I wasn't using any power, and I was used to blending into the background, so everyone ignored me in favor of keeping an eye on Blondie or Anyan.

I wish it could have stayed like that, but I should have known better.

Eventually, someone bothered to really see me. That person must have made the connection to the wallflower in front of them and the girl on television the day before. Soon I had a small half moon of curious onlookers surrounding me. Some stared openly, while others did so more surreptitiously, but all were wondering who I was and why I was there.

I ignored the scrutiny, focusing in on myself like I used to do in Rockabill, right after Jason's death and my release from the hospital, when everyone had been so gods awfully curious. Even so, I was relieved when Blondie shouted for everyone's attention, smoothly mounting a long trestle table in the middle of the floor that she could use as her speech's stump.

"Greetings comrades," she said, her strong voice carrying through the hall. "Thank you for coming so swiftly to my call. I wish this were less of an emergency, but the truth is that your speed was warranted."

"What's happening, Cyntaf?" shouted a voice from the far corner of the room. I was way too short to see anything in that crowd, but the voice sounded both scared and angry. "Was that the Red?"

"Yes," other voices shouted, various people demanding answers: what had happened, was that the Red, what were we going to do about all the human witnesses.

Blondie raised her hands, looking surprised. I don't

think she'd been expecting this much confrontation from her audience. For while she was apparently an old hat at fighting ancient evils, most of the people in this room wouldn't have been alive the last time she fought the Red and the White. Of course they were afraid, and of course they wanted answers.

"You have every right to ask questions," Blondie said. "And I'll do my best to respond. Yes, that creature you saw in Paris was the Red."

Briefly, Blondie lost control of the crowd again as everyone gasped, then started babbling. I heard people shouting "What do we do?" or "How do we fight her?" All of which were good questions.

I only hoped we could answer them.

"The Red is awake," Blondie shouted, repeating herself until the crowd quieted. "But the White is still asleep. And we need to keep it that way."

Beings looked nervously at one another, their faces betraying their skepticism.

"What can we do? We can't fight the Red!" shouted a tall goblin halfling. I could only see him because he was near me, and he stood about a head taller than everyone else. He had the yolk yellow eyes of his goblin ancestry, as well as the build, but otherwise he appeared human. For a second I thought of Jarl's Healer, the monstrous "doctor" who perpetrated awful crimes against humans, halflings, and purebloods alike. I wondered if I'd see the Healer again, and whether I or one of my friends would get to kill him.

Blondie frowned at the halfling's pessimism, her frown deepening as others took up the goblin's questions. This seemed to buoy him, and the goblin halfling called out again, "It'll destroy us without even trying. We can't fight it!"

"Not true," Blondie said. "We can fight it, and we must. Together! Together we must stand against this evil..."

The Original continued on in this vein, but she'd lost a large portion of her audience. I met Anyan's eyes, and his own features betrayed his concern. Normally Blondie was awesome at speeches and leading people, but she'd fallen apart on this one.

It's too much of a no-brainer for her, I realized. The Red and the White pop up and Blondie fights them. It's what she does. What everyone always did. But she was too good the last time...they were destroyed for so long that enough people had time to forget. Whole generations had been born since she last picked up the labrys, and the Red and the White had passed into legend. So people don't know what to do about them, anymore, the way they used to, and they didn't innately understand the threat, like they had.

While Blondie's natural charisma could sway a small group of people, as she had in Brighton, this was a huge crowd. They were feeding off of each other's skepticism rather than lapping up her natural ability to lead.

Blondie was still up there, speaking about joining together, and fighting the good fight, but I could tell no one was listening. They were all looking towards their own leaders: individual supes looking at what must have been their local leaders, the local leaders looking to the regional leaders, the regional leaders looking towards Jack, who stood near me. The rebel leader, for his part, was watching Blondie with a placid expression. He wasn't undermining her directly, but neither was he throwing his weight behind her.

Instead, he was letting her sink or swim on her own.

I sighed, pulling on Anyan's elbow. The barghest looked down at me, and then nodded before I spoke.

"You better do something," he rumbled. "Show 'em the ax or something, before we lose 'em."

I nodded, and then began to push my way slowly through the crowd. It took forever, and it was ridiculously slow going, but eventually I was at Blondie's table. I looked up at her enquiringly, and she almost appeared relieved. Taking my outstretched hand, she helped me up on to her platform.

"Hello folks," I said, repeating myself again and again until my voice was loud enough to carry over the whispers, grumblings, and smatterings of full-volume conversations.

"Help, please?" I asked Blondie. She nodded, and then she did what she would never have done for herself, as it was too cheap and she believed in winning people over with charisma rather than power.

But for me, maybe thinking I needed all the help I could get, she let her power free.

The first few rows of creatures took a visible step back, and even people in the back of the room scrunched up their faces like they were in a strong wind. For that's what it felt like—a sudden tornado in the room, emanating from Blondie.

Petals on a wet black bough, I thought, as Blondie subdued her mojo and, one by one, I saw all those faces turn to watch me expectantly.

"Um, hello everyone," I said, "Can you hear me?"

Faces amongst the crowd nodded, even as someone else grew impatient. "Who are you?" shouted a voice to my left. I couldn't help but smile.

"My name's Jane," I said. "And I've come to help you fight the Red and the White."

There was a sharp, uncomfortable silence until some-one laughed. That laugh spread through the room, till there was an almost universal roar of humor at the sight of me, claiming that I was there to defeat some legendary bad guys.

The laughter stopped just as quickly as it had started, however, when I pulled out the ax.

The labrys showed up in my hand, glowing like a star. Again exhibiting that uncanny sentience, as if it were aware of the situation, it didn't just light up. Instead it blossomed with power, a force so palpable that even Blondie was forced to back up a step.

This time, the people in the first few rows didn't move back, they were shoved.

Slowly, the force of the ax waned even as the light it emitted grew until everyone's eyes averted, including mine. Some of the beings that had once been crowded near the table and had already been shoved back now fell to their knees. Granted, it was less out of a desire to wor-ship me and more because of the bright light. Seeing them genuflecting like that made me distinctly uncomfortable, however, no matter the reason.

Only after I'd well and truly blinded everyone in the room did I dim the labrys, pulling in its power as I did so.

"Like I said, I'm Jane True. And I've come to help you fight the Red and the White."

With that, I waited. But this time, no one laughed.

"I'm not from here, obviously. I'm from America, from what used to be Orin and Morrigan's territory, on the East Coast. But I didn't know about any of that until recently. I didn't even know I was a halfling. And now I'm your champion."

All faces were turned towards me, now. I read an interesting mixture of emotions: curiosity, admiration, confusion, fear. I'd always hated public speaking—hated anything that drew attention to me. The thought of all those people watching made my mouth go dry, so instead there was only one face I spoke to, and that was Anyan's.

He was smiling at me from where he'd moved to lean against the wall, with his arms crossed. I concentrated on the curve of those lips, on how his eyes watched me with a combination of pride and affection. Imagining the crowd was all made of Anyans, I started to move more, trying to appear comfortable by making my table into a stage.

"You laughed at me, and I don't blame you. I would laugh at me. I'm easy to underestimate, but I also *didn't* want this. I didn't want *any* of it," I repeated, and for a second my voice caught. I regained control, and then continued.

"But it doesn't matter what I wanted. The woman you now know as the Red was my queen, and she used her power to betray everyone who trusted her. She killed indiscriminately—her own kind as well as those she looked down upon. She used her position to consolidate her power and to find what she needed to release the Red. And then she let that monster take over her own body."

I paused, looking around at everyone in the room. They were listening, some nodding along with my words, others still looking skeptical. I looked towards Anyan and he gave me an imperceptible little nod of encouragement.

"Without anyone ever knowing what she was up to, Morrigan nearly brought my territory to its knees. But that was before she was the Red. That was Morrigan, on her own. And now she's let herself become the vessel to a power so huge it can't die.

"What she wants now is to give that same power to her consort, Jarl. For those of you who don't know, Jarl was the front for Morrigan's evil. He was her left hand man, and he stood by as she killed their king, his brother. Imagine that evil man as the White?"

I strode over to one side of the table, looking down on that side of the crowd.

"In some ways I'm lucky," I told them. "Morrigan and Jarl left my territory." I crossed back over the table, to let that side see me. "My family is safe. My friends are safe. I have no reason to be here."

I moved back to the front of the table, looking around with as much gravitas as I could muster.

"But I *am* here. I'm here because Jarl and Morrigan need to be stopped. I wish I were here just because I want revenge, or because I'm such a good person that I want to help you. But that's not it. I'm here because I know that those two will never stop. They're starting here, certainly. They'll do what the Red and the White have always done, and destroy Britain. Destroy *your* friends, *your* families.

"But they're not just the Red and the White anymore."

I straightened the arm that held the ax, to bring it back into the picture, slowly raising its light and power like it was on a dimmer switch as I spoke.

"The Red is also Morrigan. She's smarter then she was. She's more resilient. And she's more ambitious. If she succeeds in making Jarl into the White, they won't self-destruct after Britain. They'll take the world.

"So I'm not fighting because I want to. I'm fighting

because I have to. Because otherwise those monsters are going to bring this world to its knees."

"But how can we fight them?" shouted a voice from my right. It wasn't antagonistic, this time, but serious. Whoever had yelled that question really meant it as just that—a question.

"We'll fight them the only ways we can," I said, my voice growing sad despite my intentions. "We'll fight them with everything we've got in us. And some of us will die. I might die. But we have no choice. It's either fight now, and have a chance at living, or die later, with everyone we love."

It wasn't exactly an optimistic speech, but it was the truth, and I realized that fact even as I said the words.

At that moment I realized I had to be in that room, with those people, telling them we had to fight.

It was my role. Which was as close to the idea of destiny as I was willing to get.

With that thought, the ax's light and the creature's power filled the room. For the first time since I'd arrived in the UK, I felt at peace. My calm radiated from me, taking tangible form with the creature's power and washing through the crowd so that more than a few people suddenly looked as if they'd follow me to their graves. But I knew whom I really needed to sway.

I looked over at Jack, who'd dropped his politician's facade. Instead, he was watching me with the intensity of a hawk, obviously assessing whatever it is that people like him assessed in these sorts of situations. I wished I could believe he was thinking through what was best for his people, but I'd become too cynical for that.

"What do you say?" I asked the crowd, although I

knew Jack really *was* the crowd. "Will you join me in this fight?"

Jack didn't reply, and all eyes went between the two of us. The silence was oppressive, and I felt sweat trickling down the back of my neck and down along my side.

"You have our support, halfling," rang out a clear voice.

The problem was, that voice wasn't Jack's. It had come from behind me, and it belonged to a whole 'nuther political contingency altogether.

I turned slowly, to where Luke and Griffin stood in the doorway that led to the stairs.

Rebels hissed and spat as the Alfar used their power to clear a route to where I stood on the table. Once beside me, they used their air and earth power to levitate themselves up next to me, and then they addressed the crowd.

"Rebel scum," Luke said in his flat voice, "your Leader greets you."

My eyes flew to Anyan's even as I sighed, internally. Leave it to an Alfar to offend everyone in the room through his salutation.

"You have no rights, here, Alfar usurper," countered Jack, as he strode towards us, his people moving around him in a way that expressed their solidarity.

"It is I who grant the rights in this territory, halfling," was Luke's reply. Jack jumped athletically up onto our trestle table, which wobbled alarmingly. Lyman didn't bother to join his brother, but he stationed himself at the end of our improvised stage in a way that left him free for action.

"Boys," I said, holding up my arms between the two to keep them away from each other. "This isn't time for a pissing contest."

Luke looked at me as if I were speaking Hungarian, but Griffin nodded. "True, Jane True," he said, and I wondered how long he'd waited to pull that one out. "That is not why our distinguished Leader has graced this rabble with his presence."

"Then why are you here?" I asked, before Jack could react.

"We are here to conscript you," Luke said, and I swear Griffin winced. Jack started to freak out just as the Alfar second interrupted.

"What my lord means," Griffin said, smoothly, "Is that we are here to throw in our lot with yours against the Red and the White."

"You will fight for us," Luke clarified, totally oblivious to his second's attempts at diplomacy. It would have been funny if it didn't make me want to punch Luke in the face.

"We will never fight for you," growled Jack, making me also want to punch *him* in the face. I looked to Griffin for help. He put a hand on his Leader's elbow, drawing him in to speak to him as I turned to Jack.

"We need them," I growled. "We need their power."

"Bollocks we need them. They'll use us as cannon fodder while they claim all the glory."

I frowned, seeing the wisdom of his words. In fact, that was exactly what the Alfar would try to do, just as they had in every other war.

Turning back to Luke and Griffin, I saw that Griffin had maneuvered himself to stand just in front of his leader. Luke, meanwhile, looked like he'd already forgotten why he was there in the first place.

"What are you offering?" I asked Griffin.

The Alfar second arched an eyebrow at me. His were

nearly as expressive as my former lover's, and this one clearly read, "and what makes you think I'm going to offer anything?"

"You need to offer something," I told the eyebrow, and the thick elf to which it was attached. "We need to go into this fight as equals."

"We will never be equals," scoffed Griffin.

I bit back the sharp retort I wanted to use, saying instead, "Fine. Then as partners, if not equals. We need to go into this as partners."

Griffin eyed me shrewdly. "You need us more than we need you. Why should we offer anything?"

I crossed my own arms over my chest, letting the labrys take center stage and amping up its power a bit.

"I think you do need me. You need the champion, at least. And the champion fights with the rebels."

Griffin eyed me, and then eyed Jack. The rebel leader looked surprised at my allegiance, but it had nothing to do with him. I'd be happy to leave Jack and his creepy brother in the lurch, but I wasn't letting his people suffer more than they had to.

"Fine," Griffin said, nodding at his leader. Luke dreamily extended a hand to Jack, but it was Griffin who spoke.

"For this fight, and for this fight only, we will act in partnership."

Jack eyed Luke's hand, but didn't take it. "What does this *partnership* consist of, exactly?" he asked.

"Strategies will be agreed upon by both parties," Griffin said, after a brief consultation with Luke, who didn't seem to care all that much. "Both sides will contribute what is deemed an equitable share of soldiers and power."

"But you can't do anything crazy like say that fifty halflings equals one Alfar or something," I warned. Griffin shot me a look that told me that was exactly what he'd planned to do. "You've got lots of non-Alfar troops to make up numbers. And you still need to contribute Alfar."

Griffin frowned, undoubtedly coming up with a million reasons not to trust Jack.

"Formal agreements can be struck later," I said, realizing this was silly. We would negotiate all day at this rate, and still the Alfar would manage to stick in something weaselly and horrible. Better formal contracts were drawn up, done with thought and care.

"Shake on an initial agreement to do real talks," I said. "Then go do the talks."

Jack and Griffin eyed each other, weighing up the enemy. Luke had been standing with his hand outstretched the entire time, and I was waiting for a pigeon to land on it.

Finally, however, Jack took Luke's hand and shook. Their was an odd combination of cheers and hisses from the crowd—probably cheers from people who realized how important the Alfar would be in a fight like this, and boos from people who would hate the Alfar no matter what.

I watched the two men shake, and I wondered if they meant it. A lot fewer people would die if we could all work together against Morrigan and Jarl.

But when I turned to step down off the table, I caught Lyman's expressions. He was still smiling, but the way the light was shining meant I could finally see his eyes that had been constantly hidden behind his glasses.

They burned with an emotion I couldn't read, stem-
ming from seeing his brother shaking hands with an
Alfar.

I hoped the emotions were positive ones, as we needed
every competent soldier we could get our hands on.

Or I'd just convinced a room full of people to become
dragon kibble.

CHAPTER TWENTY-TWO

After I'd done my little speech, and then stuck around to meet individual leaders and show off the labrys, Blondie took pity on me. I think she was also very pleased with my actions, as she apparated Anyan and me to a lovely stretch of stony beach. I had no idea where we were, and I didn't care. There was ocean, there was barghest, and after a day like that, I wanted both.

"Swim hard, recharge, and call me when you're ready. We'll leave for York tonight, but take your time," Blondie said, before apparating away with a soft pop and a shimmer of power.

"I officially declare this a date," I said, turning to Anyan. He cocked an eyebrow at me.

"Oh really?" he asked.

"Yes. I think I need a date right now. And by 'date' I mean you. It is our second date, right?" While I talked, I moved towards him.

"Yes, I think it would be. Why?"

" 'Cause you know what they say about what happens on third dates?" I took off my shirt.

"Um, yes, I think I do," he said, eyeballing my chest.

"Well, I'm easy. So let's consider this a third date, wrapped in a second date package. And speaking of package…"

Anyan's lips bowed in a wicked smile as I took off my bra. He moved towards me, and the look of lust in his eyes nearly knocked me over.

Needing very little encouragement, I took off my pants, kicking off my shoes as I did so. When the underwear joined everything else on the pebble beach, I started in on his clothing.

"Heartworm medicine," I said, shaking my head at the advertisement emblazoned upon his T-shirt. It was much better off lying on the ground, so I made sure it got there. Stat.

Unable to resist the sight of that chest in front of me, I ran my fingers down through the light smattering of hair on his pecs, converging my hands so my nails dragged gently down his happy trail. Stepping even closer, my mouth found his nipple as my hands found his belt.

"Are we finding a wardrobe?" Anyan asked, his voice even more gravelly than usual.

"No. But I do have plans for you. And you must not attempt to resist me. For I am the champion," I said, very seriously. His brow furrowed, and I think he would have interrupted me if I hadn't had my hands at his crotch—a powerful incentive to go with the flow. And then his pants were undone, as if by magic. I'd done it delicately, carefully on purpose. For some reason I didn't want to touch him that intimately till I had to—till we were just at that stage. I believed in doing things in stages.

I gently pushed my hands under his underwear's waistband on either hip, stroking his skin with flat palms as I pushed his jeans down his legs. His thighs were tight with muscle, the skin scratchy with hair but deliciously warm. Keeping my gaze locked on his, I saw the strain around his mouth as—already hard—he popped free of his underwear. The soft skin of my own belly was there to meet him, and I purposely rubbed my way up his body as I stood on tiptoe to kiss his chin and then his mouth. His hands found my ass, pulling me against him as he kissed me with soul-curling intensity. My libido stood fanning my virtue, which was about to faint.

I disengaged myself from Anyan's kiss, stepping back from his embrace, much to his evident consternation. But his look of confusion turned to anticipation as I knelt before him. I sat back on my heels, bending low to unlace his motorcycle boots, helping him step out of them and his pants so that he was entirely naked before me.

It was only then that I allowed myself to look up, taking in all that magnificent male beauty with the appreciation of a true connoisseur.

"People say that men have silly bodies," I said, just loud enough for him to hear. "But that's a terrible, horrible lie. You're so beautiful."

Anyan reached forward, stroking a hand through my hair as I continued to eat him up with my eyes. I think he was self-conscious, which was ridiculous.

He was perfect.

He was actually less cut than Ryu had been—less fitness model perfect and more real, more rugged. It's not

that Anyan wasn't in incredibly good shape—he was,
ropey muscles evident throughout his body. But he was
thicker, less defined but bigger, and very Anyan. His body
was like everything about him: it spoke of a man who
loved life and lived hard, but didn't live for fashion or
trends. His was a body carved by running, working, and
riding—not a body carved out in a gym by a personal
trainer.

My eyes were perusing him slowly, taking him all in—
from the grace of his smoothly muscled calf to the breadth
of his shoulder, but I was purposely keeping myself away
from the main event. Slowly, lingeringly, I allowed my
eyes to trace down that strong chest, down that flat stomach, to the magnificent cock that jutted, hard and proud
and tempting, right in front of me.

And by jutted, I mean I was pretty sure we were going
to need to hollow out one of my legs, or something, when
we did finally have sex. Don't get me wrong—he wasn't
porn-freak big and I didn't have a lot of experience. But
big is big, and I was a relatively small person.

"Oh puppy, I hope you have a shoehorn," I murmured.

"What?" he asked, as I took his hands to stand. He
watched me, curiously.

"Nothing. But before we do anything else, I need a
swim," I said. "After which, we can play."

I let a lazy finger trail down his chest before I pulled
him to the water. But he was immovable, his feet anchored
to the sand.

Curiously, I turned back to see a look of shame on his
face. He must have seen some of my answering worry
because he pulled me back against him, touching my face
gently.

"It's not you," he said. "It's just..."

I waited, but whatever he had to say must have been really serious, because he stayed silent. My imagination went supernova, imagining secret families, supernatural venereal diseases, a latex fetish that would soon find me encased in an inflatable cat suit.

"What is it?" I asked.

"It's just... erm..." He took a deep breath. "It's just..."

"Spit it out, puppy," I said, my voice threatening all sorts of punishments if he didn't start talking, and soon.

"I can't swim," he said, blurting it out so fast I could barely make out his words.

"You can't what?" I asked.

"I can't swim," he said, looking down at his feet and blushing almost purple.

I couldn't help it. I started giggling. Then I was laughing. I don't know if it was relief that I wasn't going to be donning an inflatable rubber romper, or that it was just a much needed break from the crazy stresses of the week, or if I couldn't believe that Anyan—Anyan who could do everything!—couldn't do this one thing I took entirely for granted.

"Are you kidding me?" I asked, when I'd finally stopped laughing.

"No," he said, obviously rather put out by my having treated his confession so lightly. "Why would I need to learn how to swim? I grew up in the Midwest, for the most part, where there wasn't a lot of water. And there's never any fights in the water."

"Yeah, the Sea Code," I said, referring to the set of rules the water-supernaturals lived by, partially because the Alfar never bothered to police the seas themselves.

"And I'm an earth and air elemental," Anyan complained. "Why would I go into all that...that...wet?"

"Oh, I hadn't thought of that." Of course he'd dislike the water, especially deep ocean water, as it left him cut off from recharging his powers.

"It's all right," I said, standing on tiptoes again to kiss him gently. He looked relieved, letting go of my hands to indicate I was free to swim without him.

I took them back up, determinedly.

"Oh, no," I said. "It's not all right you can't swim."

He looked stricken, causing me to giggle again.

"Which is why I'm going to teach you."

His eyes widened as I pulled him down the beach, his feet dragging like a man going to his own execution.

And here I'd always thought it was cats that didn't like the water.

A petrified barghest was no easier to move than if he really had been stone.

"It's okay, Anyan," I said, my voice as soothing and calm as I could make it. After all, I didn't want him to know I was contemplating how to knock his legs out from under him. "You're doing fine."

I was debating the relative merits of a karate chop compared with a kick to the back of knees, when Anyan took another, faltering step forward.

"Good puppy," I murmured. But he still looked as though he'd rather be anywhere else on the planet. Including Turkish prisons and/or very traditional baby showers, replete with games involving chocolate bars smeared in diapers.

And yes, there was a special circle of hell for whoever invented things like that.

Another few faltering steps forward and Anyan was nearly waist deep in the water. His hand in mine trembled, and I saw a shiver rack his body.

"Are you cold?" I asked, unsure whether he had forgotten to regulate his temperature or if he was afraid. I couldn't imagine him afraid.

"I'm fine," he said, through gritted teeth. Which meant he was scared.

Resisting the urge to say, "Awwwwww," at the sight of Anyan shaking like the cowardly lion, I instead squeezed his hand.

"You're doing beautifully," I repeated, urging him forward even more. Eventually, a thousand baby steps later, we were at an impasse. I was using my power to keep me afloat, but he was still standing, straining to as great a height as possible so his face was out of the water. Little waves kept splashing him, though, and he looked as miserable and bedraggled as I'd ever seen him.

"C'mon, puppy. Time to get your head wet."

He gave me a gimlet eye, steadfastly refusing to budge.

"It won't be bad. I'll make sure you're safe. This is my element, remember?"

His lips compressed even more and his nostrils flared, but he still didn't move.

I swam forward, wrapping myself around him, our wet bodies slick and soft against one another. Anyan probably found all that water less erotic than I did, but I kissed him anyway, letting my power envelop us both. The kiss was as raw and passionate as I could make it. Yes, I'd wanted to go swimming as I'd really needed a recharge. Yes, I'd interrupted our canoodling to drag him into the water, especially after I found out he couldn't swim. But that didn't mean I wasn't just about as horny as I'd ever been, my libido practically sitting in a corner and rocking it was so worked up. So I put all that emotion into my kiss—all my passion, my need for him, the fact I'd been aching for him for so long, now.

The fact that my bringing him into my ocean wasn't about torturing him, but about my sharing myself with him, before I shared myself with him.

Whether he gleaned any of my nuanced intentions from that kiss or not, something was definitely working. His mouth on mine was fierce, and his hands had moved to cup my buttocks. I wrapped my legs around him and kissed him for all I was worth, rubbing against him like I was part jellyfish.

He moved his right hand from my butt around to my front, slipping it down between us to find the aching flesh between my legs. I shuddered against him, careful not actually to gasp, as his fingers found my clit, rubbing gently before slipping inside of me.

I let him finger fuck me, keeping my eyes locked on his to let him see all of my pleasure. He thought that was hot, obviously. But keeping him distracted like that also meant that he hadn't noticed we'd slipped entirely underwater, my power keeping us "breathing" and afloat, at the same time anchoring us so we didn't float too far away on the tide.

Feeling the first waves of an orgasm building inside of me, I regretfully pushed away from him. It's not that I didn't want to come, but I didn't want to lose my carrot. If he wanted my body, he was going to have to swim for it.

It's only when I pushed away that he realized he was already well underwater. Those beautiful stern eyes widened, but my hand squeezed around his, reminding him that I was there, that we'd been underwater for a while, and that he was fine. When he'd calmed himself, I smiled, and then pulled him to the surface.

It was time for the lessons to begin.

When I'd suggested a swim, the last thing on earth I'd expected was to discover the barghest was a landlubber to the core. I'd pulled him to the water as more of a reflex action than anything else—the idea of Anyan not being able to swim was just unacceptable, and I'd reacted. It was as simple as that.

I would never have dreamed that it would be so incredibly awesome to give him that first lesson.

Maybe it was the role reversal—Anyan had always been the teacher and I'd always been the student. Maybe it was the simple fact that there we were, naked, in my element. Maybe it was the fact I loved swimming the way other people loved their children, and I got to teach something so important to me to someone who was becoming equally important. Whatever the combination of pleasures, I'd never felt closer to the barghest than at that moment.

After I showed him how to use his arms, Anyan's second lesson was how to kick his legs, and we were doing that age-old swim teacher technique where he was face down and horizontal in front of me. My arms were under his belly, helping him float and keeping him from actually swimming away. His arms were outstretched in front of him, his strong legs growing more confident in their paddling kicks. Again, whatever the combination of things, in that moment I fell utterly in love with that damned man. My heart swelled at seeing him vulnerable, and trusting me, and trying something new.

Admittedly, the feel of that gorgeous body in my arms probably didn't hurt, either.

When we were ready to try some real swimming, he took my hand again with that combination of trust and nervousness. I cocooned us with my power, and we swam together, side by side. Granted, my magic was doing most of the work, but he was still doing a fabulous job for his first time in the water. And he looked magnificent, all long lines and smooth flesh.

But this time, as much as I wanted his body, I realized how much I wanted his heart. I found that just as scary as he found the ocean.

Soon enough I could tell he was tiring, even with the help of my power. Swimming was hard, especially for someone who wasn't used to it, so we headed back towards shore.

A few strides up the pebbly beach and Anyan used his own power to create a lovely cushion of earth that he flopped down upon, pulling me down on top of him.

"You survived," I joked, gazing into his iron-grey eyes.

"I actually enjoyed that," Anyan said, his hands buried themselves in my hair. "Eventually," he added, as his mouth found mine.

I giggled, and then kissed him back thoroughly. The kiss quickly became something more, however—something heated, something raw. We'd had such a day, and I still had about a thousand emotions roiling inside me from that last meeting, especially. The swim had been a fabulous escape, yes. But it had also driven home all those times today I'd relied on Anyan, or let Anyan help me, or been buoyed by Anyan. He was a very, very good puppy.

And good puppies deserved a treat.

Placing small hands on his thighs, I shifted up onto my knees, maneuvering myself so that I knelt between Anyan's legs. He was half sitting up, undoubtedly wondering what I was playing at, and I kissed him one more time before beginning to move my lips down his body. I savored the taste of the sea on his skin as I moved down his chest, his belly, lingering over his hipbones, before moving lower.

Anyan was already hard, no mean feat after the cold water we'd just been swimming in. When I was where I wanted to be, I let my warm breath serve as a warning, causing him to give a low, throaty growl. *Another reason he deserves a treat*, I thought, as my tongue went next. I lapped gently at the drop of liquid on his tip, savoring the taste of him. Then I moved my head lower, seeking out his heavy balls with my mouth. He moaned, his hands tightening in my hair.

"Jane," he whispered, repeating my name as I sucked and licked at his soft, hair-brushed skin, "Oh, Jane."

When he was panting—and might have howled a few times—I moved back upward. My libido sang Lil Wayne's "Lollipop" as I did just that—treated him like he was ice cream on a hundred-degree day.

Granted, Anyan's Klondike Bar was more of an Entire Continent of Antarctica Bar, but still, if I was enjoying Anyan, Anyan was definitely enjoying me. The sounds he was making were driving me wild. That I'd made this strong man mewl like a kitten, and to know I was giving Anyan that much pleasure was almost too much for me.

He tried to pull me away, warning me that he was close, but that's what I wanted. I wanted him to break, to lose himself in me. So I answered his pleas by meeting his iron-grey gaze with my own eyes and taking him as deeply into my mouth as I could, reaching up a hand to caress him. His protests grew weaker as my lust swept up both of us, and the hands in my hair trying to pull me away now drew me tighter to him.

Soon enough he was shuddering, gasping my name. Then his body stiffened and he came, crying out inarticulately. I drank him down, loving the sound of his pleasure and the taste of him. I kept up the gentle strokes of my tongue and lips, until he pulled me up to kiss me roughly. Then he cuddled me close.

"You *are* easy," he said, after he'd gotten his breath back.

I chuckled, pinching his ribs gently in retribution.

"Hey, I like it," he amended, finding my lips with his, again. We kissed gently, then, for what felt like decades. His gentle, sucking kisses and the weight of his arms around me felt like home, and I could have lain there necking with him forever.

But Anyan had other ideas.

Too soon, he manhandled me till I was cradled in his arms, the top of my head tucked under his chin. He held me then, like that, for a long moment. This time I let myself think of everything we'd been through today: my knowing he was there for me in that crowd, him supporting me through everything, and then having him trust me swimming.

There were so many things I wanted to say to Anyan at that moment that I couldn't, or wouldn't, articulate. It had been harrowing enough wanting him. The idea of loving him was terrifying.

So instead I stroked a hand gently across his chest, swirling my fingertip gently around his nipple. He sighed with pleasure, his own big hand stroking down my side.

I raised my head to meet his gaze, kissing him lightly. He smiled at me.

"Thank you," he said. "I enjoyed that."

"I know you enjoyed that last bit," I teased. "But did you really like swimming?"

"I did. It was scary at first. But you're a good teacher." With those words, his lips twitched in a smile as his hand found my breast, squeezing gently. I sighed while he watched my mouth with hunger in his eyes.

"Yes, well, I learned from the best."

He smiled, acknowledging his role. Then he shifted me about so that I was lying across his lap, and he had full access to my body. For once I didn't resent being treated like a sack of flour. He could toss me around all he wanted if it meant I got to be sprawled like this before him.

He had one hand supporting my neck, but his other hand was free to rove my body. Anyan did so, his fingers gentle but insistent as he touched me everywhere: stroking my stomach, behind my knees, up the tops of my thighs, up and down my sides. It was like he was memorizing me. For my part, I let him see all of my reactions, holding nothing back.

"Now I'm going to give you your own lesson," he told me. "And then we're going to go back."

With those words, his fingers stroked the insides of my thighs. I shivered, opening myself to him.

"We're not going to have sex, yet," he said, pushing my knees even farther apart. I obliged, keeping faith with the word "yet."

"It's not that I don't want to, but this *is* only our second date. And I, for one, am not nearly as easy as you are."

Before I could protest, his fingers parted my folds, finding the center of my pleasure. He dipped into me, wetting his finger before gliding it against my clit. I gasped, clutching at his calf that lay underneath my arm.

"Instead, I want to get to know your body. Get to know everything that makes you scream. So that when we do have sex for the first time, I'll know exactly what you need."

"Anyan," I gasped, my overtaxed body already shuddering beneath him as his fingers drove me towards orgasm with insistent dexterity.

He smiled. It was an implacable, knowing, and very sexy smile.

"We'll start by discovering how many times you can come, Jane, with just my fingers. How's that for a lesson?"

I cried out, seeing stars, as he brought me for the first time that evening. I had one last coherent thought that night, before Anyan's clever hands broke me into a thousand pieces, putting me back together again only to break me apart one more time.

Teacher's going to deserve more than just an apple for this one.

CHAPTER TWENTY-THREE

And again," came Anyan's patient voice. Last night, those demanding "and agains" had driven me into paroxysm of pleasure, but this morning they were not nearly so fun. Arms aching, I raised the labrys and imitated the movements he'd taught me a few minutes ago, for what must have been the hundredth time. It was a complicated series of swipes using both sides of the double-headed ax, and it was by far the most difficult thing I'd learned yet. A lot of ax fighting seemed to consist mostly of bashing, but this took some technique.

"Excellent form," Anyan said, prowling around me in a circle and keeping his eyes on my body. There was nothing lewd in his gaze—he was fully in teacher mode. But I couldn't help but react to his eyes on me in a way that was very inappropriate for a student.

Focus Jane, my virtue warned. My libido backed down without a fight, rather surprisingly. I think it understood I would have to survive a battle with the Red in order to have as much sex as possible with Anyan.

We were already in York after a few hours drive in the white van through the dead of night. So far, I loved what I'd seen of the medieval walled city. York was a fabulous combination of old and new, with tons of history. We hadn't seen too much yet, but what I had was gorgeous.

Especially our current accommodation. We were staying at an awesome boutique hotel named after Winston Churchill. We didn't have the presidential suite—that went to Luke and Griffin. But we did have a really cute room with a four-poster bed. The hotel also had this amazing grand stairway that seemed to go up and up, forever, and had hugely tall bookcases on the ground floor, and then the walls were covered in pictures on the higher floors.

It also had a large lawn in front, perfect for weapons practice, and an adorable little smoking hut, complete with a telephone into the bar, for people to enjoy a cigar. I think even Churchill, himself, would have approved.

Smoking hut or sex hut? my libido queried, reminding me that it wanted to fit in some good bouts of nookie in case we were, indeed, killed.

Hush, I told it. *We have to practice.*

To be honest, the practice felt good. I'd been pretty sedentary, for me, for a while, so the workout was needed. It also felt like I was bonding with the labrys, in a weird way. The more time I spent with it, the more I felt like it approved of me. It was a strange feeling, and even weirder to think I cared whether an inanimate object liked me. And yet I couldn't help but like the labrys right back, an emotion made stronger by our time spent practicing.

"Good. You can stop now."

I brought my movements to a halt, working out a crick in my neck as I waited for more instructions.

"We've done lots of blade work, which is important. But remember your weapon has more than just the blade. It has the haft," and with this, Anyan came and stood behind me, encircling me in his arms as his hands grasped the warm wooden haft right below my own. "And it has the butt of the haft. Both are important, as offensive and defensive weapons."

Soon I was working on another set of drills, these focused on teaching me to use the haft of the ax to block an attack, and the butt as a pummeling tool. I couldn't help but smile, imagining knocking the wind out of Stuart, back in Rockabill, with a swift punch to the stomach using my labrys. It was petty, and I had way bigger, badder enemies, but the thought was still satisfying.

After a dozen rounds of that exercise, I was well and truly sweaty. When Anyan called it quits, I vanished the labrys with a pained grunt, holding out my hands for the barghest to heal. He came over and did so, watching me with a contented expression on his face.

"You did great, Jane. You move well."

"Thanks. But I think the ax helps me, to be honest."

"I think it does too. You're way better than you should be. But all that matters is if you're good. You want a beer?"

"Huh?" I asked, still focused on his compliments.

"Do you want a beer?"

"Um, sure," I said.

Anyan looked around to make sure no humans were watching us, and then he carefully pulled his glamour. We were standing in the middle of the front lawn of the hotel, but we'd been under a heavy glamour so no passersby could see. When we were all revealed, he headed in to the hotel. I gave one last long, full body stretch, then walked over to one of the tables set out on a small terrace next to the windows looking into the bar. I took a seat, leaning back with a contented sigh. The sun wasn't too strong, but it felt good on my skin. I very much missed basking on a rock after my swims.

After only a few minutes of me lapping up the warm day, Anyan was back with two pints of lager and a pint of water. I gratefully sucked down the water, and then started in on the pint.

We clinked glasses, and I sighed contentedly as I raised the drink to my lips.

"You were superb last night," Anyan said.

"I know," I said, archly, giving him a naughty smile.

"You were superb then, too, but I meant speaking to that crowd."

I shrugged. "Oh, that. I was all right. Blondie got everyone together, and everything."

"But still, you were great."

"Thanks. But…"

"Stop saying 'but' and take a compliment," Anyan interrupted, his affectionate tone undercutting the commanding nature of his words.

"Sorry," I said, with a self-deprecating laugh. "I'm bad about that. Seriously, though, I know I did a pretty good job. But you and Blondie are the ones that always set everything up. I'd be lost without you two."

"Yes, well, did you ever think we'd be lost without you?"

I took a long draught from my drink, feeling a warm flush of happiness heat my cheeks. Hearing that Blondie and Anyan thought of me as important kind of choked me up.

But not enough that I couldn't down about half of my pint in one go.

I hadn't been drinking at all recently, and I'd just been exercising on a light breakfast, so the pint went almost immediately to my head. Leaning back in my chair, I enjoyed my faint buzz as I smiled at Anyan.

"We'd all be lost without each other," I compromised. Anyan, however, didn't react, except to scoot his chair a bit closer and draw my legs up onto his lap. His fingers toyed with the laces on my new red champion's Converse as he focused his gaze on my feet.

"I'd definitely be lost without you," he said. I felt my throat close briefly at his words, my brain going into overtime that he'd just admitted what he had. But while what he said made me want to leap up and do the Hammer dance, his tone and the expression on his face told me he wasn't entirely happy about feeling the way he did.

"It's kind of scary, isn't it," I said, carefully. "Loving someone."

He looked up at me, acknowledging what I'd just hinted at, but not pressuring me to say more.

"It is," he said, stroking a gentle hand down my denim-covered calf.

"What happened, Anyan?"

The barghest remained silent, and he'd gone back to looking at my shoes. His hand lay heavily on my shin, seeming to weigh a ton.

"I know something had to have happened. The way you talk about love, and the things you've said about your past. You lost someone didn't you?" When he still didn't speak, I made another leap. "Does it have to do with Ryu?"

Anyan snorted, shaking his head. "It's nothing to do

with Ryu. Well, at least, not really. What happened was way before Ryu's time, although I guess it's at the heart of why he and I don't understand each other."

"So what did happen?"

"Are you sure you want to know?"

"I dunno ... did you kill all your wives, like Bluebeard, or something?"

The smile he gave me was sad. "No, nothing like that. But I did love someone, before."

It was my turn to snort derisively. "Of course you did, Anyan. I managed to love someone before, too, and I'm like an eighth of your age. I imagine you've cared for a lot of people in your lifetime."

"I know, I know," he said, placatingly. "It's just that some people don't like to hear about this stuff."

"As long as you don't take to scrapbooking albums of All the Women I've Loved Before, I'm fine hearing about your past. I want to know you. You know my entire life, and I know nothing about yours."

"You were a very cute baby," he said playfully, as I made an ick face.

"That's both disgusting and rather disturbing," I said. "Now spill."

He took a long pull from his pint, then, using my shin as a coaster, he started talking.

"First you have to understand where and when I was born. My parents were some of the first foreign supes to come over to the New World, and I was born here. There were lots of opportunities that came with moving, but things were definitely not settled in terms of politics. There were native forces to contend with, obviously. Plus powerful Alfar kept coming over in waves, thinking they'd be able to carve themselves out a kingdom. They often did, but then they had to defend it.

"My parents had come over with an initial wave from the human Scandinavia. Some, although not all, of the rumors of Viking explorers in the New World came from them. Anyway, they'd been seeking asylum away from the crazy leader of their own Territory, and had been taken in by the local native Alfar leader, who ran her Territory like a Native American tribe.

"The Alfar that followed in our wake, however, were strong, and soon my childhood leader fell. My parents and I were left without a place in our own Territory, so we moved east. There, we joined a human tribe that knew about supernaturals, and who sought out my parents as shamans.

"I loved living with the humans. There'd always been a lot of interplay between supes and the humans in my former territory, but living entirely amongst humans was different. Better. It's there I first learned I had a gift for art. I'd always been good with my hands, good at making things, and my parents apprenticed me to the weapons maker of the tribe. But he considered himself an artist. He's the one who first taught me where art comes from: that place in the soul where experience meets imagination. He also taught me to see beauty in the grotesque, and the grotesque in beauty. He was a good man."

Anyan's smile was affectionate, but his expression was distant. He was really immersing himself in this story. I had the feeling it was something he didn't share often, if at all, and he was as caught up in his seldom-explored memories as I was.

"It was his daughter whom I fell in love with. She was very young when I began my apprenticeship, and a very annoying little chit of a thing. She would drive her father and me crazy with her incessant whining about wanting to 'help.' He finally apprenticed her to a woman in the village, and we had some peace. I didn't pay any attention to her after that, until one day we're sitting near the fire and up walks this goddess, bearing food."

I kept my face neutral at the word "goddess," reminding myself that I'd asked for this. And I already knew the story couldn't end well.

"It was his daughter, of course, all grown up. I fell in love with her almost immediately. She was everything I wanted at the time. Keep in mind that I was as young as she was, in many ways, at least for my people. I was..." Here Anyan paused, pursing his lips as he thought about how to describe his youthful self.

"I was a lot like Ryu, actually. Which I think explains what happened between us, later. I was so ambitious. Already I was itching to make something more of myself, and by that point I was tired of always being with humans. There were so many things happening. The colonists were encroaching on our human tribe. There was talk of revolution amongst the colonists, themselves. And there were powerful Alfar throughout the continent, conquering all of the small, native territories and piecing together the huge ones we have now.

"As for the girl, she was everything a man like I was then could want. She was sweet, and kind, and gentle, and had been well trained to be a wife. She wanted nothing more than to serve, and she expected her husband to leave her for long periods of time."

I think I must have made a strangled sound, because Anyan looked up to grin at me.

"I warned you," he said. "But keep in mind this was lifetimes ago. I was a different man, then.

"Anyway, I took her as my wife, marrying her as her tribe's tradition called for. I loved her so much, and I vowed to protect her and her people. And between my parents and me, we did try. The colonists came, and we fought like demons. But when my parents were eventually killed— first my father, then my mother—we knew we were lost. The tribe moved on."

"Oh Anyan, I'm so sorry to hear about your parents."

He patted my leg, his smile sad. "Thank you, but it was a long time ago. And they died as warriors, which was all they'd ever wanted, really. They were an older generation, used to fighting. I can't imagine how they would have survived in today's world, had they made it."

"Still, I'm sorry. But I didn't mean to interrupt." Anyan gave me another gentle pat, before picking up where he'd left off.

"The tribe went west, but I was given another opportunity. Rumors of my abilities as a warrior had spread, and I was approached by the Alfar who would eventually create the Territory we live in, now. He wanted me to fight for him. At first I was reluctant, but he was so persuasive and he told me everything I wanted to hear. How I would lead, how I would finally be amongst my peers, about how I could become a real power in his kingdom.

"I let him sway me, and eventually I took my wife and moved into the interim Compound he'd created. It was only then I realized my devil's bargain. I was treated like a god, especially as I grew more skilled as warrior and, more important, as a spy. But my wife was treated like dirt, and only then did I learn of the newly arrived Alfar's contempt of humans, brought with them from the Old World. The Alfar that had always led us were close to the humans, and we all relied on one another. There was mutual respect. But the new Alfar brought none of that with them.

"Somehow, however, I was able to tell myself that everything was fine. My wife never complained, and I let myself believe it was because she was okay, even though I knew it was really because she was taught to bear suffering in silence. Looking back, I realize she had to have been miserable. But I ignored what should have been obvious, because I was happy and I was getting what I wanted."

Anyan's voice was soft, but I could hear his pain. He may not have talked about this issue often, but he'd obviously done a ton of pretty intense soul searching over the years.

"Everything came to a head in our newly forged Territory. We were under attack from the neighboring Alfar monarch, who was trying to do the same thing we were doing. They wanted our land; we wanted theirs. I was made into a general. I was so proud of myself and I loved being in command. I really felt like I was a part of something important, and I believed all of my Leader's claims that he loved me, too, as his best soldier. That's when my wife became pregnant.

"You know how hard it is for us to conceive, and my wife and I had been trying for years. She was over thirty by this time, a very old age considering the times. We'd given up on having children by then. So we were both surprised by the baby."

I felt my heart palpitate. Anyan had children? Why had he never told me?

Then I put together the fact I'd never heard about any children with the idea that this story didn't end well, and my heart sank. I was definitely going to be crying by the time this was over.

"I was ecstatic, and so was she. Children were as rare then as they are now, and we assumed everyone would be over the moon for us. But everyone seemed curiously distant about our good news. It was only later I understood they weren't happy about her being human. As a general, a leader within our Territory, I was supposed to lead by example, and knocking up humans wasn't on the agenda. That I loved her and that she was my wife didn't matter— all that mattered was that she was human.

"Of course I only understood this later. At the time, I just thought everyone was jealous of our fertility. She definitely must have known what would happen, though, which is why I hate myself for leaving her.

"But we were at war. So as much as I wanted to be with my wife, I also wanted to be with my warriors. No, that's a lie. As much as I wish I could claim I wanted to be with my wife as much as I wanted to be on the battlefield, the fact was that I wanted to fight more. I was so caught up in the power and the glory. I'd try to get back to my wife as much as I could, but she spent most of the pregnancy alone. Every time I'd see her, she'd have gotten so much bigger. And yet when I was with her, I wanted to get back to my leader, my war.

"She was very heavily pregnant when it all came to a head. I'd been home with her when we got word that everything was falling in place for a mission we'd been working on—an assassination, basically. We could end all the fighting, take the lands, and create our new world order, that sort of thing. As I prepared to leave that time, my wife asked me to stay.

"That was the only time she asked for anything, in our entire marriage. She asked me to stay. She didn't beg, she just asked. Of course I told her no, and she didn't even argue..." Anyan's voice broke as he said that, just for a second, and my heart broke with it. I waited patiently as he regained control.

"So I went to battle, and we won. We won everything. The other monarch was dead, and we had his territory. We owned the East, just as we'd dreamed."

"Is this the battle that the cartoon in your bathroom is about?" I asked.

"Yes," he said, his voice bitter. "It was a very important moment for our people."

"And your wife?"

"She was dead when I came home, carried in on the shoulders of my warriors. She was dead, as was my son." His voice was stone, but I could see pain in every lineament of his body, his face.

"How?" I asked. The one place a human woman giving birth at that time should have been safe was with the Alfar and their healers.

"They let her die," he said. "I learned then that every time I left, my wife was basically entirely ignored. She'd be given food if she went to the kitchens herself, but that was it. She took out her own chamber pots, cleaned her own rooms, and was entirely alone every time I was gone from her. I thought these people were my friends, my family, and they did that to my wife."

Even after all this time, his face had gone white with anger.

"When she went into labor, she was entirely alone. And she died alone, as did my son. Almost anyone in that Compound could have saved them without even lifting a finger, but no one did."

"Why?" I asked, completely baffled. I could understand Alfars hating humans and halflings, as I'd been on the receiving end of such prejudice myself. But why had they thought Anyan would have been fine with what they did?

"For all the reasons I learned to loathe them," he said. "Because they live one way of life and can't imagine any others. And because they can't *imagine* any other ways of living, they can't *accept* other ways of living. So if *they* didn't respect humans, of course *I* didn't respect humans. If *they* didn't think halflings should exist, they assumed *I* didn't really care about my human wife or our baby.

"But I did care. It was only because I was so heartbroken and exhausted that I didn't go on a murderous rampage when I found them lying in our bed. It was soaked with dried blood. She looked like she died in agony..."

Anyan's voice shook, and he fell silent. I took my legs off of his lap and scooched my chair closer, so I could cuddle against him. He kissed my forehead gently before continuing.

"I went...a bit crazy after that. That's another reason I felt for you so much after Jason died. I'd been there. Like I said, I was too exhausted to go on a rampage, so I just sort of turned inward. When I came out of it, everyone expected everything to be as it was. They had arranged a celebration, of all things. I left the Compound hours after I woke, vowing never to return.

"I did, of course. The Alfar that ruled us were heartless bastards, but they weren't really evil. So when ones that actually *were* evil did attack, I'd let myself get roped in. I fought *against* worse enemies, but I never fought *for* our leaders. That was a few Alfar ago, anyway, but still. I'm good at holding a grudge."

With that Anyan took my hand and played with my fingers, idly.

"So that's my story," he said.

"Thank you for telling me," I said, fervently. He now made so much more sense. Then I had another thought. "What was her name?"

He smiled at me, as if glad I asked.

"It was Manera. It means 'light.' And I named our son Samoset, before I buried him."

And that's when I lost it. I'd been processing everything as he spoke, and I'd welled up when he said the thing about understanding my pain at Jason's death. But hearing him say his wife's name, and knowing he'd had to name his son even as he buried him…

My face crumpled like a used Kleenex and fat tears started rolling down my cheeks.

"Shh," he whispered, drawing me close. "Shh…"

But I didn't shh. I buried my face in his chest and kept right on crying. For him and his ideals and the person he'd been. I also cried for the man he'd become, who carried such guilt for a boy's actions.

"I'm just so sorry you had to go through that," I said, feeling stupid for crying when it was his wife and child who'd been lost. But his expression was affectionate when I looked up at him.

"I know," he said, wiping away my tears with his thumb. "But these things happen all the time. And it definitely taught me about priorities."

"So why do you and Ryu hate each other?" I asked. I'd always been convinced there must have been a woman, or something.

Anyan chuckled. "I don't hate Ryu. He just reminds me so much of myself, before Manera died. I want to shake him. And I know he looks at me, and sees this person who could have everything he's always wanted, in terms of power and status. But I constantly hand it back when it's offered, and go back to my little cabin. He thinks I'm nuts."

"So he's never actually done anything?"

"I wouldn't say that. I had a bedmate during our last big campaign. She was beautiful, a vicious fighter, and a bit of a bitch. He seduced her away from me, thinking that I'd be devastated. But while I'd respected her and had been attracted to her, I didn't really *like* her all that much. So I wasn't bothered. I think that really pissed him off."

Torn between a pang of jealousy at the hot but bitchy woman he'd slept with and amusement at Ryu's attempted machinations, I settled on laughter.

"Oh, Ryu," I said. "That sounds like him."

"But I was not amused when he took up with you," the barghest said, his tone gone dark.

I blinked up at him. "Why not?"

"It was like with Manera," he said. "You were this girl. Sweet and definitely cute, but a girl. When I'd visited you in the hospital, I just wanted to comfort you. I didn't see you as a woman," he admitted. I reminded myself that he obviously did see me as a woman now, and kept my mouth shut.

"But then everything hit the fan, and I saw you with Ryu. I realized you'd grown up, and that you were awesome."

I gave my unladylike snort at his calling me awesome. "Yeah, awesome," I said.

"Seriously, you were. You'd recovered from this huge trauma, and you were still totally open. And you'd gone from cute to hot, and it was even sexier that you had no idea. I got so mad because I knew I could really see you, and that all Ryu saw was someone he thought he could shape into something else. I wanted to punch him in the face," he admitted.

"And is that when you realized you liked me?" I teased. Well, it was half-teasing. Part of me just really wanted to hear that he did, indeed, like me.

"Yes," he said, pulling me tight against him to kiss me gently. When he withdrew his lips, he kept his eyes on mine. "That's when I realized I liked you. And then you kicked my ass that time at my cabin, to make us take you with us when we investigated your mother's death, and I realized I more than just liked you."

If I'd felt a few palpitations before, now my heart practically seized. So it wasn't the sort of declaration of undying love heroes made heroines in books. But coming from Anyan, after everything he'd just told me, it felt bigger than that. More real.

So, typically, part of me wanted to run away, or make a joke, or maybe tip my chair over backwards to escape. But another part of me recognized that what we were facing now, with Morrigan, meant we didn't have time for games.

"I more than like you too," I said, softly, feeling my face go red with a mixture of embarrassment and trepidation.

"When?" was all he asked, before kissing me.

"For a while," I said, "I think. But swimming yesterday, the way you trusted me. I knew I was a goner."

"So just yesterday?" he asked, his eyebrow arching. "I've loved you for months, and you just realized yesterday?"

"Shut up," I told him, the word "love" echoing in my ears, before going in for a proper kiss.

We only came up for air when a couple entering the hotel went past, harumphing at our PDA session. We'd forgotten a glamour.

Holding hands, we both settled back in our chairs to finish our pints. We'd been through a lot in these last weeks, but I don't think any battle or confrontation that had happened up until now had felt this big.

And I, for one, finally felt like a winner.

CHAPTER TWENTY-FOUR

So why are they protesting, again?"

"Who knows," Blondie told me, with a sigh. "Humans are weird."

"You're human, technically," I reminded her.

"And I'm weird. Ergo..."

I shook my head slowly, and then went back to peering through the binoculars at York's cathedral, the Minster. It was a magnificent structure: all Gothic grandeur, replete with buttresses and stained glass and all the other necessary architectural trappings.

Marring its beauty, however, was a small, but growing, crowd of humans standing around holding protest signs against idolatry and the pope.

Meanwhile, we were standing atop Clifford's tower, a squat little structure smack on top of a hill in the center of York. We had a commanding view of the city, so it was the perfect place to come up with some strategies. In attendance were me, Blondie, Anyan, Griffin, Luke,

Lyman, Jack, and a newcomer whose presence very much surprised me.

"It's because the cathedral is Anglican, and the relics are technically Roman Catholic," said the newest member of our little group. "The Minster is the only non–Roman Catholic cathedral to host the remains, and there are those who see the bones as idolatry and their visit as popish interference."

We all processed what our new man said. It wasn't surprising that he knew so much about human religious politics, after all, as he was both human and part of the British government.

Daniel Rankin was a high-ranking member of a very secret part of either MI5 or MI6, I couldn't keep them straight. He was part of the hidden organization within the hidden organization that knew about supes, one of the liaisons between Britain's human ruling party and the Alfar Powers That Be. That said, Daniel also seemed to be on quite good terms with Jack, something Griffin noticed with narrow-eyed interest.

"Oh," I said, to Daniel. "That makes sense. Well, it doesn't, as I can't imagine wasting my day caring about where a bunch of old bones visit, but whatever."

Daniel gave me the same look he'd been giving me since we'd met a few hours earlier. The look said, "Who the hell are you, small woman, and what are you doing here?"

But other than that, he seemed like a nice man. And he certainly knew his stuff, at least when it came to the supes.

"So how is this going to work?" Blondie asked, crowding closer to Anyan to look at the pamphlet he had in his

hand. It was from the cathedral, and was for the visit of
the saint's remains. We'd taken one to help us strategize
how to steal said remains, or at least keep the Red from
stealing them.

Daniel, Jack, and Griffin crowded in as well, eager to
get their own two cents in, no doubt. Luke stayed back,
his eyes blank with Alfar distance, and Lyman kept his
focus on the Alfar leader. The wyvern-halfling had kept a
wary distance from Luke and Griffin, but had otherwise
gone along with our cobbled-together group's decisions.
For that he deserved credit. It must be incredibly difficult
to one day have to switch sides and work with your sworn
enemy. That said, it made me a little warm and fuzzy
inside at the thought of rebels, Alfar, and humans working together to defeat the Red.

"The remains arrive in York via armored hearse, from
where they were visiting in Leeds," read Anyan, from off
the pamphlet.

"I have a team of my strongest Alfar guarding that caravan," said Griffin. "Er, my Leader has a team. They have
been in place since we learned the bones' true identity.
They check in every half hour. So far they have seen
nothing."

"Morrigan's undoubtedly nursing some wounded pride
along with her actual wounds from our last encounter in
Paris. She'll be a little more cautious this time," said
Blondie.

"But she has to have people here too," I said. "Even if
she plans on swanning in at the last minute, they have to
be doing what we're doing."

Blondie nodded. "I've got Hiral on it. He's got a talent
for nosing out a spy."

"So the relics are in a caravan. What happens then?" Jack asked Anyan.

"When the relics arrive," Anyan read, "an honor guard removes them from the hearse and formally places them into their display case. Then there's a mass for invited local dignitaries and media, and then the exhibition begins."

"So when do you think Morrigan will make her move?" I asked.

Anyan shrugged. "She's definitely going to be more cautious after Paris."

"But she obviously doesn't care about being inconspicuous," Blondie warned.

"Yes, but being conspicuous did not work out so well for her last time," Griffin added. For once, I agreed with an Alfar.

"I don't think she'll let the dragon out again," I said. "At least not initially."

"Not after you whooped it," Anyan agreed, giving me a wink.

"How did you whoop it, again?" Daniel asked. His voice was carefully neutral, and I told myself he was only asking out of academic interest and not out of complete and utter disbelief.

"Water," I said. "The Red's made up of fire and air. It's vulnerable to water, at least in that dragon form. Not sure about its human form, although I would think it would be immune, then. Morrigan did take showers after all."

"I'll mobilize the local fire brigade," said Daniel. "They can be at the ready with hoses. And we've got the local territorial army ready to engage. We're using the excuse of the protesters to up the 'police presence,' but the police are really my men in disguise."

Daniel stepped away to make a few calls, and I caught Blondie watching him with a predatory smile on her face. Only then did I realize Daniel was a good-looking man, and I'd seen no sign of a wedding ring, or anything.

I think someone's going to end up in the wardrobe, I thought, as we turned back to the pamphlet.

"So we need lots of water, in case Morrigan comes as the Red. Fire engines will be good," I said, "but any chance we can do this…"

I trailed off as Blondie's phone went off. She pulled it out, telling us Hiral was calling.

"Hello?" she said. Then she listened, her lips curving into a smile.

"Brilliant news. We'll be there in fifteen. Keep an eye on him, yeah? Call me if he makes a move."

She hung up the phone and then beamed at us.

"Hiral's caught our spy. He's holed up right across from the Minster, keeping an eye on everything. He used the same kind of nullifier we use, so Hiral just looked for a blank spot."

I shook my head. "Clever Hiral."

"He is, at that," said Blondie, as we mobilized to troop down the hill. The walled inner city of York was tiny, and it was only a ten-minute walk to the Minster from Clifford's Tower, but it took us fifteen as we dropped off Jack and Luke at the hotel. Their seconds didn't want to risk them on an actual operation. Daniel insisted on coming with us, however, although I think that was partially because he just wanted to see some real mojo in action.

When our remaining group was just in sight of the Minster, Blondie stopped and scanned the locale.

"Dampen your magic," she warned, just as Hiral popped up right in front of us. I jumped about a foot in the air, only just managing not to thwap the little gwyllion with a mage ball.

His grin revealed rotten, black teeth, and he looked quite pleased with himself.

"Your man's up there, in the York Minster Hotel," he said, jerking a thumb towards a building a few blocks away. "He's in the loft room facing the cathedral, number thirty-two. There are two staircases, main and servants', and an elevator."

Having told us his info, the gwyllion strode off without a backwards glance.

"Good work, Hiral!" Blondie called after him, and he acknowledged her words with a perfunctory backwards flap of his hands.

Keeping our magic down, we moved towards the hotel individually or in groups of two, trying to blend in with the crowd or, better yet, stick to the shadows or under awnings of the buildings. We didn't want to tip off Morrigan's spy.

Once we were all huddled around the door of the building, we did a quick strategy session. I would take the elevator with Anyan while Blondie and Lyman took the main set of stairs, leaving Griffin and Daniel to take the back stairs. That way, even if our man decided to wander off just as we went in, he wouldn't get too far.

"What do we do when we get to the room?" I asked.

"What we usually do. Claim to be room service," said

Blondie, right before she turned on her heel and stalked forward into the building.

"Is that the whole plan?" I asked Anyan, as we headed to the elevator.

The barghest nodded, seemingly unperturbed by the fact our "plan" consisted of a single idea.

The elevator came soon enough, and we listened to it creak and groan—it was an old elevator—carefully keeping our magic banked. When the door pinged for the top floor, it opened up onto a small hallway. There was a sign marking that rooms thirty to thirty-four were to our right, so we headed that way. Motion behind us made me turn around, and I saw Blondie and Lyman breach the top of the stairs. When we got to the T in the hallway, Daniel and Griffin joined us from our right, and we all turned left as another sign, marked 33-34 with an arrow to the left, told us to do.

Soon we were all standing in a semicircle around Blondie, we looked at her expectantly. She rolled her eyes at us, and then stepped forward to give the door a confident knock.

All that greeted Blondie's knock was silence.

So she tried again, even firmer this time.

"Room service!" she called, using what I think was supposed to be a French accent but made her sound like she was imitating Pepe Le Pew.

Blondie had just raised her hand to knock one last time when Anyan hissed out a warning.

"Shields up!" he cried, pulling me backwards towards him even as he pushed the others away.

Then everything went dark as a huge mage ball came crashing through the hotel room door, slamming into the wall behind us with a fiery, smoking thud. Fire poured forth from where it had landed, blackening the hallway, but Anyan and Blondie were already pushing their way in the room. I could feel a huge exchange of power going on in front of me, and I pulled the human, Daniel, towards me and behind my shields. He was white-faced and wide-eyed, but he was also eagerly looking towards the door as if he wanted to get in there too.

Griffin made sure Daniel was safe with me, and then he walked forward, his Alfar power blossoming around him in a wave of force. Within a few seconds of him entering the room, Anyan shouted "All clear!" and in walked Daniel and me. Lyman came in last, protecting our backs.

"Holy shit," I said, before I started coughing. Someone wasn't getting their security deposit back. If they charged two hundred pounds for smoking in a room, I could only imagine what they charged for lighting the room on fire.

Then I saw who it was Griffin was pinning to the bed using his immense Alfar strength.

"Funny seeing you here, Graeme," I said, once I'd stopped coughing. As I walked towards the incubus, his beautiful blue eyes watched me, burning with malevolence from out of his waxen features.

The incubus wasn't able to move, so instead he spit on my shoe. It landed on the plastic toe of my Converse, luckily, which I wiped off easily enough on the carpet.

Add that to his bill, I thought.

"So you *are* working for Morrigan now," I said. "I figured you were. I hope she's paying you well because you've landed yourself in quite a pickle."

Graeme ignored me, but he wasn't able to ignore

Anyan's picking his head up by his hair and forcing him to look at Blondie.

"What are you doing here?" the Original asked, her voice mild. Yet the hair on my arms rose, nonetheless.

Blondie meant business.

"I repeat, what are you doing here?"

Graeme ignored her words, but it was Blondie's turn to get spat at. His aim was better, this time, and she had to use her magic to bat his phlegm ball away before it hit her face.

"You are going to tell me what I want to know," she said, acting like the spitting had never happened. "Either the easy way, with you volunteering the information, or the hard way, with me taking what I want. But you are going to tell me what I want to know."

"Fuck you, cunt," was all Graeme said.

"Um, it's actually pronounced cunt-*uph*," I replied, helpfully, as Blondie crossed the space to where Griffin kept Graeme pinned to the bed. She knelt in front of him, motioning for Anyan to hold his head up higher. Then she met the incubus's eyes, and I felt her reach out for Graeme with her power and her mind.

I knew Blondie hated doing the mental mojo on people—stripping out of them what she needed to know. But considering that Graeme did something far worse to his victims by making them crave his abuse, I couldn't help but feel that this time the ends more than justified the means.

"Tell me. What. You know," the Original ground out, her power expanding until I had to throw up shields to protect Daniel and me from being knocked over by it.

Graeme didn't stand a chance.

"She wants me to watch and report back what I see," he said, in an eerie, distant voice.

"Who does?" asked Blondie.

"Our Red Queen," Graeme answered.

"What are you watching for?"

"Signs of enemy movement. Rebel or Alfar. Anyone who would stand in our way."

"In your way for what?"

"The relics. The last remaining pieces of the White. When we have that, we can bring her consort back to her."

I glanced at Anyan, but he was too busy staring at the incubus.

"That's not what you really feel," Blondie said, after a full minute of staring at Graeme in silence. "Tell us what you feel."

Like chicken tonight? My brain murmured much to my libido's amusement and my virtue's chagrin.

Graeme gave the Original a murderous stare, but his mouth moved anyway.

"Jarl is unworthy," said the incubus, his voice snarled with rage. "He doesn't want his place as White, and he doesn't deserve it. He tries to betray our queen daily. He is a traitor to our cause."

"Is there someone else you had in mind, to be the White, other than Jarl?" asked Blondie, wryly.

Graeme didn't answer, and I felt Blondie's power push harder.

"Me," the incubus spat, eventually. "I would be her consort. We would rule the world . . ."

I couldn't help it. I laughed. Graeme's furious eyes shot towards me, but the anger in them only made me laugh harder.

"You idiot," I said. "She's not just the Red, she's also Morrigan. She'd never choose a mere incubus, an essence drinker, for a consort. Only an Alfar would do. You must know that."

Graeme's eyes narrowed, but I knew he had to realize what I said was the truth. Morrigan might be all mixed up with the Red, but she was still Morrigan.

I heard a grunt behind me, and I turned to see that Lyman had joined the party. He was nodding his head at what I said about Alfar purists, and for once he wasn't smiling.

"So how is Morrigan planning on gaining the relics?" Blondie asked, and Graeme's eyes flashed back to the Original. I felt his power push against hers, but he was no match. She overwhelmed him quickly and his gaze turned inward as he answered without intention.

"She'll come in as a penitent. She thinks you won't stop her. She thinks you won't risk revealing more of yourselves in front of the humans. She thinks she can walk in and take the relic, if it's low key and public, and that you'll let her leave with it, hoping to fight her where you won't be observed."

We all looked at each other, then Graeme, in disbelief.

"Is that it?" asked Griffin, eventually. "She will refrain from using that army she has amassed?"

Graeme, back to himself, stared at us with hatred. His silence answered our question.

"It's sort of genius," I said. "She knows we're scrambling, after her last public outing. And she thinks we'll do anything to keep any more proof from being aired. I'm assuming the arrival of the relic will be well publicized?"

Daniel nodded his head. "Coverage by all the national networks, and quite a few international ones, as well."

"So how do we keep her from succeeding?" I asked, rhetorically. No one answered.

"Thanks, Graeme," Blondie said, ruffling the incubus's blonde hair pseudo-affectionately as she plopped down beside him on the bed. "Now what do we do with you?"

For his part, the incubus looked crushed. He knew he'd given away the farm.

"I'll guard him," Lyman volunteered, glaring at Graeme malevolently. Blondie gave the wyvern-halfling a grateful smile.

"Thanks, Lyman," she said. Lyman's glasses flashed as he nodded to her. "Now, I'll apparate the prisoner, if you guys can just follow..."

"Why are you doing this?" Graeme asked, suddenly defiant again.

"Imprisoning you?" Blondie asked. "Because you're the bad guy. Of course, we'll have to figure out a way to control your tongue if your superiors call for a report..."

"Really, why are you doing this?" Graeme asked. "You're all going to die. You realize that, right?"

"That's enough," Blondie said, sharply. But Graeme was on a roll.

"Easy for you to say, Original," said the incubus. "You're the only one who's ever fought the Red and the White and lived. Every other warrior, even those who defeated them, died. That's what's going to happen to all of you. Even if you do win, even if you destroy the Red and the White, you will also die. It's happened to every other creature stupid enough to take them on. You're going to your deaths..."

Anything more that Graeme had to say was cut off as Blondie apparated him, Lyman, and herself out of the room with an audible pop.

That left the rest of us to stand in silence, Graeme's words echoing in our ears.

CHAPTER TWENTY-FIVE

Not wanting to put a damper on the evening, I tried for bluster.

"Graeme and his death threats. They're like Elvis and his pelvis."

Anyan and I were back at our hotel, having an early night in preparation for the arrival of the relics tomorrow. I was standing by the window, fiddling with the neck of my black, V-necked, long sleeved T-shirt, watching as he unlaced his heavy boots. He was sitting in an armchair in the corner, right underneath the window, and when he leaned back the soft evening sun shadowed his brooding features. When his boots were off, he leaned back in the chair, stretching his long legs out in front of him and wiggling his socked toes.

"At least Elvis had good hair," he said, eventually.

I moved from the window to the edge of the bed nearest the barghest.

Anyan stood, then took a long stride that brought him

to me. The room, after all, was very small and he was very big. He sat down, cuddling me close.

"Just because Graeme's right about the history doesn't mean we're all going to die," Anyan said, cutting to the chase in typically barghestian fashion. "Besides, there's only been one other champion, and she lived."

"But what about you? And Blondie? And all the rest? I've got the ax, but you guys have nothing."

Anyan smiled. "I wouldn't say I have nothing, Jane."

"I know. I didn't mean it that way. But it's hard not to worry."

His only response was to kiss my forehead. Wanting more, I raised my mouth to his and when his lips found mine it was all I could do to remember we were having a serious talk.

"I believe what I told everyone the other night. I do think we have to fight, and I know we can't just run away and avoid this. It'll come after us."

Anyan nodded, his hand finding the nape of my neck to knot my hair into a rough queue. By that point, I knew what was coming, but I still shuddered in pleasure when he tugged, none too gently.

"And I think I'm ready to be a hero now."

"You are?"

"Yup. I think I get it. It's about doing what I gotta do, not just because I have the ax, but because I can."

"That's deep."

"No, it's kinda stupid, but it's true," I said, laughing.

Anyan chuckled, pulling away just enough to look me in the eyes.

"So you're okay?"

"I wouldn't say that. I'm still terrified of the whole situation. Scared I'll let you down. Scared I'll do the wrong thing. Scared it'll all go to shit. But there's only one thing that really bothers me."

"What's that?"

I took a deep breath, finding my nerve. "That we haven't even had sex yet."

Anyan's lips twitched, but his expression was as predatory as it was amused.

"That is one situation that's easily remedied." His voice was husky.

Suddenly shy, I gave him a long side-eye. "Anyan Barghest," I said, my own voice tight with a combination of nervousness and lust, "are you suggesting we find a wardrobe?"

"Why do we need a wardrobe?" he asked, rhetorically, as he half-lifted, half-pulled me so we were lying, him hovering over me disconcertingly, "when we have this lovely bed?"

Then he kissed me, his lips gentle at first, then more demanding as I wrapped my arms around him, pulling him tighter against me.

I licked at his lips, seeking entrance, and he let me in, growling as my tongue slid against his. Our kiss deepened exponentially and my hands found his hair, dragging him infinitesimally closer to me as if I couldn't get enough.

Because I couldn't, in truth, get enough.

Finally, however, he broke away. We stared into each other's eyes, each of us panting.

"Are you sure?" he asked. "We're not rushing things?"

I thought of how long we'd known each other, how long I'd wanted him, and how much he meant to me. My libido suggested I reach down and give him a wedgie for asking a stupid question, but I refrained.

"Yes," I said, simply. "I'm very sure."

And I raised my lips to his, again, and this time I knew there was no going back, for either of us.

He was the first to break our kiss, his hungry mouth finding the sensitive skin of my neck. Anyan's jaw was rough with his usual light scruff, and I giggled as he tickled me inadvertently. The giggle soon turned into a gasp, however, as he sucked and bit gently at my neck, his tender ministrations growing rougher when I asked, breathlessly, for more.

My demands were silenced, however, by his mouth again finding mine as he moved on top of me.

I'd never wanted to be naked so badly in my life and I fervently wished that sudden nakedness was my superpower.

It wasn't, however, but that was easily remedied. My legs wrapped around his hips as my hands went to his grey flannel button up, his fashion concession to the damp English weather. I unbuttoned it quickly, pulling it off of him when he let me go long enough to do so. Before he could wrap his arms back around me, I grabbed the bottom of his T-shirt—one he'd picked up here, advertising the Crufts dog show—and swiftly pulled that over his head.

My hands stroked down his chest, loving the feel of his warm skin. His chest hair crinkled under my palms, and I felt as if I could pet him all day. But when my fingers found his nipples, pinching lightly, the look of pleasure that suffused his face, along with the low, throaty growl he gave me, made me want so much more.

He kissed me again as I stroked his chest, his sides, his back, thrilling again at the moan he sounded when my fingernails raked lightly over his back. My hips rose against him as my thighs pulled him tighter to me. His teeth found my neck and I answered his lust with a deeper set of scratches down his back.

It was my turn to moan as his mouth sucked away the sting of his bite, and then he was pushing my shirt over my head. I made short work of getting my bra off, Anyan's hungry eyes watching my body as I did so. Seconds after my flesh was bared to him, his mouth was at my nipples—sucking and pulling, nipping and biting—my hands buried in his hair as I pulled him tight to me, moaning a steady contralto in harmony to the aria of pleasure rushing through my body.

But what was good for the goose was good for the gander, and I'd wanted the barghest for far too long to lie back and let him have all the fun.

Using my puny arms and my powerful magic, I pushed him onto his back so my mouth could rove over his torso. I discovered, to my delight, that while his nipples were sensitive, so was his neck, and the taught skin over his ribs, and the softer flesh above his delicious hip bones. He responded to every questing foray of my mouth, tongue, and teeth with noises that set my body and my heart aflame.

I licked my way up his chest, back to his neck. Feathering my own kisses over his face, my hands went to work on his belt buckle. Busy returning my kisses and in no hurry, he let me fumble, his hands cupping my breasts while his fingers pinched gently at my nipples.

Finally his belt was undone, and then his pants. I had

to pull away, at that point, kneeling next to Anyan as I carefully lowered his zipper. He was too big to blithely pull down his zipper without risking a trip to the emergency room.

Very, very big, I thought, as I finally had him unzipped. The tip of him winked up at me from where it had escaped his black boxer briefs.

You're the champion, I reminded myself. *You have to fight a dragon. You're not allowed to be scared of a penis.*

So I stretched out next to Anyan, my small hand reaching down to grasp him through his underpants. We both gasped at the contact, him in pleasure and me, shortly thereafter, in surprise.

For, after a few soft strokes, I realized that it was still growing under my hand.

"Jane," Anyan said with a snarl, pulling my hand away for the few seconds it took for him to shimmy out of the rest of his clothes, including his socks. When he was naked, he lay back where he'd been, replacing my hand on his cock.

His skin was so hot, so soft and delicate over the hardness, and the tip so wet that my mouth watered. I was also, however, confronted again by the size of him.

Heroes do often walk like they just got off a horse, I told myself, while I tried to figure out the logistics of this situation. *Maybe if I had some ribs removed, and rearranged my internal organs . . .*

Some of my trepidation must have shown through in my gaze. Anyan stroked a finger down my cheek.

"Are you all right?"

I looked up at him, my hand still moving on him.

"It's just . . . you're rather large," I admitted, feeling like an idiot.

He smiled a rather smug little moue, before his hand closed over mine on his shaft. He pumped our hands over himself, letting me feel all that hard flesh, closing his eyes as pleasure suffused his face.

Then he pulled my hand away before moving to flip me onto my back. He was over me again, kissing me as he began undoing my own jeans.

"I'm not that big," he said, "but don't worry. I won't hurt you."

When my jeans were undone his lips left mine. Then he knelt up, scooting backward till he could pull off my Converse and socks. Then I put my feet flat on the bed, lifting my hips obligingly as he pulled down my pants and my purple cotton thong.

When I was naked before him, his eyes feasted over me, followed by his hands roving over my body.

"The trick," he said, leaning down to whisper in my ear, "is to get you as wet and ready as you can possibly be."

I *meep*ed, an undignified little sound that was about all my overtaxed brain could come up with. It made him smile again with a combination of hunger and affection, as his gaze locked on my mouth. His expression swiftly changed to one of feral hunger, so I was hardly surprised when he crawled forward just enough to bring his hard length within inches of my lips. His hands were still roving my body as I licked at him, loving his moans as my hand found him to draw him further in, caressing him with my tongue.

Anyan's hands remained busy, and he was so much longer than me that he was barely even reaching to find the heat between my legs. Although it was still a shock when he first touched me, his thick fingers suddenly sliding between my slick folds.

"So wet," I heard him murmur. I groaned my assent around his flesh, wondering if I'd ever been this turned on in my entire life.

But his clever fingers moving against me made me wetter still, and I wondered whether we'd need to build an ark.

When his fingers skidded against my clit, I was lost, and then those same fingers were inside of me, stretching me delightfully. My mouth lost him as my back arched, pleasure coursing through me.

Anyan took that opportunity to pull me up the bed, giving himself room to kneel between my thighs. His mouth on me made me gasp, then cry out, fireworks going off behind my eyelids. He had learned well, that night when his fingers had brought me, over and over, to the peak of my pleasure, before pushing me over the edge to let me tumble into orgasm. So his mouth moved against me with delicious confidence, knowing exactly what I needed to come.

But nothing had prepared me for what he did next.

At first I thought he was just using a glamour to muffle my nearly incessant whimpers, the touch of his power was so whisper-soft against my skin. The hairs on my body rose, but the feathering didn't stop. If anything, it got stronger, more sure.

He's doing it on purpose, I realized, as fingers of power moved over my flesh.

Stroking, kneading, tickling little hands caressed every inch of me, even as Anyan's actual hands were anchored on my inner thighs, pinning me open as he feasted on my sex.

Lost in a haze of sensation, I felt ghost fingers pinch my nipples and stroke through my hair, while Anyan's real fingers dipped into me. Another hand caressed my back; while another held my throat gently, possessively; and still other hands were on my buttocks, massaging them before spreading me to stroke intimately.

I couldn't take it. I broke, shattering into a thousand pieces as my orgasm overtook me. And still those fingers worked me, sustaining my pleasure until I thought I really would break.

Pulling Anyan up by his hair, I kissed the smug smile off his face, tasting myself on his lips.

"Good gods, puppy," I said, my voice harsh from crying out so many times. "Are you trying to kill me?"

Chuckling, Anyan answered me by spreading my thighs farther apart with his big hands.

"I told you," he said, his iron-grey gaze latched on to my own eyes. "The trick is to get you so wet, so ready..."

And with that, he pushed into me.

His magic went first, preparing me for him. My skin tingled delightfully, reacting to his mojo, as his power spread me open for him, stretching me with a delicious ache. But nothing could match the feeling of him—his skin, his soft flesh stretched over hardness—pushing into me.

I cried out and he held me close, kissing my eyelids, my forehead, my cheeks and chin. He dissolved his fingers of power, then, so it was just us in that bed. Just our hearts beating wildly against each other's chests, just our sweat mingling while our blood pounded in our ears, just our own whimpers and cries echoing in the small space.

I felt, for a split second, as he moved in me, like I didn't know where he ended and I began. We'd go back to being Anyan and Jane when this was over, surely. But for that moment, we were one being, intent on each other's pleasure.

He was crashing into me now, letting himself go as his own need mounted. I answered him thrust for thrust, pulling him into me deeper, wondering where I was putting him even as I squeezed myself around him. Anyan's groans filled my ears as his fingers found the center of my own pleasure, stroking me roughly till I came, my cries mingling with him as he, too, lost himself in climax.

We lay there in a tangle of sweat-streaked limbs, our hair clinging damply to our necks, our foreheads, unable to move. I was just happy to still be breathing.

But eventually my leg started to fall asleep, and I pushed the barghest gently. He moved, sliding out of me and shifting around so that I was lying half on his chest, his arms draped loosely around me.

His heart thundered beneath my ear, but the look on his face was that of a very contented man.

Wondering if my own expression matched his, I reached out tentative fingers to stroke down his outrageous, gorgeously big nose. He snapped at them playfully with his teeth, and then gathered my hand to his lips for a kiss before lowering it to his chest.

He played with my fingers as he sighed.

"And now, I can die happy," he said. He'd meant it as a joke, but something dark in his tone made me realize it wasn't. I also realized just how I felt about that idea.

"We're not going to die," I told him. And I meant it. I wasn't saying it to be conciliatory, or placating, or because I thought it's what I should say. I said it because I meant it—there was no way in hell I was leaving him, or letting him leave me.

"We are not going to die," I repeated, and this time Anyan nodded, although he was probably just humoring me.

"I love you," he said, cuddling me closer.

I stroked a hand down his chest, smiling lovingly as I looked him full in the face.

"Well I just love your doggy style," I told him. His eyes snapped open and he frowned at me.

"I'm kidding. I love you too."

He sighed. "It's too late. You said you loved my doggy style, and yet we've only done missionary."

His hands ran down my flanks as he slid me off of him, moving me onto my stomach.

"I can now think of only one way to preserve your honor," he told me, his breath tickling my ear as he rubbed his body against mine from behind.

"And that's make it a reality."

His teeth found my nape as his hands slipped, once again, between my legs. For the second time that night, I saw stars.

And then he proceeded to prove to me, twice no less, that I wasn't lying.

I really did love his doggy style.

CHAPTER TWENTY-SIX

My wig itched.

It was short, curly, and brown. Coupled with large sunglasses and a baggy overcoat, my only accessory a large sign that read "Down with Idolatry!" I looked quite the nutter.

Which was our intention. After a long night of strategizing, we'd decided to trump Morrigan's disguising herself as a penitent by disguising ourselves as protesters.

Meanwhile, we were slowly but surely taking care of the real protesters.

"You're hungry and your feet hurt," whispered Blondie to the woman next to me, as Anyan suggested to another that he might have forgotten to turn off his oven that morning. I watched the woman's hand go to her stomach as she looked around for a café, her weight shifting on suddenly sore feet, and the man looked up, startled, before dashing away from the crowd. He was quickly replaced by one of our own.

The tiny puffs of magic used by my friends were covered up, meanwhile, by Griffin standing front and center near the news crews. He was sending out a massive glamour, but even that glamour was a ruse.

The news crews, you see, were really Daniel's men, with massive guns disguised as cameras. The real news crews had been taken care of that morning, sent on various mad dashes across Britain chasing after stories suggested by my supernatural friends.

So Griffin was acting very official, surrounded by a small cadre of other Alfar, and glamouring the shit out of the area. It wasn't to keep off prying eyes, however. It was really to act as a shield for any small magics the rest of us might do, clearing the rest of the area of civilians and replacing their numbers with our own. Any stray tourists were taken care of by placing small, but effective, repulsion wards around the very far perimeter of the area. They looked like tiny mage lights placed on random flat surfaces, but they sent off a powerful glamour that made humans not want to wander near. As for those living or working near the cathedral, Daniel's "police" had already warned them to stay indoors and to close up shop, with the excuse that there was intelligence the protesters planned on using violence to stop the relics from arriving safely. For most of them, that had been enough to keep them away for the day, and the rest decided it was a good idea to go home once the repulsion wards had gone into place.

So we'd created a supernatural playground out of the cathedral grounds. Even the Minster's staff had been replaced by those of our supes who could effectively dampen their magic for long periods of time.

Not that anything could be felt over Griffin's outrageous waves of power.

I couldn't help but smile as I watched him moving dramatically about the perimeter, waving his arms and gesticulating madly. The theatrics had been his idea, and I think he was enjoying them despite his protestations they were just "to distract the enemy."

Blondie, meanwhile, was perched precariously and very visibly on the very top spire of the Minster. Our goal was to make the Red think everything was just as she'd planned it: a big human event, surrounded by human media and tons of spectators sporting cameras. Instead, everyone in that square was somehow ours, including the apparently random people dressed as tourists, strolling through and pointing at the "protesters." In fact, they were all our people, or Daniel's, and the fire trucks were parked close by and ready to roll.

"Ten minutes till the cavalcade arrives," Anyan murmured from next to me. He was dressed in a Halloween monk's robe, hood up, and carrying a sign suggesting the Minster go ahead and invite the pope to tea.

I nodded, and then found myself yawning inappropriately.

"Tired?" Anyan asked.

I wasn't feeling weak, as I'd had a filthy but recharging swim in York's river Ouse this morning, so I was more than brimming with power. But I did feel a bit sleepy.

"Someone kept me up all night," I reminded the barghest.

"Whatever," he replied, teasingly. "Someone kept *me* up all night, but you don't hear any complaints."

"It's because I did all the work," I lied, loving how his long nose twitched at me in irritation.

"I'm gonna give you a workout, later," he said, in what was possibly the worst threat ever made.

"You better. Or I'm getting my money back..."

Before I could finish, our phones beeped with a message. It was Blondie. She'd spotted the cavalcade bearing the relics. A second later, we received another text from Griffin, saying the relics were arriving early.

"Any sign of Morrigan?" I wrote back to both of them, receiving negative replies from both Original and Alfar.

"Where are you hiding?" I murmured, peering about me cautiously.

On cue, everyone started moving about. First our people serving as cathedral attendants started fussing with the carpets and other fripperies they'd laid out to invite in the relics. They were doing everything to the letter, just as the cathedral had planned, which meant welcoming the dead saint like he was a living dignitary rather than a pile of old bones. Everyone was kitted out in the real religious men's fanciest robes.

You can't greet a skeleton in jeans, after all, I thought, but then I realized how silly my cynicism was. After all, yes, the pile of old bones the people thought they were worshiping was really just that: a pile of old bones. Meanwhile, we were ready to fight and die over another pile of old bones, these imbued with tremendous power and evil. It was hard to be too critical when the humans weren't really wrong, they were just placing their bets on the incorrect pile of bones.

With the cathedral's attendants getting ready to greet the cavalcade, the rest of our people could also adjust themselves accordingly. Daniel's soldiers began fussing with their fake cameras, no doubt throwing off safety mechanisms, and gearing up for a firefight. Those of us posing as protesters fanned out, waving our signs angrily but being careful to keep our magic dampened.

Griffin's Alfar, however, did no such thing. Their own glamouring power swept even more powerfully over the square. It made sense they'd do so, knowing that some kind of fight was probably imminent. But it also meant that any one supe who slipped and flared magic where it shouldn't be would have their signature camouflaged by all the power whipping about the square.

It was then that I saw her.

I pinched Anyan hard, and he jumped before realizing I wasn't just torturing him. He followed the finger that I'd pointed surreptitiously towards the far corner of the square, swearing softly.

Morrigan, dressed in a pretty white sundress, was watching everyone mill around from under the safety of a parasol.

She looked absolutely enchanting—her long blonde hair swirling down her back and her expression one of rapt attention. I also *felt* enchanted, part of me wanting to make my way towards her, to touch her, to kneel at her feet. But now that I knew those feelings were really the Red's unholy charisma, they were easy to ignore. I did notice, however, that the creatures nearest her—under strict orders not to confront the Red should she appear— all too unconsciously stepped towards her. I doubted if any even recognized her, as most only had our verbal descriptions of Morrigan. And yet still they couldn't help but draw nearer, peering around as if they were suddenly reminded of something.

"Here come the bones," murmured a voice next to me.

It was Magog, her wings contained in an overcoat similar to mine and her mad emo hair wrapped under a floral head scarf. She looked like a local from the *League of Gentlemen*.

Gun-cameras pivoted as the first car in the cavalcade entered the cathedral's grounds from between the buildings flanking it on all sides. It was a black sedan, and another followed it. Finally there came a hearse, with two more dark sedans guarding its rear.

All eyes were on the caravan except for mine. I was texting Morrigan's whereabouts to Griffin and Blondie in case they hadn't seen her, while I kept my own eyes glued to her white-clad figure.

"Got her," texted back Blondie, even as I saw in my peripheral vision Griffin scan the crowd, find me, and give me an almost imperceptible nod.

Our former-queen-turned-dragon was sauntering towards the doors of the Minster at a leisurely pace, but the face she turned towards the hearse was filled with such utter love and longing that I might have cried, had I not known she was mourning a lover with whom she planned to destroy the world.

Again.

So it didn't take much hardening of the heart to surge forward with the other protesters, waving our signs and chanting some gibberish about idolatry. Meanwhile, some of our strongest rebels and Alfar soldiers—dressed as penitents, priests, nuns, and local dignitaries—began to form an orderly line to attend the small private mass that was supposed to be conducted before the relics officially opened to the public.

Ballsy as ever, Morrigan joined them, smiling around

beatifically at those who looked too closely. Everyone
behaved beautifully, however, not betraying a trace of
supernatural power or letting the proximity of the Red
panic them in any way.

Our plan was to get Morrigan in the church, put it
under magical lock down, and take her out then. As everyone started to process inside, Anyan and I would scamper
over to a side door where I could confront Morrigan with
the labrys. If all went the way it was supposed to, Morrigan would already be taken down by the welcoming party
awaiting her, which included Jack and Luke, along with
Blondie and some other very strong Alfar. I'd just have to
do some hacking with the ax, a job that I wasn't looking
forward to but that I was pretty sure I could handle. Violence wasn't in my nature, but Morrigan had crossed too
many lines. If she hadn't been evil before, as the woman
who would murder her own husband, she was certainly
evil now that she'd invited the Red to share her body.

"They're going in," Anyan murmured. "You ready?"

I nodded, and we started to make our way through our
own people towards the side entrance. Everyone moved
aside, quickly filling back in the space left by our passing
so that we moved through the crowd invisibly. Anyan kept
craning his head around to keep an eye on things, reporting back to me.

"Everyone's lined up to watch the bones. They're
nearly to the door. Morrigan's at the head of the line to go
in. She's only a few feet from the relics, but she's not making a move yet."

We kept walking, nearing the side door that would take
us in when we were called.

"Blondie's coming down. She's going in the back

door." The barghest took a deep breath, tasting the air. "Jack and Luke are already there, waiting."

"It's all going according to plan," I said, then remembered to rap myself on the head, to knock on wood. I had just raised my fist, in fact, when I heard Anyan swear.

"What the fuck?" I whipped around, pushing in front of the barghest only to swear, myself.

"What the fuck is Graeme doing here?" I almost screeched. Last I'd been told, Blondie herself had set him in a special cell in a rebel hideout in York, guarded by Lyman.

So what the hell was Graeme doing here, running across the square towards Morrigan?

I swore again, reaching for my phone as Anyan ripped off his shirt and his man shape flowed downward into dog shape, and he launched himself forward. Four feet were way faster than two, and I'd just dialed Blondie's number when Anyan hit the wave of fake protesters. He was shouting for them to move, to stop Graeme, but unlike when we'd moved through them going the other way, they were neither anticipating us nor were they facing the right direction. So Anyan's forward progress was significantly slowed by the crowd.

Meanwhile I got ready to create a mage ball, but I wasn't sure what to do with it. If I took Graeme out Morrigan would notice, and see where the shot came from. But he had to be stopped. I was just about to throw it anyway, when Blondie picked up her phone.

"Graeme's here!" I shouted, before she could even say "hello."

"What?"

"Graeme's here! He's free, and he's here!"

"Stop him," Blondie barked, and I let fly with my mage ball even as a black form swooped down to try to tackle him.

Magog.

But the raven wasn't quick enough, and Graeme managed to dodge both her and my mage ball.

I swore, starting to run towards the action, before I reconsidered and entered the cathedral's side door behind me. Instead of trying to dart through the crowd, I pelted down the empty aisles toward the main doors, pulling my ax as I did so.

Framed in the doorway a few yards from entering, I could see the men in livery carrying the coffin bearing the relics. And just a few yards behind them was the flash of white indicating Morrigan, with Graeme hurtling towards her.

Also in front of me was Blondie, who'd had the same idea as I had, and was running a few steps ahead as we both slid through the open doors into the sunshine, blinking after the gloom of the church's interior.

Just as my eyes adjusted enough to see, I saw Graeme reach Morrigan. He was only a few paces from her, and her eyes were on him. He shouted, she frowned, and then Anyan was on the incubus, landing on him in dog form and bearing him to the ground.

But the damage was done.

An earsplitting roar rent through the square. A sound so huge coming from such a dainty woman might have been comical, if Morrigan hadn't also reached over to grab the "priest" behind her. Before he had a chance to throw up shields or react in any way, her hand was around his throat as she lofted him above her head.

I watched in horror as scales slid up that arm until Morrigan's hand became a grotesquely large claw, squeezing the life out of the supe in her grip. Her other hand, also a scaled claw, came swiping out in front of her, gutting the man with a wound I knew couldn't be healed.

She threw the man's body out towards the crowd, roaring as she did so. Everyone was running away from the Red, ganging up on the periphery behind mutual shields, facing the Red with mage balls at the ready.

Morrigan, meanwhile, was laughing maniacally, her head thrown back as scales kept traveling up her body. She was also growing larger, and I saw Blondie motion towards Daniel who raised a walkie-talkie to bring in the fire trucks. We had water ready for her transformation into a dragon, and I prepared myself to help that water along.

But somewhere between Red and Morrigan, between dragon and human, she stopped her transformation.

Her white dress had long since ripped off, and her body was entirely covered in ruby red scales. Her legs and arms had lengthened, and her back had stooped, ready to elongate into that of a giant lizard. But it hadn't elongated, and she stayed on two legs as she surveyed the crowd through those eerie green eyes.

Anyan was closest to her, crouched over a motionless Graeme. Head low and hackles raised, his slavering mouth emitted a low growl and I knew he'd attack.

"No!" I shouted, pushing past Blondie and raising the ax even as Anyan sprang. Morrigan had her talons raised, waiting for the barghest, but it was my own wave of power that knocked him flat, and safe, feet from where she stood.

"Ah, young love," Morrigan crooned in a voice edged

with fire. Her words seemed to burn in the air, and I smelled sulfur. I was edging around her, towards Anyan, and she watched me with a ridge that used to be an eyebrow elegantly raised.

"Silly girl," she said as I crouched over Anyan. He was snarling at me and healing himself, but I refused to back away. Heroism didn't have to take the form of suicide, and I wouldn't let him throw his life away at this stage of the game. For while Anyan was used to doing what he was now—taking on a formidable foe and then healing himself of any damage even as it was incurred—he wouldn't be able to do that with the Red. Her cuts would sink deep, and they'd stay deep, something I don't think he'd remembered in the heat of the moment.

"Leaving me to my prize, just because you fell for a dog," said Morrigan, and I realized she was right. I'd saved Anyan, yes, but I'd put her between myself and the White's remains. Not that it mattered, though.

"They're hardly unguarded," I told her, nodding towards where Blondie stood, her fists clenched at her sides.

"Ah yes," said Morrigan, her throat working as she easily pronounced the series of unintelligible grunts and clicks that was Blondie's real name. "There you are. But you're no longer the champion, are you? You've given your power to a child."

Blondie raised her lips in a humorless smirk, cocking her hip and raising a mage ball ripe with power. "I've seen you die at least a dozen times," Blondie said. "Why don't we make it one more?"

And with that she unleashed hell, battering at the Red with a flurry of mage balls so powerful Anyan and I were both pushed back by their force. The Red answered with an equally ferocious volley of mage balls and fire, bathing the square around the Minster in a thick coating of smoke.

I coughed, before I felt Magog and Anyan bring in their own power over the element of air, swirling a strong wind to clear the area. When they'd succeeded, I saw that Blondie and Morrigan, still battling, were steadily closing in on each other.

What happened next occurred so quickly, I barely made it out. One minute the Red and the Original were feet from one another, then I saw Morrigan's arm—gone impossibly long—lash out. Blondie fell with a cry, her magic drawing inward so quickly it felt as if she left a vacuum. Then, within seconds, Morrigan had let her transformation finish. Where she'd stood before was a full-sized dragon, which roared in triumph as she reached forward to grab the coffin with one giant, taloned claw. Then she launched herself up into the air, taking her booty with her.

Yelling her name, I sprang toward Blondie, who was holding her thigh. Her face was white, and she wasn't standing, but she waved me away.

"Go," she said, shouting at Magog. "Take her, follow them. I'll be behind you in a minute. Barghest, I need a tourniquet!"

Anyan, naked in his man form, ran to collect the belt from his jeans even as I felt Magog's arms under my armpits. I vanished the ax for safekeeping as I felt her launch us both into the air. She soared away after the diminishing figure of the Red, but all I could see was the scene played out beneath me, as Anyan did his best to get Blondie back on her feet.

CHAPTER TWENTY-SEVEN

Being carried by the armpits hurts, and being carried by said armpits at the height a small plane flies is really, really fucking scary. Squeezing my eyes shut, I held on to Magog's wrists with a viselike grip.

We were flying impossibly high, so much so that my breath rasped shallowly in my lungs. I could feel Magog's air magics wrapped around us, pushing us forward and insulating us from the worst of the cold. She was using her power to fly just as I used mine to swim, although I wouldn't swap our elements for the world.

Especially after I made the mistake of opening my eyes to see the landscape—gone countryside, now, as opposed to the city and suburbs of York—blurring far below us. Vertigo hit hard, and my stomach flip-flopped nauseatingly, causing me to emit a long, low groan.

"Don't chunder, Jane," Magog warned, her magic carrying her voice to my ear. "You'll end up wearing it."

I groaned again, then spoke, trying to keep my mind off the vertigo.

"Where's she going?" I shouted, not knowing if Magog's voice trick worked for me, as well.

"I don't know," Magog answered. "But if she keeps going this direction, we'll be at the seaside, soon. Scarborough, or Whitby, maybe. In fact, Whitby makes sense..."

"Why would she choose the seaside of all places?" I asked. After all, the Red was vulnerable to water in her dragon shape.

"Whitby means something to them, they've been defeated there a few times," Magog said. Her dark eyes flickered down to my white face, and I think she realized how badly I needed distracting. "The first time was when the abbey was still standing; there was a terrible battle there. Henry the Eighth had helped resurrect the Red and the White, and they'd paid him back by driving him barmy with hatred of the Catholic Church and whispers of his own ascendancy to head his own, new religion. He executed over seventy-two thousand of his own people during his reign."

"Wow," I said, momentarily forgetting the earth whizzing by below. "I didn't even think there'd be that many people to execute in that time. So were they last defeated in Whitby, as well?"

"Yes," said Magog. "That's where Blondie hacked them apart."

"So why keep returning? And why return now? It's where they were defeated and by the sea..." Then I fell silent, as I'd just answered my own question.

"The ground is soaked with the White's blood," Magog said, answering me anyway.

"Do you think Blondie's all right?" I asked, my voice strained. I couldn't do this alone.

"You'll have to ask her, she's coming up behind us."

I let out a breath I hadn't realized I was holding, trying to crane my neck around. Sure enough, there was Blondie, on her huge white wings, following close behind. But she wasn't alone.

"Tricky puppy," I murmured, seeing the huge shape of Anyan in his dog form running beside her. He hadn't grown wings, or anything, but still he ran beside the Original, far above the clouds. He was one of the rare creatures able to utilize more than one element: in his case, earth and air. I hadn't thought much about what he could do with his air mojo, as I'd only really seen him using his earth powers.

So that's how he'd chased Conleth, I realized. *And why he's such a good spy. And why he doesn't make a big deal about his control over air. He wants to keep this ability a bit of a secret.*

I didn't think I'd ever stop being surprised by the barghest, no matter how long I knew him.

Blondie and Anyan were gaining on us, the Original's huge wings and the barghest's enormous strides eating up the sky. Magog never slowed, however, and together we were all gaining on the Red. Hampered by having to carry the awkward box in which the relics were kept, she couldn't grow in size to cover more ground.

By that time Blondie and Anyan had caught up with us, and I cast a grateful glance towards both of them.

"She's going to Whitby!" Blondie shouted, figuring out what we already had. "Let's cut her off at the pass!"

With that she banked left, and I saw that her jeans were

soaked in blood. I also saw Anyan's belt wrapped around her left thigh, very high up, so that it was snuggled, basically, in her groin.

That can't be good, I thought, wondering how badly the Original was hurt but knowing, from dating a vampire, that there were some major arteries in that area.

Her wound didn't slow her down at all, however, and the rest of us followed her as she sped up, pushing the three of us with her powerful mojo. I also drew from the water-saturated air, glad, again, that we were in Britain and not the Sahara. Using my power stolen from the clouds, I also helped motor us along, till we were gliding along at a pace that made me shut my eyes against the sting of the wind.

Soon I felt us descending, and I opened my eyes to see what must have been Whitby below us. A small town built around the mouth of the River Esk as it ran into the sea, from my aerial view Whitby looked far more like the fishing villages I'd grown up around, in Maine, than it did the other British seaside resort I'd been in, Brighton.

But we weren't headed for the town. Instead, we banked a hard right, again, to head towards the burned out bones of the abbey on a cliff far above the town.

Blondie and Anyan landed first, and Anyan helped catch me with his earth magics as Magog dropped me low to the ground before landing herself. Anyan changed back into man shape as Blondie threw him his jeans, which she'd had rolled up under her arm. He slid them on quickly as she began barking commands.

We'd somehow managed to fly in under the Red, but her winged form was looming on the horizon. We needed a plan, and we needed it fast.

"Jane, get some water up here. Magog, help her move it. Anyan, start loosening up this cliff. She can't get to his blood if it's washed away in the sea."

I looked around frantically, sensing water everywhere but not quite seeing it. We were standing just under the shadow of the abbey, with one of its skeletal walls looming behind us and a large expanse of cliff in front of us.

Then I felt a massive exertion of power from Anyan, and a few feet of earth at the very end of the cliff broke off and tumbled into the sea.

Blondie, meanwhile was setting up a hugely powerful repulsion glamour, the likes of which I'd never felt. I almost wanted to leave, it was so strong. But I understood why, when I looked to my right and saw a random assortment of cottages, probably only about three, making up what used to be a farmhouse and its converted outbuildings.

Another surge of power from Anyan, and I saw another few feet of cliff tumble into the sea. Meanwhile, sleepy humans emerged from their houses, saw what was happening—Blondie glamoured them so they didn't see why—and quickly gathered together their families and a few belongings before beating a hasty retreat in their vehicles.

There was a good chance that, after this was all over, they wouldn't have a home to come back to. But at least they'd have their lives, which was more than the Red would grant them.

I moved towards where Anyan stood, and to where I could now see the ocean, surging wildly below us. The winds were powerful in Whitby, and the sea was manic. When I called to it, its answer was swift and strong in my bones. It wanted to play.

Raising my arms I pulled, as hard as I could, and the ocean answered me with an enormous wave. Carefully, I cradled the wave in a net of power, one that Magog helped me pull up, like an enormous magical bucket, to where we stood on the cliff. Anyan helped by crumbling a few more feet of earth, so we had less land to avoid on the way up, and soon we had a net of water trapped high in the air.

The Red was nearly upon us, and I hastily did the same thing with three smaller nets, watching as the dragon released her burden. The relics crashed into the ground, midway between us and the abbey, breaking free of their gilded casket. Bones rolled everywhere, but before Magog could dart in, the Red had settled her bulk on top of them.

On the one hand, if that was where she needed to be to resurrect her lover, we were shit out of luck when it came to crumbling it away. It would take Anyan masses of time to make it that far back on the cliff. But, if we kept her busy long enough or, better yet, won the day, that could be our first move to keep the bones safe.

In the meantime, we had to keep her busy. Or destroy her.

I sort of liked the latter option, especially as I really didn't fancy an even more evil Jarl running around.

That's when I realized they were missing something rather important.

"Jarl's not here!" I shouted to the others. "She's got nobody to resurrect the White! We need to attack now!"

Taking my own advice, I pulled my magical water balloons closer to the dragon. Magog helped, pushing the air around them and buoying them along. Seeing what we were planning, the Red roared her disdain before pummeling our pockets of water with gouts of fire that whittled them down to nothing. We had a few though, and we were moving them in more quickly than she could dissipate them. We'd nearly gotten the largest to hover right over her, ready to drench, when a mage ball crashed into me from behind, knocking my shields hard enough to send me crashing to the ground.

"What the fuck?" I groaned, turning over to see my worst nightmare.

Skimming over the ground came the squirming, struggling form of Jarl. He was carried by a creature that looked to be the unholy combination of a snake and a man: the top half man, the bottom half snake. But this creature had wings, and was lit from within by unearthly blue flames.

It was only when I saw his glasses did I know who it was—the wyvern halfling, Lyman. Our supposed ally.

And that's how Graeme escaped, I realized, wondering how deep this deception went. Was it only Lyman? Lyman and Jack? All of the so-called "rebels"?

But when I looked over at Magog, she appeared as confused and furious as I felt.

Power was blooming from Jarl, but it was weak, uncontrolled. I saw his head loll on his neck and I wondered if he'd been drugged. If he had been, however, they hadn't given him enough as he was clearly reviving.

Blondie, meanwhile, was keeping the Red busy. They were blasting at each other with waves of power so strong the earth was being riven from ricocheting force.

"Stop Lyman!" I shouted to Magog and Anyan, both of whom moved in to attack. It was Jarl, ultimately, who saved himself, however. A massive mushroom cloud of magic bloomed from him in an untidy explosion, knocking all three of us back on our asses. It also sent Lyman shooting upward, minus one Alfar, and then hurtling back to the ground. He landed with a thud, and that's when I had my umpteenth nasty surprise of that day.

Jarl came hurtling towards me, crying out for help.

Obviously still not quite with it, his steps were erratic and his shields were at their bare minimum. They wouldn't stop a whisper, let alone a mage ball. I had my chance.

I could kill him, right then, without even blinking. All of that suffering, all of that grief he'd brought me, would be revenged.

But instead I let the power fade within me, not creating the mage ball that would have killed him. He'd asked for help, and he was powerless. I had changed in a lot of ways, mostly because of Jarl. But I hadn't changed that much.

So it wasn't my mage ball that smashed into Jarl's face, blowing up his head like that mad comedian Gallagher blowing up watermelons.

Just like that, the man I once thought was my greatest enemy had died.

I turned around to see Blondie, Jarl's executioner, watching in triumph as the Red trumpeted her grief. Whatever of Morrigan remained in that form was obviously distraught, and she went lumbering towards his body, leaving the relics uncovered.

Like a raptor, Magog was in the air and then shooting downward to claim two of the largest bones. The rest of us were racing towards the gruesome pile as well but, realizing her mistake, the Red spun about, blasting at us with a wave of power.

Blondie took the brunt, and she staggered, but her shields held. I pulled the ax, which jumped into my hands, eager to meet the enemy it was created to fight. Its power streamed forward to replace Blondie's, and she fell back gratefully, sinking to the earth. Anyan went to attend her as I took a few faltering steps forward, the power of the ax helping me gain on the Red.

I heard the cry from behind me, but it was Magog who later told me how she'd been attacked by the now conscious Lyman. He'd managed to knock her out of the sky and reclaim the bones she held, bearing them back to the pile.

"Stop him!" snarled Blondie, who was back on her feet, being held up by Anyan. Together, they held the Red while I turned on my heel to chase after Lyman. The wyvern halfling was having none of it, though, and he was strong. He was also experienced in offense, and even with the aid of the ax I was having trouble dodging or absorbing the powerful magics he sent winging my way. That said, I was coming at him from the side, and didn't have far to cut him off.

Meanwhile, Blondie and Anyan were managing to keep the Red busy, but that was all. In fact, she was gaining on them, closing the distance between the two. Torn between returning to help them, especially since Jarl was out of the picture for Morrigan to use as a vessel, I skidded to a halt. Even though I was really close to Lyman by then, who cared about stopping Lyman from making a new pile of bones if my friends got themselves eaten?

Out of my peripheral vision I kept an eye on Lyman, who was closing in on the impromptu cairn. I was just about to add a swath of power to Blondie and Anyan to help them hold the Red till we could figure out what to do, when her enormously long, barbed tail lashed through the air.

For a split second, I thought she'd speared Anyan. I

cried out, but then I realized she'd hit his shields, instead of him, with the flat side of her barbed tail. Any relief, however, was short lived as the barghest went sailing through the air.

Right to the pile of bones.

Suddenly understanding we'd been outwitted, again, I lunged, screaming, with the ax aloft. It cut through Lyman's wrists like they were thick slices of cake, but I was too late. Either propelled by Lyman, the Red, or their own terrible awareness, the last few bones of the White sailed through the air to land on the pile just before Anyan's form crashed on top of them. Then the Red was shouting something in sounds that predated language, and her magic hit like an atomic bomb. I was knocked onto my ass as everything went black.

What felt like hours later, but could only have been seconds, I raised my head. The cliff had gone from a lush green lawn to a barren, dirty moonscape. What had remained of the abbey was knocked down, and the houses next to it were smoldering.

My head was spinning and my ears ringing as I looked around, confused. Then I saw the Red, hunched over and panting into the ground like she'd just run the dragon version of a marathon.

Remembering through the haze of what turned out, later, to be a concussion, I lurched to my feet. I tried to run to Anyan but only managed a few faltering steps before my knee gave out in a blaze of pain that made my vision go red. I must have twisted it when I fell, and I'd never felt such agony. I nearly puked, but I managed to pull myself together and do a sort of agonizing, three-limbed crawl towards my lover.

He'd been motionless this whole time, and I prayed to every god I'd ever heard of that he was all right. I cried out when I saw him move.

His hands clenched suddenly, and I saw him arch his back spasmodically. He breathed in harshly before settling back down. I managed to crawl forward a few more feet before he slowly, painfully sat up.

I was weeping openly then, unsure what had just happened but glad he was alive.

He touched his face, his arms, then peered down at himself before looking around. He clapped eyes first on the Red, and I saw him smile like he'd just seen something of infinite beauty.

And then he turned those beautiful green eyes on me.

Green eyes, I realized, my heart turning to stone.

The man who had been my lover stood up, shaking himself like he was getting used to a new skin. At that point I'd collapsed, mewling piteously. My knee was on fire and my brain was just done, trying to process what I knew had happened but was completely unwilling to admit.

I could only watch as what had been my Anyan and was now the White King strode over to where the Red lay, watching him and purring. I hadn't known dragons could purr, but I wasn't able to be surprised anymore.

He laid a hand on her head reverently, and then he began to change. Going through the strange, horrible process Morrigan had at Borough Market, Anyan's limbs lengthened, his back crooking as glittering scales the color of pearls replaced the flesh I'd loved so dearly. Soon enough the White stood, in its true form, eager to meet its mate.

It nudged the Red, sending her a wave of power that she received gratefully. She got to her feet, spreading her wings. They nuzzled each other, and I felt their enormous magic combine as they launched themselves into the sky.

I don't know why they didn't kill those of us left alive on the ground. I guess they were just that happy to see each other.

I watched them fly away, my head and heart still numb, and then I looked around. My eyes roved dispassionately over Lyman's bled-out body, the headless form of Jarl, and the wreck we'd made of another British landmark, and then I heard the keening.

I was able to ignore it at first, still too heartsick to process anything. But then I understood I should see what else had happened, and I looked around.

Magog was cradling the white-faced form of Blondie. The Original's lower half was soaked in her own blood.

I watched, emotionless, as the raven stroked my friend's dead face. It would be hours before I would understand she was really gone.

And that I was totally alone.

Acknowledgements

As usual, a ton of people to thank. My family, as ever, comes first. Thanks for the constant support. And thanks to all my writerly families! To everyone at Orbit and McIntosh and Otis, thank you! And to everyone at the League and at Pens Fatales—you keep me smiling. Also, thanks to my work family. Everyone at Seton Hill University has been wonderful.

But this book gets some special shout outs. Besides the usual support they give me, a lot of friends helped piece this book together logistically. Huge thanks to Ruth, Linda, Judith, and Kristin for "forcing" me to go to France. I had never dreamed of Jane in Paris until then. And thanks to you ladies for giving me some good ideas about London sites as well. Also thanks to Roger, my guide to the wilds of York and Whitby. Again, Whitby wasn't even a gleam in my eye till you inspired me. And, finally, thanks to Andrea Cornwall, who not only rented me her lovely flat, but gave me tons of ideas for local sites that all worked their way into the book.

extras

orbit

meet the author

Nicole D. Peeler received an undergraduate degree in English Literature from Boston University, and a PhD in English Literature from the University of Edinburgh, in Scotland. She's lived abroad in both Spain and the UK, and lived all over the USA. Currently, she resides outside Pittsburgh, to teach in Seton Hill's MFA in Popular Fiction. When she's not in the classroom infecting young minds with her madness, she's writing Urban Fantasy for Orbit Books and taking pleasure in what means most to her: family, friends, food, and travel. To learn more about the author, visit www.nicolepeeler.com.

introducing

If you enjoyed TEMPEST'S FURY,
look out for

BLOOD RIGHTS

House of Comarré: Book One

by Kristen Painter

*Born into a life of secrets and service, Chrysabelle's body
bears the telltale marks of a comarré—a special race of
humans bred to feed vampire nobility. When her patron is
murdered, she becomes the prime suspect, sending her
running into the mortal world... and into the arms of
Malkolm, an outcast vampire cursed to kill every being
from whom he drinks.*

*Now, Chrysabelle and Malkolm must work together to
stop a plot to merge the mortal and supernatural worlds.*

If they fail, a chaos unlike anything anyone has ever seen will threaten to reign.

Paradise City, New Florida, 2067

The cheap lace and single-sewn seams pressed into Chrysabelle's flesh, weighed down by the uncomfortable tapestry jacket that finished her disguise. Her training kept her from fidgeting with the shirt's tag even as it bit into her skin. She studied those around her. How curious that the kine perceived her world this way. No, *this* was her world, not the one she'd left behind. And she had to stop thinking of humans as kine. She was one of them now. Free. Independent. Owned by no one.

She forced a weak smile as the club's heavy electronic beat ricocheted through her bones. Lights flickered and strobed, casting shadows and angles that paid no compliments to the faces around her. She cringed as a few bodies collided with her in the surrounding crush. Nothing in her years of training had prepared her for immersion in a crowd of mortals. She recognized the warm, earthy smell of them from the human servants her patron and the other nobles had kept, but acclimating to their noise and their boisterous behavior was going to take time. Perhaps humans lived so hard because they had so little of that very thing.

Something she was coming to understand.

The names on the slip of paper in her pocket were memorized, but she pulled it out and read them again. *Jonas Sweets,* and beneath it, *Nyssa,* both written in her aunt's flowery script. Just the sight of the handwriting calmed her a little. She folded the note and tucked it away.

If Aunt Maris said Jonas could connect her with help, Chrysabelle would trust that he could, even though the idea of trusting a kine—no, a human—seemed untenable.

She pushed through to the bar, failing in her attempt to avoid more contact but happy at how little attention she attracted. The foundation Maris had applied to her hands, face and neck, the only skin left visible by her clothing, covered her signum perfectly. No longer did the multitude of gold markings she bore identify her as an object to be possessed. She was her own person now, passing easily as human.

The feat split her in two. While part of her thrilled to be free of the stifling propriety that governed her every move and rejoiced that she was no longer property, another part of her felt wholly unprepared for this existence. There was no denying life in Algernon's manor had been one of shelter and privilege.

Enough wallowing. She hadn't the time and there was no going back, even if she could. Which she wouldn't. And it wasn't as if Aunt Maris hadn't provided for her and wouldn't continue to do so, if Chrysabelle could just take care of this one small problem. Finding a space between two bodies, she squeezed in and waited for the bartender's attention.

He nodded at her. "What can I get you?"

She slid the first plastic fifty across the bar as Maris had instructed. "I need to find Jonas Sweets."

He took the bill, smiling enough to display canines capped into points. Ridiculous. "Haven't seen him in a few days, but he'll show up eventually."

Eventually was too late. She added a second bill. "What time does he usually come in?"

The bartender removed the empty glasses in front of her, snatched up the money, and leaned in. "Midnight. Sometimes sooner. Sometimes later."

It was nearly one A.M. now. "How about his assistant, Nyssa? The mute girl?"

"She won't show without him." He tapped the bar with damp fingers. "I can give Jonas a message for you, if he turns up. What's your name?"

She shook her head. No names. No clues. No trail. The bartender shrugged and hustled away. She slumped against the bar and rested her hand over her eyes. At least she could get out of here now. Or maybe she should stay. The Nothos wouldn't attempt anything in so public a place, would they?

A bitter laugh stalled in her throat. She knew better. The hellhounds could kill her in a single pass, without a noise or a struggle or her even knowing what had happened until the pain lit every nerve in her body or her heart shuddered to a stop. She'd never seen one of the horrible creatures, but she didn't need to in order to understand what one was capable of.

They could walk among this crowd without detection, hidden by the covenant that protected humans from the othernaturals, the vampires, varcolaci, fae, and such that coexisted with them. She would be the only one to see them coming.

The certainty of her death echoed in her marrow. She shoved the thought away and lifted her head, scanning the crowd, inhaling the earthy human aroma in search of the signature reek of brimstone. Were they already here? Had they tracked her this far, this fast? She wouldn't go back to her aunt's if they had. Couldn't risk bringing that danger to her only family. Maris was not the strong young woman she'd once been.

Her gaze skipped from face to face. So many powdered cheeks and bloodred lips. Mouths full of false fangs. Cultivated widow's peaks. All in an attempt to what? Replicate the very beings who would drain the lifeblood from their mortal bodies before they could utter a single word of sycophantic praise? Poor, misguided fools. She felt sorry for them, really. They worshipped their own deaths, lulled into thinking beauty and perfection were just a bite away. She would never think that. Never fall under the spell of those manufactured lies. No matter how long or how short her new life was.

She knew too much.

Malkolm hated Puncture with every undead fiber of his being. If it weren't for the bloodlust crazing his brain—which kicked the ever-present voices into a frenzy—he'd be home, sipping the single malt he could no longer afford, maybe listening to Fauré or Tchaikovsky while searching his books for a way to empty his head of all thoughts but his own.

Damn Jonas for disappearing without setting up another reliable source. Mal cracked his knuckles, thinking about the beating that idiot was in for when he showed up again. It wasn't like the local Quik-E-Mart carried pints of fresh, clean, human blood. Unfortunately.

The warm, delicious scent of the very thing he craved hit full force as he pushed through the heavy velvet drapes curtaining the VIP section. In here, his real face, the face of the monster he'd been turned into, made him the very best of their pretenders and got him access to any area of the nightclub he wanted. Ironic, considering how showing his real face anywhere else would probably get him locked up as a mental patient. He shuddered and inhaled without thinking. His body tensed with the seductive aroma of thriving, vibrating life. The voices went mad, pounding against his skull. A multitude of heartbeats filled his ears, pulses around him calling out like siren songs. *Bite me, drink me, swallow me whole.*

Damn Sweets.

A petite redhead with a jeweled cross dangling between her breasts stopped dead in front of him. Like an actual vampire could ever tolerate the touch of that sacred symbol. Dumb git. But then how was she to know the origins of creatures she only hoped were real? She appraised him from head to toe, running her tongue over a set of resin fangs. "You're new here, huh? I love your look. Are those contacts? I haven't seen any metallic ones like that. Kinda different, but totally hot."

She reached out to touch the hard ridge of his cheekbone and he snapped back, baring his teeth and growling softly. *Eat her.* She scowled. "Chill, dude." Pouting, she skulked away, muttering "freak" under her breath.

Fine. Let her think what she wanted. A human's touch might push him over the edge. No, he reassured himself, it wouldn't. *Yes.* He wouldn't let it. *Do.* He wouldn't get that far gone. *Go.* But in truth, he balanced on the edge. *Fall.* He needed to feed. *To kill.* To shut the voices up.

With that thought he shoved his way to the bar, disgusted things had gotten this dire. He got the bartender's attention, and then pushed some persuasion into his voice. "Hey." It was one of the few powers that hadn't blinked out on him yet. Good old family genes.

His head turned in Mal's direction, eyes slightly glazed. Mal eased off. Humans were so suggestible. "What'll it be?"

"Give me a Vlad." Inwardly, he died a little. Metaphorically speaking. The whole idea of doing this here, in full view of a human audience, made him sick. But not as sick as going without. How fortunate that humans wanted to mimic his kind to the full extent.

"A shot?"

"A pint."

The bartender's brows lifted. "Looking to get laid, huh? A pint should keep you busy all night. These chicks get seriously damp over that action. Not that anyone's managed to drink the pint and keep it down." He hesitated. "You gotta puke, you head for the john, you got me?"

"Not going to happen."

"Yeah, right." The bartender opened a small black fridge and took out a plastic bag fat with red liquid.

Mal swallowed the saliva coating his tongue, unable to focus his gaze elsewhere, despite the fact he preferred his sustenance body temperature and not chilled. A few of the voices wept softly. "That's human, right? And fresh?"

The bartender laughed. "Chickening out?"

"No. Just making sure."

"Yeah, it's fresh and it's human. That's why it's two-hundred-fifty dollars a pop." He squirted the liquid into a pilsner. It oozed down the glass thick and viscous, sending a bittersweet aroma into the air. Even here in the VIP lounge, heads turned. Several women and at least one man radiated hard lust in his direction. The scent of human desire was like dying roses, and right now,

Puncture's VIP lounge smelled like a funeral parlor. He hadn't anticipated such a rapt audience, but the ache in his gut stuck up a big middle finger to caring what the humans around him thought. At least there weren't any fringe vamps here tonight. Despite his status as an outcast anathema, the lesser-class vampires only saw him as nobility. He wasn't in the mood to be sucked up to. Ever.

The bartender slid the glass his way. "There you go. Will that be cash?"

"Start a tab."

"I don't think so, buddy."

Mal refocused his power. "I've already paid you."

The man's jaw loosened and the tension lines in his forehead disappeared. "You've already paid."

"That's a good little human," Mal muttered. He grabbed the pilsner and walked toward an empty stretch of railing for a little privacy. The air behind him heated up. He glanced over his shoulder. A set of twins with blue-black hair, jet lips, and matching leather corsets stood waiting.

"Hi," they said in unison.

Eat them. Drain them.

"No." He filled his voice with power, hoping that would be enough.

They stepped forward. Behind them, the bartender watched with obvious interest.

Damn Sweets.

The blood warmed in his grasp, its tang filling his nose, but feeding would have to wait a moment longer. Using charm this time, he spoke. "I am not the one you seek. Pleasure awaits you elsewhere. Leave me now."

They nodded sleepily and moved away.

The effort exhausted him. He was too weak to use so

much power in such a short span of time. He gripped the railing, waiting for the dizziness in his head to abate. He stared into the crowd below. Scanned for Nyssa, but he knew better. She only left Sweets's side when she had a delivery. The moving bodies blurred until they were an undulating mass, each one undistinguishable from the next until a muted flash of gold stopped his gaze. His entire being froze. Not here. Couldn't be.

He blinked, and then stared harder. The flickering glow remained. It reminded him of a dying firefly. Instinct kicked in. Sparks of need exploded in his gut. His gums ached, causing him to pop his jaw. The small hairs on the back of his neck lifted and the voices went oddly quiet, save an occasional whimper. His world converged down to the soft light emanating from the crowd near the downstairs bar.

He had to find the source, see if it really was what he thought. If it was, he had to get to it before anyone else did. The urge drove him inexplicably forward.

All traces of exhaustion disappeared. The glass in his hand fell to the floor, splattering blood that no longer called to him. He vaulted over the railing and dropped effortlessly to the dance floor below. The crush parted to let him through as he strode toward the gentle beacon.

She stood at the bar, her back to him. The generous fall of sunlight-blonde hair stopped him, but the fabled luminescence brought him back to reality. So beautiful this close. He rubbed at his aching jaw. *You'll scare her like this, you fool. You're all fang and hunger. Show some respect.*

He assumed his human face, and then approached. "Looking for someone?"

She tensed, going statue still. Even with the heavy bass, he felt her heartbeat shoot up a notch. He moved closer and leaned forward to speak without human ears hearing. Bad move. Her scent plunged into him dagger sharp, its honeyed perfume nearly doubling him with hunger pains. The whimpering in his head increased. Catching himself, he staggered for the bar behind her and reached out for support.

His hand closed over her wrist. Her pulse thrummed beneath his fingertips. Welcoming heat blazed up his arm. A chorus of fearful voices sang out in his head. *Get away, get away, get away...*

She spun, eyes fear-wide, heart thudding. "You're..." She hesitated then mouthed the words "not human."

Beneath his grip, she trembled. He pulled his hand away and stared. Had he been wrong? No marks adorned her face or hands. Maybe...but no. She had the blonde hair, the glow, the carmine lips. She hid the marks somehow. He wasn't wrong. He knew enough of the history, the lore, the traditions. Besides, he'd seen her kind before. Just the once, but it wasn't something you ever forgot no matter how long you lived. Only one thing caused that glow.

She bent her head. "Master," she whispered.

"Don't. Don't call me that. It's not necessary." She thought him nobility? Why not assume he was fringe? Or worse, anathema? But she'd addressed him with the respect due her better. A noble with all rights and privileges. Which he wasn't. And she'd surely guessed he was here to feed. Which he was.

She nodded. "As you wish, mast—" Visibly flustered, she cut herself off. "As you wish."

He gestured toward the exit. "Outside. You don't belong here." Anyone could get to her here. Like Preacher. It wasn't safe. How she'd ended up here, he couldn't fathom. Finding a live rabbit in a den of lions would have been less surprising.

"I'm sure my patron will be back in just a—"

"We both know I'm the only real vampire here." For now. "Let's go."

Her gaze wandered to the surrounding crowd, then past him. She sucked her lower lip between her teeth and twisted her hands together. Hesitantly, she brushed past, painting a line of hunger across his chest with the curve of her shoulder. *Get away, get away, get away...*

She was not for him. He knew that, and not just because of the voices, but getting his body to agree was a different matter. Her scent numbed him like good whiskey. Made him feel needy. Reckless. Finding some shred of control, he shadowed her out of the club, away from the mob awaiting entrance, and herded her deep into the alley. He scanned in both directions. Nothing. They hadn't been followed. He could get her somewhere safe. Not that he knew where that might be.

"No one saw us leave."

She backed away, hugging herself beneath her coat. Her chest rose and fell as though she'd run a marathon. Fear soured her sweet perfume. She had to be in some kind of trouble. Why else would she be here without an escort? Without her patron?

"Trust me, we're completely alone." He reached awkwardly to put his arm around her, the first attempt at comfort he'd made in years.

Quicker than a human eye could track, her arm

snapped from under the coat, something dark and slim clutched in her hand. The side of her fist slammed into his chest. Whatever she held pierced him, missing his heart by inches. The voices shrieked, deafening him. Corrosive pain erupted where she made contact.

He froze, immobilized by hellfire scorching his insides. He fell to his knees and collapsed against the damp pavement. Foul water soaked his clothing as he lay there, her fading footfalls drowned out by the howling in his head.